CONSEQUENCES

"This is not how science works," Tyler said. "People don't just stick things together and come up with other things."

Justin stopped what he was doing to glare down the ladder. No one ever believed that he came up with his ideas out of the blue and then built them. "I took notes. I researched materials and made calculations. I drew schematics. I recorded the whole process, just like this."

He pointed at the monitor that showed a composite 360° view of the workroom. His image waved pliers.

Tyler wiped sweat from his forehead. "I know. I still don't believe it."

Justin tuned out the grumbling and got back to work.

Then he was lying flat on his back, staring up at an impact crater on the wall about two meters above his head. A broken web of cracks surrounded the dent in the coating on the metal wall.

He sat up. A charred lump bounced to the floor beside him: the fried remains of the power cell he'd been working on. The entire testing rig had catastrophically shorted out.

The overload should've electrocuted him. The power cell should've pulverized his insides when it rocketed loose, and the wall should've broken his back when he hit it. The blast should've killed him three times over.

He couldn't stop to feel relieved or puzzled about being alive yet. He hadn't been alone.

"Tyler?" He thought he shouted it, but no sound reached his *ears*. "Tyler! Are you all right?"

His racing heartbeat was all he could hear.

CONTROLLED DESCENT

K. M. HERKES

GEN CON
2021

Electronic Format:
ISBN-10: 1-945745-03-7
ISBN-13: 978-1-945745-03-4
Print Format:
ISBN-13: 978-1945745027
ISBN-10: 1945745029

Second Edition 2016
Dawnrigger Publishing, Illinois USA

Cover Art by Niina Cord: niinascoverdesign.weebly.com
Series Logo & decorations designed by Rachel Bostwick

DEDICATIONS

Paul, without you I would be only a dreamer, not an author. Your steadfast support made this happen.
No dedication, no acknowledgement, no words will ever be sufficient to express my gratitude and love.

Berni, Blynn, Cathy, Dan, Deb, Doug, Emily, Hugh, John, Lisa, Lynn, Susan, Tess—you are all awesome, and I want the world to know it. At various points in the gestation of this novel, each of you offered critical feedback, monumental editing help, necessary encouragement, or pivotal plotting solutions.
Thank you all.

BOOKS BY K. M. HERKES

The Stories of the Restoration

In recommended reading order

Controlled Descent

*Turning the Work**

Flight Plan

*Joining In The Round**

Novices

*collected in paperback as

Weaving In the Ends

The Rough Passages Tales

Rough Passages

The Sharp Edge of Yesterday

CONTROLLED DESCENT

CHAPTER ONE

MACHINES WERE JUSTIN WYATT'S LIFE. The only thing he loved more than building them was putting the finished product to work, and the big, fast, noisy widgets were always the most fun to test in the field. The world might not need a revolutionary new snowmobile design, but he was having an immensely good time giving it one.

He checked his safety straps and braced for the day's third trial run. The rented helicopter lifted his prototype sled towards the top of the mountain, and icy rocks flashed by, far below. Watching engine readouts had kept him preoccupied during the first two lifts, but this time he enjoyed the scenery instead.

The view across the desolate peaks of the Brooks Range was stupendous. The biggest drawback to being rich was money's tendency to attract people and responsibilities that he would rather avoid. Privacy was a luxury he was more than willing to purchase. The freedom to indulge his whims was the only real benefit of having more money than he could ever spend.

The helicopter dipped lower, and the sled cleared the top of the run. Justin released the tow cable. Thin cold air seared down his throat as the sled plummeted towards the steep slope. A thumb flick brought the motors online, and they whined as the gyros kicked in. Snow flared upwards on landing, the impact jolted through Justin's body, and the sled roared as snow churned through the intake chamber.

The mountainside flew past in a celebration of swooping turns and wrenching drops. Justin leaned into a sharp arrest at the end of the run, only meters from the waiting helicopter. Echoes bounced off the valley walls.

He peered upslope at the trails he had carved. The modified jetfoil was doing an excellent job. The sled would never be able to share a hill with skiers, but a groomed slope would survive reasonable traffic without damage. His client would be pleased.

The sound of rotors thumped overhead while he checked over the displays and reviewed the telemetry from the run. When he looked up, William Clooney was waiting for him beside a second helicopter at the far side of the pickup zone.

The rotor blades of both vehicles were lazily spinning at idle. The downdraft ruffled William's stylish overcoat and made a mess of the man's expensively cut gray hair. His expression was a courtroom blank, and the presence of his briefcase was a bad sign.

Justin stripped off his goggles and popped the safety harness. "Aren't we on vacation? What brings you here?"

William glanced at the helicopter, and then approached awkwardly over the snow. "I brought you a problem."

"I thought you and your pack of feral lawyers were supposed to tend to problems so I could ignore them." Justin powered down the sled. The idle turned rough, developing a dissonant rattle that threatened to shake the engine cowling loose. He reached underneath to pull the plug. "Disaster can wait."

William sighed indulgently a few minutes later. "Was it a successful test drive?"

"More or less. Wait a second." Justin finger-tightened a questionable bolt and punched up the power again. The machine responded with a rumble. "Did you see me? How'd it look?"

"Terrifying, but I'm neither an adrenaline junkie nor addicted to snow sports. I don't understand how you do it, honestly."

"Practice. Ride the drop, keep your balance, and correct course so that things break your way. It isn't hard."

"Not for you, perhaps." William paused. "Are the new power cells still meeting your expectations?"

Justin retrieved his toolbox from the helicopter and pulled out the diagnostic kit and a set of instruments. "They're not technically power cells."

"I don't think the public will be comfortable with ferroceramic electromagnetic storage capacitor," William said. "We can let Marketing decide."

"Marketing will never see these. Wyatt R&D isn't getting them. They bitch about my methodology too much. For now the patents stay sealed in my name. I might toss them to Dawnstar Foundation, once I work out the bugs." Justin finished a few more adjustments to the motor before defeating the temptation to ignore his responsibilities. "All right, what's the dire crisis? Another directive from an unhappy ex-Wyatt?"

William shook his head. "Not this time, although ex-Wyatt the Second will be involved."

"Then it must be another licensing request from what's-his-name over at Martin-Hong. Tiff's been hounding me about expansion again."

"His name is David Hong," William said. "And he's their director of R&D, as you very well know. You've invited him to dinner more than once."

"No, I didn't. Tiffany planned all those. She likes him. I think he's a weasel. I don't remember weasel names."

"In any case, no, it isn't a licensing issue. This is official trouble, and dire enough that I've scrounged up a backup pilot. Entirely too many people saw you drinking beer for breakfast for you to legally fly second seat. We don't need the scandal of Civilian Security Bureau officers arresting you for violating flight regulations as soon as you get home."

Justin stopped dead in the middle of repacking the field kit. "Home today? That bad?"

"Bad enough. Extremely bureaucratic."

"What kind of bureaucracy? Audit red tape? Insurance? Asset taxes?"

William settled a long-suffering glare on Justin and refused to answer, which meant it had to be a regulatory issue. William was touchy about those.

"Articles of Restriction again?" Justin sat back on his heels. "Does the Fed want to drive growth or not? Is the US part of a global economy or isn't it? Isn't the government ever going to get tired of changing its own rules? Maybe it's time for another Restoration. Maybe we could get it right the *third* time around."

William said stiffly, "Speaking on behalf of everyone who was out of diapers during the last round, I'll thank you not to make light of that option."

"I'm not joking. The never-ending new regs are choking us. We can't sit back and let a pack of bureaucrats—"

"Dammit, Justin, shut *up*." William folded his arms and deliberately turned his back. "You know I think that the Fed isn't holding the reins tight enough. I am in no mood for this. You have no right to joke about Restoration. You didn't live through it."

Justin's anger dissipated in an instant. "No, I didn't. Sorry."

William had lived through the riots and the militia-driven coups and the societal collapse that preceded Restoration, and the scars ran deep. He'd been nearly as old as Justin was now by the time the worst of the chaos was beaten back.

The man brushed at his coat in a finicky gesture. "The Fed's regulatory powers are nothing, compared to what they were, and the dangers of corporate or privately driven rebellion are still very real. Yes, we glued the broken pieces of the world back together, but it's still fragile, and it needs corporate cooperation to survive.

You know that, when you're not acting like a child who's been told to clean his room."

"I said I was sorry." Justin turned to finish packing. "You know I'm stupid about some things."

"I'm sick and tired of that particular stupid," William said. "Ignorant pouting was excusable when you were sixteen. It's an embarrassment now. I hate it when you mock what my generation went through. I *hate* it. We built something good from the ruins we made of our country, and people died to make it real. Don't even joke about tearing it down for your damned convenience."

"I'm not mocking anything, William. I've helped rebuild it, thanks to you."

The self-inflicted financial and physical damages of the Restoration years had stifled growth and innovation for a long time, but overall the United States had come out ahead in the wake of the global meltdown. From its incorporation, Wyatt Enterprises had ridden the crest of a surging economic revival.

Justin walked around William to face him down. "Look, all I'm saying is that we never could've gotten off the ground today. The Restoration changes in patent law and tax structures, the consolidation of services and loosening of regulatory oversight—those are what made Wyatt Enterprises possible. Now the government is smothering everything again."

William sniffed. "They can't smother me."

"Nothing keeps you down." Justin caught William's eyes and made sure his gratitude was visible. "Anyone who could take a fifteen-year-old's crazy patent application and build an empire out of it can do anything. I'm sorry I pushed your big red button. I don't know what I'd do without you."

"Without me you'd own a mechanic's shop in Lincoln, Nebraska," William said. He added with exasperated affection, "Finish up before we both freeze to death. I'll give you the full brief in the helicopter."

"Should I give you my phone?"

William responded with an outstretched hand and a grimace. They had learned together the expensive consequences of expletive-laced phone calls made in the heat of the moment, but William had borne the brunt of the recovery work. Justin surrendered the device that had empowered so many impulsive rants.

Once the sled had been wrestled into its carrier and both helicopters were on their way back to the lodge, William transferred the documents to Justin's account and handed over a folder stamped with official seals.

Before finishing the first paragraph, Justin could feel his blood pressure spiking. He kept his mouth shut and kept reading. His temper was developing a sharp edge, but he refused to hit William with it again so soon. When he was done, he set down his datapad and took a deep breath.

"You'd better keep the phone for a while," he said.

THE FORTIETH DAY of Alison Gregorio's job search started badly, with frizzing hair, a late bus, and a disastrous encounter with a greasy seat. While an elevator lifted her to the upper floors of Seattle's newest skyline addition, she did her best to repair the damages and rebuild her confidence.

The odds were against her getting a foot in the door at any law firm, much less one as prestigious as this one. Being offered this meeting was like hitting a lottery jackpot; she needed to count her blessings and pray that she didn't blow her winnings. If she did—if she failed here—she might as well settle back into the well-worn ruts of her life for a few months and consider whether her ambitions were too big for her limitations.

Her current boss and landlord would dance with glee if she took a break from career advancement. He wasn't having much luck finding a potential replacement for her. Alison smiled at the mental image of him pretending to look doleful while he grinned behind his moustache.

As the elevator doors opened, she was still grinning like an idiot. She found herself facing a tall elegant woman who carried her stunning brunette looks with an air of nonchalance.

"You must be Alison," the woman said. "The security desk downstairs said you'd arrived. I'm Nicole Avon. Welcome to Clooney and Associates."

They exchanged the obligatory firm handshake, and Nicole said, "The guys are waiting down the hall. Would you like to freshen up before we start?"

Interviews started at first contact. Alison had already lost her opportunity to make a good first impression, but there was no sense in declining the chance to make a better second one.

"Yes, thanks," she said.

The restrooms were as pleasant, clean, and welcoming as the rest of the place. The application of warm water, comb, and cosmetics worked wonders on mood and appearance, and Alison gave the mirror a stern look.

The suit looked cheap because it was, even if the body inside had curves where curves looked good. Her long hair was a serious dark brown and contained in a practical knot, but the unruly bits needed smoothing down, and the ends were split. She looked soft and fragile. No one would take her seriously.

Determination rose through the insecurity. "Think first, talk second," she told herself. "You got this far, and that's a miracle. Don't waste it."

Nicole was waiting in the foyer. A sweeping concierge desk curved away to the left, and the right opened outward to an atrium under a dim gray skylight. Rain was a perpetual feature of February in the Pacific Northwest.

They went past an open arrangement of cubicles to a conference room: maple paneling, table for twelve, inset lighting, and a stupendous view of Puget Sound. Alison was introduced to the three men waiting there and prayed she could keep their names straight.

All three had been stamped from the same tall, blond, well-tailored, well-groomed mold. Mark's hair had a slight curl, and he had sad eyes. Derek was barely taller than Alison, and he had a dimple. Frank's hair was the lightest, so pale that his eyebrows were nearly white.

They all had white straight teeth. They all also looked to Nicole for direction, which Alison found encouraging.

"Now that we're all here, let's get started," Nicole said. "We've done a little research already, and your application was recommended to us, so we feel like we know a lot about you."

She looked to Mark, who smoothly took over. "Instead of engaging in tedious chitchat to confirm that you're civilized and can speak coherently, we'd like to skip straight to the hard stuff. How does that sound?"

Alison was mentally stuck on the comments about research and recommendations. If the point was to throw her off balance, it was working like a charm. She went with her gut response. "It sounds different."

"We are different," Mark said with a nod. "Derek, why don't you start with what we know?"

"Sure." Derek glanced at his datapad. His voice was a lot deeper than Alison would've expected, given his short stature. "Tell me if I've missed anything. You're currently employed in food service and pulling a Subsistence stipend for admin work. You've applied for positions not only at three law firms, but also at two banks and five corporations with offices in the area, but you've never held any jobs in the private sector. Any corrections or additions?"

"I'm not employed at my landlord's restaurant. I lend a hand, but no money changes hands. That would be illegal while I'm drawing Subsistence. I fulfill my Sub obligation at Lakeside Life Clinic. It's an inpatient mental health facility."

She fought to keep her consternation out of her voice. Learning those details about her life would have required more than a *little* research.

"I know I'm aiming high for someone holding down a Subbie admin job," she said. "But managing communications, people, and projects takes talent and skill, and I have both. I see no point in undervaluing myself."

A lot of people in Alison's position would be plodding away at Subsistence jobs their entire lives. The social safety net met basic needs in return for labor. In a perfect world there was fair return on investment for both sides, but no system designed by flawed humanity would ever be perfect.

In large part the business community only tolerated the existence of governing bodies because the public sector could provide services for a shared and lesser cost. Providing people with health care, housing, and other necessities ate into private profits. Building and maintaining common infrastructure was also expensive. Employment in the civic sector, mainly in medicine and maintenance, occupied most of the Subsistence workforce.

All companies above a minimal income bracket paid a Subsistence tithe to fulfill their end of the social contract, and most had to fill a Subsistence jobs quota as well. Many businesses filled the positions with trainees. Others restricted Subsistence job slots to menial or unskilled service positions.

In theory those with ambition or talent moved up the bureaucratic chain or out into the world of free enterprise. In reality inertia was a strong force, and incentives to excel were weak. Getting stuck in the system was easy. Alison had been born in the social safety net. She had no intention of staying there any longer than it took to cut her way loose.

"Tell me about these transcripts," said Frank. He smoothed his thumb across one white eyebrow as he consulted his datapad. "You qualified for Tertiary Ed to fulfill your government service requirement, and certified in support sciences and history. That's an unusual balance, with a lot of electives. You spent seven years on it, too. Four past obligation."

Alison had chosen to explore topics she might never have a chance to pursue again. It seemed to baffle people who saw education as a means to an end. She'd hedged her bets. Even if she never got off Subsistence, she would've had those years.

"I qualified for Tertiary Ed admission in lieu of other service, but I didn't qualify for scholarships. It's expensive. So I was off Sub, but I couldn't get loans or a decent job because I'd been on Sub all my life. I had to scrape together class money a little at a time."

"Catch-22," Mark said. "It's a flaw in the system. One of many, in my opinion."

That was a conversational hot potato Alison had no desire to pick up. "I could've done extra government service time to qualify for money, but I decided to scrape though my 'three and free' for citizenship on my own, stepped straight into a Sub internship and split time between the job and studying until I finished. I maximized electives, yes. Being well-rounded used to be an asset."

"Still is, in some quarters," Frank said. "But even with your admin background, you barely meet the qualifications for the entry-level job we posted."

Alison abruptly tired of the game. She pushed back her chair. "You don't want a fresh face who only has paper skills. If you did, I wouldn't have gotten this far. The position is open because you're burning out *experienced* people. The job description is brutal. You need a ringmaster who can work magic: push papers, juggle clients, and prepare presentations for all four of you and more."

She made eye contact with everyone in turn. "Right?"

"Right," Mark said. "That's it in an unattractive nutshell."

Alison sat back. "You want me. I can do it, and—just as important—I want to do it. I work hard, I work smart, and I learn quickly. My record shows that. Ask anyone who's employed me and they'll tell you the same. Hire me and put me to work, and I'll prove it."

Another awkward silence followed.

"We did say we wanted to skip the boring preliminaries," Derek said. "Do you have any questions?"

She did, and she asked them, and polite handshakes wrapped up the session. Nicole accompanied her to the elevator, where she asked, "May I ask a strange question?"

Alison censored her first response, which was, "As opposed to the other strange questions?"

Aloud, she said, "Of course."

"Do you have plans this afternoon?"

"Tea at Pike Market." She deserved a treat. "Then a long bus ride home and a few hours helping in the kitchen at Mario's."

"It's an Italian restaurant, isn't it? And your boss is named Mario?" A smile lit Nicole's eyes. "Truly?"

"Scout's honor. He calls me his mouse in the attic and says he feeds me to keep me from gnawing on the wiring. I'm surprised you didn't know. You seemed to know everything else about me worth knowing." Unwise, to say the last part, but she couldn't help herself.

This time Nicole didn't try to suppress the smile. "Oh, surely not. We couldn't know whether you had a sense of humor until we met, could we?"

On the descending elevator trip, Alison tried to assess her performance. It was impossible to tell whether she'd made her case or blown it. Only time would tell.

CHAPTER TWO

ALISON SET ASIDE ALL THE doubts and what-ifs once she was seated in the tea shop with a steaming pot, a plate of tidbits, and a book from the shop's eccentric collection. She was just starting on the indulgence of a cream-filled cake when a shadow fell across her table.

One of the three men from Clooney and Associates nodded to her. His raincoat's tailored lines were being ruined by the stained and weathered leather messenger bag slung across his body. Alison recalled the dimple. She said, "Hi, Derek," a half beat before he offered a resigned smile and said, "I'm Derek Sutton."

Her reply of "I know" emerged in sync with his "You remembered my name," and they both ground to a halt.

Derek slid into the seat across from Alison and set his bag on the table, where it dwarfed the tea tray both in size and significance. "I'm sorry to interrupt," he began, and then his voice took on a mournful note. "No, I'm very sorry. I'm about to ruin your treat."

Alison swallowed a queasy surge of nervousness. Rejections were delivered electronically, not by courier. Derek pulled a thick folder from his bag and laid it in front of her. "Payroll paperwork.

Benefits information. Extensive fluff on the firm's history and organization and so forth. These are yours. I also need you to fill out the official file copies now." He reached into an inner pocket and produced the datapad and a stylus. "And then I need you back at the office, digging up precedents and stemming a rising tide of backlogged filing."

Alison drew the folder to her and looked over the payroll information. Her jaw dropped.

Derek said, "That includes a hiring bonus for immediate onboarding. I'm authorized to wheedle, beg, or grovel. I am not allowed to take 'no' for an answer. We've been swamped for two months now, and we've gotten a call from the boss that means we're going to be neck-deep in work for the foreseeable future."

"The answer is yes, of course. Do I look insane?" Alison flipped through the rest of the paperwork.

Derek said, "In case you're wondering, the pay's commensurate with expectations. Expect to be treated as—and to behave as—a professional equal, or you won't last. It's the way Nicole runs her unit, the way Clooney runs the firm. You're not trained in law, but none of us can do your job. Clearly. We're all specialists. You'll be expected to take classes too. You'll work for every cent."

"Who recommended me? I've been wondering."

"Bill Clooney handed Nicole your app and thought you 'might do.' Sign. Please." Derek pushed the datapad forward with two fingers until it clinked against the teapot.

The casing was still warm from his pocket and it made a friendly hum when Alison touched stylus to screen. She finished her tea before she finished the paperwork, and she asked for a carryout box for the rest of the cake. Derek ordered a box of pastries at the counter while he waited.

"It might be the best food we see tonight," he said as he rejoined her at the table. "Never can predict whether the partners will order good food or good-looking food. Either way, sugar treats earn brownie points."

Alison glanced at him. "Brownie points? Seriously?"

Derek laughed. "No pun intended, for once." He gestured towards the door. "Are you ready to dive in?"

"Ready." Alison took a breath. "Ready as I'll ever be."

BY THE TIME Justin worked through all the briefs in their entirety, the helicopter trip was long over, all the equipment he'd brought along had been reloaded into the belly of his private jet, and the plane was loaded and prepped for the long trip home. The details only fueled his frustration.

The core of the crisis was a cease-and-desist order that blocked all sales of any Wyatt Enterprises products to any company operating in an attached list of countries. The list was long enough to destroy the company's international trade; the injunction was clearly meant to be punitive, based on perceived violations of laws prohibiting export of sensitive technologies. The rest of the documents outlined fines due per offense and suggested costly provisions for compliance.

Justin concentrated on mundane activities like farewells and apologies to the disappointed lodge staff to give his temper more time to settle. When he could finally trust himself not to yell about the issue, he reopened the conversation with a question. "Wasn't this resolved when Tiffany settled that export challenge last year?"

By then he and William were both seated in the plane cabin with takeoff behind them. William turned away from the window and shrugged. "*Your* company," he said, with an emphasis reminding Justin that accountability still fell on the controlling shareholder, "reached equitable terms on an older version of one of those items. The rest are recent hobby projects that you funneled into corporate R&D after you were done playing. I'm sorry, Justin, but I have to side with the bureaucrats this time.

Whether you admit it to yourself or not, you dig into fields with dangerous applications."

"Dangerous?" Justin cast through his memory for the pertinent facts. "I did a high-altitude glider for a German celeb, and a dune buggy for a South African banker. I build toys these days, William. Expensive toys for grownups, granted, but toys all the same. That was the whole point of ceding ops control to Tiffany. I wanted the creative freedom."

"Yes, but you don't see what you're creating. It's maddening, and Tiffany is taking advantage of it." William rose and paced the length of the plane, bent to look out the last window at the darkening sky outside. "She pushed into production as fast as possible, to milk as much profit from sales as she could before she was reined in. You've allowed this to happen. It's your responsibility to resolve it. If I can think of dangerous applications for your work, anyone can."

When Justin let rationality have its say, he could admit that William was right. A small voice of conscience argued the same points. He could see the fundamental logic of the restrictions. Logic rarely won any battles against territorial instinct, however, and prudence seldom defeated pride. He disliked the injunctions on principle. They were his ideas, and he should decide who got to use them and how.

Negotiating wiggle room on compliance was time-consuming and boring, and Justin was too tired and angry to deal with it now. Tactics were Tiffany's strong suit anyway. So was strategy, when push came to shove.

If Justin supported the projects out of sheer territorial stubbornness, as usual, the company would spend time, money and goodwill lobbying for lenience. Tiffany was going to get what she wanted—a fat bottom line—because she knew *him*.

Thinking about that gave his anger a new focus and sparked an idea.

"I'll resolve it," he said. "Let me take a second look at the concessions they want."

"Thank you." William settled on the couch that lined one side of the cabin, pulled out his computer and got to work. "Is it safe to use the phone?"

Justin stifled the urge to roll his eyes. "Yes, it's safe. The plane is new, and so are the phones, and all the systems are shielded and certified clean. We're safe as houses."

The lawyer muttered something about houses not falling out of the sky. Justin served himself a drink from the well-stocked cabinet and prowled back to the galley to find out what kind of treats the lodge had catered aboard the plane.

The tall young man who hopped to his feet from the attendant's jump seat was not what Justin was expecting. He cataloged denim and flannel, sandy hair cropped short, fine bone structure, and a dark tan. The other man returned the appraisal with a piercing sky-blue stare, and his eyes said he found the view less than impressive.

Justin's temper took a backseat to his sense of humor. For some reason everyone expected him to look impressive. Disappointment inevitably followed introduction to the reality of a smallish physique, untidy dark hair, and a beard that needed shaving twice a day to restrain its exuberance. An indifferent fashion sense only amplified the handicaps.

Fortunately for his social success, he could always count on avarice or curiosity to compensate for his questionable physical charms. In this case it was a moot point. He said, "Usually the pilots bring girlfriends to crew the cabin. To each their own, of course, but it's a little disappointing from the flirting perspective. Is there coffee brewed yet?"

A fierce blush stained the man's chiseled cheekbones. "Why? Are you planning to bring me some?"

"Ouch. You're not working the flight, are you?" Justin turned toward the main cabin. "William, I've accidentally insulted a total stranger. Do we have a stowaway?"

"That's Tyler Burke," William said. "He's Harry's little brother, and he's humoring me by riding along for an interview with Analytics. Flash your doctorates at each other, why don't you?"

"Harry's my relief pilot, right?" Justin snagged a sandwich from the ridiculously large stack piled on a waiting plate. "You find talent for Wyatt R&D in the strangest places, William. How do you do it?"

"I'll never tell," William said. He delighted in inflicting prospective hires on Justin unannounced. It was his idea of a filtering process. Sharp minds and active imaginations too often came encased in egos that cracked under the demands of team design. William felt that meeting Justin constituted a test of patience and tolerance.

It was less than flattering, when Justin thought about it. He grinned at Tyler. "Which should we duel over first? Credentials or coffee?"

One corner of Tyler's mouth twitched in a stifled smile. "I think you'd win a diploma war, but I make a mean pot of caffeine. I don't mind brewing some up, if you're working."

He was evidently as easygoing as his wide-eyed wholesome looks implied. "You get bonus points for that," Justin told him. "Yell when it's ready, thanks."

From the look of things, the lodge had packed enough food to sustain a family of eight for a month. Justin dropped off a plate at William's seat as a peace offering before retreating to his own workstation.

Ruddy afternoon light spilled through the windows over the right wing, and the twisting ladder of the Wyatt Enterprises logo on the screen teased his peripheral vision. Suddenly he just didn't care about the regulatory interference. His interests were diverging more and more every year from the business that bore his name.

Since the divorce, he'd spent more time on fund-raising for his non-profit foundation than he had on Wyatt Enterprises itself.

Let the government have its paranoid way. Tiffany could deal with it.

Tyler brought a mug of coffee and retreated after setting it on the desk. Justin let the caffeine flow into his bloodstream and started rereading the injunction with an eye towards finding quick resolutions to each disputed item.

When he finally finished, he smiled at his reflection in the screen and sat back. The sky outside was pitch black now. "William," he said, "I'm being a good boy for once. I crossed every 'T' and dotted every 'I' for the Fed."

"Oh?" was the wary response.

"Why not? It'll cost Wyatt Enterprises an arm and a leg. I just sent you my notations."

The silence from the rear of the plane grew thick. Justin looked over his shoulder and savored the unusual sight of William struck speechless.

"That will drive your ex-wife up a wall," the lawyer finally said. "I'll alert the firm."

His tone conveyed approval tempered by resignation. Justin raised an eyebrow to invite the scolding he knew he deserved for making a serious business decision merely to aggravate Tiffany. William pulled out his datapad without comment, and that was censure enough.

Justin called up the avionics so he could check the flight time. He would still have to attend days of meetings and review tons of paperwork to get this cleared up. The sooner it was done, the sooner he could do work he enjoyed.

The map splashed onto the screen, and apprehension sent chills up his spine. He cupped his hands against the window to look outside at the dark sky off the wing, then checked the sidebar of data beside the blinking icon.

Four hurried steps brought him to the cockpit door, and two

faces turned to him when he opened the hatch. The glow of the heads-up display flickered over black glass. There were no ground lights anywhere to be seen, no surprise in this part of the world.

Scott, his regular pilot, turned in his seat. "Sir?"

"Take us up to the ceiling, Scott." Justin glanced over the controls from readout to screen to light board, and the sinking feeling became a frigid rush of fear. "*Now*. Sharp as you can."

While the man scrambled to obey, Justin turned to Harry. "What was your last beacon? What about ATC?"

"Anchorage passed us off to Juneau a few minutes ago. On course and on time."

"We're heading east into the Coastal Range, not along it. I'm absolutely certain of that."

"The instruments—"

Turbines roared, and the floor pitched steeply as Scott pushed for altitude at the steepest climb the plane could handle. Justin grabbed the doorframe. "The instruments are *wrong*. What's fuel consumption look like?"

The plane rolled wildly to the left, throwing Justin against the doorframe again. Scott started swearing, and the pitch of the engines rose to an angry whine. Harry rapidly adjusted controls, and Scott said, "Strap in, we're—"

They lost altitude in a stomach-dropping lurch. Justin fell. His left shin hit the edge of the cockpit door with his full weight behind it. The pain was a distant explosion, muted by adrenaline, but the whole limb went useless under him, unresponsive from the hip down.

He dragged himself to the seating area. The cabin lights flickered, and another violent plunge threw him into a wall. Loose items in the cabin rattled, air howled against the skin of the plane, and the shriek of the engines rose ever louder.

William's frantic queries were barely audible. Justin struggled into the seat beside him, fumbled the seat belt into place, and hunched over. He couldn't see Tyler anywhere, hoped the man had gotten—

The world spun upside down, turned inside out, and then disintegrated in a roar.

IT TOOK ALL of Alison's remaining energy to strip off the uncomfortable interview suit before she flopped onto the welcoming surface of her bed. The workday had stretched into the wee hours of the next morning. Her job orientation had consisted of Derek escorting her past the security desk at the building entrance for biometric recordings and badge assignment.

Frank had pulled him away before he could finish explaining the office network. Alison had figured it out with a lot of help from other people.

An initial frenzy of pulling records and sorting messages eventually slowed to a steady flow of other demands. Request chased after request for files to be pulled, printed, collated, or transported from one conference room or another.

The work was similar to her office duties at the clinic, in the same way a pack of wolves was similar to a litter of puppies. This world was bigger, faster, and much more dangerous, and it was terrifying as well as exhilarating.

The flurry of activity revolved around a pending government censure of Wyatt Enterprises. The core disagreement involved information rights, and the firm was working on negotiation tactics and damage control. Lucrative data-sharing negotiations were at risk.

Learning that Clooney & Associates was the counsel of record for Wyatt Enterprises had caught Alison by surprise.

She had noticed the name on C&A's list of clients when she did her research for the interview, but there had been no reason to assume it played such a central role. A company as big as Wyatt

Enterprises employed hundreds of attorneys from dozens of firms.

C&A provided legal representation for one of the country's biggest industrial conglomerates. Alison had won the employment lottery, hit the job jackpot, and kissed the career frog-prince all in one lucky day.

Now her body hummed with a peculiar combination of fatigue and nervous energy. Sleep was impossible. Alison stared at the cracks in her plaster ceiling and made plans.

She needed to thank a dozen people and draft apologies to a dozen more whose territorial toes she had inadvertently squashed. She also needed to memorize the layout. Accidentally walking into a private conference because she'd gotten room names mixed up had been embarrassing today. It might be a firing offense if she did it again.

The cracks in the ceiling blurred. Mario had promised to repair the damage for a year now. He could've set up the unit as housing for a Subsistence employee. He could've taken the subsidy in return for boarding and training. Instead, he'd chosen to let Alison nest here, skirting the letter of the law while upholding the original spirit.

She would be able to pay him rent tomorrow. Pride made her dizzy.

A new wardrobe would be another necessary cost; her chef's jacket covered anything, and her Sub coverall was required for her clinic job, but suits were expensive. She should also look into joining a ride-share. All signs pointed to the next few days being hectic, and the midnight bus ride had exceeded her tolerance for creepiness.

She could look into the luxury of her own automobile. It would take a year of saving, and first she would have to qualify for a license, but there was no point in dreaming if she didn't dream big.

Before she knew it, she fell asleep. The phone startled her

awake. She groped around in the dark until she found her shoulder bag where she had dropped it. "What?"

"Alison?" her caller asked.

"Sorry, yes. Nicole?" Alison blew a strand of hair off her face and checked the clock. Her new boss was calling her at 3:00 a.m.

"There's been a—" Nicole paused for several seconds. "Sorry. I'm at the airport. I need you to bring me a secured unit from the office. Right now."

"Ah." Alison swallowed. "Nicole, I'm halfway across the city, and I don't own a car."

"Call a taxi. It'll be reimbursed." A background mumble. "No, never mind. Mark's setting up a taxi for you now. We'll have to issue you an official expense account too. Later. Ready to accept a list?"

Alison grabbed her datapad. "Go ahead," she said, and watched access overrides and titles appear on her screen. "Got it. I'll get to the office ASAP. Can you tell me what I'm collecting?"

"All our Wyatt contracts and privileged statements. Grab the upcoming agendas too. Things we scheduled tonight might not be on the board yet. Derek and Frank will be there to hold down the fort by then, and they'll make sure nothing's missing. I also need our media contacts. Pull all the boilerplate for Wyatt press releases too, then join Mark and me here at SeaTac. Got all that?"

"Yes." Alison caught sight of herself in the mirror across the room. Rat-nest hair, puffy raccoon eyes, rumpled clothes. "Um. Do I dress for work?"

"I don't care what you wear as long as you dress fast. Nobody will be watching you. Get here as soon as you can."

"Nicole, are you all right? Why are you at the airport?"

"Oh." The exhalation carried a heavy weight of emotion. "I'm sorry, Alison. I'm not being clear. I was still at work because Dr. Wyatt pitched a childish legal tantrum that put Mrs. Wyatt into a snit and that sent Development and Mergers into a round-the-clock marathon uproar, and then we got—"

Tears choked her voice. "I'm out here talking to the Feds because we just received word that our founding partner and our biggest client—their plane's missing and presumed down. Nothing's going to be all right for a very long time."

Alison was climbing into a taxi ten minutes later.

TYLER WAS DELIGHTED to see dawn arrive, not only because it was beautiful, but because it meant that he was still alive to see it. The sunrise was gorgeous. A flame-orange orb was rising through candy-pink cumulus over layer after layer of jagged blue-black peaks lined with snow.

Wind rose with the sun, a steady flow of air that pushed icy particles along the ground in waves. Drifts were already creeping over the wide swath of charred rubble and chewed-up ice nearby.

Tyler lowered his eyes from the scenery to contemplate more practical matters.

He was sitting on a ledge just below the lip of a deep crevice in the ice field, and he'd bolstered its protection with a sheet of fabric pinned in place by debris. A paltry fire flickered and spat on a metal slab at his feet. Cushion stuffing and splinters of wood fed the flames, and ragged pieces of metal crowded close on three sides. They were packed with snow and ice, and water trickled slowly into the cups Tyler had jammed beneath them.

He had fire and water and a semblance of shelter. He might survive until a search-and-rescue team found him.

Might.

Tyler rested his forehead against his bent knees. The frigid air was so thin that he was always short of breath, and every inhalation dragged a painful course past raw sinuses into lungs already abused by smoke. Even when he held his hands to the flames his fingers were so cold they ached, and when he sat still, his toes went numb. If he built up the fire enough to get warm, the fuel would run out in a day. Of course, if he stripped naked, he would go hypothermic in minutes and be dead in an hour, so he wasn't complaining.

He would've frozen already if luck had not spared his luggage and then put it where he would literally trip over it in the fiery aftermath of the crash. Metal pinged nearby, and a gust of wind carried the acrid scents of aviation fuel and burned plastic to him. The odor still held hints of a roasted-meat scent that was going to give him nightmares for the rest of his life.

If he lived long enough to sleep.

If he did sleep, no one would complain about the way he snored. Harry would never complain about that again, would never bitch about Tyler's lack of ambition, would never again call him an undisciplined moocher because he would rather ski than write grant proposals.

His brother was dead.

Tyler sucked in a painful gulp of air, rose to his feet, and emptied the water collectors into an insulated coffee flask that was missing its handle. Five minutes of self-pity were all he could spare. Harry was dead, but he was alive. If he'd really wanted to take the easy way out, he would've done it before putting so much effort into not dying.

Water in hand, he moved to the far side of the fire, where he knelt beside the other two occupants of his refuge. Neither William nor Justin had shown any sign of consciousness since Tyler had found them. Both men were bundled in the same long stretch of cloth he had used to build the lean-to. The fabric was too tough to cut with the only knife Tyler had found, so he'd basically mummified both men in it and hoped it would be enough to keep them from freezing.

William Clooney's skin was ashen, and his eyes were deep-sunk in their sockets. Tyler had found him pinned under an interior bulkhead, with one corner of the unit jammed nearly to his spine. He was not visibly bleeding, but his insides had to be pulped.

Tyler stripped off one of his mittens and laid fingers against the man's throat. His heart nearly stopped in shock when William opened his eyes, and he said the first inane thing that came to mind. "Good morning."

"Thought I was dead, didn't you?" William looked past Tyler's shoulder at the sunrise and smiled. "Not quite yet. That's a nice view to go out with."

"Don't say that." Tyler sat back on his heels and tucked his hands under his arms for warmth. "Just don't."

"I'm a realis—" Sweat broke out on William's forehead, and the sound he made would have been a scream if it had been louder than a whisper.

Tyler's gut knotted in sympathy. "I'm so sorry. I don't have a first aid kit, I couldn't find …"

He fell silent. There was nothing to say. After a few minutes, the worst of the pain seemed to pass. William swallowed and licked his lips. Tyler slid a hand behind his neck and raised the flask to his lips, but the man turned his head away after just a few sips.

"Save it," he said as he closed his eyes.

"For what? Are we having a party later?"

"For yourself. For Justin."

Justin looked worse than William did. The right side of his face was massively bruised, and the napkin serving as a pressure bandage on the gash above his right ear was black with dried blood. A huge lump had risen under the cut.

In addition to the head wound, his legs had been pinned beneath the same bulkhead that had crushed William. The left tibia was definitely broken; bone had been poking through skin. Tyler had reduced the fracture and splinted both legs after pulling Justin out of the wreckage.

Now he tried to get some water into the man. His hands were

shaking, and more water went over Justin's skin than down his throat. Tyler took a deep breath to steady himself before trying again. The dry air caught in his throat, and he coughed until he had spots in his vision.

He gave up and took a drink himself. The water was bitter enough to make him choke, but it soothed the rawness. He gave the rest to Justin.

"How is he?" William lifted his head, then let it drop back with a groan. "He was mumbling earlier."

"He was talking? Great." Tyler hesitated, caught between offering comfort to a dying man and lying to one. Honesty won out. "He took a hard hit to the head. I don't know—it looks bad. He also lost some blood, broke some bones. I'm doing everything I can."

William sighed. "Do you have a way to take notes?"

"Sure, let me pull out my crash-proof calligraphy set."

The sarcasm fell into a disapproving silence, so Tyler went scavenging. Charred plastic whittled to points made readable marks. He even had paper, from an old graphic novel in his bag that he'd intended to reread while awaiting his interview.

William began dictating as soon as Tyler was ready. By the time he finished, Tyler had covered every margin and bare spot of the book. There were breaks for sips of water, breaks to feed the fire, and breaks for Tyler to warm up stiff muscles. Justin stirred once or twice, and he swallowed readily when Tyler gave him water, but he didn't wake.

Tyler watched him uneasily while he folded the papers and tucked them into the interior pocket of his coat.

Those notes would give anyone holding them access to a substantial fortune and to a lot of unpublished research that could be turned into more money. They included everything from account numbers and file search codes to security protocols and verifications. William Clooney had handed him the keys to Justin

Wyatt's personal kingdom, an act that had to be so far past unethical that the line would no longer be visible.

Tyler took another look at the sky and considered his priorities. The sun was well above the mountains now, and the temperature had become more bearable. The light reflecting off the snow was blazing bright. He would need a way to cut the glare, or he'd be blind by sunset.

It was time to walk the wreckage again. Scavenging in the daylight might be more productive. He stood up.

William opened his eyes. "No questions?"

Tyler shook his head. Anyone could tell Justin was in bad shape. A decent and honorable man would want someone to benefit from materials that might otherwise be lost in legal limbo for decades if his client was no longer living—or could no longer remember them.

It was the kind of gesture a good man would make. Tyler didn't need to pester William to know that. He'd been raised by a man whose mind worked the same way. Harry would've approved.

A thick bank of clouds was rising over the western peaks, but the sky to the east was a pure and empty blue. No contrails anywhere in view from north to south horizon.

The crash should've triggered an emergency beacon. There had been a flight plan, and Wyatt was a moderately high-profile public figure. There should have been some response by now.

"Have you heard any planes?" he asked.

"No."

"Me neither." Tyler walked away.

CHAPTER THREE

MOVING OVER THE UNEVEN ICE pack was time-consuming and used up a lot of energy. Tyler worked in a fan pattern, returning regularly to stoke the fire, collect and dole out water, and pester William about potentially useful salvage.

The scrap heap grew to include two more bags of clothes, several boxes containing sandwiches and bags of pulverized snack chips, an intact container full of liquid that smelled volatile and would probably burn, and a torn sleeping bag. Then William sent him digging into the buried tail section, where he uncovered an expedition-quality medical kit that was still mostly intact.

He returned with that auspicious find to discover that the lawyer was fading fast. William only roused when shaken hard, and he refused both water and the offer of the painkillers.

"I can't feel anything now," he said. Tyler couldn't think of a good reply. William managed a faint smile. "I know. I don't have long now. Tell me again what you said earlier."

"What I said—" Tyler cast a glance at Justin, who was now tucked into the sleeping bag beneath the cloth sheet. The hidden splints kept his legs slightly bent, and the head injuries were hidden from this angle. It looked as though he had settled back for a nap, but he hadn't stirred even when being shoved into the confines of the bag.

The longer he remained comatose, the worse his chances were. Tyler said, "I swear I will take care of him as long he needs it, as well as I can. Is that what you want to hear?"

"Only if it's sincere."

"It is."

"Good man," William whispered. "Thank you. I think I'll rest now."

Within the hour he was gone.

The unpleasant practicalities occupied Tyler for some time. He knew he couldn't sit beside a corpse and stay sane, but neither could he hack a grave into solid ice. He settled on burial by crevasse. A cairn of ice chunks and debris to mark the spot was the best he could offer as a monument.

There were no words to express his feelings, so he said nothing. He raised his chin, took as deep a breath as he could, and walked away.

He had fire, water, food, and shelter. That was better than nothing, but if no one was searching, then there would be no rescue. A waiting game would only prolong the inevitable. It was time for a change in plans.

ALISON NOTICED Frank hovering at the edge of her peripheral vision long before she acknowledged him. He was keeping his hands hidden in the pockets of a dark suit that set off his pale hair, he was rocking back on his heels, and he wore a bashful smirk.

It was a look Alison was already coming to dread.

"I have a surprise for you," he said finally.

"Of course you do."

In two days Frank had been responsible for three deliveries of documents whose disposition he failed to share prior to their arrival, two postponed meetings that threw off everyone's schedules, and four meeting attendee additions who required presentation packages at the last minute.

"I'll let you in on a little secret," Alison said. "I don't like surprises. See this?" She nodded at her desk. "It's called a workstation. It facilitates many useful tasks, one of which is communication. Try using yours to pass along news as you receive it—unless your real motive is dropping bombs on the firm's effectiveness, that is. "

"Wow." Frank laughed a little too heartily. "I should've expected that after what Derek said yesterday."

Alison's heart sank. She had given Derek a similar speech. He'd deserved it too. This was what happened when she got too comfortable too fast. "Should I apologize?"

"No, it's why we hired you." Frank rubbed at his eyebrows as if trying to get them to drop back into their normal positions again. "I'm only saying ouch."

He bent to pick up the file box resting at his feet. "You might like this surprise. It isn't strictly work-related."

The box contained hardware that Frank proceeded to deposit on her desk. "Phone," he said, "plus an earpiece and desk headset to replace that junk you're using. Datapad. Notebook unit with workstation connectors. Satlink. Charger. Connectors for home systems. That's the full set."

He paused. "You do have a home unit?"

Alison gave the question serious thought. Before she lost her temper, she really ought to get a few more facts. And yet when her mouth opened, what came out was: "Where do you think I live? A cardboard box? Subsistence doesn't mean subhuman. I have running water and electricity, and, yes, a computer system." She made her eyes big and round and let her voice go twangy. "Ah kin even plugs it together proper. Ah has smarts jes' like reg'lar folk."

Frank's complexion was so light that the rosy blush made his hair and eyebrows glow. His mouth opened and shut, and then he snorted back a chuckle.

He swallowed a second one and then gave up, laughing out loud. Heads popped up all around to see what was going on. Frank sat down on the floor, put his head in his hands, and giggled without shame.

He was wearing purple socks. That detail quelled Alison's temper. She waved away the curious onlookers, and sat back to wait until the storm of mirth passed.

Frank pulled out his handset and aimed it her way. "Can you say all that again? Please? It was worth immortalizing, and I couldn't ever do it justice."

"Not a chance." Alison made herself frown. It wasn't easy. He could've taken offense, and then she would be back to transcribing psych evaluations for a living. Instead, he seemed completely delighted.

Her attention wandered to the workstation. "Frank, I'm needed for Nicole's meeting with Vladimir somebody from BLW in three minutes, there's a contact call with the search-and-rescue coordinator, and I'm still trying to shovel out three months of filing. Do I seriously look so poor that I need donations?"

"No, no. God, I needed that laugh. Let me start over." Frank continued in a too-bright voice, "Hi, Alison. So sorry we dropped you in the deep end of shit creek on your first day, but hey, I've finally brought you a paddle."

"Still not making sense," Alison said. "Two minutes."

He pointed to the equipment with a twirl of one finger. "Staff equipment. Standard. Should've been issued to you day one."

"Ah. Oops." Alison felt her face heat up. "That was a waste of a perfectly good classist smackdown, then."

"Apology accepted. Thirty-second summary: no matter what you had for personal use, pitch it. You use these. The details are all in that employee contract you didn't read."

Alison made a hurry-up gesture, and Frank nodded. "All the

components have hardwired C&A network IDs and real-time syncing between units and the net here. You might need all the adapters to transfer your own files to the new system if your home unit is more than ten years old. That's when the industry standardized component design."

Alison picked up the phone handset. It was a terrific upgrade, but she would die before she admitted that. She could and did say, "C&A goes all out for its staff."

"Top shelf," Frank said. "But we'll see things in the next few years that'll blow this away. It took ten years to get properly back online after the chip-rot plagues, and another five to get the industrial side clean enough to support decent R&D again, but the consumer market is catching up fast. If we ever find a way to kill the plague bugs, then we'll really be on our way."

He slapped his hands together. "Now you know my shameful secret. I am the resident amateur technology nerd. If you'll excuse me, I shall take my thoughtless, insensitive self off to my own office and commence communicating."

His first note was waiting on the workstation when Alison got back from the meeting. "Look, Ma, I found my homework!"

He'd forwarded his schedule for the rest of the week and the next, as Alison had requested on her first day. His meeting agendas were updated, and he'd added hours for completing backlogged filing to Derek's and Mark's schedules as well as his own. The man knew how to make amends.

Alison was weighing the potential disaster of flirtation turning into a doomed office romance against the potential for flirtation to turn into something nice and short-term when her workstation chimed with a call from Nicole's direct line.

Protocol sent calls to her when Nicole flagged her account as unavailable. She tapped acceptance. A woman's face appeared on screen, and Alison's audio headset delivered the end of a shouted question: "—can't it be voided? This will cost us millions! You people are incompetent!"

Alison let her face freeze into "executive-professional extra-icy" mode. "Clooney and Associates, Nicole Avon's desk. She's unavailable. Would you like to speak to another partner?"

"Who the hell are you, and why are you on this line?"

The demands were delivered with a first-class glare and a heavy dose of antagonism. The woman had honey-blonde hair and vibrant hazel eyes, and she was dressed in a gold suit. It was a striking combination, and it looked like furious was her default expression.

Alison kept up the mask and spoke in a stony-hard calm voice. "My name is Alison Gregorio, and it's my job. I'm on Ms. Avon's staff. I can redirect—"

"Don't you dare. Push this through. I'll leave a message for the bitch myself."

"One moment," Alison said, because the other comments that came to mind would get her fired. She also sent Nicole a heads-up: "Anonymous explosion on the private line."

The response came a few minutes later: "Please set up new private account soonest. And congrats on surviving first contact with Tiffasaurus Wyatt."

JUSTIN'S WORLD was a place of blackness, howling noise, and endless pain. Lying in the darkness and existing without reason or purpose was all he did for some unmeasured length of time.

Memory returned on a tidal wave of imagery and sensation. He thrashed, responding to past danger before rationality could veto the idea, and that was a second too late to prevent his learning the hard way that moving was a bad idea.

Vertigo swelled over him, pain clamped tight around his skull, and the blazing nervous system response between knees and toes was beyond labeling.

Even breathing hurt. He lay still, gasped for air and fought back the nausea with all his might, because if he threw up while lying on his back then he would drown in vomit.

The air was bitter cold. His sense of smell awoke at last, to inform him that his invisible surroundings stank. A crackle nearby caused him to flinch with agonizing results. The noise became the snarl of a parting zipper, and a gust of smoky air washed over him. The zipper whirred again, and a weak greenish light began to glow to his right. It revealed cloth overhead.

He was in a tent.

"Hey," a hoarse voice whispered. The glow resolved into a chemical light stick, and a man's face emerged from the dark. Blond stubble darkened a delicate jaw, and his eyes were hollowed pits of shadow under sweat-flattened hair. A pair of goggles made from tape and tinted plastic hung from a cord around his neck.

"Well," the man said. "You look awake."

Justin licked lips that were chapped dry enough to bleed. "Who are you?"

"Do you know who you are? What about where? Do you remember how you got here?"

"My name is Justin Wyatt. The last thing I remember is that someone sabotaged my airplane." He swallowed back bile. "I don't know the date, the time, or my location, I can't move my legs, I need to piss, and I still don't know who the hell you are. Do I pass the test? Do I get a gold star?"

The man's smile was barely a twitch of lips. "Sounds like you've cracked your head before. Welcome back. You've been drifting in and out since yesterday, but that's the first time you've had the answers. You were down for three days. I'm Tyler, by the way."

"The guy William talked into an interview." Justin pulled together memories. "Where is William? Where—"

He didn't bother finishing. Tyler's face told the whole story. He looked years older than he had on the plane, wearied beyond exhaustion, but he would still be an easy mark in any betting game. A whole new pain coursed through Justin. "Shit," he said. "Shit, shit, shit, shit."

"I'm sorry," Tyler said. He lifted a plastic cup. "Can you raise your head?"

Justin got as far as resting his weight on his elbows before the throbbing in his legs made his head whirl, and the resulting dizziness propelled him into a helpless bout of dry heaves. He couldn't even roll over, much less sit up properly.

Tyler swiftly changed hands, pulling the cup away and moving a wad of fabric into position where it would keep Justin from completely fouling himself.

The maneuver was too smoothly performed for it to be Tyler's first time doing it. If Justin had hurt any less, he would've felt humiliated instead of merely grateful.

Tyler brought the cup to Justin's lips afterwards. "Swish and spit first. On the cloth. And sip slow, otherwise you'll puke it right back up again. Don't move your legs. They're broken."

The water tasted foul. When Justin grimaced, Tyler said, "I'd blame the taste on the antibiotics I dissolved in there, but it's just as nasty plain."

If there were antibiotics, there might be painkillers. "Don't suppose you salvaged any aspirin?"

"Aspirin, morphine, and naproxen. You get nothing until I'm sure your brain's not going to shut down again."

"The morphine would kill me anyway. Allergies." Justin gingerly ran one hand down the outside of his legs. The knees had been slightly bent and then encased in something rigid. Lots of tape had been sacrificed to the effort. "You a doctor?"

"Skier. Ski guide. Wilderness first aid. Also, I broke my right tibia a few years back. Not as bad as yours, though. I tried to splint it up like they did mine."

Justin scratched at his itchy chin and refused to think about the long term consequences of amateur medical attention. He was alive now. That had to be enough. "What's our situation? Start with the crash."

The most interesting aspect of Tyler's account was its lack of drama. He related the story of three days' survival, two of them alone but for an unconscious invalid, as if it were mundane. His improvised solutions to the environmental challenges had been inspired, but he made them all sound obvious.

A hint of satisfaction shaded his voice when he mentioned finding the tent in the back of a cargo pod, and he finished with a shrug. "I'm glad you're awake. I was planning to head out, tomorrow. We can't stay here."

He fell silent, stared into the glow of the light stick.

Justin wondered if he'd been planning to head out alone. "Trying to figure out how to move a man with two broken legs?"

"No." Tyler's tone dismissed that issue as irrelevant. "I cobbled together a sled for you. It's the whole—" He broke off, shook his head.

Justin let it drop. There was more than enough to occupy his attention. The longer he was awake, the more his legs and head hurt. For another distraction he had the burning questions of how and why he'd ended up here.

Then there were the even more pressing matters. The light stick faded, and in the comfort of darkness Justin worked up his courage. "Tyler," he said. "Remember when I said I needed to piss?"

"Yeah."

"You have a genius solution for that problem?"

It raised a chuckle. "We'll work it out."

TYLER EXTRICATED himself from the tent as soon as he could see the sides against the sky outside. Every time he shut his eyes, he relived the crash, heard screams, and felt a looming sense of failure and loss. Being awake was easier.

He unearthed the few remaining red coals from the fire's ashes and blew them to life. The sky was bright over the eastern peaks, silhouetting clouds, and the wind was only a rustle of air. The silence was eerie. He nearly jumped out of his skin when the tent zipper opened behind him.

Justin raised himself on one elbow and dragged himself forward to reach the door. The head wound was scabbed, but purpled bruising still covered half his face, and blood had stained the dark brown hair all around it to a weird muddy purple. He was ghastly pale under the bruises, and pain had drawn deep lines around his mouth and nose. His sunken brown eyes looked glazed.

"I'm ready to check out," he said in a mushy voice. "This hotel sucks."

He raised a hand to stroke at a four-day beard that looked almost full already. Tyler scratched his own much sparser stubble while he thought. Either the man was delusional or he was joking. His speech was slurred. Maybe he was delirious.

Justin's smile widened to a grin. "Wha', nodda des'clerk?"

Half frozen, brutally injured, but determined to make a joke out of it. There were worse ways of coping.

"Funny," Tyler said. "See me laughing. Get out here, and I'll show you what we have to work with."

Justin got halfway out of the tent before he made an awful choking noise and twisted to one side in an ultimately unsuccessful attempt to keep from vomiting on himself. He sounded like a cat with a hairball. The first time it had happened, Tyler had lost the contents of his own stomach. Repeated exposure was improving his resistance.

"It was easier when you were unconscious," he said a few minutes later when Justin batted at his arm for the fifth time. "You weren't such an asshole about cleanup."

He also hadn't whimpered. The bottled-up sound knotted Tyler's gut nearly as much as the retching did. He got Justin untangled, dried off, and more or less upright by the fire, and they ignored each other in self-defense.

Tyler was beginning to wonder if Justin had fallen asleep sitting up when the man finally said something that might've been, "I think I'm done being disgusting."

Tyler handed over a cup of water, naproxen tablets, and an antibiotic capsule. "Swish and spit first, remember. If it all stays down for a few minutes, we'll try food to keep it there. Everything's packed except the tent."

The sled was little more than a section of bulkhead equipped with a tow rope. Tyler bundled the tent onto it and dug up a sandwich for each of them. Along with the meager provisions from the galley, clothes, and the roll of mystery fabric, he'd added the rest of his scavenged finds.

A crate of twelve metallic cubes the size of his clasped hands took up a lot of space, but William had said they were important. The hoard also boasted a dented and unresponsive laptop computer, a zippered kit of precision tools, and a battery for his phone, which was also dead.

Justin said, "Ima s'posed a ridah *that*? Nuh-uh."

"I'm open to better ideas." Tyler handed over the food.

Justin ignored it. "Can you drag it here for me?" he asked.

At least that was what Tyler thought the mumbles meant. He pulled the roll of cloth out of the piled salvage and helped Justin unfold it. "What is this stuff? I couldn't cut it, couldn't poke holes in it, couldn't even mark it."

Justin inspected the dark gray material closely, tilting it towards the bright light now bouncing off the snow. Then he demanded the tools, one of the cubes, and some wire by pointing at them.

Every action had a strange slow-motion look to it. Changes in position were minimized and, if unavoidable, plotted out and performed at snail speed. Muttered commentary was incomprehensibly slurred. Finally he looked up.

"There was a little gray container, looks like a glasses case. Did you see it? About the size of your hand?"

It took Tyler a minute to make sense of the words, and when he did, he nearly lost all self-control. Justin glanced up without moving his head when the silence dragged on.

Tyler realized he was clenching his teeth and his fists, and he forced jaw and fingers to relax. "Maybe you're still in shock. You think sunglasses are a priority? I'll give you the damned goggles if you want stylish shades."

This silence dragged on even longer before Justin said something Tyler translated to, "*Looks* like a glasses case. It's a solar collector for the laptop, which has a secure satellite link."

"Oh."

"It was in the same cargo pod as the cloth, if that helps. Keep the goggles. You're no help to me snow-blind." Justin mumbled to himself past a wire gripped between his teeth. A few moments after that, he snorted. "Sunglasses."

His air of superiority was grating, but it might not be arrogance so much as the deep confidence that came from accomplishment. Harry had been irritating that way too, about flying and the military and a million other things.

Much to Tyler's surprise, he found the charger wedged under the rock where he'd found the cloth on the night of the crash. Nearby, the burned remnants of a small vehicle sat upside down, guts bare to the sky. This time he saw the pair of storage boxes behind its seat. Inside he found a crash helmet decorated with garish yellow and chartreuse flames, a pair of gloves, and another set of machine tools.

He returned to find Justin up to his elbows in cloth. A thin strip was peeling off the edge as Justin drew it along a loop of wire. The wire was connected to a panel of inputs and outputs on one of the cubes. Its sliding cover lay discarded nearby.

Tyler watched long enough to realize he would be ignored forever. "I found stuff," he said.

He received a grunted response and sat down, setting the helmet to one side. When it was clear the charger would also be ignored, he set it up and connected it to the computer, which remained dead.

Justin puttered on, and the resulting improvements included stabilizing struts and cargo strapping. Soon, Tyler was on his feet again, under orders to locate string or zip ties. Improved, it appeared, did not mean finished.

The project came together with a clear purpose, and Tyler marveled at the difference a little engineering made. The rigid handles and a harness would without a doubt make the sled easier to maneuver, and Justin had somehow fused the fabric to the bottom as runners to reduce friction.

By sunset, the results even looked good.

Justin raised his head. "What happened to the light?"

"The same thing that happens every night." Tyler hauled the sled out of reach before it could be subjected to any further inspiration.

He contained his annoyance within a cage of humor. Amusement took less energy than aggravation, and getting angry at an inventor for being inventive was like getting angry at water for being wet. A day's delay meant nothing. Their chances of survival were too near zero to calculate anyway. Both sled and occupant were now much more likely to survive the planned excursion long enough to die of some other cause.

Justin winced as he shifted his weight. Then he moaned and bent over his legs, both hands gripping tight just above the knees. Tyler moved to help, only to be brusquely waved off. He worked on the fire instead and listened to Justin's breath whistle between clenched teeth.

Tyler distinctly remembered sobbing like a baby from the pain when *his* broken leg was healing. He'd been in a proper cast in a warm hospital bed. With a morphine drip.

All he could offer now was distraction. "You're not what I expected," he said.

Justin blinked back tears and squinted at him.

"Endurance," Tyler said. "Pain tolerance. And fit. I expected corporate lab-rat flab when I had to clean you, but you're all muscle. You're a runt, but you're tough."

The awkward silence returned. "I like fast things," Justin eventually said. "Cars, skis, planes, boats. If you're not in shape, fast things kill you." After a pause for breath, he added, "Look who's talking about expectations. How many mathematicians spend their winters guiding backcountry skiers?"

"The ones who have outdoorsy older brothers with spare beds? Had. Had a brother."

His throat closed on grief. Justin looked away, and his expression brightened at the sight of the laptop. "Hey, y'foun'it."

"Not. Now." Tyler moved the computer out of reach, handed over the helmet instead. "Does this ugly thing belong to you?"

Justin made a face at his reflection in the visor. "Horrible, inn't it? Never let a three-year-old pick your safety equipment."

He raised the visor, lowered it and mumbled.

"What?"

Justin said, "I wanna tessa'puter."

"I want to go around the world in my own yacht," Tyler said. "Disappointment for everyone."

He assembled food scraps and snowmelt into a meal and held onto his temper by the thinnest of margins.

"I have a yacht," Justin said slowly and carefully. "A ten-meter single-hander. I'll trade you."

"Nice try." Tyler handed over a share of the meager rations. Justin eyed the computer over the rim of his cup. Amusement had its limits. So did Tyler's temper. "Quit it, will you? You need a nanny, I swear."

Justin took a deep breath. "Had'un. Y'buri'dim."

Tyler dropped the subject with all possible speed and pretended a great interest in packing everything useful so that they could leave at first light.

He was going to need his rest.

CHAPTER FOUR

"HOW'S YOUR HEAD?" TYLER ASKED. The words came spaced between breaths. Pulling the sled would have been hard work at sea level. Conversation at this altitude took heroic effort. Tyler refused to stop trying.

The noise pulled Justin's attention away from all the things that hurt, back to the outside world. His body was made of pain. There was no isolating one particular agony from the rest. They consumed him until there was nothing left but the will to endure.

"I'm fine," Justin answered through gritted teeth.

"Liar." The smile was all in Tyler's voice.

"How're you holding up?" Justin asked.

"Fine." The smile was still there.

"Liar."

The ritual carried comfort in its consistency. Reach a point where the terrain required a turn, skid through a maneuver, engage in call-and-response. Sometimes Tyler asked after Justin's legs. Sometimes Justin spoke first.

The sled jerked. Justin bit his tongue and tasted blood.

"How're you doing?"

"Fine."

"Liar."

Hours passed, one bump, one slide, one jarring drop at a time. With every shift Justin recalculated exactly how much pain he could endure.

"Who's the three-year-old?" Tyler asked.

Justin licked his lips and struggled to make sense of the new question. "The one who picked my helmet? Ryan. My ex's son by her new husband. The first ex. He's six now."

The whole chapter of the past around the boy's conception still rankled. Justin had been unhappily buried in the tedious minutiae of Wyatt Enterprises' day-to-day operations, and Helen had been on location for her first big feature production—having quickies with her costar between scenes. She'd filed for divorce the day after the news broke.

Justin had taken a long time to recover from that hurt, and it could be argued that bouncing into a second disastrous partnership didn't count as recovery. He'd definitely learned his lesson that time. Relationships free of legal ties were safer. Celibacy was easier on the ego.

The top of the ridge fell away to another long slope cut by diagonal ridges of rock. At the bottom the basin spread into a long and nearly flat valley heading off to the right. That was promising. Tyler stopped to rest halfway to the curve. Justin handed him a bottle of water. Neither of them had much of an appetite left, but thirst was a constant.

"Didn't know you had kids," Tyler said once they started moving again.

"I don't. Her kid, not mine. I spoil him because it drives his mother bugnuts. He calls me Mister Justin."

Skid, drop, bump. The world disappeared behind a red curtain of agony. Tyler maintained a diplomatic silence for several minutes before asking, "How's your leg?"

"Fine. How are you?"

"Fine."

"Liar."

NIGHTFALL BROUGHT A STUDY IN BALANCES.

On one hand, pressure near Justin's head wound still produced debilitating vertigo, and any sharp movement caused him to black out. On the other hand, by the end of the day he could sit up without immediately vomiting.

On one hand, he had to concede that the computer was dead. On the other hand, the power cells worked fine, and after cannibalizing the computer and its charger, he worked up a heater of sorts from one cell and a light from another. Tyler was thrilled with both gadgets until he learned that there had been a minor possibility of explosion. Then he got pissy. Plus and minus. Light and heat were good things, but once they had heat, Tyler insisted on checking Justin's injuries. That wasn't good.

One look at the seeping scabs and the black bruising under the wrappings on the left leg turned Justin's stomach. Tyler had tried to realign the bones, but it looked subtly misshapen. It hurt when he used any muscle below his neck, and even thinking about touching it made him sweat.

Tyler insisted on wiping down the whole thing with disinfectant from the first-aid kit. Justin threw up on him. Balance again. While Tyler cleaned up, Justin sat by the door of the tent, scrolled out some of the gray fabric, took one of the power cells, and made a cylinder he could flex or drop into rigidity with a touch of current. He wormed it onto his leg before dressing and locked the new cast in a more comfortable position.

"What the hell is that?" Tyler asked. "And I deserve an answer this time."

Justin didn't remember him asking at all. "It's mushroom shit."

"It's what?"

"It's an organic matrix permeated by electromagnetically

responsive fungal proteins. Behaves like a lightweight extruded polymer. Somebody in Wyatt R&D came up with it. Rao? Patel? I don't remember. I fired them. Bastards committed umpteen separate genetic research violations, among other things."

The original research team had been aiming for a ballistic-resistant reactive fabric. They'd succeeded too well in durability and not at all in reactivity, and producing it even in a lab setting had been a regulatory nightmare.

Failure wasn't justification for firing, though. Justin had booted the project leaders because they had misrepresented their product in the original proposal. Police and military were the only serious markets for bulletproof camouflage, and Justin wasn't interested in supporting those markets.

Early in his relationship with William, the lawyer had threatened to quit if Justin ever pursued the arms market. Having grown up hearing Restoration horror stories, Justin had never been comfortable with it himself.

The world had plenty of people who enjoyed building bigger, better death machinery. It didn't need him. If the country fell apart again, as William had seemed more certain it would do with each passing year, then Justin wanted no part of its destruction on his conscience.

"It was an expensive gimmick," he said. "I bought the patents so I could tinker with it on my own budget, hoping to find an equally expensive use. Never considered the medical market."

"Shortsighted of you," Tyler said.

The right tape splint came off without pain, and the shin was bruised but not swollen. Justin tried putting his foot on the ground, leaned onto it until the tingling came too close to hurt. The leg would almost hold his full weight. Small victories were still victories. They toasted that one with icy water and ate a celebratory meal of snack chips.

Neither of them slept well.

The next morning Justin decided to adapt the heater into something he could jam into the bottom of the sleeping bag without melting it, burning off his feet, or exploding.

"How long will this take?" Tyler asked as he waited for completion of the task. "Be nice to get below tree line before we starve."

That had to be a joke. They were starving already. Tyler would know that. The inadequate rations might last three more days, and three days might not even get them off the heights. Tyler knew that too. They were both simply too stubborn to give up.

Justin gave the heater a last tweak and squirmed onto the sled. "I'm ready."

A half day's travel brought them to the end of the wide-open snowfields and onto a narrow, steep slope where they lost the sunlight and gained a brisk wind. The snow went from hard-crusted pack to deep soft drifts. Both Tyler and the sled bogged down time and again.

And then Tyler went full-length into a hidden pocket and took a half-hour to climb out again. His hair and face were sopping wet when he emerged. By the time he pushed the sled a safe distance away from the hazard, he was shuddering. Justin insisted that they swap places so that Tyler got a chance to rest and dry out in the warmth of the sleeping bag.

Justin sat next the sled, leaning against the heater, and worked to keep his weight balanced so that he didn't pass out from the pain. Exhaustion reigned in silence for a long while. The breeze riffled Justin's coat, crept under his collar, and chilled his neck and chest. The air smelled like sulfur and sweat. He sneezed.

Tyler didn't open his eyes. "How're you doing?"

"Do you smell that?"

Tyler's eyebrows went up at the departure from their usual litany. "You smell like a dead skunk. So do I. Why?"

"The air smells warm. Warm and wet."

Tyler's eyes popped open, and he took a deep breath of his

own. A second inhalation ended with a cough, and he wrinkled his nose. "Like a locker room."

"That would be nice. Showers, saunas, maybe even a pretty masseuse. I'll settle for water and a windbreak."

They started moving again, casting for the scent every time the breeze shifted direction. The trace whiffs brought them through the rock cut, across the next wide valley, then up to a snowy dip between two heights.

Tyler stopped in his tracks and fell to his knees with a strangled groan. Justin struggled to see what was wrong, and the sled teetered and slid into Tyler's back.

"Hey, watch it. If you break your legs, then we'll—" Justin stopped when he too caught sight of the next valley.

Steam drifted up from open pools of water. Ground fog drifted between scrubby bushes and over tufted grass. Flat steps of rock ranked down one sidewall like steps into a pit of bubbling mud, and the remaining snow on the slope above it was stained a sooty yellow.

A small square building sat on the side of the valley farthest from the mud pits. The steeply pitched roof was metal and free of snow, and the walls were solid gray slabs of siding that harmonized with the rocky surroundings. There were no visible windows, but the door was sheltered by a screened porch. It had a prefab look, as though it had been air-dropped and assembled on-site, and it was the most beautiful thing Justin had ever seen in his life.

The air stank from the hot springs, but it was no longer silent. A bird was singing somewhere down there. Where there were birds, there were probably bugs. Where bugs and birds could survive, so could two men.

"Damn," Justin said after a moment of reverent silence. "I bet there's no masseuse."

TYLER SAT on the floor of the little cabin's screen porch while sunset colors crept up the high peaks to the east. Steam rose from the cup of hot chocolate cradled in his hands, and if it tasted stale, at least it smelled good.

His mood was not nearly as sweet as the drink. Now that he was warm and had a full belly for the first time in days, he had enough energy for things like emotions, and he was so angry at Justin he wasn't sure what to do about it.

He'd unearthed a standard emergency beacon from one of the cupboards soon after their arrival, and for a few hours he'd been wallowing in fantasies of rescue, because he'd left the device on the couch next to Justin as soon as he'd found it.

As soon as his back was turned, Justin had pulled the batteries from the beacon and put them somewhere. Tyler was grateful to be here, but he didn't want to stay any longer than necessary. He couldn't understand why Justin did. Maybe he was sharing a roof with a crazy man.

The main room held a freestanding heater stove, and counters lined one wall under a row of cupboards. A metal bench, a table, four chairs, and an empty water cistern were the only other furnishings. The cupboards were stocked with cookware and an eclectic assortment of canned food.

Two metal bunk bed frames with mouse-nibbled foam mattresses occupied a smaller second room. A modern outhouse sat outside in the back of the building, next to a lean-to sheltering a supply of solid-fuel blocks. Tyler's explorations had given him no clues to the cabin's original purpose, but the weathered bricks looked as if they'd been there for years.

Tyler did not want to be here for years. He'd relied on Justin to take care of ensuring that they didn't end up lost here like the building, and Justin had done just the opposite. The idea of hunting down the batteries and triggering the beacon against Justin's wishes made Tyler sick to his stomach, but he didn't want to die here either.

He was willing to listen to any rational explanation, but a rational person would've already said, "Tyler, we need to hold off, and here's why."

Justin sat with his cocoa and said nothing.

A heavy fog soon obscured the valley floor, and noise rose along with it until Tyler could barely hear himself think. The sounds they'd heard from the valley rim came not from birds, but from frogs who were engaged in a frenzy of peeping and mating in the small open ponds.

"Weird, hearing frogs," he said. "We're above tree line."

"That's what you call weird?" Justin turned to him with a frown. His heavy beard added a menacing aspect to his face. "We chance onto a shelter stocked with food in the middle of nowhere, and you're curious about frogs?"

It took Tyler a moment to decipher the words. Justin slurred all the time and often refused to repeat himself. Sometimes he didn't respond at all to questions, not even when poked to get his attention. He always said he'd been lost in thought, once Tyler managed to get him to react. It was nearly as annoying as the man's air of smug superiority.

Tyler said, "I wonder about a lot of things. I even get lost in thought. I'm just not rude about it like some people."

Justin looked bewildered instead of ashamed or angry. Tyler gave up. Sugar wasn't helping his mood. There was no point in putting off the confrontation. He went inside and brought back the lantern, a bowl of hot water, and the medical kit. He tucked the emergency beacon into his coat pocket.

Justin made a face at the first-aid supplies and unwrapped his leg. It looked as good as Tyler remembered his own appearing at this stage, which was to say ugly and frightening. The break site was thickly scabbed but not streaked with red, hot to the touch, or swelling. The leg was a little crooked, and the skin was discolored near both the ankle and knee. The darker skin had the rough texture of a weathered suntan.

Justin slapped Tyler's hand away. "Stop'itickles."

"Fine." Tyler got a grip on his temper and went through the tedious process of washing and rewrapping the healing limb. A moment later he had the answer to one question: where the batteries had gone. He pushed aside the bowl and picked up the batteries that were hidden under Justin's chair.

"Are you going to activate it?" Justin locked up the cast and swung the leg up onto the overturned sled.

Tyler set the device between them. "Why isn't it already screaming to the world that we're here?"

Justin stared at the potential for rescue with a haunted expression. He touched the locator beacon with a finger, and his hand trembled.

"I'm scared." He closed his eyes. Tyler ground his teeth together and squeezed hard on his patience, and finally Justin said, "Or maybe I'm crazy. The plane was sabotaged. I can't remember why I believe that, but I'm sure of it. The computer would've been a secure contact. We don't know who'll answer this call, and I'm too scared to decide what to do."

Fear was a feeling Tyler understood perfectly. "Why didn't you just say that?"

"Do you understand the word scared?"

"Scared of what? Me? Did you think I'd argue? I can use logic too. Four reasons for a crash: mechanical failure, pilot error, weather, or sabotage. That was a fine bird, in my brother's words, the skies were clear, and he did not make mistakes. Call it a working hypothesis: someone is gunning for you, and they may try again. If you want to build up some strength before you face it, then fine. That's your plan, right?"

Justin turned the seat around to use as a walker, grabbed the lantern, and went indoors. Rational discussion was clearly not on the table. Tyler decided to take a different approach. Actions spoke louder than words anyway.

The power-cell heater was sitting in the middle of the

bunkroom when he reached it, and the room temperature was positively toasty. He tossed his coat onto a top bunk. Everything else went on the bottom one.

Justin was lying on his back on the other bottom bunk with one arm draped over his face and the sleeping bag crumpled at his feet. His lamp sat on the floor beside him. Tyler borrowed it and got to work building one of his own.

The room was much brighter when he finished. He returned the first lamp to Justin's bedside. The remains of the beacon remained on the floor next to the new lantern. A second heater would've been even more useful, but Tyler didn't want to shut down the one they had to copy it, and he wasn't about to experiment without a model. Potential detonation was a powerful deterrent.

He wanted to know how the little power gadgets worked, wanted it so much he could taste it, but he was in no mood to ask about it. Justin's lack of faith in him still stung too sharply. He tossed the graphic novel containing all the notes William had dictated onto Justin's chest and flung himself onto his bunk for a good long sulk.

William had seen the good in him after five minutes. Justin's distrust, after all Tyler had done for him, was insulting.

He was drifting off to sleep when Justin said, "I can't."

"Can't what?" Tyler glared across the room. "You can't do without me? Can't stop me from doing what I want? Can't believe I won't betray you? What?"

Justin was sitting up now, right leg bent, with the notes in his lap. "I couldn't do it," he said. "Decide, I mean. Couldn't."

"You say yes. You say no. It's simple, unless you're afraid I won't back you up. Unless you're scared of me, which is so insulting I don't have the words for it."

"No, Yes, I know it's that easy, but it isn't. You decided, and I still can't wrap my brain around it." Justin stared at the wall for a while before he spoke in a low voice that sounded torn out of him. "I *couldn't*."

Maybe it wasn't about trust or fear. Tyler sighed. "Forget it. It's shelved for now. We can rebuild the beacon whenever you want. Canned pasta is disgusting, though. Keep that in mind."

A long silence. "I like the light."

"Me too."

Another silence. Justin rubbed the frayed binding of the graphic novel with a frown. "Can you leave it on a little longer? I want to finish the story."

Tyler watched Justin read long enough to convince himself that he wasn't being mocked. Comics were not something grown men read. Not comics with men in capes and women in tights. Harry had said as much on many occasions.

Justin shifted his weight and made one of the choked noises he sometimes made, the ones that never quite turned into whimpers. He shut his eyes momentarily before he turned a page.

"No problem," Tyler said. His throat tightened. "Stay up as late as you want."

CHAPTER FIVE

TYLER FINISHED COOKING BREAKFAST LONG before Justin emerged from the bunkroom the next morning. The stove heated fast, and canned tomatoes and pasta didn't take long to prepare.

Justin leaned against the wall and watched Tyler serve it up. When two bowls of pasta and two cups of boiled coffee went on the table, he stared at them.

Tyler sat down. "Join me, or go sleepwalk somewhere else. Eat. Drink. Talk. Simple concepts."

Justin dragged his chair-walker to the table, sat down, and blinked. He did not pick a topic for conversation, so Tyler chose one for him.

"My brother's name was Harris," he said. "He did two tours in a CAF air unit, and he raised me on the side. I was a late-life surprise; my parents loved me, but they didn't push. Harry did. He loved flying, loved life, and I respected him more than anyone else I've ever met. I loved him, and he's dead. I had to say that."

"Why were you living up there with him at the ass-end of nowhere?" Justin mumbled after a long, long silence. Most of the words even sounded normal.

"I was sponging off him while I tried to decide what to do next with my life. He had his cabin and his bush piloting, and I had him. Except that now I don't."

Justin made a face. "Do we have to talk about this today?"

"No, not today," Tyler said. His throat closed up. He swallowed the lump of grief. It burned, going down. "But you need to know this: if I ever find out who got Harry killed, whoever looked at him—and your friend, and me—as nothing but collateral damage, then I will rip him into a million pieces."

He paused for a tasteless bite of pasta. Harry would've laughed at that declaration. Boxing lessons had been a fiasco. Tyler knew how to handle himself in a crisis because his brother's idea of bonding activities had included winter camping and hunting, but Harry had been the brave one.

His brother was dead. He wanted to cry.

"When." Justin's voice was hard. "I promise that. When we find them. Not if."

"Yeah?" Tyler looked up to Justin's eyes and felt his shoulders rise and hunch in the instinctive response Harry had never been able to drill out of him. Justin's brown eyes had gone cold and hard, and he was frightening, for all that he was sitting there scruffy and bruised with a coffee cup cradled in hands that looked none too steady. The force of personality inside the physical shell carried an intensity that hit like punch to the gut.

"I swear to you, we will get them, whoever they are," Justin said. "I will make it happen."

Tyler held his breath until Justin looked away, breaking the spell. The man's voice lightened. "The assets I hid from Tiffany should give us enough money for a decent war chest. Notice that I'm not asking where you got those gateway codes? I'm trusting you. That's trust, right?"

"They're from your lawyer," Tyler said. "Where else? It was a nasty-looking head wound, Justin. I think he was worried that you wouldn't remember it or be able to use it."

Justin concentrated on his coffee.

When he finally set down the cup, he said, "You need to know more about those power cells if you're going to start pulling them apart." His smile had an edge. "I haven't shared them with anybody yet. How's that for trust?"

Tyler felt unaccountably humbled. "It'll do," he said.

IN ALISON'S opinion the public areas of Clooney and Associates had been designed by a genius. Seattle could be gloomy when the skies turned gray and rainy for days on end, but C&A's warm color palette soothed and inspired.

The same could not be said for the spaces assigned to those who toiled away their days and sometimes nights in the support area. That was a utilitarian corporate maze. Personalization violated no regulations—it was even encouraged—but days turned to weeks before Alison found the time to begin adding some luster to her lackluster workspace.

She stayed after hours and pulled out her supplies, losing herself in a happy creative reverie until someone spoke behind her.

"Whatchadoin'?"

Frank was looking even more washed out than usual in a pale gray suit, but his eyes were gleaming with good humor. Alison did a mental check of his schedule.

"You were due in a meeting with Caroline Nguyen at Garfield Limited an hour ago," she said. "If I have to reschedule you for that for tomorrow, who's going to take the morning—"

"Whoa there, chief." Frank raised both hands in a placating gesture, then lowered them to Alison's shoulders and steered her to her chair. "Relax. Caroline called a couple of hours ago. Their new project hit a snag. We set a tentative date, and I copied you on it."

Alison shrugged off Frank's hands and rested a hip against her desk. He gave her a hurt look.

Flirtation had indeed resulted in a lovely weekend fling, and they were now negotiating the rocky aftermath. They'd mouthed all the right words at each other about respect and professionalism on Sunday afternoon, but now it was Wednesday, and life was complicated. Alison kicked herself in the hormones. Half a loaf was more enjoyable than none, but it only had been a romp. She had been clear about that.

She brought up the schedule. "You should've told me sooner."

Frank looked over her decorating efforts. "Where did you get all the images for this collage?"

"I take a lot of snapshots. I took a class once." The habit of recording life had persisted long after the lessons of composition, elements, balance, and perspective slipped from memory. "Does it break any rules?"

"No, you'd be sworn in or asked to leave any session where privilege applied, and there'd be disclaimers if recording was prohibited. Laws, you know."

"Funny, finding those in a law office." Alison said as she finished the adjustment. Frank was aiming for friendly-collegial. Maybe things wouldn't be as awkward as she'd feared. She grabbed another handful of pictures and waited for him to leave. Frank sat down in her chair. She went to work and ignored the intrusion the way a friend would.

"That's amazing," Frank said. "It looks simple, but I know intellectually that it isn't. Where'd you learn it?"

"Art classes. And storyboarding in theater." Alison stepped back to evaluate the effect. Three weeks seemed an impossibly short span to contain all that had happened. She smoothed down a few curling edges and really looked at the captured memories.

She'd started with an image of Nicole in profile looking into the distance, tear-filled eyes at odds with a smile. The airport lounge was a blurred background. The picture had been selected from a host of similar shots. Nicole's elegant poise always made an excellent impression, and as—apparently—William Clooney's hand-picked successor, she was the partner who did the most to keep the media machine running smoothly.

Alison worried about her. Driving ambition and a hard, forceful presence were admirable in combination, but they came coupled with a vicious temper and a brittle ego. Everyone had fears and doubts, and Alison was often the one providing tissues and sympathy for the stormy private breakdowns that Nicole pretended had never happened once they were over.

News printouts and headlines drew the eye to the rest of the candids: Mark, Derek, and Frank talking on their phones in the office hall in a row like triplicate dolls; Frank asleep at his desk, display glowing with names and faces from a conference call; Derek and Nicole shouting and red-faced, fighting over the right to monitor the Alaska search effort in person. Derek had won the argument. He'd shipped home a whole smoked salmon in a strange kind of apology.

Happier images were included too: Mark holding up keys and smiling the afternoon Alison's company car was delivered, and a group shot of the whole team seated at one of Mario's tables with three bottles of wine and two courses of a meal inside of them.

Only three weeks. It was so short a time, but it was surely too long for anyone to survive in the Arctic. The search and rescue effort was prohibitively expensive, and the government would not allow it to continue forever.

"What are you thinking?" Frank asked again. "You have this Mona Lisa smile, not quite happy, not quite sad."

"I've been here three weeks today." She let her fingers drift over the printed faces of people she would never have a chance to meet.

"Ah." Frank cleared his throat, and his phone chirped. "Hey, guys, where are we going to celebrate our savior's three-week anniversary? Decide before you get to her desk, and get here fast; I'm starving."

She turned and let a glare convey her disapproval of his presumption. Frank pulled the mischievous-boy face again, and Alison said, "Not that I'm ungrateful, but why did you stop by to see me now? Please don't say it was just to say hello. We talked about not doing that."

His expression turned serious. "We did. I stopped by with office news and got distracted. Word's come down that the SAR efforts are being scaled back. That really means shut down. It will hit the news tonight."

"The ex-Wyatts will be impossible without the search to distract them," Nicole said as she arrived. She offered a sad smile to Mark and Derek when they showed up a few seconds later from opposite directions.

Mark said, "If anyone's interested, Gordon Lee is handling the office pool."

"Hey, thanks," Derek said. He raised his phone and stepped away for a private conversation.

"Pool?" Alison asked.

Nicole said, "The office pool on the date someone will petition to declare Bill and Dr. Wyatt dead. And who petitions first. Bonus for guessing both right."

"I'm down for the seventeenth," Frank said. "I hedged my bet and took wifey one *and* wifey two."

"Ghoul," Nicole said. "Alison, your number one job the next few weeks will be running interference. Clooney and Associates is handling Wyatt's personal estate and the corporate succession. Helen thinks I got my job by sleeping with her husband, and Tiffany hates anyone who interferes with her. I will need you to be a brick wall."

Derek tucked away his phone. "Bad news, everyone. T. Wyatt Rex has officially killed the pool. Gordon says she's broadcasting right now."

"Now? Already? They haven't even been missing a month! Cold-blooded, gold-digging—" Nicole flung up both hands. "No. I will not do this. She will not make me lose my temper."

"It's got to be the Martin-Hong mess," Frank said. He blushed at a warning look from Nicole before continuing, "I'm only saying that even Tiffany needs a reason. It has to be the deal she's been trying to green-light. She wants the proxies."

Mark said, "There's a new stock inheritance law in the House, too. She might be worried about securing her cut before it hits the books."

"That's never going to pass," Frank said. "The corporate sector's already sponsoring protests. If it goes through, the riots would be like Restoration all over again."

"That's it. Restoration came up, discussion is over." Derek made a broad gesture towards the hallway. "Away we go. Alison, I can see you're dying of curiosity, but now is not the time and here is not the place. We'll tell you all about it—everything that isn't privileged, anyway—over dinner. Gossip always goes better over drinks."

"IT STILL TICKLES." Justin shifted his weight in his chair, lifted one foot, then the other. The material encasing his left leg flexed as he bent the knee, then stiffened in response to the controller in his hand. The power cell on a strap over his shoulder hummed quietly, and static pricked at his calf.

He peered at Tyler, who was on the floor under the chair. "Where's the power bleed?"

"What? You're mumbling, Justin. Enunciate. Ah-hah."

The tingling stopped. Tyler set down his screwdriver. "That rash is all over both legs now."

"Ignore it. I do." The darkened skin did not itch, throb, or wake

Justin in screaming pain the way other things did. He picked up the improvised crutches. "Test drive."

Ten minutes later, he dropped onto the couch and groaned as he locked his leg out straight on a chair. His back and stomach were quivering from the strain. Sweat trickled down his belly and between his shoulder blades. His skull was pounding, and the room tried to spin sideways.

"Experimental success, practical failure," he said. "Guess the fun's over."

They'd managed to survive six weeks together without killing each other from sheer boredom, but they were down to their last can of tomatoes, and he was barely mobile.

"I need to bring in fuel," Tyler said. "We'll talk after. If you still can't face the thought of making contact, I'll hike as far as I can in a day, trigger the beacon, then make up some story to get someone here as soon as possible. Then we lie about who you are. That's the best I can do."

Justin laid his head back to stare at the ceiling. The ceiling had no suggestions. He closed his eyes. The decision was still impossible.

He woke up cold and stiff, with no idea where he was for several terrifying moments. Memory kicked in when the outer door creaked open and heavy steps thumped on the porch. Then the inner door opened. Justin said, "It's up to you, Tyler. I still can't make myself think about it. Where were you?"

"I—ah—" Tyler cleared his throat. "Someone did a flyover, and I saw parachutes."

"What?" Justin sat up with a jerk. The world dissolved into pain. When he could see again, Tyler was kneeling in front of him. The view swam and wobbled through a filter of vertigo.

"You've been staring again," Tyler said. "Have you heard a word I've said?"

"No." Justin fought to think past the sick headache.

"No. Here's a summary: looks like this place is a seasonal

research post. A supply drop came down a valley over. A ton of food, including six cans of everything we've spent the last eternity using up, and another ton of reagents and bio-sampling packs, seismometers, and two of these."

Tyler lifted a computer case, set it next to Justin's leg, and opened up the shock-absorbent shell. A rolled-up solar charger was visible in the back of the container, and the case was insulated as well as reinforced.

Energy surged into Justin's muscles. "That's a purpose-built field unit manufactured by BLW Research," he said. His voice shook. "Vlad makes that model exclusively for the Dawnstar Foundation as a favor to me."

It was a stupid name but a great institution, one Justin had set up when he was young enough to feel idealistic, and newly rich enough to feel guilty about it. He'd amassed a fortune making things that people had initially told him were useless, and he'd wanted to give others the same kind of opportunity.

In one of the twists that made the universe an interesting place, an organization designed to throw money at whimsical ideas regularly spun off enough profitable applications to make it a going, growing operation.

Tyler made some mental connections, then raised eyebrows. "Hard to miss the irony."

They would both be frozen corpses if not for the foundation that had built this cabin. Justin said, "I'm not sure it's irony, but those units have secured links to Dawnstar headquarters. No false stories, no shouting to the world. Just people we can reach privately, people I trust the way I trust you. Manny Bannerjee and Jiri Nemecek will get us home safe if anyone can."

Tyler's eyes went wide, and the reality of the words hit Justin hard a second later.

They were going home.

ALISON'S MOCHA WAS COLD, and her legs ached. The antique benches lining the train station's main lobby contributed to a lovely ambiance, but they were not designed for extended visits.

She sucked down the sweet dregs of the drink and went for a walk. The streets outside were as quiet as the city ever got so close to the waterfront, and Alison took deep breaths of the fresh air while she paced around the parking lot.

She had been looking forward to a quiet night at home with a book and a salad, a quiet respite before what would be a horrible day. Now she was facing the possibility of spending the night before Justin Wyatt's funeral waiting for a client.

Funerals were supposed to provide closure. Organizing this one had taken weeks of negotiations, and it would mark a hiatus in the infighting, not an end. The obstacles ranged from official reluctance to issue a death certificate to the difficulty of getting assorted family members to agree on a location for the service. Nicole had won that fight. It was being held in Seattle, because everyone involved had to meet anyway to discuss the unresolved business details.

Funerals were supposed to bring people together to grieve. This one would be combining elements of a composite explosive. Someone was certain to blow, probably in full view of the media. Tiffany had won that round; there would be national coverage.

Alison was stuck here now because she wanted to avoid as much of the coverage as possible. Getting Mrs-Wyatt-One and her entourage settled tonight should've been easy. Two months of estate-related visitations had polished the arrival routine to perfection. Most times, the use of decoys and personal car delivery threw off the press entirely, and Helen preferred privacy to publicity when it came to family. In direct contrast, Tiffany Wyatt had arrived in a flurry of press coverage arranged in advance. The horde of media had followed in a choreographed progress from airport to hotel to press conference to the restaurant where she dined in company with business and political allies.

Alison had seen the highlights on the news at the bar earlier, including Tiffany's impassioned plea that she be left "to retire and grieve in private." The act had left Alison more determined to ensure that Helen and her son got that privacy in truth. She considered and rejected the idea of touching base with Helen again. Helen would say, "Send the codes to my people and go home." Alison couldn't bring herself do that. Not tonight.

She headed inside and went downstairs to the boarding lounge. It was a dull example of bland modern design, unlike the historic lobby, but it had a clear view of the tracks through a glassed wall.

A rumble and screech of brakes hinted at the imminent arrival of the train several minutes before the line of cars halted sedately on their assigned track. The garbled tones of the paging system made the official announcement. Finally, the passengers came straggling in.

Helen Armstrong was at the rear of the moving herd, walking beside the baggage truck. Her son Ryan lay nestled against her shoulder in a loose embrace; his dark hair pressed against her cheek, his arms were around her neck, and both his hands clutched small plush toys.

Tom and Miguel in their business suits easily kept pace while maintaining an alert watch on the surroundings. Their boss, Mariana, brought up the rear and kept an eye on their employer. Alison waved to them, and her irritation over her lost evening ebbed away.

Helen hefted her son higher so she could wiggle her fingers in greeting. She was an unpretentious woman with a warm grin and bright blue eyes, and tonight she wore her blonde hair pulled back in a braid. Her loose dress and walking boots were perfect costuming for the role of "sensible traveler, maternal and gorgeous."

During their first meeting Alison had decided to confront the five-ton gorilla of income and social status sitting between them.

Passing references to the corrupting power of wealth, the debauched lifestyles of celebrities, and the lack of talent in the entertainment industry were met by remarks regarding the moral bankruptcy of the legal profession and the general incompetence of flunkies, and after they were both done laughing, they'd found that they rather liked each other.

That liking had grown over the course of visits and meetings and long-distance conversations. Most of an actress's life seemed to be spent in an elaborate artificial bubble of insincerity. Alison quite enjoyed providing regular reality checks.

As Helen reached the lounge, she let Ryan slide to the floor. He buried his face against her leg like a child much younger than his six years, and Alison knew not to expect much interaction from him. Helen said he'd been fond of her ex-husband, which seemed odd, but Alison tried to avoid judgment.

The boy was quiet and a little strange, but he also had a sweet streak of generosity. Mariana carried a stash of stuffed animals for him because Ryan was always finding people to "adopt" them but anxiously needed one in hand at all times.

Alison greeted the boy by name, got the usual lack of response. She hugged Helen, next. "I can't say I'm happy, given the circumstances, but it's good to see you."

"Why are you here?" Helen wrinkled her nose. "That sounded rude, didn't it? I mean, I told you we'd hire a limo. Now we've ruined your evening."

"No, the freight delays did that. I wanted to stay. I'm not messing with tradition at a time like this."

Helen looked around the lounge, and her smile broadened. "No press at all. Again. How refreshing."

The remarkable thing was that she meant it.

"They'll be camped out in the hotel lobby by morning." Alison handed keys to Miguel. "It's parked under the closest light pole."

He checked the vehicle and the parking lot for muggers,

bombers, or whatever other hazards might be lurking, and they met him at the door.

"How was the trip?" Alison asked as the car was loaded.

Helen lifted Ryan into his seat, hugged him, and then let out a huge sigh. "Fine except for the last bit. Rail travel is fun. You should try it for yourself."

"I doubt riding coach would be as fun as having a private compartment."

Neither of them raised the obvious point, that rail travel was an eccentric choice when a flight from Los Angeles to Seattle would take less than three hours on the private jet Helen could easily afford. Not when Ryan was sitting there listening in wide-eyed sleepy silence. Helen's first visit to Seattle to discuss her ex-husband's disappearance had been postponed because Ryan had refused to get on an airplane.

"It's far more scenic than bus or car, too," Helen said. "Speaking of cars, Alison, how are you getting home?"

"The usual. Cab out of downtown, bus for the rest."

That plan did not meet with Helen's approval, due to the late hour and the distances involved, and discussion ensued between her, Tom and Mariana on how to provide transport and escort while juggling other duties.

A stuffed giraffe landed on Alison's knee, and then a small cold hand slid into her palm. She looked down into Ryan's face. His expression was sad, and his hair was falling over his brown eyes in dark ringlets.

Alison brushed back his bangs. "Are you tired of the arguing too? Are you ready for a bedtime tuck-in?"

"I'm hungry," he said. "I want pizza."

Helen's inhalation was an understated gasp of hope.

Alison said, "I live above a very good pizza place, which would get me home *and* stop the arguing. What do you say? Shall we all have dinner together?"

He nodded, very serious, and Alison glanced at Helen again

before saying to Ryan, "If you're very good and promise to say please and thank you, Mario might cook for us himself."

Mario was thrilled to his toes to serve a celebrity visitor regardless of the hour, and Ryan captured his heart with the first whispered request for "pizza, just with cheese, please."

The boy finished his pizza and a bowl of spumoni, gifted a delighted Mario with a fuzzy stuffed elephant, and was sound asleep before the linguini with clams got to the table for everyone else. Helen said that it was the most she had seen him eat in days, and everyone else ignored the tears in her eyes.

Alison hoped it was a good omen.

CHAPTER SIX

NICOLE SLAMMED THE DOOR OF her office shut with enough force to rattle the pictures on the walls, kicked off both shoes, and stomped barefoot to her desk.

Shoe removal was a bad sign. Alison set them by the door, unpacked files, and arranged Nicole's laptop and papers on the coffee table in the conversation grouping. Throughout the tidying and straightening, Nicole stood and watched the clouds and sheeting rain outside her window. Puget Sound was all but invisible behind the fog and gloom.

Alison picked up a vase full of twigs and glass beads from the table in the seating area and set it on the desk. Then she retreated to the couch to work on her own projects.

Nicole turned and frowned at the vase. "Tempting."

"Messy," Alison pointed out.

"True."

Alison completed a letter and assigned the distribution list. A while later, Nicole made herself a cup of coffee and brought a second one to Alison. Then she sat down to contemplate the papers on the table.

The array of official legal stamps, inked signatures, and certifications of authenticity gave the documents an archaic appearance at odds with the bar codes and holographic seals that decorated the top edge of each page.

Nicole swept her fingers over the seals. "An order of dissolution the day of the funeral. I should've known."

Alison kept working.

"Thank you for not rubbing my nose in it," Nicole said. "Priorities. Partnership meeting first. We have a lot of cases and contracts in progress, and I want them in pristine, perfect order, not a dot out of place. What else? Draft an official announcement, pull everything together, take a look—" She paused. "Alison, you are not taking notes."

"There are standard protocols, and I already have drafts for press releases and announcements in a file cache called 'Restoration,' in honor of Derek's twitch. I've forwarded it to you for review and approval."

"You saw this coming?"

A snort escaped before Alison could stop it. "Hardly. No, every time I needed to train myself on a new program or format or presentation, I used being free from Tiffasaurus as a hypothetical subject. I'd been thinking of giving them to you for a birthday present, for laughs."

Nicole's expression lightened as she began scanning the files. "Bill's last gift to me, that's what you are. Make sure you remind me of how indispensable you are while I'm working you to death over the next few months."

DEREK PULLED out a chair for Alison. "Tell me again why we're here?"

Alison wrinkled her nose at him as she negotiated the tricky seating maneuver required by a formal dress. He looked fantastic in a gray suit and an electric-blue shirt that brought out the color in his eyes. "You're all doing me a favor, and you know it," she said. "This is overwhelming."

Nicole and the others had been showing the C&A flag at dedications hosted by the beneficiaries of the Wyatt estate for weeks now, but Alison had been limited to vicarious attendance through hearing all the post-banquet gossip.

Then Helen had overheard a wistful remark about missing the fun. An invitation to this local event had appeared the next day. Alison had Helen to thank for the dress as well, and nervous butterflies were hosting a party in her stomach. She'd lost sight of her social comfort zone when the limousine showed up.

Ticking off items against her mental list of expectations was a way to occupy her mind and prevent a terminal case of self-consciousness. Big round tables, eight seats each, were packed too tightly for the available space. Check. The room had a worn patterned carpet, partitioned walls, and insufficient lighting from chandelier fixtures. Check. Too many plates, excessive flatware, and extraneous crystal. Check, check, and check.

Every setting had its own themed takeaway. Derek was building a desk shrine with all the ones he'd collected from earlier events. Mark used it as a stylus-throwing target.

The tablecloths were deep forest green and gold, the logo colors for Wyatt Enterprises. The party favor tonight was a glossy sheet with biographical information and photographs. Alison slid hers off the plate but was too distracted by the other arriving guests to read it.

Tiffany Wyatt was already seated at the presentation table on a raised dais with other dignitaries. She wasn't tall or pretty, but she was incredibly visible. She dressed in bold colors and classic lines, and she had a crackling aura of confidence that drew the eye to her. When Tiffany made speeches, which she liked to do as often as possible, she was impossible to dismiss. Her neighbors looked dazzled by their proximity.

Alison recognized some of them from assorted C&A conferences: David Hong and Ferris Martin, Ken Watanabe and Vladimir Borisov from BLW Research, and both Manny Bannerjee and Lidia Park from the Dawnstar Foundation, which was hosting this event.

Nicole, Mark, and Frank all found their own seats at Alison's table and settled down with resigned expressions.

"This is the last one of these memorials, isn't it?" Mark asked as he picked up his handout. "I don't know if I can take any more praise-singing."

"Don't ruin it for me," Alison said. "No politics either. Don't make me regret asking you along."

Derek made a mournful face. "No hand-wringing over the water rights skirmish between Utah and Colorado? No teeth-gnashing about the Subsistence drawdown that got stiffed in the New Senate because corporations like the system the way it is? I was looking forward to pounding my fists on the table, Alison. What about the military cuts? Can we talk about those?"

"No. Restoration."

He put a hand over his heart. "Ah, a fatal shot. Restor-ation mentioned, topic dead."

"Spoilsport," Frank said.

"Quiet." Nicole loaded authority into the word, resulting in instant silence. She wore her stern lawyering face as well as a stunning gown. Spending time with ex–Wyatt wives ranked very low on Nicole's list of fun activities.

"Don't worry," she told Alison, correctly interpreting a worried glance. "I will play nice with Helen. You've done worse things for me."

Helen arrived on a wave of attention from the rest of the attendees. She wore an understated dress and held Ryan by the hand, and Mariana was on the boy's other side in a conservative suit that showed off her athletic good looks. Ryan looked sweet and innocent in his little-boy suit, and every few paces he insisted on being swung for a step between his mother and her security escort.

It was an adorable sight, and the murmurs didn't stop until Helen sank gracefully into her seat—the one directly facing the dais—and gave Tiffany a beaming smile.

Alison had no idea what kind of behind-the-scenes maneuvering had put Helen on the floor and Tiffany at the dais, but the effort to diminish her significance had been wasted. She was stealing the show.

Ryan climbed onto the empty seat next to Alison and picked up his butter knife. He was the only child present, and Alison wondered why Helen had brought him. Maybe the testimonials helped him find closure. Ryan put down the knife, then pressed a finger against a picture on his handout before arranging his animal companions for today—a dog and a dolphin—at the top of his place setting. Mariana removed the butter knife.

Helen kissed Ryan on the forehead and then looked to Alison. "You look great. Thank you for coming. Thank you all. I know it was short notice. I don't know which idea frightened me more: having empty seats or facing replacements Rob's producer might've chosen."

Her husband had planned to attend this event with her, along with a producer and two other actors from the project he was currently promoting. The producer had decided this morning that it wouldn't be appropriate publicity and might send the wrong message. Rob Armstrong had also sent his apologies to the sponsors. Alison gave the marriage another year at best.

Frank said, "It's our pleasure, Helen. What's a little indigestion between friends?"

Social conversation took everyone past the introductions from the dais, and the Dawnstar Foundation expressed its gratitude to the Wyatt estate and acknowledged the contributions of the Armstrong family through several forgettable food courses.

Servers cleared the tables and brought around dessert and coffee, and a speaker began a presentation about the foundation and the debt it owed its creator.

The statistics made Alison's eyes glaze. Mark made a face at her as if to say, "I told you so," and she was dozing in spite of her best efforts when Ryan tugged her sleeve.

He whispered, "What's this say?"

Ryan was pointing at a line of the biographical handout. "Geosynchronous," Alison said. "It means a satellite—"

"I know what it means. I only didn't know how to say it," he said. "Geosynchronous. Geo means rock."

Alison continued reading over Ryan's shoulder. A list of devices took up a third of one side: from a shielded antenna to a hydraulic valve used in sanitation systems. The rest of the page was a timeline. Some of the dates surprised Alison. Helen had married young; before Restoration she and Justin wouldn't have been able to legally drink champagne at their own wedding.

"Mister Justin was smart," Ryan said. "He built my first phone."

Alison glanced to the boy's mother. Helen lifted her shoulders. "It was an old prototype," she said. "Justin did love his gadgets."

Her tone said the gadgets were the only things he *had* loved, and Nicole said, "Helen, please. Can't you stow the bitterness for one night?"

The look Helen gave her was a masterpiece of emotional presentation: hurt and anger all wrapped up in martyred acceptance and tied with a smile.

Nicole said in a low voice, "You've been giving me that look for seven years, and it's been driving me nuts the whole time. I never slept with your husband. Not once."

A patter of applause interrupted them. Justin Wyatt's image was plastered across the presentation screen now. Helen put a hand against her mouth, then bent her head.

Tiffany rose to make her speech, and Alison looked down from the portrait onscreen to the child beside her.

Helen Armstrong was a blue-eyed blonde. Robert Armstrong was tall and fair-haired too, and gushing reviewers loved to call his eyes "green as moss agates." Ryan had black hair and brown eyes like the man on the screen.

He was also fidgeting and sitting on his feet and starting to fold the handout into an origami creature. Mariana whispered to him, and when he nodded she led him away with apologetic glances to everyone else. Ryan handed off the dolphin to a woman who smiled at him, and she accepted it with a thrilled laugh.

After they'd left Helen said, "I can see what you're thinking, Alison. Don't think it. Ryan is not Justin's child. He's *mine*. Mine and Rob's. Trust me, there were tests."

Alison blushed. "I'm sorry."

Derek patted her arm. "Trust me, you're not alone in wondering. There was plenty of speculation, due to the timing and the public nature of the affair. DNA tests were negative. Saved Wyatt a ton of support money."

He drew back suddenly, which probably meant that Frank had stepped on his foot, and Mark reached for the bottle of wine still sitting at the center of the table.

"By all means, let's talk infidelity and sordid personal details," he said. "It's better than listening to yet another reverent tribute to a self-centered ass who never got my name straight. You'd think he could've guessed right a third of the time."

Derek said, "I can't be sure, but I think he might've done it on purpose. He never called me Derek. Not once."

That broke the tension, and Nicole smiled. "It's my fault for not making two of you dye your hair. Helen, I would apologize, but the resentment gets to me. Your ex settled a crapload of money and stock on you in the estate when he wasn't obligated to leave you anything, and he gave you everything you demanded and more in the separation. *You* filed for release. What more did you want?"

More applause and laughter—Tiffany's amplified and grating—washed over the room.

Helen's face flushed with anger. "I wanted to be a person who wasn't 'Justin Wyatt's wife.' He forgot I existed for days. Weeks. If you weren't in front of him, you weren't real to him. I filed for the divorce so I didn't have to wait for him to notice. Asking for all the money was just a way to hurt him by making him think I didn't care."

Nicole looked supremely uncomfortable. "I'm sorry."

Helen dabbed at her eyes with her napkin. "He was kind, in his own strange way. I've been trying to remember the good, lately. Isn't it sad that it's so much easier now that he's dead?"

They all sat quietly through two more short speeches, and the party broke up with a standing round of applause for someone who wasn't there to hear it.

Helen said, "Alison, I hope the reality behind the glitz wasn't too disappointing."

"Not at all." Alison grinned. "But once was enough."

The guys were halfway to the doors already. Elsewhere in the room people were gathering into pairs and larger groups, and Alison suspected that providing a venue for unofficial business was the real purpose of such events. She wondered how many contracts would be sealed over drinks in the hotel bar later.

Nicole's attention was on someone in the milling crowd, but before she could head after them, Helen reached out to touch her arm. "I owe you an apology."

Nicole nodded, acknowledging the admission without actually accepting it. Then she excused herself to chase the deal she was intent on making.

"I believe I may owe her more than an apology," Helen said wryly. She squeezed Alison's hand. "Thank you again for filling my table tonight. We'll have to find an excuse sometime soon to have some real fun together."

"I would like that," Alison said.

TYLER WASN'T sure exactly when he'd sunk to the point where his main purpose in life was picking up after Justin Wyatt and apologizing to people for him. The downward momentum had gotten away from him over the past eight weeks. He did know when the slide had begun. It had started the moment he met Justin's friends from the Dawnstar Foundation on a private airstrip in Vancouver.

The man and woman in dark suits and dress shoes had greeted Justin with smiles that turned to worried glances as soon as his back was turned. They'd explained the arrangements for false ID and treatment at a hospital renowned for discretion and excellence, and then they'd offered Tyler a job with Dawnstar. Anything he wanted, they said, as long as he stayed off-grid and quiet.

He'd sworn to take care of Justin. His loyalties weren't for sale. Even if they had been, *Justin* was the one who had promised justice for his brother's death and a peek at some fascinating physics on the side.

Tyler had told the Dawnstar executives that he already had a job, and then he'd helped translate Justin's slurred complaints to two orderlies getting him squared away for a flight to Minneapolis. The expression on Justin's face—relief and gratitude—had made Tyler feel ten meters tall.

Right now, hiking through a spring snowstorm to a doctor's office he'd left an hour earlier, he felt exploited and annoyed. " 'Get my gloves,' he says. Do I look like a valet?"

By the end of their first month back in civilization, he'd learned to double-check Justin's vicinity before any departure, but the man still regularly misplaced items. He also issued high-handed directives, fell asleep at irregular times, and spent hours "thinking." Direct questions often yielded stares instead of replies.

Communication was becoming a major issue. Justin had left hospital custody a week ago, and Tyler still didn't know why he'd been released when he could barely walk.

The man at the reception desk of the Mayo Legacy outpatient

clinic smiled sympathetically when he saw Tyler come in. "What was it this time?"

"A pair of blue gloves." Inspiration struck. "And a copy of his medical records, please."

The gloves were under a massage table. The receptionist consulted several screens in his search for records before saying hesitantly, "Wouldn't Mr. Smith rather wait for the updated version from Rydder Institute? They received the file we sent, and they've set up an evaluation appointment for Wednesday."

Tyler had no idea what that meant. He proclaimed ignorance and played up his lackey status. Once the surprising news that he was listed as Justin's next of kin came to light, the medical data were sent to his account.

He returned the gloves to Justin, who ignored them, and then he studied charts until he developed a headache. The terminology was impenetrable. He stopped as soon as he squeezed out enough details to explain Justin's situation.

The weird skin condition Justin had developed was leaving him in medical limbo. Its cause was mystifying a host of experts, and the risk of contamination disqualified him from remedial surgery. Without intervention his leg would never hold weight properly, but he was restricted to physical therapy until the discoloration was gone.

While floundering through reports from a neurologist, Tyler came across the name Rydder again, in the context of it being Justin's only chance to make a full recovery from the head injury.

Rydder Institute's slick publicity profile was much easier to comprehend than the medical jargon. The operation was local, like Mayo, and it claimed to provide some of the world's most advanced neurological and mental health services. It held a monopoly on the small pool of talent in a breakthrough field called neopsychiatry, and a defensive attitude about its exclusive services explained why Justin hadn't been sent straight there.

The place ran extensive background checks before allowing

patients onto the grounds. Other safety measures included patient waivers and heavy official security for the practitioners, courtesy of a close working relationship with the Civilian Security Bureau.

In a minor miracle, Justin remembered to mention his appointment, so Tyler didn't have to explain how he knew about it. He got Justin through the guard stations and the paperwork on time. Then he idled away a few hours in a comfortable waiting room with books and journals. People came and went, but the conversations were always hushed and mellow, creating an enjoyable white noise that encouraged concentration.

If he hadn't looked up at the right moment, he would've missed Justin's exit. The man limped right past him, head down, blankly staring. Tyler packed away his datapad and readied himself for a low-speed chase.

Someone at his shoulder said, "There's no rush. He's been hit hard by some bad news. Give him a minute to process it in private."

Tyler turned in surprise. The woman wore a tan lab coat and an air of authority, but she wasn't much to look at: brown skin, muddy eyes, graying hair, small breasts, big hips. Her voice, on the other hand, was remarkable. Every syllable was crisply resonant.

She also had a friendly smile. "Hi. I'm Dr. Beth Clarence. I would've been the lead neopsych on Mr. Smith's case if we could've treated him. You're his caregiver, as I understand it. He spoke of you, before the test results cut short our interview."

It wasn't a question, but Tyler found himself nodding. Dr. Clarence tilted her head to one side. "God does have a sense of humor. You're an odd fit for each other, but it works. Try to be patient with him."

"I am." Tyler shook off confusion. It was easy to lose track of sentences when all the words sounded so significant. "Wait. Are you saying you can't treat Justin?"

The woman grimaced. "No, we can't. I'm afraid he can't

tolerate our proprietary drug formulations. It is a shame that we can't screen for allergies ahead of time, but it's rarely an issue. Fewer than one percent have any issues. Please convey my apologies for raising his hopes."

Tyler nodded. "I'll do that. Is there a next step?"

"He should throw himself into occupational therapy." Dr. Clarence's voice went dry. "But I expect he'll go to ground like a wounded badger instead. Keep an eye on him, or he'll run himself ragged digging himself a new den."

"Run? He's barely walking."

Dr. Clarence's smile returned. "Humor is good. He needs that. Good luck with him."

When Tyler caught up with Justin, irritation wiped away his lingering puzzlement over the odd conversation. Then he turned around without saying a word and went back into the building to retrieve Justin's coat.

Halfway back to the city, Justin announced, "Physical therapy is boring, and Manny and Jiri aren't doing a damned thing about investigating the crash. I can't work here, and neither can you. Let's pack up and head home to Seattle."

That sounded a lot like going to ground. Apparently Rydder's doctors were as perceptive as they claimed to be.

"All right," Tyler said. "Why not?"

He did his best to keep ahead of Justin's erratic progress, from collecting treatment plans from exasperated physicians and unhappy therapists to taking care of all the travel arrangements. And when Justin thanked him on the way to the airport, he felt ten meters tall again.

It was 4:00 a.m. when Tyler drove a rented cargo truck onto one of Seattle's bustling wharfs, but the area was brightly lit and bustling. A steady parade of trucks rolled through a gate to his left, and a locomotive hauling stacked containers accelerated away from the railyard.

Justin had told him to drive here, and here they were. He might wish that he knew *why*, but he might as well wish for wings. Justin liked secrecy the way seals liked fish. After a week spent in private meetings with his Dawnstar associates, he'd arrived at the hotel with the cargo truck.

"Pack your kit," he'd said. "We have to be on the docks before four thirty."

Tyler was directed to one of the interior secured yards. A sign identified it as "Mercury Shipping," and an overland truck sat inside the open gate. The contents of their vehicle were quickly added to the open container on its bed. A paunchy man wearing a baseball cap accepted a datapad from Justin and gave it a close assessment. "Which one of you is Smith?"

"That would be me." Justin offered his hand.

The driver gave it a brisk shake and shook Tyler's in turn. "Your boss warned you this is the slow boat, yeah? I hit Spokane and Helena before your offload. Safety regs make that three full days. It's no joyride."

Tyler gave Justin a hard look. Justin ignored him. "It's a free one, and the gear has to get there somehow."

Pete sealed the manifest on the datapad. "True enough. Last chance for a piss or a cup of coffee before we leave."

They sampled the amenities of the warehouse office, and on their return to the truck, a container came to rest nearby with a noise so loud that it could be felt as a physical pressure. Justin's left leg gave out when he flinched. Tyler caught him by the arm and barely kept his own balance.

"How's the leg?" he asked once he checked his shirt for spilled coffee.

"I'm fine."

Tyler gritted his teeth on a sarcastic response. The ritual was starting to grate on him. Justin was never going to be fine, but he seemed determined to ignore reality.

Dealing with him required cultivating patience the way Tyler's mother had cultivated orchids in a region where the sun barely rose for a third of the year. That meant being careful, methodical, and resigned to eventual failure.

He'd given his word, and Harry had raised him to keep it. His patience was withering with every day now, but he would nurture it as long as he could.

Justin said, "How're you doing?"

"I'm holding up." The second half of their private joke came to his lips without thought, and Justin nodded before turning away to limp towards the truck. Tyler followed behind, ready to catch him when he faltered again.

CHAPTER SEVEN

TYLER WOKE UP WITH A jerk when the truck came to a halt. The sun had set while he napped. The dark surroundings gave him no hint of the reason for the halt.

"We're here," Justin said. He opened the passenger door, and outside air wafted inside. The odors of growing things and rotting ones blended with asphalt and dust to create a scent that was hot, ripe, and thick.

Anything was a vast improvement over the stink of three-men-in-a-truck. Tyler inhaled gratefully and followed Justin outside.

The GPS showed a map for Lincoln, Nebraska. They had halted near a block of light industrial buildings. Signs flickered bright invitations to businesses a block away, but the immediate area was devoid of activity. The office park backed against an open space where scattered trees and tall grasses rustled in the evening breeze. A heavy layer of mist was rising up to the clear, dark sky.

Justin went to a two-story building whose dingy white walls were blank but for a loading dock and a single standard door on the side facing the drive. Unlike most of the other operations, this one had no commercial sign. Justin's palm print and a pass card unlocked the door.

The foyer was painted a dirty beige and was occupied by a gray metal reception desk and filing cabinets. Two narrow hallways lined with doors led deeper into the building.

"I'm not impressed," Tyler said. "Why are we here?"

A buzzer drowned out the end of his question: the truck was in the dock.

Justin limped down a hall. "If we were in one of your superhero stories, this would be my secret hideout. Help me load the toys into the freight elevator."

Justin's lair was a large underground space three stories deep. It extended well under the neighboring park, which probably explained the park's continued presence in a well-developed area. Tyler uncrated and assembled a computer array that could probably handle the launch of an interplanetary expedition before he was pulled from that office to another room and assigned the task of unpacking frames, motors, tools, wiring, and various electronic components.

Justin wandered off.

When Tyler's stomach diverted his attention with a long, unhappy growl, he checked the time, then stood up. "Time for a break, Justin. Long past time."

The sound echoed. Large as the space was, it felt cramped, a chaotic maze that testified to long occupation. Machinery fought for space with chemical tanks, and storage bins. Power runs and pipelines snaked overhead and underfoot. Tyler made an informal tally of over a dozen projects in progress.

"I'm starving," he said, raising his voice. "It's time for breakfast."

Justin's head popped into view over a 3-D manufacturing unit.

"Breakfast?" He looked around as if seeking a window. "It's morning already?"

"Yes, it is. Is there a decent restaurant in this town?"

"There's food here. Jiri had the staff stock the place." Justin ran his hands through his hair, which left it in a brushy mop. "We worked all night?"

"Yes, we did." Irritation soured Tyler's mood. Water, wet; Justin, obsessive. Pointless to rail at the nature of either, but he was too tired to be tolerant after yet another marathon session of unappreciated labor.

"Huh." Justin glanced down, his attention clearly wandering back to whatever he had been working on. More than two minutes later, he shook himself out of the reverie. "Did you get the new tech up and running?"

"Running and integrated into the existing system, which I noticed has no external linkages whatsoever. There isn't even a landline into this place, is there?"

"No." Justin scratched his chin. "I like privacy."

Tyler gritted his teeth, but it failed to keep his temper inside. "Is this the big plan? Sit in your cave and hide? Do you even care who nearly killed us, or have you forgotten all about it? Have you even been paying attention to your own company lately? Have you thought of anyone else you can trust to contact? Have you done *anything* useful? I know you weren't learning how to walk straight or speak clearly."

Justin's eyes narrowed, and the set of his jaw boded ill for the conversation ending well. Tyler stepped back mentally and looked past his own frustration. "I'm sorry; that sounded a lot less obnoxious before it came out of my mouth, but I'm serious. What's the plan? I do have a life, you know."

It wasn't much of a life, but that wasn't the point.

Justin's expression went tighter and tighter, then relaxed into a huge yawn. "Damn, I hate this," he said in the general direction of the floor. "Come on, let's get breakfast and some sleep. Then we can start fresh."

"Come *where*? Get started doing *what*?"

Justin continued walking. Every few steps he brushed against one piece of equipment or another. It gave his progress an odd emotional subtext, as if he were pausing to greet special favorites amidst the crowd of machines.

For all Tyler knew, that was exactly what he was doing. "*Justin.* Look at me, dammit."

Justin stopped and turned, one hand braced on a workbench. Grit was smeared down one cheek, and he looked defeated.

Tyler was past caring. "I am done, understand? Fill me in or I walk. Right now. I'm not your personal slave, and I'm not an idiot, and if you keep treating me like one, then we are done, you hear me? I have had enough."

"You sound like both my ex-wives rolled into one."

Pointing out that the ex-wives must have been crazy to marry him in the first place seemed cruel, but Tyler didn't trust himself to say anything else.

Justin looked away first.

"You also sound a lot like William on a bad day." He glanced back, sidelong and apologetic. "Can this wait until after a shower and breakfast? Please?"

When Tyler nodded, Justin's shoulders slumped. "Good. Come see the rest of the bunker. You would've regretted bailing out before seeing the guest rooms."

JUSTIN GOT Tyler settled in the residential quarters and took himself off to the main kitchen to start on breakfast. An hour later, Tyler was sitting down at the butcher block table in the center of the large room. His t-shirt and jeans were clean, his sandy hair was dripping wet, and his feelings were written across his face. His mood hadn't improved.

"Nice place," he said. "Secret underground luxury hotel. What is it for?"

Justin reached for plates in the cabinet. The first grab missed by a ridiculous distance, and he yanked hard on his temper. The clumsiness, the limp, the never-ending *aches*—as frustrating as those were, none of them were as bad as the dizzy lapses in balance or the way his mind dropped out from under his thoughts at unpredictable intervals. Getting angry only made it worse.

He'd tried to blame everything on being cold and weak and in pain for a long time, but the doctors had ripped away that comfortable delusion. His brain was broken, and the list of forbidden activities was a long one: piloting, hang gliding, and driving were all on it. He got the plates and focused on what he could do. He could make things right with Tyler.

"Dawnstar leases space to the government when I'm not here," he said. "The business upstairs is a cover for them. A lot of the work done here is done by people with *very* high security clearances. People like that enjoy their creature comforts. So do I."

"It's not nice enough to make up for being a mushroom." Tyler raised his chin. "Do I smell toast?"

"I promised breakfast." Justin placed a full plate in front of him and set a datapad next to it. "This is all I have on the crash. Lists of competitors, old personal enemies, the official investigation into the disappearance, a lot of records from the months beforehand. It isn't much, I know. And I haven't kept up on what Tiff's doing with Wyatt Enterprises. I don't care."

He wanted to find and punish whoever had targeted him, needed it with an intensity that worried him, but he couldn't turn desire into direction.

Tyler leaned forward to put his elbows on the table. "That is not a plan, Justin. That is a data set and a bad case of denial. It didn't occur to you that your ex's plans might contain clues?" Exasperation and amusement warmed his voice. "I should've yanked your chain about this a long time ago."

"I don't like leashes." Justin might have the self-awareness to know he needed handling, but that didn't make it comfortable. "I came here because the doctors said I need familiar surroundings and routine. If you need to go—you don't have to—I don't need—"

He did need, but he wouldn't beg. Couldn't.

"I should've reeled you in ages ago," Tyler said with dry humor. "Stop looking at me like that. I'm not going to leave you in the lurch for being an aggravating ass, Justin. I'm no prize in the personality department myself. This is as good a hidey-hole as any, but what are we doing here? Is that crap we hauled here useful for anything?"

"You said you wanted to run analysis on the power cells. I wanted to make that happen for you. You'll need to build testing equipment. The crash, though—I can't focus."

He'd concluded that the sabotage itself was a dead end. The debris was inaccessible, and the official investigations had uncovered nothing. There was still hope that the data on competitors and activities would point at a culprit. Grinding through the available information and determining who benefited most from his death would generate a long list of suspects. The approach was hardly elegant, and it would be a long-term proposition, but it might work.

Even the thought of starting it made his head hurt. He could cross out a lot of the names if he could just figure out why someone wanted him dead, but pondering motivations made his head hurt too.

Life hurt.

"Why don't you take a stab at the mystery, Tyler?" he said. "The workstations in the labs have to stay off-grid, period, but there's a data line in the living quarters."

"Add amateur detective to my duties? Sure, why not?" Tyler picked up his fork and looked at his plate for the first time. "Raisin toast and scrambled eggs with cheese."

"You order that every chance you get."

"I know." Tyler shoveled eggs into his mouth while he began reviewing data. "Never thought you noticed."

Justin had noticed, the same way he had noticed Tyler's reaction to the smell of frying bacon the first time they'd walked into a diner. Hard to miss an aversion to cooked meat in someone who had wolfed down frozen steak and beef jerky for days at a stretch. They both had their issues.

Tyler looked up and asked, "Did I smell coffee too?"

Justin poured two mugs. "I'm writing off the rest of today, all right? I'll be in the rec room if you need me. There are maps."

He was home, as much as any place had been home since the last divorce, and he'd been looking forward to visiting his pool for days now. Caffeine and the comfort of being back in a safe, well-loved environment had taken the edge off his weariness, but his body was aching with a vengeance. Hot water eased that particular pain better than anything else he'd tried.

The hinges on the old steel door into the area were perpetually in need of lubrication. Justin wrestled it open and shut it behind him to keep in the heat.

Murals of a tropical island decorated the walls, an excellent sound system provided wave noise and birdsong to heighten the illusion, and the lighting was programmed to mimic the local day/night cycle. A hint of ozone and metal hung in the air from the filtration, and the pool stretched out twenty-five meters, deep enough for diving at the near end.

Diving was inconceivable. Justin wasn't even up to swimming a lap. He stripped to his underwear, grabbed a towel from the selection on a side table, and made his gimpy, tentative way to the neighboring hot tub.

Full immersion might lead to falling asleep and drowning at this point, which would be a stupid waste. For now it was enough to sit on the edge of the tub with both legs submerged to the knee. Heat radiated through his skin, unlocking cramped muscles and relieving the heavy throbbing in the bones. He lay back, stretching his arms over his perpetually aching head, and the heated tiles pressed against his spine.

He fell sound asleep. Something metallic squealed behind him, and he came awake with a jerk. He knocked over a coffee cup. The cup shattered, and shards of ceramic went skittering into a pool.

Pool. Coffee cup. Justin concentrated on the known objects, but they were no help. He had no idea where he was. Fear rose like a choking cloud.

Soft laughter came from behind him. He turned, and his brain jolted into working order at the sight of the man standing in the doorway.

Tyler wiped a smile off his face. "Sorry, but that was one of the funniest things I've seen all year."

"Ha." Justin gathered his dignity and stood up before the spilled coffee reached him. "S'wrong?"

"Nothing." Tyler made a vague gesture. "That's still spreading, huh? Looks like you took a bath in self-tanner and forgot your arms."

"I think that's the only theory I hadn't heard yet." The discoloration didn't respond to medication and didn't act cancerous; biopsy samples lost the odd color within seconds of being taken. "Maybe if I end up all one color again, the doctors will stop worrying about it. And if nothing's wrong, why are you here?"

Tyler gave Justin the look that said he was still a few words behind, translating mumbles. "I was checking tech journals. Martin-Hong Technologies is sponsoring capacitor research that looks like your blocks. There's a draft article on storage mechanics. I thought you said you hadn't told anyone about them."

Justin's heart rate shot up, and he had to catch his breath before speaking. "I didn't tell. And I took all of my prototypes north."

He hadn't even realized the full potential of the storage cells until he started working with Tyler. It had been a personal project, not a corporate one. William had insisted on filing sealed patents, but Justin had never added them to his assets lists. Tiffany would've pestered him to throw them into Wyatt R&D if he had. His copy of the documentation was in a deposit box at a bank with a strict biometric access policy.

There was the motive he'd been unable to grasp. If he died before he published those patents, then whoever held the designs could build false provenance and file new ones—or sell them to someone who could.

His working notes must've been copied by someone who'd seen the potential Justin had failed to see, someone who had known that the work was relatively undocumented and decided to profit from it.

"Where did Martin's people get it? I know they didn't get it from me. And why do they care? They don't do power tech." Fear grew in the pit of Justin's stomach. "Shit. They've been refining their product line towards armaments for years now."

"Maybe they want to branch out again."

"I doubt it. The cells blow up, remember? It isn't significant on a small scale, but it's a cube function."

A moment passed in silence before Tyler said, "I hesitate to ask what you consider a significant explosion."

"One of the hand-sized ones could bring down a two-story building with reinforced walls. Put four of them together, and you could pulverize a bunker like this one—and I was working to minimize the potential. I'll bet you anything that Martin-Hong will shelve the battery idea and shop explosive prototypes in a year. Better pray they sell to the open market, not under the table."

"Damn, Justin." Tyler whistled softly. *"Damn."*

"I can account for every prototype, and no more than twelve people ever even heard about them. One of them stole specs and sold them to Martin-Hong."

Tyler wrote down the names and repeated them back. Then he said, "Forget about amateur sleuthing, Justin. This wasn't a personal thing. It's big. You need to call in some big guns."

"I don't have any. William always handled that kind of thing, and no one trustworthy at Dawnstar had any suggestions. Manny and Jiri—they won't take it seriously. They think I'm making up a conspiracy to give meaning to tragedy. They believe in me enough to give me money, but they don't believe *that.*"

After a long silence Tyler said, "I have a name."

The way he said it left Justin certain that he'd missed hearing it several times already. It still made no sense. "Yes, you have a name. It's Tyler. Don't tell me you're forgetting things now too."

That won him a roll of eyes and a wry grin. "No, that's your specialty. Harry gave me a call code once, made me memorize it and said that if I was ever in a jam, even the worst jam I could imagine, any kind, that this guy was the one to ask for help."

'Worst jam imaginable' seemed like an apt description for more than their current situation. "Being lost in the wilds of the Canadian Rockies didn't qualify?"

Tyler's face turned beet red. "At first, you didn't want to call anyone, and after that, we had the help from your friends, and—damn, Justin. I never even thought about it until just now. I don't know what to say. I'm a moron."

Justin raised a hand to forestall a plunge from obvious embarrassment into abject misery. "I will never criticize 'I forgot' as an excuse," he said. "Make the call."

ALISON'S AFTERNOON had been going well until Mark called. The office was running smoothly, Nicole's calendar was full but not overwhelming, and Alison found an hour of free time on her hands. She was using it to update her contact lists when the call came in.

"We need to talk," he said.

Mark had a way of speaking that made everything into a

pronouncement of doom. Alison still had to stop herself from reacting to it.

"Nicole's taking a half day," she said. "What about tomorrow? She has an hour free at ten."

"Not Nicole. You." Mark sighed. "I need a second opinion. Let's get lunch."

Every time she thought life might get boring, something new cropped up. Several questions came to mind immediately, but discretion seemed the best course. Whatever this was, Mark wanted it kept quiet. She suggested tea instead of lunch, Mark paid for the snack, and after they finished eating, he showed her the source of his worries.

His specialty was corporate real estate brokerage, and that had landed him a major role in the firm's disentanglement from its Wyatt Enterprises business. After a month spent chipping away at the list of ownerships and leases, he'd discovered some alarming anomalies: properties purchased by C&A and leased back to Wyatt Enterprises without formal brokerage, and leases held by the firm for no reason. Taken together, their value was tremendous.

"I swear no one but Clooney ever knew this was going on," Mark said, "but it looks as if we're hiding assets from Tiffany Wyatt. She will incinerate us, if it's true."

She would, without a doubt. Alison said, "Yes, but why show me? I'm not a lawyer."

"You have a creative imagination," Mark said with stiff dignity. "And you catch little details like they're going out of style. I'm hoping against hope that you'll see a detail and have a burst of inspiration. And you're *not* a lawyer."

If she found anything, Clooney and Associates would be off the hook. If not, the conversation would be protected. Mark lost nothing by involving her.

"Let me see the files again," Alison said.

She did find one item of interest. A construction firm from Chicago called Design Unlimited had been contracted to do work on nine of the twelve problematic properties, and some of the places had been renovated more than once. Their work might be that good, or it might be a red flag.

Alison brought up the company profile and passed it to Mark. "Have you talked to anyone here yet?"

Mark looked it over. "No, it looks like I should, doesn't it? Best to hit them in person, too. Would you mind coming along to help dredge files and run interference?"

"A business trip? Are you kidding? Count me in. I'll clear it with Nicole."

"Pack your passport, just in case."

"What? Why?"

"So sad. A history major with no sense of history." Mark shook his head in mock despair. "Remember the Summer Secession?"

"That was years ago," Alison said. "And it lasted, what, two months? It isn't an annual event."

"Yes, but all that commerce fuss out west could blow up nationally."

In addition to the continued posturing over water rights, several state governments were unhappy with new federal controls on commerce both interstate and international. There were rumblings about stepping out of the Republic and declaring independence to protect the integrity of their tax rolls.

Rumblings and posturing were safety valves. That was how representational societies worked. Any history major knew that.

"You're a total alarmist," Alison said.

"You never know when things are going to go sour," Mark said as he rose to his feet. "Better to have your papers than to need them. That's all I'm saying."

"I do not believe it," Tyler said. "You don't just stick things together and come up with other things! It takes people and time and meetings and tests. You have to run simulations. Test materials. Test prototypes. Run more simulations and tests. This isn't how it works."

Justin stopped what he was doing to glare down the ladder. Introducing instrumentation into the packed innards of the power cells was delicate work, and distraction was dangerous. Criticism was distracting.

No one ever believed that he came up with his ideas out of the blue and then built them mostly alone. "I took notes. I did math. I researched materials and made calculations. I drew schematics. I recorded the whole process, just like we're recording this." He pointed at the monitor that showed a composite 360° view of the workroom with its occupants entangled in the equipment and wiring. The image waved pliers. "Watch it to your heart's content."

"I have. Twice. I still can't believe it." Tyler wiped sweat from his forehead. "You just 'thought them up,' you say. "

"It's the truth." Justin stopped talking and got back to work.

These days he couldn't think at all without giving himself sick headaches. Luckily, innovation wasn't nearly as taxing as creation. He could still build testing machinery that would provide the empirical data Tyler needed.

Once upon a time he'd paid other people to do things like that. It led to independent replication, market applications, licenses, and money. It was also boring.

That was the main reason he had started a company in the first place—that, and because William had suggested it. Now he needed work that would keep him too busy to think about all the other things he couldn't do.

The next thing he knew, he was squinting at the ceiling and struggling to locate an anchor for place and time. The vertical surface against his left shoulder was scarred by an impact crater the size of a plate about two meters up. Cracks surrounded the center in a broken web.

He sat up when he remembered where he was. A charred lump bounced to the floor beside him: the fried remains of a power cell. The entire apparatus had catastrophically shorted out.

The overload should've electrocuted him. The power cell should've pulverized his insides when it rocketed loose, and the wall should've broken his back. The dent in the surface marked where his shoulders had struck. He should be dead.

Panic boiled up. He hadn't been alone.

"Tyler?" He shouted it, but he heard nothing. "*Tyler*!"

Tyler rose to his feet back by the rig. He looked uninjured. Justin's terror and guilt ebbed back to containable levels. His skin was a little itchy, but overall he felt better than he had in weeks. All the bone-deep aches had vanished, leaving behind a heady sense of well-being.

His ears popped, and a muted beeping became audible. A glance at the strobe light above the door across the lab confirmed that it was the ear-shattering claxon of the lab's alarm system. The doors had automatically shut.

Tyler reached up to disengage the alarm, which released the lock. Then he slid the panel open and looked into the hall.

"Where're you going?" Justin tried to stand up, but his sense of balance was shot. He lurched, his leg gave out, and he slid to the floor again. "Damn, I hate this. Give me a hand, will you?"

Tyler looked around the room and then whirled in a circle. His eyes settled on Justin and went wide, and he said, "What the hell?"

The near-silent words were easy to lip-read. Justin looked down and got his second shock. His body wasn't *there*. He could see floor, but not his feet. Second by second, the effect slowly wore off, until he was visible again.

"Interesting," he said.

CARL JENSON CHECKED the dash navigator once more. The indicator said they were on course, but the surroundings didn't inspire confidence. Wet gravel squelched under the tires as they approached a stand of tall grass and cattails.

"Please remember that the all-terrain in the vehicle description does not include water," he told his brother. "This is an expensive rental. Are you sure about this meeting?"

Parker grinned and took the car over a bump in the gravel road with more enthusiasm than necessary. Prospective clients often preferred to meet on neutral ground rather than in their own territory, but neutral usually meant restaurants or public buildings. Nebraska was in the middle of nowhere already. Out of town in Nebraska was overkill.

"At least tell me we're not here to knock down a wasp nest," Carl said. "I didn't bring a big stick or a ballistic vest."

Parker pulled on the brim of his baseball cap and shrugged. He was feeling cautious, not expecting treachery.

The road came to an abrupt end at the edge of a swamp. Deceleration flung Carl forward into the seat belt. The strap bit into his shoulder, and the safety lock engaged. By the time he got the latch to release and got his door open, Parker had retrieved his weapons from the trunk and was heading down a narrow trail to the left. Carl caught up a few meters into the brush. The weeds and trees opened onto a cleared meadow surrounding a tin-roofed maintenance building. One of two garage bays was open, with a muddy truck parked halfway inside the door.

A nicely paved road swung in a wide curve away to the right. Parker had brought them in by the back route. A lawn mower buzzed in the distance; closer, insects chirped in the weeds. As Carl reached the garage, Parker gave him a look over his shoulder. One eyebrow lifted: *now what?*

"Don't ask me what to do," Carl said. "You're the one who set up the interview." He got another look in response, but it was too complicated to translate. "Use words, please. Why are we here?"

"Debts owed, for one thing." Parker pulled off his cap, ran a hand over short brown hair. Shrugged again. "Man had the code. Worth checking out. Feels right."

"You and your feelings." Carl sighed. "Okay, let's go talk to the dead men."

CHAPTER EIGHT

THE GARAGE BELONGED TO THE city park system, judging from the posted memos, and it was currently empty. Carl returned to the open garage bay for the sake of the breeze and settled a hip against a workbench. "Want to order a pizza? I saw a picnic table out there."

A raised hand from Parker forestalled further sarcasm. He cocked his head to the side, listening, and a moment later Carl heard the sound as well: muttered voices getting steadily louder. Parker drew his pistol.

A door-sized section of wall inside the office slammed open, and the voices became clear. "No, I will not shoot you in the leg, so there's no point in petitioning for a gun and a license. I won't do it. Stop talking about it."

The sandy-haired young man who stepped into the room was tall and athletic, dressed in running shorts and a striped t-shirt. He was looking over his shoulder down a set of stairs. "And move faster. We're beyond late."

Someone on the stairs said, "They'll wait, Tyler."

"Not the point, Justin. Really not."

"Prepping again would've taken all day. I couldn't stop in the middle. I'm here now, aren't I?"

The speaker reached the top of the stairs and stopped. He wore long pants and a red hooded sweatshirt, and he moved with a distinct limp. His eyes narrowed with interest when he saw the audience. Carl found that intriguing.

Parker was always as tense as a wound spring, and his hazel eyes were a little too direct for most people's comfort. He was also armed. He wasn't much over average in height, but he took up a lot of emotional space. Carl was far bigger and built on a heavier frame, and his pale, shoulder-length hair made him even more conspicuous. On top of all that, he and Parker both wore outfits that were close enough to uniforms to leave an impression of military discipline. The overall effect usually impressed clients, made them nervous, or both.

Justin Wyatt only looked mildly curious. The man was far thinner than he'd been in the file images Carl had reviewed, he had at least two days' dark beard stubble on his face, and he was half a head shorter than Tyler. All in all he was a far cry from the polished larger-than-life mover and shaker portrayed in his corporate propaganda.

Tyler, in contrast, still looked exactly like the baby-faced image on his Tertiary Education ID. It was hard to believe he was as smart as those transcripts indicated, and he couldn't possibly be as wholesome as he looked.

"You are the people I called, right?" Tyler couldn't keep his wide blue eyes off the pistol. "I sure hope so, because otherwise, we are royally screwed."

Parker holstered the gun and looked Tyler up and down. "Harry did a good job with you."

Coming from Parker, that declaration was as good as a contract. Carl pulled his datapad out of its cargo pocket and brought up the appropriate files.

"Are you the man I talked to?" Tyler asked. "The situation is pretty complicated—"

Parker said, "Harry's dead. You aren't. Keep you alive, find and remove the threat. Simple."

"Yeah." Tyler drew out the word. "Anything is, when you boil it down that far. Can you help us? Or do you know somebody who can? You disconnected as soon as I gave you our names and the address."

Parker took the datapad and handed it to Tyler. He gave the contract a perplexed look, then handed it to Justin in turn before saying, "I don't understand. Consulting contract?"

Carl said, "We specialize in personal security and private investigations, and we work for hire."

All eyes in the room shifted abruptly to him, which was a reminder to keep his voice modulated for the general public. "We'll help with or without a contract, but formalities have their place. That document protects you from anything illegal we do, for one thing. Cash will also give us an operating budget. We aren't made of money."

Justin muttered under his breath while he scanned the screen, then said louder, "Relax, Tyler. I can do this."

Carl said, "Let's try this from the top with introductions. Hello, I'm Carl Jenson. That's my brother Eddie Parker Jenson. Adopted brothers, obviously."

The last comment interrupted Justin with his mouth already open. Carl softened the potential for irritation with a smile. "Everybody wonders when I say 'brother.' You really are Justin Wyatt? Not dead."

The man nodded. "Not yet. That's me, and you know Tyler, since he's the one who called Eddie."

"Not Eddie," Parker said. "Parker, Captain, or 'hey you.' Eddie's for family."

"Parker. Right." Justin frowned at the datapad. "Before we go any further with formalities, I want to look this over. Indoors or out? I need to sit down."

Parker inspected the stairwell leading to who-knew-where and looked at Carl. They ended up outside at the table in the shade. Justin spent the short walk reading and making marginal notes, and he continued reading long after they were all seated. Eventually, Tyler planted a palm over the screen.

"Sign it," he said. "There's no choice to dither and worry over. We don't have a lot of other options."

"Never sign things unread. You end up with your immortal soul included in the deal." Justin looked up. "Looks good. There's just one last point to clear up."

His expression made Carl's back tighten up. "What?"

Justin drummed his fingers on the tabletop. "I asked a friend to look into the source of Tyler's call code."

"You what?" Tyler asked.

"Didn't I mention that?" Justin kept watching Carl. "Oops. Anyway, Parker there popped right up. His life's an open book. Combined Armed Forces special combat, record not pristine but impressive, then a nice clean résumé like you listed. But you? There's nothing authentic on your account profile more than a couple of years old. Carl Jenson is a big juicy mystery. Who are you?"

"Off-limits," Parker said, and he came to his feet with his fists clenched at his sides. "No prying or no deal."

Carl wrapped a hand around his brother's wrist. Parker's defensiveness on this particular topic could get dangerous. "It's only a question, Eddie. A reasonable question."

His history had been built by experts, but money could make a lot of holes. Justin had done the digging. He was careful. Careful was good. Parker gave Carl a surprised look. *Are you sure?* Carl squeezed his arm and let go. *Yes.*

It was long past time he pulled his own weight in their partnership. Parker clearly wanted to help. Carl was willing to risk exposure for the chance to make an honest contribution.

"My past isn't pertinent to your situation," he said. "I don't mind curiosity, if you don't mind me choosing not to completely satisfy it. What do you want to know?"

Justin looked from him to Parker and back. "Everything, obviously, but I'm used to not getting everything I want. What can you —no, what *will* you tell me?"

He understood the difference. That was nice. Carl said, "I declined a job offer from some unpleasant people a few years ago. They didn't take no for an answer. The new identity threw them off the trail. When Eddie runs protection contracts, I handle paperwork. I have contacts and training that are useful for investigative cases, and I can run surveillance equipment. When he runs a combat crew, I plug gunshot wounds and powder jungle rot. We come as a set. Take it or leave it."

That description made him sound a lot more useful than he had really been much of the time. The ultimatum at the end of the summary fell into a long, tense silence.

"Suits me," Justin finally said, and he went to work on the datapad. He called up an account and signed off on the retainer. "There. Signed and sealed. Convenient that you're already using the same sketchy bank I do. We're in business. Come downstairs and get the party started."

He handed back the datapad and headed towards the garage without waiting for a response. Parker stared after him. Ignorant acceptance was one thing. Trusting acceptance was another. He slid his eyes towards Carl. Impressed and pleased.

Tyler misread the message and said defensively, "Don't take it personally. He's an ass sometimes, but he means well."

"Did I hear him ask you to shoot him earlier?" Carl asked.

"Oh, yes. Just wait," Tyler said. "He'll ask you too."

CARL STARTED his evening with a stroll around the defunct military installation that Justin Wyatt called home. The physical plant was a work of art that kept the facility synced with the outside world; the lights in the halls dropped to half strength after sundown, and the ventilation system was silent and efficient. The air smelled fresh but not antiseptic, and the temperature varied enough to prevent staleness. None of it could fully disguise the reality of being sequestered underground, and that knowledge kept Carl's nerves on edge.

Either he walked off the tension or he took tranquilizers. He hated tranquilizers. He walked every meter from the extensive warehouses to the residential wing, which had better accommodations than many hotels.

Parker loved the whole place. An inconspicuous location with clear approaches, only two obvious access points and a hidden escape route was near his ideal for defense. The buildings were even wired for surveillance. Security would be simple once their hired support arrived. In the meantime, Parker was sitting watch upstairs, and Carl really needed to sleep before his turn rolled around.

He returned to his quarters. The furnished suite was spacious, and the king-sized bed was comfortable. Sleep remained elusive. He resorted to reviewing the case particulars to distract himself.

Pinning down the guilty parties behind attempted murder and industrial espionage would not be easy. Carl had put inquiries in motion, but they would take time. His contacts were discreet and effective, but they wouldn't make this a priority unless he provided Justin's name. Carl wasn't willing to do that without knowing more about the situation than he did now.

After an hour of restless stress, he took to the halls again. His feet took him to the gymnasium and exercise area modestly labeled "Rec Room" on the wall maps that Parker had removed, and he stepped into the pool area with a sigh of relief.

The ceiling was a star-sprinkled black sky vaulting overhead.

Water glowed in the pool, lit from below, and waves lapped quietly in the gutters. A breeze rustled invisible leaves. The air was warm and wet and fresh.

It was all an illusion, but it was a near-perfect one. The jitters receded, and exhaustion shouldered its way forward. Carl kicked off shoes and socks and stretched out on a convenient lounge. His feet dangled off the end, but that was normal, and the murmur of the water was as soothing as a lullaby.

JUSTIN REGARDED his left hand with sour irritation. The white sensor pads all but glowed against his skin. He was getting used to the shade, which was no darker than a suntan, but it still looked *wrong* somehow. Different.

Numbers appeared on the appropriate screens when he touched a switch. He flexed his thumb, clenched fingers into a fist. Numbers shifted each time.

He hit another switch. The power indicator jumped, but the other readouts went flat at the same time his hand and the rest of his body vanished. A glance at the recorder screen confirmed that the session was still being recorded, but he was no longer in the picture.

He squelched the urge to giggle. Then he toggled off the first power unit and activated the second one. Every hair stood on end, then settled. He was running enough energy through his body to cook flesh now, but not only was he uncooked, he felt *good*. He was also still invisible.

Once he turned off the power, he had to wait nearly thirty seconds before he could see himself again. That was never going to get old.

Next he grabbed a knife from the tool tray. When he'd run his first test on his left foot, he'd deliberately drawn blood. The minor injury was worth the relief of confirming that he could be cut if needed. Dying of appendicitis after surviving everything else would be absurd. He tested the knife point against his hand with a long slow prod, then stabbed hard and fast. The blade skated off his skin with a grating sound, and a curl of metal peeled from the edge as it slid along his palm.

Behind him Tyler said, "That is totally freaky."

Justin jerked upright in surprise and spun around. "Stop startling me like that, will you?"

"Stop sitting with your back to the door. Or else lock it. You also might want to turn up the AC before you fry the electronics. The temp is over thirty cee in here." Tyler sat on a lab table nearby, leaning back with his weight on his arms. "I came to tell you the dynamic duo finished moving in. Parker says no more cleaning crew or grocery service, but we'll have a whole squad of guardian angels in a day or two. Oh, and Carl started reviewing all the info you gave me. I guess he's the brains of the outfit. Did you notice he doesn't even carry a gun?"

"Most people don't." Justin started the laborious process of resetting electrodes onto the right hand. That would be the last of the current set of tests. "Carl's the big one with the long blond hair, right?"

Tyler remained silent. Justin glanced up to find that he was the focus of serious disapproval. "What? Did I get it wrong? I've been busy. Was I supposed to fawn all over them the way you did?"

"No, but most people would attempt polite conversation." Tyler hopped off the desk. "There are only two of them. How could you mix them up?"

"I didn't, did I?" Conversation took energy. Polite conversation required concentration. Justin had limited reserves of both. "Did you come here at this hour to nag me about names?"

"No, I also had some new questions about those." Tyler pointed to the power cells Justin was using to power his experiment. "Remember them? The project we were working on together before you started the high-tech navel-gazing?"

Justin took a deep breath to protest, but Tyler waved away his own remark. "Sorry. Never mind. If I was turning into a sideshow freak, I might obsess too. Is it still spreading?"

The freak comment slipped under Justin's emotional armor and cut deep. He patched over the wound with a smile. "Every bit of skin is covered now, and it's testing consistent. Any electrical contact or fast impact has a full-body effect. I don't know if the source was viral or bacterial or some weird biochemical cellular thing, but it's apparently here to stay."

"Weird is the right word." Tyler snorted. "What are you going to tell the dynamic duo about it?"

"Dynamic duo?" Justin's stomach sank. "Who?"

Tyler sighed dramatically. "Carl. Parker. Damn, Justin. Do you pay any attention to the words I say?"

"Only when you aren't being insulting," Justin said. He could check his notes later to find out who Carl and Parker were. For now he would stick to generalities. "I don't like the word freak, and I'm not putting on a show for anyone. I'm trying hard to be as normal as possible."

He wasn't slurring as much these days, but he still hurt all the time, and at unpredictable intervals he had an impossible time choosing clothes or remembering where he'd put tools. The fade-outs were the worst part. Some days he spent half his waking hours staring at walls.

Normal was lying in a pile of plane wreckage on a snowy mountainside.

Tyler said, "Normal people do not ask other people to literally stab them in the back. You won't ask again, will you? Don't ask me to hurt you. I can't do it."

Justin hadn't thought of it in terms of getting hurt. "I'm sorry, Tyler. I won't ask again."

"Good. Will you help me with the power cells? I'm stuck on the math. I have a million questions."

Slogging through a few tedious calculations was the least he could offer as repayment for everything Tyler had done for him. "Fine," Justin said. "Show me what you have."

It was nearly midnight before they called it quits, and by then Justin's bones and head were throbbing too much to sleep. The pain vanished every time he juiced up his skin and made it do tricks, but it always came back.

It came back fast if he took advantage of the relief to do ordinary things like walk straight or jump or climb stairs. Fast and *hard* if he tried anything more strenuous. Writhing in agony was an effective deterrent to spending too much time charged up. It was far easier to endure the everyday discomfort.

He was slowly adjusting to his new normal. He considered that sad truth as he headed to the pool room for a soak.

CARL CAME out of sleep already in motion. The foggy remains of a dream clouded his vision, pulling his thoughts off-center into terrified incoherence. Awareness barely arrived in time to prevent him from running headfirst into a wall. He pushed off the hard surface with a slap of hands and went to his knees under the crushing weight of panic.

He was in a cowering ball on the floor by the time he was fully awake.

Someone nearby said, "That was interesting."

Justin was standing beside the lounge Carl had so dramatically vacated. Water dripped through the slats of the chair. Justin wore swim trunks, held a cup in the hand and had a towel around his neck. He tossed the towel onto the wet chair and sat on it, extending his left leg with a wince. The shin was scarred—a vivid red line—and the left leg was much thinner than the right.

Tyler's story about the plane crash and subsequent survival adventure had never mentioned a crippling bone fracture. He'd said, "Justin hurt his leg." The apparent gift for understatement made Carl wonder how to translate the breezy admission that Justin had taken 'a hard hit to the head.'

Justin looked functional enough now, which meant any damage to his skull couldn't have been major. Concussion, maybe?

Justin waved the empty cup. "Sorry. I was trying to help. It looked like a pretty awful nightmare." Then he shrugged, which was a tactful way to avoid saying, "I didn't expect you to bolt like a jackrabbit if I splashed you."

Carl ignored the implied invitation to explain himself. Full disclosure was not in the contract, and he would only make matters worse if he said, "Being brutally tortured and left for dead would leave anyone with a few quirks."

He pushed his sleeves down to hide the scars on his wrists. His nerves were steady enough to defend himself against questions until his legs stopped feeling wobbly or until help arrived, whichever came first.

Justin said, "You're not living up to the steely-nerved badass mercenary stereotype at all."

His comment was dry, but Carl heard the foundation beneath the mocking tone. This was someone who knew plenty about failing to meet expectations. Instead of intrusive curiosity he was offering empathy. Carl wondered how many people missed the self-deprecation and heard only insult. Most, he expected.

He cleared his throat. "You want badass? Wait thirty seconds."

Racing footsteps approached. Carl mentally revised his time estimate downward. Ten seconds later the door crashed open. Parker's rifle hit the tile floor with a clatter as he knelt down. Intense hazel eyes bored into Carl's. *Worry. Anger.*

"Not a reality slip," Carl said. "Basic nightmare, complicated by waking up with company in the room. You can come off red alert any time now."

Parker glanced up, as if he could see through meters of earth to the open air. Then he looked back. *Doubt.*

"I can do it," Carl assured him. "I need time to let everything settle, that's all."

Parker's brows drew together. He slapped at Carl's pockets until he found the one where Carl had stashed his medicine case. Then he jammed the container against Carl's chest hard enough to bruise.

"Take the fucking tranks," he said as he stood up. "Idiot."

He leveled a warning finger at Justin to hold him silent and watched until Carl applied the dermal patches. Then he nodded sharply, scooped up his weapon, and stalked out.

"All-righty, then," Justin said once the door clanged shut. "Badass cameo, as promised."

"That's my brother," Carl said. Warm lassitude spread through his veins. "The fists at my back and the thorn in my side since we were five."

Justin finished stretching his leg. "What, you were a shrimp when you were five?"

"No, but some bullies like a big target, and I hated fighting. Eddie loved it. He struggled with other things, ones I could do well. We adopted each other. My parents pulled him from the Restoration crèche where he was raised and made it official a few years later."

"Cute story. You tell that to everybody too? Like the adoption thing?"

"No, actually." Carl hadn't shared that tale with anyone in years. Exhaustion and tranquilizers were the mortal enemies of inhibition. Strange that Parker had left him alone here. He trusted no one easily, and clients hardly ever.

Justin headed to the hot tub, slipping into the bubbling water with a happy sigh. He sat with his back to Carl, minimizing his presence. Carl eased himself onto the lounge again and closed his eyes when rainbow halos developed around every object in view. Dizziness was only one of many reasons he despised taking the drugs.

Justin said, "Curiosity is killing me. I hope you know that."

The sardonic comment rippled with undercurrents: worry and resignation with a strong flow of suppressed anger. Ignorance sorely frustrated him, and he was putting a lot more effort into courtesy than the result indicated. Forthright honesty was a basic element of his psyche along with the curiosity. Those traits grounded an ego like a faceted diamond: goal-oriented, self-contained, and emotionally transparent.

No wonder Parker liked him.

That thought jarred Carl off his meandering mental path. Inability to focus on topic, nonverbal cues upstaging speech, elemental motivations poking at his attention: those were just three more troublesome side effects of the tranquilizer. He played back Justin's words in his head and said, "Nightmares won't interfere with me fulfilling my duties. I'm not discussing it."

"Are you kidding me?" Justin turned so he could rest his chin on his crossed arms. "We covered this, right? I asked, you answered, subject dropped. Your personal demons aren't my concern."

The dismissal was sincere. Not because Justin didn't care—he did, that curiosity was sharp in his voice—but because he recognized a painful topic and didn't want to open old wounds. The rudeness was compassion wrapped up in egotistical wolf's clothing.

Curiosity was contagious. Carl asked, "Then what are you dying to know about?"

"I want to know why your brother showed up so fast, and how you knew he would. Also, do you think I could borrow his gun?"

The hopeful non sequitur slipped through Carl's defenses and dragged a laugh out of him. "No, on the rifle. As for the rest, would you believe we always know when the other one's in trouble?"

Most people took that answer as a joke and accepted the follow-up explanation of surveillance and standard procedures, but Justin was not most people. Carl had no idea what he would ask next. It was a refreshing feeling.

His train of thought abruptly derailed. "Am I hallucinating?" he asked. "Because I would swear I can see through your head right now."

"*Shit.*" Wet puddles appeared on the floor beneath a shimmer like a heat mirage. As Justin returned to shadowy visibility he inspected himself from toes to fingertips. "Interesting," he said. "Apparently electricity and kinetics aren't the only stimuli. I never look at myself outside the lab, I guess. Unless this is a new development."

Not a single intelligent response came to Carl's mind. Justin dropped onto the neighboring lounge and bent forward. Wet hair curled over his forehead, and his eyes gleamed, dark and mischievous. "That's my big secret," he said. "I'll bet it beats yours."

His heart was in that challenge, and the blunt sincerity of it was irresistible. Carl smiled. "It might. Why don't I tell you what mine is? Then you can judge for yourself."

CHAPTER NINE

ALISON THOROUGHLY ENJOYED HER FIRST airplane trip, although she was glad she wasn't going to Salt Lake City. Everyone's credentials were being double-checked at that gate, and the line stretched across the hall. Boarding her flight to Chicago was notably swift in contrast, and the trip proved uneventful despite Mark's gloomy predictions.

Design Unlimited's main office was a gorgeous two-story confection of cream-colored concrete and metal grillwork. Its neighbors were single-story boxes faced in dull brown. Alison's efforts to remain unimpressed failed somewhere between the lobby and the pleasant conference room that had been set up for their visit.

After several hours of work, a woman came to ask quietly if Mark had time to spare for the head of the firm. Mark had discussed that possibility with Alison, and he waved her on her way now.

Adam Berenson met Alison with a broad smile and a firm handshake. His weathered skin and calloused hands testified to experience with the physical side of his business, and his mop of disheveled silver hair gave him an air of distracted inattention belied by the sharp intelligence in his gray eyes.

"I asked for the lawyer," Berenson said after they were seated in his office with drinks in hand. "I'm not complaining. You're much better looking. Only thing is, you being here means the lawyer doesn't want to share anything legal with me."

A smile seemed like the safest answer to that truth. Alison smiled.

Berenson set his iced tea on the coffee table with an emphatic thump. "How much do you know about what Design Unlimited does?"

"Only what I've read from your marketing materials and today's research. Architectural design, construction, and remodeling, all using cutting-edge materials and green technologies."

"We specialize in unique," Berenson said. "Custom work on properties that real estate agents like to call 'exotic.' A decade ago this was a five-man operation. These days I have five people on zoning compliance and permits alone. I have a gal on retainer who specializes in international law. We've been successful beyond my wildest expectations. Much of that growth is due to business steered our way by Wyatt Enterprises or through Clooney and Associates."

He paused. Alison wondered if she'd missed a question. "Go on," she said.

"The latest Dawnstar contracts have left us overextended, but if you are looking for weakness to use for financial leverage I'll make you regret it. I'm not interested in being swallowed whole. Not by you or anyone else."

That scenario was so far removed from any of Mark's suspicions that Alison answered without thinking first. "Leverage?"

Berenson scowled fiercely at the ice cubes in his drink before turning the stare on her again. There was a twinkle in his gray eyes now. "Ms. Gregorio, I suspect that you have no idea what I'm talking about."

"I have no idea what you're talking about. Honestly Mark was saying how impressed he's been with your cooperation. We're here to review property histories pursuant to an internal matter. That's it, I swear."

He took his drink over to the window. "If you are being honest, then I'll have to look elsewhere for the bogeyman currently giving my lawyers fits." He rattled ice cubes. "*Someone's* vetting us for a takeover, and I won't stand for it. This isn't just a business to me."

"I could tell that much from the write-ups and reviews," Alison said. "You must have some amazing stories."

"I do." Berenson smiled at her. "Do you have to get back to your boss right away? I'd be happy to share the histories that go with those invoices and contracts."

"Oh, I'll make time for that." Alison pulled up a chair. Mark could mope on his own for a while.

Berenson had a huge repertoire of anecdotes about the mishaps involved in converting caves, rock formations, retired missile silos, and other oddities of nature or architecture into livable, workable spaces. A soft buzz from the desk stopped him midsentence. He glanced at a flashing icon on the screen with a sheepish expression and picked up the handset. "I'm sorry, Trish. I got caught up—yes, please send him through."

The door opened, and the same woman who had escorted Alison to the office ushered Mark inside. His expression was morose, and he tapped anxiously at the case for his datapad with one hand through the necessities of introductions and seating.

"I want to offer my sincere thanks," he said. "I'm sure Alison explained that we're looking into an internal matter. Confidentiality applies. I can say that your help has been invaluable."

Berenson nodded graciously. "I was told you'd say that."

Alison asked, "Are you done already? That didn't take long."

"Once I started digging, I hit gold fast."

Berenson said, "If our finances weren't your focus, what were you tracking down?"

"I needed to verify a timeline for ownership transfers. It was a lot easier to tell who owned what when by tracing who was paying your bills. There were a lot of needlessly complicated deals, but from your side the timeline's clean-cut and aboveboard."

"There were some kind of tax breaks involved," Berenson said after a moment's thought. "Our latest projects have been remodels or upgrades on buildings Dawnstar recently purchased."

"That's not my problem," Mark said. "Making sure we hadn't dropped one of the legal balls—that was."

Berenson showed them to the door, and Alison thanked him for his time. "I enjoyed the virtual tours."

"You should try a real tour sometime, unless you're only humoring an old man." Berenson beamed at her. "I'd be happy to arrange visits if you're ever near any of the sites. Our contracts require allowances for scheduled walk-throughs up to five years after completion. It's not as though we can set up builder's models, after all."

He made sure Alison left with a business card with a private number appended to the data card.

The offer was tempting. The pictures had been amazing. And she did need to talk to Nicole about taking a vacation.

Tyler missed windows. The bunker was an incredible piece of architecture, but he'd barely seen real sky in the month since the security team had arrived. The walls of the office Justin had given him held image frames with an extensive library of landscapes, but they weren't windows. They also showed entirely too many snowy vistas.

He was deleting a scenic mountain picture when one of his number-crunching computers chirped. He wanted to scream at the results. The simulations of Justin's power cell output still did not match the empirical results on record. Not that there was much information available on the power cells' function.

Justin had abandoned his project of building test equipment to play with himself instead. Tyler had only the incomplete data collected during the cells' original design phase, and Justin never tested any feature more than once before moving on. Tyler allowed himself the small indulgence of thumping his forehead against the desk.

"How did he get away with that?" he asked the universe. "How?"

Then he changed a program variable at random and restarted the sim. No errors popped up immediately, so he left it to run. If the world were perfect, he would clear his mind with a long run himself, but the treadmill in the gym was no substitute for a real trail, and he wasn't allowed outside alone. The grounds and the building were patrolled twenty-four hours a day by the six security professionals Parker had brought in, and they didn't approve of unscheduled wandering.

Everyone on the security crew called Carl "Doc" and Parker "Captain," and four of the six were attractive young women. Kaylie was the one who'd delivered a short lesson in the economics of risk, the one time Tyler griped about being stuck underground.

She was taller than he was, wore her hair in a perky blonde ponytail, and scared the living daylights out of him. She'd juggled knives while she told Tyler that assuming anonymity would protect them from another murder attempt was the kind of assumption that got people killed.

The company name was Mayhem & Havoc Incorporated, and Tyler had no desire to get on the bad side of anyone who advertised services under that title. He hadn't challenged the seclusion since that chat even though the lockdown was scheduled to continue indefinitely. It would end when Carl's investigative contacts found a target for the team to hunt down.

Tyler hoped it wouldn't take much longer. He knew the list was down to three: Tiffany Wyatt, David Hong from Martin-Hong Technologies, and Vladimir Borisov of BLW Research. Suspicious activity had been spotted in their personal or professional circles, they all had people on payroll without specified duties, and each of them had visited Justin's labs on multiple occasions.

Pinpointing which one of them had done the dirty work couldn't be easy. Tyler pitied Carl's contacts, whoever they were. All of the suspects were highly placed within organizations that had money to burn, and all were ruthless enough to have people murdered if it brought them sufficient reward.

Justin's power cells represented a huge reward. He'd come up with the design as a shortcut to powering other gadgets more effectively, but the underlying technology was potentially a world-changer. Simply mapping out solid mathematical models and possible applications would keep a team of world-class physicists, their interdisciplinary support crew, and records staff busy for years. Tyler's frustration boiled up again, and he muttered his new mantra, "This isn't science. It's insanity." He was working alone on a major breakthrough while Justin played with his toes like an overgrown baby.

Someone rapped on the door and startled him out of the sulk. He looked up after yanking the door open. "Hi, Carl. You're up late."

Carl rested a shoulder against the doorframe. Even at this hour he was buttoned down in his semi-uniform of collared twill shirt and cargo pants. Tyler wondered if he ever rolled up his sleeves. The outfit was field green tonight, although black ran a close second in popularity. Parker favored tan. Parker favored weapons too. Carl didn't. Tyler still wasn't sure what to make of that quirk.

"Justin's up late," Carl said. "It's my turn playing babysitter on night shift. Would it be impolite to ask who you were talking to?"

"Myself. No one. I don't know. Justin drives me nuts sometimes." Even as Tyler spoke, he wondered why he was confessing to a tantrum.

He decided to blame Carl. The man's eyes were dark blue, a soft detail in a face whose crooked nose and punch-thickened skin testified to a violent past, and he *watched* things. He mostly watched Justin, which Tyler appreciated because it meant he had more time to himself, but the regard was unsettling.

Then there was Carl's voice. The smooth baritone was easy on the ear despite the man's penchant for speaking in long, impenetrable sentences, and it lulled the listener into losing control of the conversation. When he asked questions, blurting out answers felt inevitable.

An idea nudged at the back of Tyler's mind—something about that voice—but he shook off the distraction. "Basically I'm losing my marbles stuck down here in this cave. You'll lose a few too if you spend too much time with Mr. Invisible and his ever-changing freak show."

"Sanity is overrated. I dropped by because Justin wants your help and you're ignoring your phone."

"What's he tinkering with now?"

Carl raised an eyebrow. "I have no idea. It involves little black boxes, sparks, and lots of muttering and cursing. He's changed out breakers five times and broke a worktable by thumping it too hard."

That sounded interesting. "I should take a look."

As they walked down the hall Carl asked, "Has he always been like this? Not the fists of steel, I know that's recent. I'm talking about the way he's absentminded and monomaniacal at once."

"He's been like that since we met, but I barely knew him before the plane crash. He thinks sideways, you know?. Amazes me, the things he'll notice when he isn't being forgetful or rude." Tyler was reaching for the door release when he heard glass shatter inside the room.

Something nearby hit the floor hard enough to make it vibrate.

The lock indicator flashed from green to red. The absence of alarms was no comfort. Justin had turned most of them off days ago. Tyler popped the emergency release. The door squealed open, and white smoke gusted through the opening on a draft of hot air.

"Carl, is that you? Tyler?" Justin called from somewhere in the haze. A moment later he added, "Either way, come look at this. It worked this time."

Laughter bubbled up from deep in Tyler's belly. Maybe he should be toiling away in a real lab with a crowd of clever, ambitious people, but he was here instead, with someone who cared more about sharing a discovery than a threat to his safety.

He laughed until he had tears in his eyes, and then he wiped the moisture away. Then he called, "Hey, freak show, which corner are you in? Don't make me hunt you down."

Silence.

"Justin?"

"I heard you, boy genius. I'm in back near the target wall."

Tyler stopped and stared when he got there. "You quit working on that diagnostic rig after we blew it up. When did you finish?"

Justin wiped soot off his hands and looked at the snarled wiring and scaffolding beside him. "Five minutes ago. Hook up the telemetry to the lab system whenever you want. I'm sorry it took so long."

"Damn, Justin. Thank you."

The courtesy went unanswered. Justin had already started to pack away tools and tidy up the workspace. His hands were shaking, and he was listing to the left.

Tyler suddenly realized that he hadn't seen the other man all day. With a stab of guilt he asked Carl, "If he finished just now, then when did he start?"

"This morning," Justin said. "Skip the nagging."

"Only if you leave the cleanup to me and go to bed. I know your docs told you no more than twelve hours on your feet. Well, they said six, but that was ridiculous."

Justin gave him a guilty look and headed out the door. An hour later, after cleaning up the lab, Carl and Tyler found him asleep in the hot tub. More precisely they found his clothes and towel and drew conclusions from the swirling patterns in the water.

Justin didn't even say good night after they woke him up and got him into bed.

"That's normal?" Carl asked as they left his room.

"For him? Just another day at the office," Tyler said.

ALISON RAISED her glass of iced tea. "Here's to the joy of enjoying nature from a safe distance."

Rain spattered against the train window, each droplet racing away with a thin comet tail of moisture. Nicole raised her own glass, which contained white wine and a bubbly mixer. Vacation meant she could have a drink with every meal if she wanted one, she'd said. It also meant a break from formality. Nicole's jeans and tank top were clean but well-loved, her nails were polish-free, and her hair was in a ponytail. Alison had her hair down for once instead, but she wore an equally comfortable outfit.

Despite their low-key style choices, they were both collecting looks from other passengers. That was due to the now-empty third chair at their table. Helen had excused herself to check on Ryan.

Lightning flashes illuminated the dining car, followed by a crack of thunder loud enough to be heard over the wheel noise. Glassware clinked as the train rocked onto a rough section of track, and Alison grabbed her plate as it began to slide away.

Nicole said, "Here's to escaping unpleasant respon-sibilities. If not for your invitation, I would be severing C&A's last connection to Wyatt Enterprises right this minute." She lifted her glass higher. "May Tiffany get exactly what she deserves. Martin-Hong and its legal vultures are going to eat her alive."

They clinked glasses, and Nicole tossed back her wine with a contented sigh. "You were right to trick me into coming along too. This was a stroke of genius. I can't believe I'm saying that, but it's true. "

"I knew you'd never take a vacation unless I called it a favor for a client, but I wasn't sure how it would shake down. I'm glad you two worked things out."

Nicole waved away the effort it had taken to bury past resentments. Ryan's presence had helped. The boy was as accurate an emotional barometer as a cat, and his smiles were a great incentive for keeping the peace.

"She booked us a whole car and has a personal chef. What's not to love?" Nicole picked up a tiny sandwich. "What's the appeal of the next stop? Design Unlimited does amazing things, but I can't imagine anything in Lincoln, Nebraska being a prime attraction."

Alison consulted her memory instead of her phone. Her vacation concession was traveling as tech-free as possible: no organizer, no computer, and phone use restricted as much as possible. Full avoidance of her comm account was impossible, but weaning herself off the information flow was a rewarding challenge.

The news was all bad these days anyway. Terrorist threats, civil protests, and political crises were hitting one after another this year. Leaving it all in the background for a week felt like selfish luxury. "I think a missile silo is next on the list," she said after some thought. "A repurposed Cold War relic."

"Sounds dull, especially when you put it next to that incredible cave castle in Pennsylvania."

They compared impressions of the sites they had visited over the last three weeks of cross-country travel while the storm quickly passed east. Nicole glanced at the empty seat. "Do you think she's avoiding me?"

"I doubt it. Ryan's probably being clingy." Alison pulled out her phone and sent a query to both Helen and Mariana. A reply came within seconds from Mariana: check news. ASAP. Alison brought up the screen, and there it was, the third item down.

Her mind went blank, but she was hyper-aware of the way her hands were shaking, sweaty and cold all at once, the way her head felt detached from her body as if the slightest breeze would send her floating away.

Nicole asked, "Allie, what's wrong?"

Her mouth opened, but she could not make words emerge. She lost her grip on the phone. It slid across the table. Nicole captured it and scanned the screen.

"Oh, my God," she whispered. "This can't be right."

The blurb read: "Explosions Rock Downtown Seattle: Hundreds Feared Dead." The image under the headline showed C&A's office building with a smoking rubble-filled gap where its top two floors should be. The time stamp on the picture was fifteen minutes old.

By the time the train pulled into Lincoln, the sun was going down and the death toll had been adjusted to a hundred. Alison and Nicole's luggage was on the platform within seconds after the train stopped moving. That was a speed record for the porters. Alison thanked and tipped them without lifting her eyes from her handset.

She and Nicole were both trying unsuccessfully to get the firm's staff lists forwarded from a records archive. Their calls and messages were bouncing off the overloaded Seattle systems. Alison composed a new message and sent it to chase her earlier efforts while Helen's staff formed their usual protective perimeter on the platform.

The brick walls of the restored historic train depot next to the passenger station were blood-red in the slanting light, and a number of passengers were taking advantage of the brief stop to look at the scenery. A huddle of people in the railyard across the tracks had stopped work to watch the arriving train too. Alison was mildly surprised that no police were waiting as well. She probably had Helen's lawyers to thank for that discretion.

Word had spread quickly on the wings of speculation. Paparazzi darling Helen Armstrong was here in town with her legal advisor on the same day that her one-time rival Tiffany Wyatt died in a mysterious explosion at that advisor's firm. It looked suspicious to say the least.

Helen descended from the train stairs as dramatically as if she were onstage, and an imperious look over the crowd shamed a few of them into turning away. Then she gave Nicole and Alison each a hug while Ryan stood in the door and waved.

His face was solemn, and his cheeks were still blotchy from crying. He had come running to the dining car earlier to give Nicole and Alison each one of his stuffed animals. So they wouldn't be alone, he told them. Alison squeezed the soft little rabbit. She wiggled her hand to set its ears waving so that Ryan would see that she still had it. He nodded, looking satisfied.

If only a toy really could shield her from loss.

Tears stood in Helen's eyes as she took Alison's hands. "I have no words."

Words could never encompass the sudden destruction of so many lives. Alison swallowed hard. Helen added, "I would come with you, but—well. Planes. And Ryan."

"I understand. Give him a hug from me." Alison stepped forward to embrace Helen, they promised to call each other when they arrived safely home, and a short time later the train pulled away.

The ground steamed as rainwater evaporated, but the wind blowing in the wake of the storm carried a chilly foretaste of autumn. Alison shivered. Nicole gave the empty platform a ferocious scowl. "Where is that taxi? It should be here already. We need to get to the airport."

Alison had placed the taxi request less than twenty minutes earlier. "Lincoln isn't *that* small," she said.

"Then you should've called sooner."

The snarl begged for an angry reply. Alison grabbed her luggage and walked to the curb in front of the station where the taxi driver would be sure to see her.

The street was more of a cobbled square here, with a wide curbside loading area and a line of restaurants facing the depot from the far side of a parking strip. Evening rush hour was in full swing, and traffic rolled slowly through the neighboring district of restaurants and shops. The stores looked busy. People looked happy.

Alison sat down on the largest suitcase and said, "Getting angry at me won't get us out of here any faster."

The taxi wasn't the problem. The closest plane available for charter was in Omaha. It wouldn't get here for another hour. They would be lucky to reach Seattle before midnight

"I know. I apologize." Nicole wheeled her bags over to Alison's and gently bumped them together. "I can't stand being so helpless. I need to see it. I can't believe that it really happened. There must be some mistake. This can't be real."

"It is real." Alison's voice broke. "Please, can we not talk about it? Just be patient. We'll be home soon."

Home. The word had such a barren sound now. Frank was gone. Mark. Derek. Ari from Admin who made cupcakes on Fridays. Genni, the paralegal who was on a roller derby team. All gone. A small sound escaped Alison's throat.

"Oh, God." Nicole covered her mouth and turned away. "Oh, God. What am I going to do? How could this happen?"

Alison rested her head in her hands. Feeding each other's grief helped neither of them. Nicole sat down too. They waited together, taking comfort in silence. Alison kept her eyes shut and tried to find a little inner calm.

Peace was elusive. People nearby chattered and laughed, cars revved their motors to maneuver through the streets bracketing the square, brakes squeaked, and horns honked over parking spots. The breeze raised goose bumps on Alison's bare arms. The cool air smelled of fresh grass and wet leaves.

Tires screeched.

Alison looked up, and then something slammed into her, pushing her against Nicole and sending them both tumbling sideways and down.

She hit headfirst.

Carl's first warning of trouble was the sight of Parker sprinting away from the loitering yard laborers he had been harassing. The workers had prioritized celebrity-watching over loading a rental truck. Carl was content to load it himself with Tyler's help, but Parker had no patience with sloth. He had been grumpy all day.

When he took off like the hounds of hell were at his heels, Carl dropped the box Tyler was handing off.

"What the hell?" Tyler said.

Parker headed across the tracks towards the gap between a hotel and the train station. Carl hopped out of the truck and went after him at a jog. With no obvious threat in sight, there was no point in trying to keep up. Parker only acted like this when he sensed an imminent threat, but it wasn't a precision response.

"Hey!" Tyler shouted after him. "Where are you going?"

"Just follow us with the truck!" Carl called back. Dread suddenly gnawed at his insides, and he pushed into a dead run as he came around the corner of the station building.

In front of him and behind Parker, a dark sedan came around the end of the parking strip much too fast. Parker launched himself at two women sitting with luggage sets at the curb. Their backs were to the approaching car, and he was running full-tilt when he swept them to one side. They went sliding across the bumpy surface in a tangle of limbs and bags just before the car hurtled over that spot and into the corner of the station.

It hit with a boom of collapsing metal. The impact crumpled the front end of the vehicle into the rear seats.

Someone screamed, across the cobblestone square, and a ringing alarm went off inside the building. The car motor rattled and died. Blood dripped onto the folded wreckage of the hood. Dark clots slid down the interior of the shattered windshield.

One of the women—tall, leggy, dark ponytail—extricated herself from the jumble on the ground and staggered to her feet. Parker was on his back with his arms still locked around the other woman. One hand cradled her head, and he was breathing hard and staring at the sky.

Carl knelt beside them. "How bad is it, hero?"

Parker shifted his arm. "Hand," he said with a wince. "Fuck. Ribs too, maybe. That one saw me coming at them and didn't even move."

He pointed with his chin at the black-haired woman who stood shivering with her arms wrapped tight around herself. Her eyes were squeezed tight shut, her lips moved in a soundless mutter, and tears poured down her cheeks unheeded. Carl made a snap evaluation: in shock but not seriously injured. She looked familiar, but identification could wait.

The woman in Parker's arms was unconscious. She was tiny and rounded, with pale olive skin that was smeared with blood. A deep scrape on one cheek ran up past her hairline. Parker eased out from beneath her, sliding his hand free to ease her head to the ground. His knuckles were bloody, and two were swelling. Long strands of brown hair clung to them, and Parker regarded it with a scowl.

"That doesn't look good," Carl said.

Parker lifted a shoulder and made a face. He'd taken most of the impact. "We bounced."

Sirens wavered in the distance, and bystanders who had witnessed the crash were making their way across the square. Carl diverted them towards the car with a gesture indicating that he had this under control.

"What set you off?" he asked Parker.

Parker flapped his uninjured hand in the direction of the wreck: he'd sensed a threat to himself, Carl, or someone under his protection, and he'd reacted.

"Yes, I grasp that you got to four without adding up two-plus-two the way the rest of us do, but why did you get the alert? The crash wasn't coming our way."

Parker flexed his fingers, assessing damage. He admitted ignorance with a shrug. There had to be a connection. He didn't get hunches about strangers.

Carl looked at the hysterical woman again, concentrating until the associations clicked into place. Her images had featured prominently in his research. "Ah-hah. That's Nicole Avon. Partner at C&A, Wyatt's legal shark tank. I don't know her friend. What do you want to do now?"

"Scoop them up, sort it out later." Parker slowly got to his feet. "You scoop. I'll distract. Shit." The last word was directed at the mangled handset he pulled from his pocket. "Optimal outcome is zero exposure. Any sign it's a honey trap, any hint of compromise, we bug out."

"Got it." Carl handed over his phone and bent to examine the unconscious woman. Pulse and breathing were both strong and steady, pupils were even and responsive. He quickly ran his hands over limbs, across and around her body: no open wounds, no obvious broken bones. All good signs. He chafed her hand between his own. "Come on, little one, wake up."

Tyler pulled up to the curb, facing the wrong way to traffic, and one of the truck's rear doors swung forward to bang against the side. After glancing at Parker, the accident scene, and the approaching onlookers, he asked, "What do you need from me?"

He sounded calm, but his curiosity was all but palpable. His tone also warned that his patience wouldn't last.

"We're taking these two in," Carl told him. "I have this one. Help the other one into the cab. Her name is Nicole."

The woman's eyes came open at the sound of her name, and white showed all around the iris. Carl took the opportunity to smooth the way.

"Everything's fine," he said. He pitched the words just right, made eye contact, and made the words stick. "You're safe. Relax. You need to let Tyler help you. Just relax and let him tell you what to do. Don't think. Relax and listen. You can do that. Yes?"

Nicole nodded, blinking. Carl nodded back, then slid his eyes to Tyler, directing her attention there. Letting Tyler watch him do that was a calculated risk, but this wasn't a normal protection contract in any way.

Tyler gave Carl a puzzled look before crossing the sidewalk to join Nicole. His put his arm around her shoulders to help steer her to the truck, and he mouthed "What the hell?" at Carl as they walked by.

Parker tossed baggage into the truck with one hand while issuing a rapid-fire series of orders over the phone. The unconscious woman stirred. Carl held her down. "Take it easy, lie still. Can you move your toes?"

She lifted one hand to her forehead, then gingerly touched the scrape on her cheek. "Make up your mind," she said. "Lie still or move my toes?"

"Good question." Carl gave her a moment and prompted her again. "How are those toes?"

Her legs moved, and her face lost all color. "Ow."

"That's good, too," Carl said. "Motor and sensory nerves both responsive."

"What happened?" She pressed against Carl's hands, trying to rise. "Ouch. I feel like I got hit by a bus."

"Not quite." Carl helped her sit up. "What's your name?"

"Alison." She combed back her hair with one hand, then froze when she saw the crowd gathered by the wreck. "Oh, no. Where's Nicole? Is she okay?"

"She's all right." That was stretching the truth, but the priority was to secure them both. "See, she's there in the truck with my friend. Let's join her, and we'll give you a ride to the hospital."

Alison gave him a dark look from under lowered brows. "No, I don't think so. We'll wait for the police here. They'll want statements."

Her resistance caught Carl by surprise. Hurt and disoriented, she should've been easy to dazzle. The reluctance was based on rational caution and an outsized sense of duty. Carl appealed to that. "Your friend is in no shape to talk. Let us take care of you."

Alison blinked. "Thank you, but no. We're fine. Taking care of Nicole is my job." She touched her cheek again.

She went pale when she saw blood on her fingers. Carl mentally apologized, then leaned aside to give her a better view of the crashed car. The results were predictable. She turned aside to vomit up everything in her stomach.

"Enough protesting," Carl told her. "You need help. Take my hand." This time there was no resistance to the order. Carl lifted her into his arms when her right ankle wouldn't hold her weight.

An ambulance, a patrol car, and two fire trucks arrived on the square within seconds of each other. Parker finished his call and started towards them. Then he hesitated, glancing at Carl.

"She's fine," Carl said. "Barring complications, which I'll rule out later. There's plenty of diagnostic gear in the mothballed labs."

With a nod of relief, Parker continued on his mission. His idea of witness reporting would create delay and confusion, and any other legal snarls could be handled later.

Alison squirmed, and Carl tightened his grip as he looked down. Under other circumstances her glare probably sliced through anything in its path, but the pasty skin and tangled hair blunted its edge. Right now she looked as dangerous as a newborn puppy.

"Don't scream," he said. "Please don't." He didn't want to damage that sharp spirit with rough handling.

"Do I look stupid?" she asked. "You'd only stick a hand over my mouth, and then I would bite you, and it would go downhill from there. Where are you taking us?"

"Somewhere safe." Carl hefted her closer so she wouldn't see him smiling.

CHAPTER TEN

TYLER SPENT THE NIGHT IN an escalating state of aggravation. No one would talk to him. Carl was too busy getting the new arrivals settled in at first. Once they were in the hands of the medic from the security team, he retreated with four of the other specialists behind a locked door to discuss the incident in Seattle and its impact on their situation here. Parker shut himself away with the rest, when he got back from the police station.

All the avoidance made sense, but it was still galling.

Justin was no help. He collected his crates, absorbed a terse summary from Carl that left out the interesting details, and retreated to his lab. He showed no grief over the death of his ex-wife, which was perhaps excusable. His lack of interest in the others who had died was less forgivable.

Midnight came and went before Tyler gave up on the possibility of getting any answers from anyone and went to bed. Fear and irritation kept him awake all night. He got up before dawn and went to scrounge breakfast.

The kitchen was occupied.

Parker was sitting on top of the long wooden table with his boots on the trestle bench. He'd taken off his shirt, and his right hand rested on top of his head. The last three fingers were taped together. Two empty bottles of beer sat on the table, and he had another in his hand. Towels, a bowl filled with water, and a comprehensive medical kit were also on the table.

Carl squeezed a sponge over the bowl. His sleeves were rolled to the elbow, and he'd tied back his hair. Tyler finally understood why the man was always so diligent about keeping the sleeves and hair down. Bracelets of knotted scarring circled his wrists, and white lines showed against his forearms as well. Round burn marks dotted the back of his neck, up and over his ears.

Tyler wasn't sure whether to stay or go. Both would lead to awkwardness. Indecision held him motionless.

Parker's side was one long purple bruise punctuated by scabbed patches of road rash. Carl scrubbed open each scrape, swabbed it, and sprayed it down. "No shower until the sealant dries," he said. "You should've let me take care of this sooner. If it gets infected, don't whine to me about it."

Parker lowered his arm, stretched it. Mumbled.

"Of course, no swimming. Dammit, Eddie." Carl set down the sponge and put both hands on the other man's shoulders. "I know you're fast, I know you think you can take down ten men blindfolded with one hand tied behind your back, but you aren't indestructible. You have to stop doing things like that."

Parker's eyes went to Tyler, and he grinned.

Tyler would never get a better straight line. "Stop doing things like what, Carl? Things like knowing an accident's going to happen before the driver does? Things like those voodoo witch doctor tricks you pulled? Don't even try to deny that you did something to those women. I watched you order them to go to sleep."

He paused for breath. Carl was using that gentle, evaluating gaze of his, the one that made its object the center of the universe. That sent a chill up Tyler's back, and fear fed his anger.

"And you," he said, pointing at Parker. You told me to be discreet yesterday morning. You. Were. Not. Discreet. You made a huge public scene, and then you both hid from me all night long when I only wanted to ask a few questions. That was not fair. That was cheating."

He stopped there, and embarrassment colored his anger. He didn't sound indignant or forceful. He sounded like a whiny child.

He stomped over to the refrigerator, where he could vent his emotions by shoving around bottles and boxes. He grabbed a slice of leftover pizza and a beer, and he slammed the door.

Parker began to laugh in helpless pained gasps. Tyler turned to glare at him.

"Cheating." Parker bent over, arms pressed tight against his ribs. He subsided into breathless chuckles and shrugged into his shirt. "No accident," he said. "Pro hit. Stolen car, driver's ID faked. Cops think the airbag failed. I think the hitter got hit to break the blame trail."

"That doesn't explain how you knew it was happening thirty seconds early from two hundred meters away. It doesn't make up for hiding from me all night."

"Hiding?" Carl swept the towels into the trash and took the bowl to the sink. When he finished washing up, he leaned forward, resting both hands on the countertop. Every motion looked threatening. "You've got to be kidding me."

That sounded bad. Tyler retreated to the far end of the table with his food.

"It was necessary," Carl said in a voice so low that it sounded like a growl. He put his back to the counter, and the scorn in his eyes was molten hot. "Safety came first. Not your tender ego or your sense of entitlement. Not our own well-being or comfort, for that matter. Forgive me if we were too busy keeping you *safe* to sit and chat."

Tyler popped the cap off the beer and chugged it down. Liquid courage, liquid bandage for his tender ego. "That's all valid," he said when he finished. "But Justin wasn't curious about what you left out, and he's always curious. I think you've told him a lot more than me. What he knows, I need to know too. Either wiggle your fingers and make me forget all about this, or start talking."

He took another bite of pizza in hopes that it would settle his churning stomach. He might be shuffling off to his room in an oblivious haze any minute now. At least then he would no longer be wondering about it, and he might even be able to get some work done later.

Carl exchanged a cryptic look with Parker.

Tyler said, "And that's another thing. You keep having these conversations where neither one of you talks. Do you have any idea how annoying that is?"

The question startled a laugh from Carl. He ducked his head and pinched the bridge of his nose between his fingers. "Yes, I do," he said. "I'm sorry, Tyler. I'm sure it's frustrating from your perspective, but can't it wait until we've slept?"

"No," Parker said. "Sooner is better."

He hopped off the table and retrieved three more beers. The empty bottle was removed from Tyler's hand and replaced with a new one. Glass clinked. Parker sat down across the table from Tyler. Carl sighed and joined him.

"Me first." Parker drew little circles on the tabletop with the bottom of his bottle. "I know things sometimes. Didn't learn it. Can't do it on demand. Can't rely on it. No explanation. I can also find Carl anywhere. That, I rely on."

"The link goes both ways," Carl said. "Also annoying sometimes, since it's a sense of condition as well as location. I am thankfully exempt from weird hunches. It's all his bizarre talent. I'm only along for the ride."

Parker smiled and tipped back his beer for a long swig. Before

Tyler could ask any of a million other questions, Justin shuffled into the room.

He wore an earpiece and carried a datapad in one hand, and his attention was divided between listening and reading. He bumped into the table and scraped down its length without looking until he ran into Tyler's leg, where he stopped and listened, still oblivious to the audience.

Tyler was used to seeing lines of pain on Justin's face, and 'annoyed' seemed to be a baseline state, but this looked like the same face Justin had worn when he'd promised Tyler retribution. Weariness was a frothy surface layer over a cold rage so intense that the man was shaking with it.

"Make it work," Justin snapped. "Anonymous is not a difficult concept, is it?"

He set down the datapad, and scrolled up and down a list of names while he listened to the response. His eyes were red-rimmed and glazed. "Yes. Cut out the account and liquidate. I'll get you the beneficiaries list as soon as I have it." He pocketed the earpiece and pulled up a new screen.

Tyler cleared his throat.

Justin looked up. A moment later he asked plaintively, "How am I supposed to do private business when I run into people everywhere?"

"Locked doors are a good start," Tyler told him. "I wasted a perfectly good mad on you, Justin. I didn't think you gave a damn about the explosion, but you're setting up a fund for the survivors and their families, aren't you?"

"Of course I am. William started that firm—wait." Justin squinted at him, then at Carl and Parker. "It's four in the morning. Why are all of you in the kitchen at this hour?"

No one answered. Parker started picking at the grain of the tabletop.

A slow grin spread across Justin's face. It was like a time-lapse of sun melting snow. Angry pain dissolved into glee. He dropped onto the bench next to Tyler and waved a finger at Carl. "I told you so. I told you he was observant. He caught you, didn't he? Have you filled him in?"

"Not completely," Tyler said. "Carl's being evasive."

"Not surprising. Here, I put some things together for you." Justin called up a presentation program on the datapad. "I never dreamed you would tackle these two directly. I thought you would come to me. Do you remember spending a day at Rydder Institute? After Mayo?"

Facts clicked together in Tyler's head. He glanced at Carl, who lifted one eyebrow over a challenging blue stare. Tyler looked away fast. "I *knew* I'd heard that weird way of talking before," he said. "You're a whaddayacallit. A neopsych. The brain benders. I thought they all worked at Rydder."

"Neopsychs can't work anywhere else," Carl said. "Rydder Institute puts its practitioners through a monstrously effective conditioning program. Neos cannot work off Institute property, they cannot depart from approved treatment plans, and they cannot subvert those restrictions. They will die first."

"I remember reading about that," Tyler said. "But you're here."

"The conditioning keeps the general public safe from neo's. It doesn't protect neopsychs from the public."

Justin slid the datapad closer. "Read, Tyler."

Tyler skimmed over news articles and flipped through pictures. The story looked vaguely familiar now that he was seeing it again. Some enterprising criminals had gotten their hands on a few Rydder personnel, and they'd decided to test the effectiveness of the loyalty programming.

Tyler raised the screen to compare obituary to battered reality. His meal tried to come back up when he considered the kind of abuse required to account for the differences.

A nasty little thought started to gnaw at him: maybe sympathy was exactly what Carl had decided he should feel. Logic made him reject the idea. The observed data argued for trust. Big organizations were good at burying problems. Someone who didn't die as advertised might be considered a problem to be buried as deeply as possible.

"It's fun watching the wheels go around in his head, isn't it?" Justin said. "You can practically see the gears grinding."

Tyler flipped him off and said to Carl, "Your programming broke but you're not dead. And you're not at Rydder. So you're a fugitive?"

"Not exactly. I found a way to convince Rydder Admin that I died after all. No one's looking for me."

"But there's nothing to keep you from going around bending people's brains now. Have I got that right?"

"There's always my conscience. I also lack electrostim equipment, isolation kit, pharma support, and an environment conducive to therapeutic repetition, but those are the accessories, not the arsenal."

Tyler was looking at a man who had the ability to literally change minds at his whim—permanently, if he had the right tools and enough time—and whose potential was in no way fettered by outside authority. What he saw was a wounded victim struggling to build a new life the best he could. Tyler knew how that felt.

Carl's secret hadn't been Justin's to share. The exclusion was forgivable in retrospect. "Thank you for trusting me," he said, and he felt a warm sense of satisfaction when he saw some of the sorrow leave Carl's eyes.

Justin slapped the table with both hands. Everyone else jumped. "All right then. What now?"

Parker yawned and grabbed his beer bottle. Carl rubbed both hands over his face. "Yes. Beer and bed sounds good."

"Wait a minute," Tyler said. The others looked at him. He spread his hands out. "When do we start saving the world?"

The silence grew oppressive.

"Oh, come on." Tyler pointed at Justin. "You've got all kinds of mutant powers." A second finger added Parker. "You see the future." He ignored the scowling protest and opened his hand to Carl. "And you've got the witch doctor voodoo going for you. You all have superpowers. Saving the world comes with the territory. What else you would you want do?"

"Sleep," Carl said. "I notice you left yourself off the list. What's your role in this master plan?"

Tyler grinned at him. "Isn't it obvious? I'm the comic relief."

In the interests of fairness, Alison had to admit that her prison was a nice place. The suite of rooms included a small office and a tidy kitchenette with a coffeemaker and a cabinet stocked with snacks. She'd won the grand prize in the getting-kidnapped-by-total-strangers sweepstakes. If only she'd known she was buying a ticket.

Humor helped keep fear at bay. So did activity. As soon as she awakened in the silent confines of a windowless bedroom she resolved to keep very busy. She started by opening every door and peering into every corner.

One door led to a hallway occupied by a woman wearing black fatigues and a holstered pistol. Alison quickly shut that door. In a second bedroom she found Nicole lying fully dressed on a bed. She was staring blankly at the ceiling, and Alison's efforts to converse were met with impassive silence. She gave up before the effort broke her heart.

Each room was decorated with at least one camera. Alison hung a towel over the one in the bathroom. She ate trail mix and mourned the absence of tea. Going back to bed was tempting, but she took a long shower instead.

Afterwards she dressed in fresh clothes from the now-neat suitcases that she'd packed in a messy hurry. She set Ryan's bunny on the top suitcase to guard her belongings and repeated the room tour. Her aching ankle disapproved, but the rest of her body appreciated the exercise.

Her handset and datapad had disappeared, and both the entertainment screen and the workstation were locked into reception-only modes. Given those restrictions, she thought it odd that the workstation was connected to a local network. The briefs and files stored on it had an eerie similarity to preparations for a legal defense. She decided if her jailers were going to hand her information then she would take all she could get.

Much of the material was hard to believe, but she had *seen* Tyler Burke, and if he was alive then she could accept Justin Wyatt might be too. The report on their Arctic walkabout was short, choppy, and brusque: just the facts and barely those. Even the essentials made her cringe.

In bits and pieces she began to put together the facts of her situation, at least in the view of those who had brought her here. She laughed herself breathless when she realized where she was, and she worked up the nerve to open the outer door again.

The hall carpet was thick and beige. Wall sconces illuminated light green walls. Ten more doors could be seen before the corridor curved away. Another woman whose uniform bristled with weaponry was guarding Alison's door now. This woman's skin was black, and her short hair was bleached blonde with black stripes. Her eyes were smoky brown and brightly wary.

"What happens if I run away?" Alison asked her.

"I tell the captain," the woman said. "Somebody gets stuck surveilling you, in case you get lost or fall down a well. I'm Chris. You need anything in there, you let me know."

"Okay, thanks." Alison shut the door. Not exactly a prisoner then. It hardly mattered. Her ankle was not up to strenuous explorations.

A file labeled with her name showed up on the network late in the afternoon. It contained her vital records, employment files, and the comprehensive background check that C&A had done before her job interview. Its appearance sent an interesting message about her captors' resources.

She kept at her studies until the desk clock informed her that it was 20:00, when the door to the suite opened from the outside. Her heart rose thumping into her throat at the sight of her visitor. She jerked her gaze away and wrestled with the pointless urge to plug her ears.

The door clicked shut.

"I am not a vampire," Carl said in the deep, smooth voice that had sent Alison to sleep the previous day. Then his words had carried implacable power. Now he sounded amused.

"I know what you are. Were." Her voice squeaked.

The file on him should've been one of the least credible ones in the batch, but personal experience was a great leveler of doubt.

"Is that so?" Carl asked. "I didn't know Eddie was putting Justin's show-and-tell into the mix." He raised his voice and turned toward a camera. "Thanks, asshole. Why don't you rent a billboard and tell the whole damned world all about me?"

Alison said, "If you didn't want me snooping, you should've locked me off the network."

"We provided the briefs to bring you up to speed on the situation, not to leave you too terrified to look at me."

He sounded hurt. Alison raised her eyes as far as his collar. "Now you're playing on my sympathies."

"Of course I am. Next I'll hypnotize you with my beautiful blue eyes, and you'll throw yourself into my arms," he said. "Or maybe we'll have a conversation like two moderately sane human beings. Take a chance."

"I'm not feeling talkative. Now what will you do?"

"Nothing. I'm used to uncomfortable silences."

Alison looked up and met Carl's eyes, which were dark blue and worried in a sad, serious face. Her sense of humor decided to creep out of hiding. If she could worry about manipulation then Carl couldn't be doing a very good job.

"Promise me you'll never do the scary stuff again."

"I swear I will never again put you to sleep without your permission," he said promptly. "I apologize for the necessity. Good enough?"

He hadn't made a blanket promise. That was somehow reassuring. "Yes."

"Let's go from there." Carl hesitated. "I'm here for two reasons. That was one. Excuse me for a moment while I attend to the other."

He clipped on a phone earpiece and went into Nicole's room. The sound of soft conversation drifted out, and after a few minutes Nicole came running into the living room.

She was sobbing, and she pulled Alison into a tight embrace. Alison patted her on the back and wished she were a more nurturing person. She wasn't good at consolation, and incoherent bawling was no improvement on blank staring. She put Nicole on a stool at the counter and went to get her a box of tissues from the bathroom.

"*No,*" Carl said, and Alison froze in her tracks before she realized that Carl was talking to someone else again. Walking past him felt impossible. She retreated to the neutral territory of the couch. Nicole wept in the kitchen and Carl carried on a one-sided conversation with the cameras.

Between pauses, he said, "Not without a month dedicated to it. There are deep—yes, of course guilt. Don't be insulting. Send Yoshi down here."

A few minutes later, Nicole had been handed off to a friendly-looking Asian man wearing a black uniform who escorted her from the room. Carl moved to a chair across from the couch. When the closing door cut off Nicole's sobs, a wave of mixed emotions swept over Alison. Her worry was colored by gratitude for the quiet, and she felt ashamed of being glad.

"She'll get help," Carl said. "It's nothing I did to her, if you're wondering."

"Nicole is ambitious and tough, but underneath—well. She's hard. Brittle. And two big shocks in a row like that could overwhelm anyone." Alison folded her arms and looked at her feet. She was babbling amateur analysis at a psychiatrist. She needed to be busy.

Carl said, "You should know your options. We can get you temp ID and hide you somewhere if you want to lie low until we catch whoever bombed your office and targeted Ms. Avon. Or you can stay and help us with the hunt."

Alison inhaled deeply. It didn't loosen the knot in her chest, but the scab on her cheek cracked. She pressed it. Her fingers came away bloody. Her head started spinning.

Carl said, "Blood makes you woozy, doesn't it? Let's get some new sealer on that. How's your ankle feeling? It wasn't a bad sprain, but I'm sure it hurts. And the bump on the head? Is it still tender?"

For some reason all the concern made Alison feel even worse. Tears rose out of nowhere and spilled down her cheeks. She hid her face in the hand that wasn't bloody and ran towards the bathroom and privacy.

The roil of emotion was impossible to subdue. She sat on the closed lid of the toilet and tried anyway. A shadow fell over her, and then a warm hand touched her cheek, smoothed away a streak of moisture.

She hiccupped and sniffled. "I'm sorry," she said. "I'm so sorry. I don't know why I'm crying."

"Really?" The single word was a desert-dry masterpiece of sarcasm.

Anger suppressed the other rioting emotions in an instant. "Oh, shut up. I know I'm weak and useless. Go ahead, send me away too, but don't make fun of me. I can't help it."

As soon as she spoke, she wanted to bite off her tongue. Instead she stared at her hands, clenched together in her lap. Carl placed the tip of one finger under her chin and lifted it. His eyes truly were a beautiful shade of blue.

"I was not mocking you," he said. "And no one here will send you anywhere against your will. I swear it. Why do you think tears are a weakness?"

"What would you call them?"

"Healthy. You're concussed, you're in pain—you're *grieving*. You're a strong, smart, practical woman, but in the last twenty-four hours you've been knocked down by shock, knocked out, kidnapped, and imprisoned. All that helplessness needed to come out."

Alison's mouth dropped open during the recitation of her miseries. The anger drained away, leaving dregs of irritation and a weary relief. "You lied," she told him. "You poked at me until I bawled out all the stress."

One side of Carl's mouth lifted. "And then I kicked you straight in the pride to help you rebound. Be honest, Alison. You understood why I only promised not to put you to sleep, and you feel better now."

Alison always tried to be honest with herself. She satisfied pride with a scowl. "Will you please stop looming?"

He retreated to the door, and the wry half-smile returned. "Why don't you wash up? Since you're staying, I'll see about getting you some real food."

He walked off before Alison could frame a response. She splashed water on her face and regarded her puffy-eyed reflection. The scrape was still seeping blood. Her hair was frizzy and tangled. "Perfect," she said. "I'm a strong, smart, practical, hideous hag."

Carl reappeared in the bathroom doorway. "Burgers or pizza are the choices tonight. Chris can bring food to you if you aren't ready for company. I'll ask Keene to check your ankle and change the dressings on that scrape. Okay?"

The lump was trying to swell in her throat again. Normal or

not, the weepiness was embarrassing. She said, "Okay. I think I'd rather eat here, thank you."

"If you're feeling brave later, ask for an escort to the rec room," Carl said. "We're trying to hammer out an action plan, and knowing Justin, the swimming pool is where the whole crew will be."

CHAPTER ELEVEN

ALISON DIDN'T FEEL BRAVE THAT evening. Her cowardice lasted through a full night's sleep and two visits from the guards. They said they were security specialists, they insisted Alison call them by name, and they brought doughnuts for breakfast and pizza for lunch. She wondered why such nice people would work for a company called Mayhem & Havoc, but she was afraid to ask.

When she caught herself wondering when dinner would be delivered, she sat herself down and told herself to dig up some courage.

There was no one in the hall to consult when she emerged from the suite, which gave her food for thought. She limped through the hallways to an intersection with an echoing corridor big enough to drive two trucks past each other. Conduit, pipes, and wiring hung overhead beneath the high curved ceiling, and three open archways gave views into huge rooms full of fabric-draped lumps. The ends of the passage were painted to look like a tunnel through a mountainside. Alison would've sworn she could walk right through it into a sunlit meadow.

Directly opposite her was a long hallway that would have

looked at home in a university science building. Sidelights on two office doors glowed, and a yellow light flashed over one lab door. She tried the lab first. The door did not open when she pulled the handle, but a bell chimed.

She waited. The lock light flashed green, and the door slid open. The room was much larger than she had expected, and it was stifling hot. Wires and pipes twisted around tables piled high with boxes. The far wall had a bulls-eye target painted on it.

Someone said, "See that, Tyler? Door properly locked, and I wasn't even doing anything dangerous. No surprises. Aren't you proud of me?"

"I'll be proud if you want," Alison said, "but I'm not Tyler."

A short, scruffy man emerged from beneath a lab table near the back of the room. Alison's mouth dropped open.

She was in the same room as Justin Wyatt. He'd started one of the most successful companies in history, he'd followed up with a massively successful nonprofit venture, he was famous, he was brilliant, and he was right *there*.

"Hi," he said. "You're out."

Alison's brain went blank, and then her tongue ran away with her. "No," she said. "I'm Alison Gregorio. Out is a direction."

Her heart sank as she awaited a scornful reproach. Justin gave her a grin instead, ducked out of view behind some equipment, and reappeared on the near side. As he approached he pulled out a handset and typed a quick note. His hair was matted and wet, and he set down the phone to brush at it before offering his hand.

"Nice to meet you."

He was covered in grease and grime from ripped shirt collar to worn sneakers. Awe was impossible to maintain in the face of that much untidiness. Alison shook his hand, rubbed at the resulting smear on her palm, and peeked at the phone screen. "What does 'I win' mean?"

Justin stopped wiping his hand on his shirt. "Um."

"You people were placing bets on me? Seriously?" She probably ought to be outraged.

"That depends." Justin pocketed the handset and retreated behind the closest table. "Are you going to get mad or cry if I say yes? I am not—" He stopped, visibly considered options, and tried on a sheepish smile. "There's no way this is ending well for me, is there?"

"I don't see how." Alison took pity on him. "Want to start over?"

"Oh, no." He retreated further, ducking behind equipment again. "I'd screw up even worse. If I haven't mortally offended you yet, can you give me a hand?"

She went with her first impulse. "Will I get it back?"

Laughter drifted to her from the rear of the room. "Think of it as a loan."

Together over the next few hours, they built something that looked like a football mating with a centipede. All in all, it was an entertaining afternoon, if a somewhat strange one. Alison got used to long silences and being used as an equipment stand.

She had stumbled into a world where people behaved as if the strangest things were unworthy of comment. The only way to stay sane would be to accept each new experience as it came at her.

Justin dropped a hammer on his foot and didn't notice, even though it chipped the concrete floor next to his toe after bouncing. When he used the arc welder, it looked like it was floating midair after a few seconds. His hands shimmered and disappeared. He didn't notice that either.

When the gadget was finished, Justin asked, "What do you think?"

She thought he looked exhausted. He moved like her arthritic grandfather. Every motion was deliberate and careful, and his skin didn't look healthy under the deep suntan. She thought it odd that his voice went low and slow when he got excited, and she thought the way he combed unruly curls of hair behind his ears was adorable.

None of those thoughts were polite enough for sharing, so she said, "If you're asking me about the doohickey, I think it looks dangerous in a complicated way."

"It could be." Justin poked at the apparatus, and it swiveled on its base. "Carl has contacts inside the Civilian Security Bureau. We're following the official investigation. There was no sign of chemical explosive. It wasn't a gas leak, either. I'd bet my left hand C&A was blown up with something like this, and that's my fault."

"When did Wyatt Enterprises start building bombs?"

"Never. *I* designed a battery. I considered the explosive potential a flaw. Some other bastard thinks it's a feature." He frowned. "This is a test unit for Tyler. Thanks for helping me work. I know it's not what you signed on for."

"Nothing has been, lately, but this was fun." Alison decided to take the topic by the horns. "What *am* I signing on for? Don't you know who's behind—well, everything—yet? Why does Carl think I can help? What can I do?"

Justin said, "You had fun?"

Four serious questions and Justin was stuck on the one comment about him. Alison began to understand the tone of voice people at C&A had used when they reminisced. She bit her lip and pushed away that painful memory. A whooping yell in the hallway interrupted the silence. Tyler came dancing into the room with a sheaf of printouts in his hands.

"I did it!" he shouted. "I got it! Part of it, anyway. Justin, where are you hiding, you freak? Oh. There you are." He shook his hair out of his eyes and approached with a grin. "Look at this! Did it, did it, did it! We're going to get a Nobel for this, swear to God we will."

Justin squeezed his eyes shut, and one of the veins on his forehead started to throb. "Tyler, if you keep calling me a freak, I am going to sneak up on you and freak you so hard that you'll regret you were ever born."

Tyler's expression fell from elation into embarrassment. "Hell, Justin. You know I don't mean it that way."

"No, I don't," Justin said, snapping out each word. "Freak means freak."

The conversation was headed downhill fast, so Alison asked, "So you do turn invisible? All the way, I mean? It's all true?"

Justin shifted right from hurt to self-absorbed. "Not exactly invisible," he said. "It's emissions interference. Visible spectrum, mostly. I still radiate heat like an oven, plus IR and … and you don't really care, you're just talking me off the temper ledge." He fell silent, and then he twitched his shoulders. "Show me the math, boy genius."

Tyler gave Alison a grateful nod and handed his prize to Justin. An esoteric discussion ensued. Alison found a bare spot on a table, sat down, and debated leaving in search of food and reality-based conversation.

The door chimed and opened again. It went unheard by both men, but Alison waved when she spotted Carl's pale hair as he peered back and forth through the maze. Justin and Tyler both ignored his arrival. Carl settled against the table near Alison, folded his arms, and regarded them with a tolerant smile.

"You missed dinner," he said without taking his eyes off the show. "I came to rescue you."

"We were wrapping up, but this happened." She indicated the passionate argument. "That could go on all night, couldn't it?"

"Not tonight," Carl said. "There have been hints that we're compromised here. We're packing up and moving out. How are you feeling?"

"Hungry," she said. "Better than yesterday, since that's what you're really asking." She leaned sideways to bump a shoulder against him. "What was the bet?"

"The M&H crew started a pool on when you would leave your safe nest," he said easily.

"Speaking of leaving, where is Nicole? Did you turn her over to the police yet?"

She knew it was a loaded question, and the shot scored a solid hit. Carl's smile fell away, and both Justin and Tyler stopped talking. Alison asked, "Did you think I wouldn't notice that the guard disappeared when Nicole did? Did you think that I wouldn't see? Do you think I'm an idiot?"

No one answered the rhetorical outburst. Alison paused for breath as she finally recognized how bitter she felt. Admitting the treachery out loud made it real.

"I *feel* like an idiot," she said. "I did Nicole's schedules. I did her correspondence. It's clear, looking back, that she was hiding something, but she would never bomb her own offices. That place was her life. She didn't know, did she?"

No one responded. No one even wanted to look at her.

"You can't think I'm involved," she said. "I'd still be locked in, at best."

"We know you're innocent," Carl said. "And we suspect Nicole was being played too. To answer your original point, we deposited her in a private mental institution under a false name. No police. There's not a scrap of legal proof, no matter how it looks. No proof yet, that is."

"Proof is what you want from me," Alison said as one of her earlier questions resolved itself. "Communications and schedules. Data points to fill a pattern. Nicole is a minnow. You want the big fish." She wondered what they would do when they found one. "What will happen to Nicole? I can't stop caring, no matter how mad I am."

"Time will tell." Carl pushed away from the table. "And speaking of time, we've run out of it."

He pointed at the other two men. "We're leaving in one hour. Less, if you can manage it. If you can't carry it, don't pack it. Two vans, two cars, all of us and all of the team's kit. You can do the math. Alison, if you want food, get it now. We'll be meeting Eddie in Chicago tomorrow morning, but it's a long night between."

Both Justin and Tyler looked bewildered as they watched him go out the door.

"Leaving?" Justin said. "Now?"

"Notes!" Tyler bolted out of the lab.

THE SOUND of laughter roused Justin from a fitful sleep full of nightmares, and he woke shivering, with a cramp in his neck from leaning against the van window. Dim gray light filtered through the glass, and highway signs flashed past every minute or so. Subdivisions and industrial buildings lined the road, partially hidden in ground fog. It looked cold. He felt cold too, and the body aches were worse than when he'd dozed off.

The last time he'd felt this bad he'd been lying in snow.

He had the back bench of the van to himself, the middle one was unoccupied, and Tyler and a woman whose name Justin couldn't remember sat in the front now. Carl had turned the front passenger chair to face them, and they were conversing softly while their driver kept her eyes on the road.

Bags and boxes were piled beneath and between all the seats. Tyler's notes slid off Justin's lap and down into the luggage when he moved. He stifled the impulse to kick them. A kick might damage important equipment, but it wouldn't help him understand the equations. He could put a hole three centimeters deep into concrete even using his bad leg, but his brain was useless.

He closed his eyes and curled into a heat-conserving ball. Trying to wrap his mind around Tyler's mathematical models was like grasping smoke. He'd tried, last night. He'd tried until somewhere in the middle of Iowa. Then he'd lost his temper about his inability to follow the concepts. He and Tyler had snarled at each other until Carl sent Justin to the back seat and enforced total silence.

Another burst of laughter rose from the front. "Now we practice," Carl said. "Key points again: let the team do their job, and do what you're told. They're the ones who'll end up hurt if you panic. Alison, are you ready?"

Alison: that was the name. Justin settled back to listen to them role-play their way through scenarios that brought his dreams to mind. When he firmly forced his thoughts away from that, they drifted towards other worries.

Money was becoming a critical concern. Two new costs were fixed: discreet additional protection for Helen and her family, and the C&A survivors' fund. One was necessary insurance, and the other was the least he could do to make amends, but the expenses were going to suck his savings dry.

Until now he'd been able to draw on outside money, but leaving the bunker took them out of Dawnstar's aegis and off their books. Upkeep of even a small security detail would be a major financial drain. Outgo would outstrip income in a few weeks unless Justin found someone to play with his money. That would mean finding someone who could be trusted.

If he'd enjoyed that type of work, if he'd been any good at it, then he never would've signed over Wyatt Enterprises' daily operations to Tiffany in their settlement. She'd wanted the company, and Justin had been as happy to be rid of the hassles as he'd been glad to be rid of her. Now Tiffany was dead, Justin couldn't even put the blame for her death where it belonged, and if he ever did find the culprit, then he would have to decide what to do about it.

"Morning, Justin. Are you feeling okay?"

Justin winced at the unexpected sound of Alison's voice. "I'm fine."

"Are you sure?" she asked. "You're shaking like a leaf, and you're getting all faded too. Is that the transmissible thing? What did you call it?"

Justin looked at himself. The growing daylight was too bright, and the moving landscape did bad things to his sense of equilibrium. His hands were shaking, and his sleeves shimmered with a refractive aura. He folded his arms against his chest and squeezed his eyes shut again. "I doubt it's transmissible." He clenched his chattering teeth. "But who knows?"

If Alison ever ended up with an open comminuted leg fracture, they could try wrapping it in experimental organics, expose it to subzero temps for a few days, and run current through the mess off and on. It might catch twice. More likely she would succumb to one of the many grisly complications that he'd miraculously escaped. There was a list. The doctors at Mayo could all recite it.

"Sorry, no," Alison said. "I meant, 'Why is it doing its thing right now?' Transmitting. Or did you call it emitting? I don't remember."

"I said emitting, and I don't know why. It happens when I get hot, but I'm freezing back here."

"It is a little chilly." A warm hand pressed against his forehead. It felt nice. "You're burning up." Fabric rustled. "Hey, Carl?"

A more substantial presence joined Alison, and the temperature check was repeated. Alison smelled better, and her hands were softer. Carl exhaled in a long, thoughtful sigh. "Do you have any idea when the fever started?"

"Fever? I'm not sick. I'm tired and freezing and I hurt like hell, but that isn't sick. It's normal."

"No, it isn't. Hang on a little longer. We're almost there. We'll get you to a doctor if we have to." Carl moved away to speak in a whisper to Tyler.

Alison stayed behind. Justin could hear her breathing.

"Sorry I snapped at you," he said. His head ached, but that was no excuse for being rude, even if his brain was wandering. Women liked apologies. Helen had taught him that much before she gave up on him.

"You really need to stop talking. That fever's taken down all your filters, I think. It's kind of sweet, but you're going to feel horribly embarrassed about it later."

Justin didn't recognize the woman's voice. The blanks hit like that sometimes. Worst case, he lost time. Other times he lost words, names, facts, or himself.

Forget being embarrassed later; he was mortified right now, and dropping dead would be much less humiliating than admitting that he didn't even know where he was at the moment. Then again, if death by embarrassment were possible, he would've died ages ago.

He had death on his mind. Maybe his subconscious was trying to send him a message like: "Life's a bitch and then you die." That was the kind of profound sophistication he expected from himself these days.

Fever. Filters. Reality slid sideways, and Justin's eyes popped open. They started watering from the brightness, and he blinked away moisture. "Shit. Was I saying all that drivel out loud?"

The look on the woman's face mingled pity with amusement. "I think everything for the last few minutes has gone straight from mind to mouth." She brushed his hair back. "You really are sweet."

"What's left of me, you mean? I know you, right? I hate this shit. It *sucks*."

"Okay, that's enough talking. You're getting worked up over nothing. Relax." She moved again, and somehow Justin ended up leaning against her shoulder, with his nose in her hair and his cheek against the soft skin of her neck. It was restful and warm, and he drifted off to sleep.

THE VAN CAME AROUND one last twist in a maze of residential streets and pulled into a driveway. Tyler opened the van door as soon as Chris nodded permission from the driver's seat. His shoulder bag bumped against his side as he hopped out, and the notes inside it made cranky crumpling noises.

Their new home sat on a winding street lined with other nondescript ranch houses. Worn-out toys sat abandoned in weedy lawns, seedlings sprouted in sagging gutters, and broken glass glittered everywhere. Quite a change from Justin's bunker, but it had the same advantage of anonymity.

Parker yanked open the graffiti-tagged front door before Tyler reached it. "Problem."

"Justin's sick. I'm supposed to ask you to help carry him in through the garage, and then I'm supposed to get out of the way."

Tyler knew he sounded sulky. He felt sulky. He'd offered to hand over the medical files he'd squirreled away, so that Carl wouldn't need to submit a formal request and wait hours for approval. He would've kept his mouth shut if he'd known Carl was going to blame him for Justin being sick. He'd looked angry enough to kill someone after reading Justin's charts.

It wasn't fair. Tyler felt bad that he hadn't understood how badly hurt Justin was, but Justin hadn't told him, and medical jargon was incomprehensible. "It isn't my fault, I swear," he said.

Parker rolled his eyes and walked off.

One dim ceiling light illuminated a room furnished with a stained couch, rickety wood chairs, and a tile-topped kitchen table. Grocery bags lined the counters in a corner kitchen area, and a camp chair and a duffle bag sat by the front door. Futons were visible through the open doors of three tiny bedrooms down a short hall. The air smelled musty, and the carpeting was stained.

A computer displaying security camera imagery sat near the front door. Sliding glass doors on one wall led to a deck that held a built-in hot tub full of green water. The small weedy lawn was surrounded by a head-high fence.

Alison came through a door into the kitchen. A murmur of unhappy voices rose behind her. Tyler grabbed a bag of chips and a bottle of soda and fled to the yard before the voices got any closer.

He found the switches for the hot tub and set it bubbling to drown out any noise from indoors. He couldn't concentrate on meaningful work, so he followed the tedious but now-familiar precautions to secure his online access and tried to catch up on his journals.

One interesting bit of news popped up right away: Martin-Hong was shuttering their capacitor program. Preliminary results had disproved the concept. Tyler found that unlikely, given that he knew the things worked. Justin's paranoid suspicions might be right after all. If civilian development were being stifled, that would leave the field open for military sales—assuming the military was willing to sink money into development. R&D was expensive, and the armed forces were stretched thin these days, between domestic unrest and overseas obligations.

The sliding door squeaked as Alison closed it behind her. Bad mood or no, Tyler drew the line at being rude to friendly women. "Hi," he said. "What brings you out here?"

"I'm hiding too." Alison sat beside him. "The security team is fighting about whether to plot assassination or a kidnapping. Don't ask for details, my ears shut off when they mentioned torture. Carl is still trying to figure out what's making Justin so sick. They can't wake him, and the fever's bad."

Tyler's anger cooled, leaving behind the ashes of the guilt that had fueled it. "He was sick and I was yelling at him. Nice, huh? Some friend I am."

"You didn't know." Alison smiled at the chip bag. She wasn't pretty unless she smiled, but then she was extraordinary. "I was waiting for you both to start thumping your chests and hooting last night. You are both such *boys*."

"He gets under my skin."

"Of course he does. Ten years more life experience, a billion dollars in the bank, and a zillion inventions to his name? Who wouldn't be intimidated?" Alison set aside the chips and ran her fingers through her hair. The wavy strands tangled in a knot. "The real question is, why don't you see that you get under his skin?"

"I don't," Tyler said, puzzled. "Do I?"

"Hmm." Alison picked at her hair. "Who's David Hong? That's who everyone in there is discussing with such a scary amount of hostility. I guess there's some kind of proof that he was after Justin?"

Pain twisted in Tyler's chest. "Hong is an exec for one of Wyatt Enterprises' competitors. If he is the one who brought down our plane, then I'd like nothing more than a chance to burn him alive over a slow fire."

Anger burned away pain. When he was angry, he didn't want to bawl himself to sleep. When he was angry, he could pretend he was brave.

"Hostile," Alison said, drawing out the word.

"Sorry." He couldn't hold onto the heat for long. "Are they sure?"

"They seem sure," Alison said. "I answered a bunch of questions about Nicole's schedule for Carl. He called people who sounded excited. Are they serious about torture?"

"I hope so." That was what he had to say. It was what he should want, even if the idea made him sick. "He killed my brother. He should pay for that."

A few minutes later Alison said, "Do you think Justin will be okay?"

"I don't know. I try to keep an eye on him, but he's impossible. He forgets to eat, he forgets to sleep, and he's never completely recovered from the plane crash and all."

"I can't believe you both survived all those weeks in the Arctic." Alison shivered. "I get cold on days like this. I guess you're tough, though. You're not even wearing a jacket."

"Yeah, but Justin still turns up the heat every chance he gets, and I swear he spends half his nights up to his neck in hot water. I would bet you ten bucks he'd already be in this nasty tub if he knew about it. We wouldn't be able to see him, with his freaky skin thing going on—"

He looked at the tub, then at Alison. "He's had a hot soak every night since we got to the bunker," he said with growing apprehension. "At least an hour or two. Except last night, because we ditched out. And I was distracted and didn't notice that he forgot his coat until Iowa. The truck was cold. We turned on the AC when it got stuffy, remember? Those are all variables."

Alison leaped to her feet, and they reached the door together.

CHAPTER TWELVE

JUSTIN SAW FLASHES OF LIGHT, smelled chlorine, and heard raised voices. Then a shock of heat obliterated it all. The overload seared through his nerves. He dimly knew his whole body was jerking and thrashing, but he was too busy gasping for breath to care.

The tide of sensation slowly subsided to a familiar feeling of warmth and gentle enveloping pressure. He was floating on his back in hot water, and something was holding his head above the surface.

When he opened his eyes, Parker was staring down at him from directly overhead. A gray, gloomy sky was behind him. His bright hazel eyes had the odd focus of someone working by feel, and his hands were loosely gripping Justin's chin and hair. His expression was bleak.

He let go when Justin patted his arm. His clothes were soaking wet, and he flicked water off his hands at Carl, who stood frowning just out of splashing range.

Carl said, "Yes, they were right. Stop gloating. If they'd been wrong, it would've boiled what's left of his brain. I let you do it, didn't I?"

The deck was covered in puddles. Parker jammed a baseball cap over his wet hair and stalked off in a swirl of irritable energy, adding a wet trail of footprints across the deck to a dilapidated one-story home.

Justin turned and brought up both arms to support himself on the tub's edge. His muscles were quivering with fatigue, but he was warm to the core, the aches were gone, and the terrifying confusion had loosened its grip. All he'd needed was a little heat.

"Great. I'm a tropical plant."

"It could be worse." Carl poked at one of the puddles with a boot toe.

Justin planted a hand against the cool deck, watched it waver into visibility. "It puts a big fat check mark in the symbiosis column. Prolonged drop in temp sent me hypothermic, but whatever's sharing my skin likes being warm so it triggered a fever response to generate heat, and things got out of control. Unless the water was the controlling variable. Shit, I hope I'm not amphibian. That would be inconvenient."

Silence warned him that he had erred, and he noted that Carl was looking through him. Conversation without visual feedback took extra effort. "Carl, relax. I'm fine."

"You were not fine. You were *dying*." Carl stomped the puddle, splattering water everywhere. "I really, truly, deeply hate working for idiots."

"Hey!" The insult smashed into Justin's ego and left it bleeding.

Carl turned and left. Justin dragged himself out of the tub. The water stank of algae, and so did he. Shivers started again by the time he reached the house. Warm air met him at the door. So did Parker, with a stack of towels and a brusque nod.

Four members of the security team were milling around the room, and an array of ammunition boxes, weaponry, and bags made the floor an intimidating obstacle course. Once upon a time he'd run slalom snowmobile courses at a hundred kilometers an hour. He'd raced sailboats. He'd flown airplanes.

Once upon a time he'd been able to *walk*. Now crossing an unfamiliar room without hurting himself was an insurmountable challenge. He wanted to sit down and cry.

"Shower. Clothes. Decisions," Parker said. He steered Justin past all the activity, and deposited him in a bathroom with the duffle that contained most of Justin's worldly goods.

Justin took a shower that filled the bathroom with steam, struggled into clean warm clothes, then sat on the edge of the tub until he thought he could walk without falling over. He looked at his hands: translucent within gray sweatshirt sleeves. He clenched them into fists and watched the effect wear off.

"Freak," he said, trying it on for size. The label still did not fit comfortably, but neither did "cripple" or "idiot." Facts did not disappear merely because he hated them.

His head began to throb, a familiar subliminal pulse of discomfort. The ache in his bones reawakened too, swelling to the usual background misery. The shower had helped. Sleep would help more. First he had to face up to the ominous-sounding decisions Parker had mentioned.

Parker was with Carl in the kitchen nook. Both men were wearing black fatigues now, and they looked like a pair of patient vultures. Carl was standing, while Parker had perched on the counter so he could kick his heels against the cabinets. The living room was empty except for rows of stacked boxes, and Justin doubted his memory. He was too tired for subtlety. "Weren't there other people here?"

"They're busy with scouting and supplemental shopping," Carl said. "Alison was distressed by the omission of vegetables from the supply chain. How are you feeling? Are you hungry?"

"No." He took a deep breath and moved to the wall for support when his leg trembled. "I didn't know heat regulation was an issue," he said. "There's a lot I don't know about this skin thing, and it may kill me yet. That doesn't make me an idiot."

Parker stretched out a foot and poked Carl with it.

"Yes, all right, I apologize for calling you names," Carl said. "You still should've spoken up when you started to feel sick."

"Carl, I always feel sick." The confession burst out in a gush of self-pity. "I hurt all the time. All day, every day, I hurt. Painkillers don't touch it, at least none I can take safely without living in a haze. It's a constant. I didn't say anything because I didn't see the point."

"Of course not." Carl rubbed his forehead. "I suppose that's the reason you never mentioned those drug allergies, the hairline skull fracture, or the three-day coma? You didn't see the point?"

Justin twitched. He'd known that contract clause would come back to haunt him. "You pulled my medical files."

"I should've dug them up when I saw your leg, but it's a violation of privacy, permissions or no. The clause is only there for emergencies, which this was, dammit. Damn Tyler for downplaying the damage, and damn me for not trusting my instincts. You and 'fine' are barely on speaking terms."

"I'm alive. I'm coping. Don't you dare pity me."

The last sentence was unintelligible. Justin took several deep breaths and blinked back tears.

"Pity has nothing to do with it," Carl said, more gently now. "The point is that we need to know everything. We can't protect you properly if we don't know your limitations."

"How could you miss them?" Justin's legs went from wobbly to boneless, and he slid to the floor. Getting up again was going to be a bitch. "Tyler teases me about them every day. They're obvious."

"No, Justin, they aren't." Carl's voice gentled almost to a whisper. "You compensate incredibly well, given the extent of the injury and your limited treatment options. Miraculously well with chronic pain involved."

He was qualified to judge. Justin couldn't trust his voice, so he shrugged.

Carl added, "I will say that ditching physical therapy two months into a two-*year* recovery plan wasn't the smartest decision you could've made. And hiding it all from your caregiver is turning him into an abusive jerk."

"I was bored. Therapy hurt. And Tyler—he's only trying to cheer me up. He just sucks at it." Justin forced out the words and kept going. "Can we not talk about me? I won't be your problem much longer anyway."

"What's that supposed to mean?"

"I have about a month before I'm broke, relatively speaking. I shouldn't have shunted as much as I did into the C&A survivors' fund. It put a big kink in the cash flow, but I couldn't stand back and do nothing. They were William's people."

Parker growled.

Justin looked up from the dirty carpet to find that he was the focal point of a stare so intense that its force erased whatever emotion it was meant to convey. "What? You said you wanted to know everything. That's everything."

The floor shook when Parker came off the counter, and he slammed the front door on his way out.

Once he was gone, Carl said, "A month is more than enough time to see this finished. Even if it wasn't, we would still stay—Eddie and I, at least. Mayhem & Havoc can't afford to work pro bono, but we aren't doing this for money in the first place. Did you forget that detail?"

"Maybe." Of course he had forgotten. "Then why is Parker so angry at me?"

"He isn't mad at you. He's mad at David Hong. He wants a kill order."

The announcement was made so casually that Justin nearly missed its significance. He swallowed a surge of cold ferocity when the name sank in. "That damned weasel is the one behind this whole mess? You're sure?"

"We don't have the whole story, but Tiffany Wyatt and Nicole Avon were off their grids at the same time he was, and he's the only one left standing. It looks like the lawyer was brokering a deal to yank the new tech away from both their companies for a shared private venture. I have people confirming details now."

"Good. Take him down." Hatred spread like black ice inside of him, an emotion so cold that it left Justin shuddering. "I don't want him dead. I won't stoop to his level. There's been enough destruction already. I want him to *bleed*."

"Speaking of destruction," Carl said. "You'd better know this sooner than later. We were compromised, back in Lincoln. Someone broke into your bunker an hour after we pulled out, and the building dropped into a sinkhole an hour after penetration. Rescue crews have pulled out five bodies already. No IDs yet."

"Somebody blew up the data lockers?" Justin's heart stopped dead and then thudded painfully against his ribs. "How could anyone be stupid enough to do that?"

The silence grew very cold. Carl said, "If you were irresponsible enough to set death-traps, I will walk out of here right now and take everyone with me."

"Of course I didn't—" Justin stopped and fought back tears. The bunker was gone. Neither rage nor grief would bring it back. It was only one more pain to go with all the rest. "I would never play with other people's lives. Not intentionally."

"Of course you wouldn't." Carl closed his eyes and rubbed at the bridge of his nose. "What did you mean, then?"

"It was security for the hush-hush government programs. Big flashing signs and audible alarms stating that data breaches and equipment tampering could blow demo charges. Believe me, they were impossible to miss, and they left plenty of escape time at every stage. Anyone who ignored those warnings out of greed or stupidity got what they deserved."

The last of the anger gave Justin the strength to shove himself to his feet. "If the weasel sent them, then their deaths are on him. Let him live with the guilt. What are the other options for dealing with him?"

"First we complete the evaluation of Hong's security. We didn't pick Chicago at random; it was here, Seattle, or Atlanta. We got lucky. He's here now. We grab him, find out exactly what he did, and then see if we can come to an agreement. Blackmail is an effective negotiating tool."

"Whatever works. I am past ready for this to be over."

"Over? Justin, we can neutralize the primary personal threat, but your reappearance will start a new round of problems. There will be a hellacious inheritance mess, for one thing."

"Not if I don't challenge the payouts." A new wave of fatigue washed over Justin. "A bequest is a gift. You don't ask for gifts back. I can't take back what Hong stole either. Even if Parker did kill him, there's no putting the chick back into its egg. I can only challenge under patent and make him bleed money for it. That'll help with the finances eventually."

He started to estimate income and evaluate rebuilding costs. Some of his other licenses might revert without too much hassle. That would add up fast.

"You are a very unusual person." Carl said, startling him out of the calculations. "I keep underestimating exactly *how* unusual you are."

"Just call me a freak. It's simpler." He yawned again, and then again. "I'm also an exhausted freak. Help me to a bed, will you?"

Carl offered a hand up. "I am sorry I called you an idiot. Anger is my recoil response when people I care about frighten me. I don't think you realize how close we came to losing you today. It caught me by surprise."

"So you have a temper like everyone else. Big deal." Justin's toes lost contact with the floor as Carl got a grip around his chest and lifted him. "Shit, you're strong."

"You're missing the point."

Carl half-carried him to a bedroom and left him there to sleep. It wasn't until Justin was drifting off that he realized that he never did hear what the point was.

THE SHOPPERS RETURNED. Parker didn't. Carl sent two of the team assigned to the house off to retrieve him; Parker was heading for the group gathering intel on Hong's movements, and they wouldn't welcome the interference.

Tyler made himself a snack, and Carl put together sandwiches so there would be food on hand for the guards on duty. Afterwards they both ended up watching Alison slowly construct something involving greens and bright crunchy things. Once she finished she spent ten more minutes fixing tea and tidying up.

"We'll only be here a week or two," Carl said. "Do you think you'll be done eating before then?"

Alison bestowed a dazzling smile on him and so pointedly didn't say "Men!" that she might as well have shouted it. Then she took her meal and retreated to a bedroom to eat in privacy.

That was when Carl realized that his datapad—which he'd left open with Justin's medical report on display—was still sitting on the counter where he'd left it. Alison had spent the last twenty minutes skimming the files right in front of him.

Carl secured the device and warned himself never to underestimate Alison again. Tyler flopped onto the couch and grinned. "I like her," he declared.

Parker came prowling into the house through the garage door and went straight to the sandwiches. When he was done wolfing down food, he stared at the empty disposable plate. Muscle worked at the corner of his jaw.

"Eddie—"

Parker started folding the edges of the plate. "Blind."

"I know. We'll work on it."

"Idiot."

"No. Do us all a favor and don't call him one. It's a raw, bleeding wound."

Tyler said, "You have to be talking about Justin. What did he do this time?"

"Nothing new." Carl stretched out his legs. The chair creaked. "Thank you for the quick thinking, earlier today. I was ready to pitch him into an ER and pray. You saved his life."

"I wish I'd noticed earlier that he didn't have a coat." Tyler grimaced. "Never mind. I hear there's good news, too. You've pinned things on David Hong. What comes next? Burning him alive would be poetic justice. I like that idea."

"Really?" Tyler's words and tone were a total mismatch. What he thought he should feel and his real feelings flatly contradicted each other. He did want justice, but as an intellectual ideal, bloodless compared to the savage emotional depth of Justin's vengefulness.

Tyler looked away. "Well, it would be poetic."

"It won't happen. Justin vetoed deadly force."

"That figures. He probably forgot what justice means."

Parker growled under his breath.

Tyler's eyes widened. "What is his problem?"

The short answer was that Parker had a homicidal temper. Carl took the long route, hoping to pick up an attitude adjustment for Tyler along the way. "You know that we only took this job because Eddie knew your brother."

"Yeah. Harry, my brother who burned to death because David Hong didn't care who else he killed as long as Justin went down. So?" When neither Carl nor Parker responded, Tyler flung up both hands and let them drop again. "Oh, great. Justin can't be bothered with matching socks or remember to shower half the time, but he gets to make the life-or-death decisions? Why him?"

Carl let the silence run long enough to strip the bitterness down to its petty roots. "My point was that based on knowing your brother, Eddie thought you were worth potentially dying for. I'll be damned if I can see why, at times like this."

Parker had the sense to not interfere. He went for another sandwich. Tyler tried to regain control of the conversation with a glare, but Carl held him pinned from across the room.

Alison's voice broke the tableau. "Come on, Carl. He's barely out of Tertiaries, and math is his native language, if I'm remembering right. He's pretty people-savvy, considering." She carried her empty dishes to the trash. "Sorry to interrupt."

"No, please do." Tyler made space on the couch and waited until Alison sat down beside him. "Me being dense about people is nothing new. I still don't even know why I bug Justin. Will you give me a hint now?"

Alison smiled. "You're young, attractive, healthy, and supersmart. Just looking at you reminds him that's he's a mess. Honestly, the way you pick on him is a little hateful."

Her observations were astute, and the straightforward presentation dodged right past Tyler's ego to his sense of fairness. He looked stricken. "Hateful? I don't hate him. He's an aggravating ass, but he's Justin Wyatt. How could anyone not respect that? Oh."

He looked to Parker, who was still radiating murderous intent from the other side of the table. The paper plate was in shreds. "Okay, I think I see where this is headed. If I'm worth dying for, then Justin's worth killing for, and he's pissed because Justin won't let him do it. Why didn't you just say that?"

"Because this way Eddie got to hear you prove you understood the situation. Start using that smart brain of yours before that smart mouth gets you killed."

Tyler's cavalier outlook was not only cruel, it was also potentially hazardous to his health. If someone had set out to design a package guaranteed to trip every serve-and-protect trigger in Parker's brain, it would look a lot like Justin. The man had an unusual clarity of spirit, a generous heart, and courage to spare. If the hypothetical designer had added "female" to that package then Hong would be dead already, orders or no orders.

"I'm entitled to my opinion," Tyler said in a voice that shook slightly. "I miss Harry. I miss my *life*. Hong should pay. I want that. That's all I'm saying."

"He'll pay," Parker said, which was a good sign. If he could form a sentence, then he was stepping off the brink.

Justin chose that moment to come out of his bedroom and limped into the kitchen through the middle of the conversation. He had a blanket draped over his clothes like a cloak, and he looked dead on his feet, with dark circles under eyes that were glassy and bloodshot.

Carl felt a deep pang of regret. He tried to respect the mental privacy of those around him, and Justin was so emotionally transparent that there'd been no reason to look deeper. As it turned out, even the clearest crystal could distort perception. Breathtaking intelligence and an honest disdain for social niceties had been obscuring some serious cognitive issues.

Alison poked Tyler in the arm. He scrambled to his feet. "I'm sorry I yelled at you, Justin. Are you feeling better?"

"No." Justin stopped dead in front of the refrigerator.

His jaw worked slightly. Carl kicked himself again. He'd seen that reaction and a dozen others like it far more times than it should've taken to recognize their significance.

Staring silences followed by careful comments that established location and the passage of time weren't creative reveries. Justin's brain was seizing up on him. His propensity towards distraction and his impatience with conversations were both rooted in an inability to follow abrupt changes in topic.

No one expected a genius to be conventional. Justin had hidden everything from minor memory gaps to major sensory processing problems by looking preoccupied while he struggled.

The energy and determination he channeled into acting normal was staggering to contemplate.

He had forgotten what he was doing, but he planned to stubbornly stand in that spot until he remembered or someone intervened.

Parker opened the refrigerator and handed over a sandwich and a glass of water. Justin silently limped away with the food, his full attention consumed by the simple task of keeping a broken, exhausted body from betraying weakness.

Tyler spoke in a voice gone acid with pent-up frustration. "See, that's the kind of thing that makes me crazy. You're welcome, Justin. Enjoy your lunch. We're so happy you appreciate the effort."

Justin paused at his door. "I suck at appreciation."

Carl was certain that no one else had caught the hurt undertone until he heard Alison sigh.

"Nice job not listening to a word I said." She patted Tyler on the knee. "Next time just kick him in the balls. You'll hurt him less."

"It was a joke. He joked back. How is that hurtful?"

"Are you blind? What—"

She stopped when Parker pushed himself out of his chair and headed into the hall. Justin's door banged open and shut. Tyler opened his mouth to shove his foot down his throat again, but Carl stopped him with a look.

Alison said, "And that's my cue to retreat. Something tells me you'll do a better job explaining the facts of life than I could. Can I join the gun-toting mute, or will he shoot me if I startle him?"

Carl smiled at the description. "He won't shoot you. He could use the assist."

After Alison's departure Tyler moved to the patio door. It put the length of the room and the barrier of the couch between himself and Carl, and he adopted a textbook defensive posture:

arms crossed, body hunched, head down. "Why is everybody always on his side?"

"Tyler, it isn't about sides. It's about damage. Those aren't jokes. I'm sure it started that way, but it's gone toxic. Stop slapping him with his flaws every time he turns around. He would change if he could. He is doing the best he can."

Tyler worked his way from indignation to guilt, and his face reflected every stage of the transition. "I know I'm a jerk," he said, which earned him major points for self-awareness. He lost them all on the next breath. "But it's stressful, dealing with him."

Carl found himself fumbling for words that would not flay the man's ego to pieces. Emotion muddied responses, warped observations, destroyed objectivity. His feelings were running high enough to drown.

"You want stress?" he said. Anger rose, guilt about his own mistakes escaping as rage. He crossed the room, leaned in close as Tyler backed away. "Try living in a body that's turned traitor on you. Try coming to terms with brain damage when intelligence is the cornerstone of your identity. Try owing your life to someone who treats you with utter contempt. You're a selfish whining *child*."

Tyler's shoulders hit the wall. His eyes were dilated, pupils swallowing the blue iris, and he was shaking like a leaf. A few steps away brought Carl to the middle of the room. "Justin would let you gut him with a dull knife. I won't. Respect that if you can't respect him. Watch your tongue, or Eddie will cut it out. Don't think he won't do it. Don't think I won't let him."

Tyler shook his head, not in refusal but in surrender.

Any more pressure would crush him. Carl knew that, the same way he knew he needed to leave, but he could not resist one last squeeze. "You miss your brother?" The soft question slipped easily past demolished emotional defenses. "Ask yourself if he'd be proud of you right now."

The sound of crying followed him out the front door.

ALISON PAUSED in the bedroom doorway to consider the tableau inside. Justin sat bundled under his blanket, empty plate and glass on the floor beside him. He must've inhaled the sandwich to be finished already, and he looked determined to ignore the world until it left him alone.

Parker stood to the left of the door with a scowl on his face, one hand nervously scrubbing over his cropped hair. He looked determined to keep Justin from feeling abandoned. It was an interesting standoff.

"Hi, remember me?" Alison asked Justin. The flicker of confusion in his eyes was enough answer. He ducked his head to stare at the bedspread.

"Oh, that's mature," Alison said. "I won't be offended if you've lost my name, but don't ignore me. It's been a crappy couple of days. Don't make it worse."

Parker made a small amused sound, and Alison looked his way. He gestured: keep going. She handed the dishes to him. "More food, please, and a deck of cards if you guys have one. Any kind of simple game will do."

He slipped out the door. Justin remained silent long enough that Alison wondered if he'd dozed off. Then he raised his head. "Alison Gregorio. Right? I'm awful with names."

She kept her gaze steady on his dark, vulnerable eyes. "That wasn't the problem, and we both know it. You don't have to make up excuses. I know you have serious memory and processing deficits from a brain injury."

"Why do I try to keep secrets?" he said after a few seconds. "Did Carl tell you?"

"No, the files were sitting open, and I got nosy. Yes, it was rude and unethical and probably illegal, but I was curious, and I could tell something was wrong. Sorry."

He took his time working through his reactions. The wheel

stopped on "resigned acceptance." "'S'all right, I guess. Better that you know up front why I'm a rude, forgetful bastard."

Alison heard echoes of Tyler in the words. "Here's what I know. You need to stop taking tall-smart-and-sarcastic so seriously. He doesn't mean it. Not the way you think. You intimidate the hell out of him. Oh, and while I'm showering you with unwanted advice, stop taking out your frustration about your head on your poor abused body."

Justin sighed. "Is that what I'm doing?"

"Carl said so at one point. What do you think?"

"I think that you probably irritate most people as much as I do." The words stung until Justin added, "Sorry, that's my rotten sense of humor. I meant it as a compliment. And Carl's probably right."

Parker came back in with sandwiches, beer, and two decks of cards. After a considering pause, he sat down cross-legged at the bottom of the bed, made a flat spot in the blankets, and started shuffling. Justin stared at the process as if he'd never seen it before in his life, and he kept staring after Parker removed the cards. He twitched when Alison squeezed his hand. And then he blushed.

"I keep hoping that will stop." He rubbed his temples. "Some days are worse than others."

"Routine and familiarity make it easier to maintain focus. You haven't had much of either, have you? Eat. It'll help the headache."

He stared at Alison instead, and she waited, because she wanted to know what *Justin* knew. "Mental health clinic," he said after another of those long thoughtful pauses. "Where you saw a lot and learned it all because you couldn't stand not knowing everything about everything."

Alison chose to take that as a compliment. Justin demolished the sandwiches and started on the beer before asking, "Why cards? Therapy?"

"No, but if you sleep all day you'll be up all night." Alison smiled at him. "And I'm bored. Will you play a game or two with me? Or is it 'us'?"

She directed that at Parker, who lifted one shoulder and let it drop. He dealt out pinochle hands, and they played cutthroat. Justin held his own except when he reneged or forgot how to bid, which was about one hand in ten. They worked out house rules to accommodate it and played on.

When Carl checked in on them after a couple of games, they moved to the kitchen table, which convinced Alison that she would never play against Carl or Parker in any bidding game that involved money. Both of them were devastating, and in tandem they were unstoppable. At some point Alison started to feel terribly odd, having a good time when the world had fallen apart so recently, and she had to excuse herself to go cry in her room.

Laughter and voices drifted to her when the game attracted an audience of off-duty security specialists. She put a pillow over her head. Later, Carl brought her a huge bowl of popcorn and a datapad—with a page of instructions on how its layers of security worked—and left them both beside the bed.

She took it out to the couch and joined the party.

ALISON COULDN'T BE sure what the security team did while off duty, since they were bunking in the house next door, but with one or two of them underfoot at all times, she had learned their workday routines quite quickly. She also learned that firearms and surveillance systems were complicated, stun guns were finicky, and gunpowder smelled nasty. The other women indulged her curiosity with welcoming tolerance and infinite patience.

Something big was happening this morning. A quiet parade into and out of the garage was in progress when Alison took her morning shower, and it was winding down as she finished. She dried her hair and went in search of explanations.

Terry was at the kitchen table as usual at that hour. The head of Mayhem & Havoc was a fit, middling-height, middle-aged woman with brown skin and black cropped hair. She had an aura of supportive, patient confidence, and she bore an uncanny resemblance to one of Alison's primary school teachers.

Her seat gave her clear views of the hall, the yard, and the surveillance monitor by the front door, and the scents of fresh pastries and fried meat emanated from bags on the counter. Alison sat down with tea and a muffin.

"Yo," Terry said. "Up early again."

"It was noisy." Alison nodded at the garage as vehicle motors revved to life. "Should I be worried?"

Terry shook her head. "No cause for alarm. Celebration, maybe. We're setting up the scoop on Hong."

"Thank God. I'm ready to get back into the world again." Yesterday had made three full weeks of mourning and wishing she could contact friends and family. Three weeks of learning to make do with clothes that could be bought at convenience stores. Three weeks of watching people plan sinful acts with good intentions. It felt like eternity.

"This is my real world." Terry smiled and looked through the sliding doors into the backyard. "Now hush. You're interrupting my favorite show."

Parker was doing t'ai chi exercises out on the lawn, and it did make pleasant viewing. He wore only a pair of loose shorts, his body was all working muscle, and he executed every form with perfect, fluid grace.

Justin stood across from him in gray and black sweats. Rain or shine, every morning, Parker dragged him out of bed and coached him through the routines with results that varied from amusing to hilarious. He was far from graceful, but he was almost as much fun to watch.

When today's show came to an end, Justin headed straight for the bathroom. Parker tossed on a jacket and went out the front door. Neither of them acknowledged their audience even in passing.

Kaylie entered the house with her head turned over her shoulder to observe Parker's departure. Terry stood and yawned, and they conversed quietly before Kaylie settled by the door. Things were back to normal, at least for now.

Alison consulted her datapad over breakfast, and she soon lost herself in the limitless realms of news, trivia, and entertainment. There were three new shows she wanted to see, Seattle's media had moved on from the C&A explosion to a sports scandal, and she wasn't going to be visiting Utah or Arizona any time soon. The state governments were both petitioning the Fed for assistance asserting water rights against Colorado. Shots had been fired. Mark would've been insufferable. He'd predicted it.

"I find you in the same spot every morning," Justin said, startling her.

He was sitting on the far side of the table. He wore clean sweats and had recently shaved, and he had a steaming cup of coffee in both hands. The picked-over remains of an omelet sat on a plate in front of him.

Alison checked her clock to find that she had lost nearly two hours to an online daze. Parker and Carl were conferring over diagrams posted on the living room wall, and Kaylie was pulling hairs from her ponytail and splitting them with one of her knives while she watched the security monitors.

Outside, a cloudy sky promised rain.

Tyler was outside too. He spent every waking moment sitting in a deck chair with his computer or pacing the yard, and he hadn't spoken ten words together in days. It was either an impressive sulk, an extended bout of creative thought, or both. No one else seemed concerned. Alison tried not to worry, but she couldn't help herself.

"I am a creature of habit," she said to Justin. "I have a nice routine now. Catch up with the world after breakfast, play cards in the afternoon. Write letters I can't send at night. Wake up thinking about dead people."

A flicker of emotion crossed Justin's face. "I'm sorry."

"Me, too." Grief was a strange thing. She would forget people were dead; then it would hit her as if it had just happened and she started hurting all over again. "It's hard to move on. This isn't real life, it's life on hold. Limbo."

Justin looked away. "What would you be doing now, if your life wasn't on hold? If none of this had happened?"

Alison gave the question some thought. "I was looking for a new apartment, before all this. Someplace with room for craft supplies and windows on the mountains. I guess I'd be decorating it now. Maybe buying a cat. I always wanted one."

Her throat closed up. Half the people she would have invited to a housewarming were dead. The rest didn't know she was still alive. "I suppose I'll still need to find a new place. I'm sure Mario must have rented out my old one."

Justin said, "I will get you out of limbo and back to your life, I promise. My fault you lost it, after all."

He put down his cup and glanced down as he tapped his fingers on the table: checking to see if they were visible. Alison was sure he didn't realize he did that. *She* knew, which meant she was watching him a little too closely. Getting emotionally involved was a bad idea. She knew that, but she couldn't help herself.

She laid her hand over Justin's fingers to stop the nervous tapping. "How are you handling all this?"

"Small steps. I'm still a fragile hothouse flower, but I can balance on one leg these days."

He was deliberately misinterpreting the question, but joking about his body was a sign of progress. Alison said, "Hothouse I'll accept. Fragile and flowery, not so much."

"I showered. I have it on a checklist."

"Yes, but you aren't flowery. You smell nice."

"Oh." He shrugged off the compliment. "I'm sticking with fragile. Heat regulation still sucks. I had an idea about ..."

He never finished the sentence. After a few minutes, he rose and headed to his room.

Parker turned away from Carl, stepped into his path, and shoulder-checked him into the wall. Justin bounced off and continued onward without noticing the course alteration. Parker picked up a heavy duffle and went out the garage door with a grin on his face.

Alison smiled into her tea. Two weeks ago, Justin would've fallen. He was getting better.

Carl came into the kitchen. "Eddie says the team's confirmed a window in Hong's schedule tonight. We'll be meeting them at their rally point and head to a lockdown location from there."

"He never said all that," Alison said.

"A direct quote would be: 'Game time. See you at the ORP.' I've had a lot of practice translating. Tonight could get ugly. Just to warn you."

On that cheerful note, Carl got a mug of coffee and sat down at the table. The kitchen suddenly felt crowded.

Alison began cleaning up the morning's collection of cups and plates and empty bags. Standing up while Carl remained seated minimized the man's overwhelming presence.

"How's Justin?" Carl asked.

"I don't know. Why don't you ask him?"

Carl tilted his head, and then he smiled. "Sorry. I was trying to ease into a difficult topic with a neutral one, but evidently he's not neutral for you."

Alison went to rinse out her tea mug. "Talking to you is like carrying a can of tuna through a room full of sleeping cats. Please don't tease me."

"Then don't make it so damned easy."

Alison looked back, surprised.

Carl said, "Alison, I am not omniscient and I am not a saint.

The more you evade and self-censor, the harder I dig for reasons. I can't stop myself."

"You don't even try o stop most of the time."

"True," Carl said. "But we're getting off topic." He leaned his chair back on its rear legs so he could stretch his legs straight. He sat with his arms folded and his chin tucked in, and the floor under the table got a serious scowling. "Tyler and Justin want to be part of what happens tonight," he said. "I was wondering if you'd be coming or not. It's filthy work, and Yoshi will stay back with you if you'd rather not witness it."

Alison had a duty to seventy ghosts to see this through to the end. She had the *right* to see it through. She let her resentment show. "Of course I want to be included. Do I look like a frail, fragile flower whose nerves need protecting?"

"Hardly. More the opposite, which is why I'd like to ask a fav—"

Carl abruptly tipped his chair upright and stared at the security monitor. Kaylie began staring as well, and then she reached for her sidearm.

CHAPTER THIRTEEN

CARL GESTURED SHARPLY, AND KAYLIE sat back with a puzzled look. Alison wondered what they were watching. All she could see was Tyler sitting on the deck and gnawing on a fingernail while he drew on his screen.

The back fence wavered. Seconds later, Justin was visible, crouching barefoot and motionless less than a meter from Tyler. Carl flashed another signal to Kaylie, and she flipped a switch on the system control board. Tyler continued working in blissful ignorance. Sound hissed from the speaker beside the monitor. Fabric rustled as he shifted position.

"How did he do it?" Carl asked quietly.

"He pried off the window boards and came around the side," Kaylie said. "But the ghost act? No idea. House systems flagged a power surge and a popped breaker, and he vaporized from the camera feed."

Carl sat back again. "This should be interesting."

Justin leaned forward like a sprinter about to start and shouted, "BOO!" less than a foot from Tyler's face. The datapad flew one direction, papers went another, and Tyler's chair went over backwards with him in it. He landed on his back with a strangled yelp and struggled up onto his elbows.

Justin got to his feet, staggering slightly, and padded a few steps forward to look down at him. "I told you if you called me a freak again that I'd make you regret it."

Neither of them moved for several seconds. Justin glowered from above, Tyler gaped up at him in shock. Then Tyler let his head drop back and started laughing. Justin turned the chair upright, gathered up the scattered research materials, and sat down on the deck. The chuckles died into a quiet broken only by breathing and scraping noises as Tyler accepted his belongings from Justin and returned to his chair.

"This isn't how it works, you know," he said. "I'm not the comic relief, after all. I'm a rotten bully. I should run off and become your evil archenemy."

"I already have one of those." Justin began rubbing his leg. "I don't need two. I need a friend who isn't afraid to tell me when I'm an ass."

Tyler bowed his head over the computer for several minutes before saying in a grudging voice, "Becoming an evil mastermind would be time-consuming. My schedule's pretty full these days."

Justin said, "Do you have time to check some numbers for me?"

Tyler's head lifted fast, and silence spun out again, a long stretch of quiet that eventually snapped on his sigh. "Depends. Will you let me bounce my ideas off you in exchange? I promise to use small words."

Everyone was pretending to be working by the time the door slid open, but it was an unnecessary precaution. Tyler and Justin were too busy talking math to notice anything else in the world. Once they were safely inside Justin's room, Carl said, "Nice. Tug on the shared history, offer a treat, let him fuss, reestablish balance. That was a very nice job of ego patching."

"Isn't that your specialty?" Alison asked.

"Yes, but in this case, I did the damage. Accidentally."

Alison considered Carl's brooding scowl. The man wasn't a saint, and he wasn't angry. He was frightened.

"What kind of favor did you need?" she asked.

THE COMMERCIAL GARAGE Parker's team had repurposed for the night had enough open floor under its leaking tin roof to generate echoes, but its row of offices could be reached only through a narrow interior hall.

Justin arrived there late, since either Chris or Yoshi had typed the wrong address into the GPS, and he moved as quickly as he could with Tyler's help to get to the open office door where Alison and Carl were supposed to be setting up an observation area.

Carl had briefed them earlier on the basics of running an effective interrogation that didn't rely on torture for results. Justin had been left with the chilling realization that prying information out of people was a science. It was an uncomfortable revelation.

The first thing he noticed when he opened the office door was that the problem of access to the garage floor had been solved by breaking a picture window. Sparkling pebbles of safety glass fanned over the office floor. Tape covered the edges of the hole in a rough frame.

Beyond the window, bright lights glared down on one small area of the garage, creating deep shadows around a semicircle of plastic sheeting. The shrouds provided a rough but effective cover for entrances and exits, and they moved and shifted ominously in the gloom.

In the center of the lit stage sat an empty chair.

The office had a counter along one side wall. Alison sat on one of four bar stools, near the window. She wore the same style of black coveralls over her clothes that Justin, Tyler, and everyone else had on. They minimized the need for forensic cleanup, Terry had said, and Justin had been afraid to ask for details.

"Wait there," Alison said.

Justin stopped in the doorway.

"Okay, that's good. Now come in, but slow."

Her fingers picked nervously at the end of a roll of tape, and she was looking to Justin's left. He leaned into the room to see what was bothering her before committing to action.

A desk had been shoved into the back corner of the office, and Carl sat on its dented metal top. He was slouched forward with his weight on his hands. His attention was on the window, and his heels thumped against the side of the desk.

Justin's spine tingled as all the hair on his body stood straight up. Something about Carl's posture looked fundamentally wrong.

"She said slow, Justin, not stop." Tyler edged around him and settled at the counter on another bar stool. "Sorry we're late. It wasn't our—whoa. What the hell?"

The office door squeaked when Justin shut it. Carl stopped watching the improvised interrogation area and looked at Justin instead. His eyes held no sign of conscious recognition; the blue stare reflected nothing but terror on the cusp of panic.

Justin held his breath. Carl's gaze drifted back to the window. His attention moved from the circle of lights to the empty chair at the center. To the video recorder on its tripod, back to the chair. To the armed figures in the shadows. To the chair. Cloth-shrouded crates, glint of metal tools. Chair.

The tap of his feet against the desk punctuated every shift of focus, and he was gripping the desk so hard that his arms were quivering.

Justin joined Alison. "What is going on?" he said softly.

"The lights came up and he—blipped." She sighed. "He said he wanted me here because I wouldn't register as a threat. In case, he said. I think he knew he'd get like this but couldn't admit it to himself, much less anyone else."

Some of the blame had to rest on Justin's shoulders. He should've realized that an interrogation would raise grisly associations. "Does Parker know?"

"He called and said, 'Don't touch.' Which I knew already. Carl said *if* this happened and you barged in, that he might hurt you because he went out swinging."

Tyler glanced between Carl and the brightly lit chair awaiting an occupant, and when comprehension dawned, he shot Justin a mortified look. "Oh, crap."

"Yeah." No one had gotten lost. Carl had made certain they were delayed until he knew how he would react to the situation.

Parker arrived at the hall door. He was dressed in the same black coveralls that the rest of the security team were wearing, only he wore a comm headset instead of their face-shielding helmets.

"Fucking complications," he said. "Hold for my mark," he added over the headset. "Twenty minimum."

Then he unbuckled his weapons belt and dropped it onto the floor outside the window. His headset joined it, and he frowned at Carl. "*Meds,* stubborn fuck."

"No. Wait." Alison looked at a note on her handset. "I'm supposed to tell you, he took the tranks and the blockers. I hope that means something to you."

Parker glanced at her. "That's fugue. Flashback on max. Blockers prevent fugue, mostly."

Alison made a helpless gesture. Parker's mouth worked silently as he stared at Carl, and then he said, "Then what it means is this: he'll stay like that for God knows how long unless someone pushes him, and *then* he'll go fucking berserk. It means you get out. He's dangerous, and he can pin me, some days."

"He asked me to stay," Alison said while Justin was still absorbing the novelty of hearing complex sentences from Parker. "I'm staying."

"In his head there are only enemies here. He won't see you."

"He said he could, underneath. That it helped. Do what you need to do. I'm staying."

Tyler glanced at Justin for guidance, and Justin shook his head. He wasn't leaving either. This was his mess, and he wasn't leaving Alison to clean it up. Tyler looked sick but refused to retreat alone.

Alison was still matching Parker stare for stare. Seconds dragged past, then a minute. Another minute. Parker sighed and pointed at the tape. She tossed it to him.

It made a loud ripping sound when he pulled a strip loose. Carl's head snapped back as if he'd been hit, and when Parker moved sideways, his eyes glittered, following the shift. Parker bared his teeth. Moved one step closer.

Carl lunged for him.

Parker was faster. He turned at the last moment, captured an outstretched arm, wrapped the strip of tape around it. The dangling shackle became a pivot point, and two meters of muscle went crashing into the wall beneath the counter. Carl bounced off and skidded on his hands and knees through broken glass. Sharp fragments scattered in all directions, and then he was diving at Parker again.

Justin pulled Alison back, out of range of fists and feet. Tyler jammed himself into the corner by the window and sank into a crouch with both arms over his head.

Parker ducked inside a punch that would've broken his jaw, took two hard hits to the body, and snaked a second strip of tape around Carl's other wrist. Carl's feet went out from under him again when momentum betrayed him, and he landed with enough force to knock him breathless. In short order Parker pinned him prone, planted a knee against his spine, and secured his wrists behind his back.

Start to finish, less than thirty seconds. Blood from tiny glass cuts stained the tape and soaked Carl's sleeves. Parker went still, head bowed. His eyes were shut tight, and the tears dripping down his cheeks in no way diluted the determination on his face.

Justin realized with a sinking heart that the fight wasn't over yet.

Parker grabbed Carl's bound arms in one hand and yanked them straight up. The leverage forced him flat against the floor. A second jerk produced a shriek of defiant, mindless anger.

It was the first sound either of them had made. Tyler shifted his arms to cover his ears. Alison crammed a hand against her mouth, and Justin hated himself for wondering how much torque a shoulder joint could take before dislocating.

Parker got a grip in Carl's hair and bent to whisper in his ear. He nearly ended up with a nosebleed, but he pulled back an instant before the back of Carl's skull smashed into his face. He bent close to whisper again. Dodged again and wrenched Carl's arms hard enough to make him scream until he ran out of breath and sobbed.

Then Carl nearly twisted his own shoulders out of their sockets trying to curl up into a ball. Parker pulled the taller man across his lap and bent over him, still whispering while he stroked Carl's hair with one hand.

The response was a barely audible murmur.

"Knife." Parker scrubbed his face against his arm.

Justin turned to grab a blade from the weapons belt. As soon as Carl's hands were loose, Parker gathered the other man close and rested his chin on top of Carl's head. Carl slowly went limp within the circle of his brother's arms.

Alison gathered up the rest of Parker's discarded gear and brought it to him. He eyed the equipment and her with equal wariness.

She said, "Come on, Captain Karate. Let's play to our strengths. I'm an excellent pillow. You excel at soldier things. We're still on a schedule, right?"

He sighed agreement, moved his arms. "He'll need half an hour, maybe more, to pull himself together."

"We'll stay with him. I promise I won't faint over the blood.

Cross my heart."

"Wait." Justin knelt in front of them. The concrete felt bitter cold through both layers, jeans and coverall, and the draft against his wrists raised gooseflesh. Parker's bleak, red-eyed glare was almost as cold. Justin said, "I need you to know something first. If I'd realized—if I'd understood there was a risk—I would've let you murder the weasel outright rather than put Carl through this."

"I know." Parker allowed Alison to relieve him of Carl's weight and then slung his weapons belt over his shoulder. "*He* knew and he tried anyway. He hadn't pushed, hadn't risked anything, hadn't cared in years. I was afraid he never would. This is better. This means he isn't dead inside yet."

Multiple complete sentences. It was disconcerting, and Justin could not think of anything to say in reply.

Parker headed for the window, grabbing one of the bar stools on the way. He planted it on the floor in front of Tyler's corner with a solid thud. Tyler twitched. His arms were still wrapped defensively over his head, and he said in a thick voice, "Leave me alone, or I'll throw up on you."

Parker rapped knuckles on the top of Tyler's skull and left through the broken window. As he walked away he said to someone else, "Go on backup. Warm-ups in ten."

Tyler slowly uncurled to glare after him. Alison nudged Justin with her foot. He took the hint and limped across the room. Tyler's skin was greenish and sweaty, and his eyes were red and wet with barely contained tears.

Sympathy might hit hard enough to send him over the edge, and crying in public would only embarrass him even more. Justin said, "This is a strict no-vomit zone."

Tyler swallowed hard. "What about fainting?"

"No. Fainting and vomiting are not funny. You're the comic relief." Justin helped him to his feet. "There you go, funny guy. How's that feel?"

The question sounded as ragged as Justin felt, and as he spoke he heard the chord of familiarity. Tyler met his eyes, and the pinched unhappiness in his face eased a little.

"I'm fine," Tyler said, then repeated more confidently, "Fine."

"Liar." Justin forced his voice to stay solemn.

"How's your head?" Tyler asked, the answering phrase in a ritual that had carried them both through a situation far worse than this one.

"Fine."

"Liar."

They regarded each other with pleased smiles. Alison stared at them both as if they were insane, and it didn't matter in the least.

David Hong walked into the interrogation area like he owned the place. He shaded his eyes against the glare with both cuffed hands and looked around with a calm and critical eye until his two escorts took him roughly by the arms and secured him in the chair. A bruised lump discolored the skin of his forehead, and the silvering black hair was a mess, but his face was devoid of emotion.

Tyler wondered why the man wasn't shaking in fear. He knew how he would handle the threat of personal violence: he'd just failed a dramatic demonstration.

He could face danger without flinching, but only the impersonal kind that pitted him against his own limits and renewed his spirit with sweat and adrenaline. Facing human malice required a kind of courage he couldn't seem to acquire.

Hong's wrists were cuffed to the back of the seat and his ankles to the front legs, which left him splayed back, uncomfortably exposed. He made it look as though he were reclining by choice—quite a trick, since he was nearly naked. Tyler had expected someone exotic or visibly evil, but Hong was just a big round middle-aged rich man stripped of all his expensive accessories. He wasn't a pretty sight, but he inspired only disgust, not hatred.

Tyler's rage flickered and died, burned out at last. That was a human being out there. Murder and torture were more than words. They were real. *This* was real. He couldn't say it was wrong, but it wasn't righteous, either.

He'd wasted a lot of time and energy trying to hate when all he really felt was empty. No matter what he wished or did, his brother wasn't coming back. He could no longer hide the ache of loss behind a blaze of anger.

He shifted his weight on the bar stool, rested his elbows on his knees and locked his hands behind his neck. He no longer felt any desire to be here, but he was going to have to watch anyway.

Parker stepped into the lighted zone and stopped precisely where his shadow would fall over Hong's face. "You know why you're here," he said.

"No, I don't." Hong's voice was rough. A livid hand-shaped mark on his throat was only one of many fresh bruises. None of the damage looked permanent. All of it looked painful.

He squinted, eyes watering. "Could you be any more clichéd? Isolation and humiliation. Beatings and bright lights and cryptic threats. What did you do, read *Kidnapping for Dummies*?" His tone was cool. "This is ridiculous. Martin-Hong is insured. Take pictures, record a ransom request, and call the negotiator. All this theater is unnecessary."

He cleared his throat, licked cracked, dry lips. Parker leaned in so close that his breath moved Hong's hair, and his smile was a thing of bare teeth and manic eyes. Hong squeezed himself as far back as he could get in the chair, the only retreat he could make.

Parker walked around behind him. "That's in your book too, isn't it? You see your kidnappers' faces, your survival chances drop to zilch."

He leaned close again, from behind, whispering at Hong's ear. "No rules. No ransom. No negotiators. No one even knows you're missing. If you cooperate, you're home by lunch tomorrow, and no one ever knows you were gone. If you keep being a total dickhead, you'll die before dawn."

He wrapped a black piece of cloth around the man's head and walked into the dark outside the circle.

CARL FLIPPED through the limited selection of drugs remaining in his kit and picked the best of the bad choices available. He had no business popping painkillers on top of the other pharmaceuticals in his system, but his shoulders hurt so much he was past caring. The pills scratched their way down his throat. After swallowing, he said, "Show's over for an hour or so. Are you going to ignore me the whole time?"

Dead silence.

Parker had just disappeared offstage, beyond the window. The bright scene was ringed in a fuzzy halo. Carl blinked. Three sets of wary eyes looked at him from closer in, faces shadowy against the spot-lit performance behind them. Worry, guilt, and turmoil: Alison, Justin, and Tyler sitting shoulder to shoulder.

Carl swung his heels against the desk, generating sensory feedback to keep himself grounded. There was never a good time to get lost in body language and contextual cues, and right now he was far too vulnerable to both.

The others all reacted to the sound with uncomfortable shifts in weight. That was understandable. Carl felt uncomfortable too. He wanted desperately to hide alone in the dark like the violent wounded animal he'd resembled recently, but their concern trumped his embarrassment.

The transition back from a fugue was often a nightmare in its own right. Warm body contact anchoring him to reality had been a welcome change from woozy memory-fractured disorientation. He'd awakened with Justin sitting rock-solid on one side and

Alison on the other. Their presence had given him the strength to hold back the panic he'd felt at the sound of Parker's voice making threats. They'd moved as soon as he sat up, though, and the silence was growing awkward now.

He leaned forward and braced his hands on his legs to ease strained back muscles. Across the room Tyler sat up straight. Justin moved closer to him in response, support offered and received without conscious thought.

Carl fought to concentrate past the distractions.

"Can you even see us?" Justin asked. "Your eyes are dilated. Wouldn't pinpoint pupils be normal, considering?"

Inquisitive Justin had done some research on the pharmaceuticals. Carl said, "I have some atypical responses. I can see you here. Out there, that would be another story."

Hong was out there, marinating in fear and uncertainty. Carl should be out there too, gauging the best time to step back in. He couldn't do it. The lights were making him dizzy from here. He would be blind under them.

Carl jumped when Alison laid a hand on his arm. Her steady brown eyes caught his in a look that offered friendly sympathy and a touch of curiosity. She tucked her hair behind her ears and said, "You still want to do—that. Why? How can you even consider it?"

"Breaking someone's will, terrorizing him, shattering his ego—they're all different skills." Carl had those differences engraved in his flesh and etched into his brain. "If I could get what we need with minimal trauma, collaborating with Eddie, then I'd do it in a heartbeat, but I'm mush-mouthed and dizzy. Eddie's style is more direct, and that means blood and ugliness. I'll expedite things as much as I can for him from the sidelines."

Alison looked to Justin, who said, "How?"

"I'm more analytical in this state than when I'm clean and sober. One of life's painful ironies. Another reality slip is highly unlikely. Chemistry's on my side for a little while."

For a while. The aftershocks would be less than enjoyable.

"Could you help someone else help Parker, then? Tag team with threat and projection, like you planned?" Alison said. "Justin and I, we talked it over. Can one of us do it?"

"Are you all insane?" Tyler blurted out. His indignant posture deflated under a dry look from Justin. "Sorry, but look at him. He's obviously higher than a kite and he's already had one raving fit. There's no way this will work."

"Nobody's forcing you to help," Justin said.

Thoughts chased over his face so quickly Carl was suddenly reminded of just how *intelligent* the man was. Justin nodded to himself and then slapped Tyler's shoulder. "Let's follow Alison's advice about playing to our strengths. I want those things we discussed this morning, and you're wasted here. Two problems, one solution. You can run errands. Look at me, making decisions."

He dragged Tyler into the back hall and returned alone a few minutes later. Another look passed between him and Alison. Again, Carl missed the nuances. Justin was a major distraction.

When they'd met, Justin had been a struggling invalid, an injured animal licking his wounds in hiding. He was still wounded, still struggling, but he was done hiding. The outward manifestations were minor, but in some critical way he was stronger than he had been.

Something had changed tonight.

Alison curled her fingers around Carl's wrist. "Focus, Carl. I know he's cute and distracting, but you need to walk us through your plan again so we can avoid any more blood and screaming."

"That's a worthy goal," Carl said.

And Justin said, "Cute? Me?"

Laughing hurt almost every muscle in Carl's body, but he didn't even try to stop. It was worth the pain.

Alison checked the fit of her earpiece one last time and shook her sleeves into place. The motion settled her nerves into a semblance of calm. Then she walked forward as if she knew what she was doing, and she yanked the hood off David Hong's head.

The man blinked away tears, turned his head aside as if expecting an attack. The lights were generating a lot of surplus heat. Hong's face shone with sweat, and heat radiated through the black uniform Alison wore.

Sweat broke out along her neck and face, and her heart rate rose on a flood of adrenaline. A little voice in her head whispered that she could still change her mind.

Hong would know her face, after this. None of the Mayhem crew were willing to risk identification. It was a big line to cross. Alison's ghosts had prodded her to leap right over it.

A real voice spoke in her ear; a low baritone whisper that shook at the edges. "Don't hesitate," it said. "Execute the plan. No, don't look at me."

Alison stopped an instant before turning. Carl was right there in the shadows with Justin, just behind the plastic barrier. They had moved up much closer than they'd originally planned.

Hong was staring at her now, as much as he could see anything in the glare. Alison smiled her best smile. Surprise gleamed in Hong's eyes, and in her ear Carl hissed, "Nice. Now—exactly like we laid out."

Alison let her smile freeze and tried out her best cold-hearted-bitch tone of voice. "Are you ready to chat, or should I leave you to my partner's tender mercies for a while longer?"

Parker moved forward on cue to stand at her shoulder. He made Alison feel steadier, even though she knew precisely how dangerous he was. He wasn't safe, but he was on her side, and the depth of his relief when she and Justin had presented this plan made all this heart-pounding stress worthwhile now.

"Who are you people? What is this? What is going on?" Hong's voice rose with every question until it broke. "Why am I here?"

Alison pushed up the sunglasses, hiding her eyes again. Hong had said exactly what Carl had predicted. Scary.

She said, "What you're doing is asking stupid questions when you should be begging to know what I want. I'll give you a second chance. Go ahead. Ask."

Hong's face went red and then pale again, emotions raw and intense flashing over his face. Carl spoke. "Furious, resentful, frightened—but not confused. That's odd. Frustrated, embarrassed that you're—ah. Vanity. Go for his balls, literally, and tell him he's pitiful."

Alison circled the chair, slow and deliberate. She gave Hong another sneer. Then she tugged at the waistband of the man's boxers. She didn't have to fake her disgust. The elastic snapped back against skin. Hong jumped.

"Pitiful," Alison said. Her stomach turned. The man smelled like rank fear and greasy hair. "You're grotesque," she added on her own initiative.

Carl whispered, "Good. That's good. Dammit, I can't think of words. *Damn*. Threat, lifeline. Sympathy."

That was why he wasn't out here himself. Alison took the instruction and ran with it. "You're so pitiful I'll give you another chance, David Hong. How's that? Are you going to ask me the question or not? Do you want to die?"

Hong was breathing heavily now. Sweat ran into his eyes. He blinked rapidly. "No, I don't want to die. What do you want? Please, God, what do you want from me?"

"Perfect." Relief sang in Carl's hoarse response. "Now give him some praise. Lay it on thick."

Alison beamed at Hong. "There, wasn't that easy? You asked the right question. Very good. Maybe you'll live through this after all."

Hong shook his head, but he was relieved despite himself. Alison knew that without anyone whispering in her ear, and Hong said, "I don't understand."

"He will," Carl whispered, and Alison said, "You will."

She waited while Parker brought out another chair and one of Justin's strange little power cells. Hong cringed when Parker moved past.

After dropping off the props, Parker stepped back. White showed at the edges of Hong's eyes as he strained to keep the other man in view without looking away from Alison.

She swung the chair so she could sit on it with her legs splayed wide around the back. Carl made a soft hissing sound. It sounded approving. Whoever was working the video recorder shifted position to the side to get all three of them in the shot. Alison caught sight of herself on the display screen.

The uniform coverall was too big, and rolling up the sleeves had made her look childish. She'd cut ragged cuffs instead, adjusted the fit to make the most of what nature had given her and put her hair in a slicked-back ponytail that left her face sharp-edged and harsh.

The small metallic cube in her hands rolled over in her fingers, framed in the rungs of the chair back. It caught Hong's attention and held it as if Alison were a hypnotist.

"He's wavering," Carl said. "Huh. Tell him what you want him to do. Reel him in."

Alison smiled at Hong again. "I want you to talk to me about this."

Carl pulled her off after an hour spent delivering his lines and riffing off his improv cues. Hong had given up on evasion, trapped too many times in his own words, and he begged Alison to stay when Parker sat down in her place.

She made it past the hanging tarps into the dark before her hands started to shake, and she got out of easy hearing range before she fell to her knees and retched up everything in her stomach. Her skin broke out in a clammy sweat. The memory of Hong's pleading face flashed through her mind, and her empty stomach rebelled.

Once she had nothing left to heave, she got herself to her feet and took refuge behind one of the vans, leaning against the tire. She was sweaty and jittery and more than a little frightened of herself, but she also felt so alive it was as if all her nerves were on fire. She heard murmurs of the conversation with an echo, one ear live, the other a fraction of a second later through the earpiece with Carl's commentary between answers.

"Jesus, Mary, Joseph, and all the angels," she whispered. Mario would never recognize his mousy tenant today. He would cross himself three times and head straight to the closest church to pray for her soul. She'd enjoyed herself.

A cool draft touched her cheeks. "Hi," Justin said.

That was it. Nothing more. Alison raised her head. "What do you want?"

"Nothing. Do you need anything?" Justin's appraisal took a few seconds longer than usual to rise above her chest. "Ten minutes with hair gel, tape, and scissors, and then, pow. You were impressive. And frightening." He stuck his hands in his pockets. "Did you scare yourself?"

"Did Carl send you over here to check on me?"

"No, I got worried about you on my own initiative," Justin said. "Which should've been a sign that it was a stupid idea. No insult intended. Forget I asked."

He limped away.

"Justin, wait."

He stopped without turning back. "I'm getting cold."

"Be careful where you step. I lost my lunch over there somewhere."

Justin waved a hand and disappeared into the gloom. Alison took out her earpiece, closed her eyes, and tried to convince herself that she'd only pretended to be a sadistic bitch.

Justin kicked Alison's foot when he returned. She looked up at him, but she couldn't speak.

He handed over a bottle of water and a wet cloth, wrapped a

thin emergency blanket around his shoulders, and lowered himself to the floor beside her. "Swish and spit first," he said. "Sip slow."

The cool cloth felt soothing against the back of Alison's neck. She opened the bottle and drank as directed. "That sounded like you were quoting someone," she said.

"Tyler. Every time he gave me water after I puked he'd say the same thing. Even the times I puked on him." Justin snorted. "Which I did a lot. Head injuries suck. Sometimes life sucks worse."

His shoulder was warm and only a little higher than Alison's. Perfect for leaning. She leaned there for a while. Justin adjusted the blanket to cover her too.

"How many of them did you know?" he asked. "The ones who died at William's firm."

Tears welled up. Alison wiped her face against her arm. "More than thirty by name. Three good friends. Plus Nicole, for all intents and purposes. Carl only gives me updates when I nag him because I cry every time...the guilt is killing her. It makes me so angry. When I looked at that sweaty, nasty man over there, and I knew he only saw Nicole and everyone else as pawns, I wanted—"

She could barely keep talking past the hurt of it all. "I wanted him dead. Yes, I scared myself."

Justin rested his cheek against her hair. "I would've made the weasel cry and beg a whole lot more without half the excuse. If that helps."

Alison nodded. Pain melted into sympathy and affection. Hong had destroyed nearly every aspect of Justin's life and crippled him in the process, and he truly thought that Alison had a better case for bitterness. His sigh gusted over Alison's scalp, and he shivered. She took his hand. "Thank you, Justin. Let's go back now."

The air was warmer in the prep area. Carl was hunched in a

folding chair with both bandaged hands turned palms-up on his thighs. The interrogation was visible through a gap in the plastic sheeting. Carl stopped squinting at Parker long enough to glance at both of them. One hand moved in his lap, and he smiled just a little.

Alison steered Justin to the empty chair next to Carl. "Sit."

His blanket crinkled as he complied. His shoulders came down from their defensive hunch, and he released his death grip on Alison's fingers. She found another chair, wedged herself between the other two, and felt comforted.

THE NIGHT DRAGGED ON, one slow, painful hour at a time. Justin's temper gnawed harder at his self-restraint with every confession that Hong made. Being cold and hurting to the center of his bones didn't help matters, and every glance at Carl made him feel guilty about the self-pity.

The toxic soup of emotions bubbled away inside his head, stirred up by one fundamental truth: he'd been a fool, and his foolishness had killed people. He'd been willing to give up half of everything he owned to get away from Tiffany, once he realized that his things were what the woman loved, but it hadn't been enough.

It never would've been enough, and he should've known that. He'd been overpowered by Tiffany's charisma, and he'd been happy to let her muscle into his life because he needed people like her, people who thrived on the social interplay of business, who lived for the games of negotiation and dominance.

Justin had loved the woman for all the traits they didn't share. She had never loved him. She'd loved his money and his prestige, and he should've understood how far she would go to win it all.

Carl continued to coach Parker through the process of squeezing the story from Hong, and a specialist from the

Mayhem & Havoc team accessed and collected data from his personal and professional accounts. Other team members were working elsewhere to obtain material that wasn't electronically accessible.

When Justin could no longer bear to sit still and listen to the interrogation, he wandered over to look at the dirt being collected. The Mayhem tech working the electronics suite had black-and-white hair. Her name was Chris, if Justin remembered correctly. She smiled and let him read over her shoulder.

Shame and embarrassment joined the pity party. He had never dreamed that Tiffany felt the kind of acid hatred and frustrated ambition that seethed in her correspondence with Hong. The more Justin read, the angrier he got.

His predictable reactions during an uncomfortable party had given Tiffany the opportunity to steal the power cell data. One slip in casual banter at an awards dinner had piqued Hong's interest. Weeks of oblique correspondence between the pair had blossomed into conspiracy.

Once Justin was removed from the picture, Hong and Tiffany were free to openly pursue a commercial connection. That made it easy for them to develop their private plans for a separate shared venture. They had worked on the public Martin-Hong merger and the clandestine partnership right up to the day that Tiffany, sixty-nine other people, and a chunk of Seattle real estate were also removed from the picture.

Details came together on the timeline Chris was developing, and Justin began to regret his decision to let Hong live. Tiffany had been maneuvered every step of the way to the meeting where she died. Mass murder had been *expedient*. The explosion had efficiently removed Hong's co-conspirator and created doubt about the value of the power cells within his own company at the same time.

Military budgets were tight; an unreliable weapon wouldn't be worth the cost of development. The technology that had seemed like a brilliant opportunity now looked like an expensive mistake for Martin-Hong.

When Hong offered to sever the partnership and sell out his share for stock and patents, Martin thought it was driven by guilt and happily took advantage. Hong secured additional capital through an intermediary, and a private venture was in the works. He seemed to think Parker wanted a stake in his new operation, or that he represented someone who did.

A walk around the garage cooled down Justin's body, but not his temper. When he gave up and came back, Hong was sitting hooded and silent while Parker and Carl spoke together at the edge of the work area. Alison offered a weak smile when Justin rejoined her.

"I don't know what's going on," she said. "Hong said he was sorry, and Carl sat up like someone poked him with a stick and yelled for Parker."

She was running her hands through her hair, curling it around her fingers. Justin stuck his hands into his coverall pockets to keep them to himself.

The discussion ended with Parker heading over to talk to a woman with striped hair. Carl eased himself back onto his seat with a groan. "He shouldn't be this docile this fast. It's like fingernails on a blackboard. It's as if he expected to be kidnapped and shaken down. I can't pin down what he's thinking. We're missing a piece."

Missing pieces: the communications that Justin had been viewing flashed through his mind, and facts came together in a rush of insight like nothing he'd felt in months. He jolted upright at the shock of it. "Shit. "

Alison gave a breathy laugh and put her hand on Justin's thigh. "You're twitching too? What is it?"

"Hong isn't working alone. He isn't even in charge."

The timing was off. Hong had only begun buying up facilities and hiring staff for power cell development right before the C&A

blowout. No scheming backstabber worth the cursing would have delayed that long without a reason. The delay would make sense if he'd lacked capital, but his first deal with the firm backing his new venture was dated well before Justin's plane had gone down.

He'd established a relationship with a capital investment firm called Enduring Technologies around the same time he and Tiffany began plotting. He could have tapped that well far earlier than he had—which implied that he hadn't known until later that Tiffany would be eliminated.

An outside partner would explain another gap as well: the connection to whoever had attempted to murder the stray lawyer who'd been traveling with Alison. People who committed murders for hire did not rub shoulders with people in Hong's social and professional circles.

Enduring Technologies was based in Dubai, and it specialized in serving those who wanted to gamble on risky ventures without revealing their identities. No amount of international regulation could prevent all abuse of anonymous investment. Criminals who needed a convenient channel for money laundering were also likely to know professional murderers. Hong must have found one of them, or one of them had found him.

Without a name, without knowing who was backing Hong's moves—or controlling them—Justin would never put this behind him. He had been ready to give up rights to his own discovery as long as Hong bled money for it every day of his life.

Tonight's small sufferings and the fear of exposure were not nearly sufficient retribution for mass murder and attempted murder, but Justin would've swallowed his anger and let it go.

He'd been willing to give up vengeance in favor of justice, but the sacrifice would be meaningless. Hong might not even know the name of the devil who held the rights to his soul.

But he *might* know.

The cold air wasn't the only reason Justin was shivering. Fury shook him bone-deep. He wanted answers.

CHAPTER FOURTEEN

HEAT ROLLED OVER JUSTIN AS he hit the edge of the lit circle, and then he was at Hong's side and felt wet skin under his fingers. He lifted Hong up off the seat by his throat and paused to study the weasel's face.

A red hazy veil distorted Justin's view of features that were contorted with horrified incomprehension. Not afraid enough. Not yet. Justin shoved him back. The chair tipped over and hit the floor with Hong still on it, and Justin went to his knees in a clumsy lunge to stay with him.

"Who was it?" Justin snarled. "Who did you hire to bring down my plane? Give me names, and maybe I'll let you live long enough to regret ever meeting me, you greasy lying murderous motherfucker. *Who*?"

Hong's face was turning red. Justin squeezed harder.

An arm came around him from behind and hauled him off, and no matter how much Justin kicked and squirmed, he couldn't break free. He had to release his grip, and Hong crashed to the floor again.

Something hit Justin below the ribs. He barely felt the impact, but he heard a breathy, "Sonofa*bitch*," and he was shoved off-balance. A sideways step to reclaim his center of gravity left him face-to-face with Parker over Hong's thrashing, screaming, wailing body. The haze slowly faded from Justin's vision, but he could still feel his pulse in his teeth. Every muscle still shook.

Parker was holding one clenched hand in the other. The knuckles were scraped bloody. *"Fuck,"* he whispered. Then he shouted, "Shut up!" at Hong, which resulted in immediate silence.

Parker levered the man upright with a one-handed grip on the chair. "Needed air to answer," he said, and with a wave he ceded the floor.

Justin swallowed rage. "Don't make me repeat myself."

"I don't know who did it," Hong whispered. "They hired people; we never met. Jesus, please, this can't be happening. This is a nightmare or a hallucination. A trick. You're dead. You have to be dead. You're dead."

Justin spread his arms wide. "Here I am, with two live fists, two live feet, and a serious need to kick your ass into next week. Talk. Who's calling your shots?"

Hong shook his head, flinging droplets of sweat everywhere, and his lips quivered. "I don't have a name, I swear. They used cutouts, we only met once, and there were no names, and I swear I don't know, I *didn't* know, I thought you were them. I wanted to keep a little control. That's why I held back the spec data I bought from Martin, and we agreed to negotiate, that's why I was going to Atlanta next week. But then I thought—I don't know."

His voice dropped into a wordless moan, and he rocked against the cuffs, twisting in place. "Why aren't you dead? I tried, I did. I did everything I could do, I'm so sorry, sorry, sorry…"

The chair wobbled from the force of his struggles. Parker grabbed the back to keep him from tipping over, and he looked into the dark prep area with a frown. "Losing him," he said.

"I see that." Carl pushed past the plastic sheet and walked out into the light. He raised one hand to shield his face. "Damn, that hurts. Eddie, get me to him."

Parker lent him a shoulder for support, staggering when his brother's weight came down on him like a sack of bricks. Carl leaned in, took Hong's face between his bandaged hands, and managed to catch his eyes. "Look at me. *Look.* Yes, good. Now listen. I know what you're feeling, but it's a lie. Fight it." There was a hint of desperation in his voice. "Fight it. You aren't an —*dammit.*"

The last was a comment on Hong shuddering into convulsions that went on for over a minute. Afterwards he fell limply unconscious, breathing heavily. Carl cursed under his breath and then stood straight and closed his eyes against the glare.

"What the fuck is going on?" Justin asked.

"I thought the drugs were throwing me off." Carl's voice lost all character from one word to the next, from expressive to flat in a single sentence. "Drugs were throwing him off. We'll be lucky if he comes out of this with only half his synapses fried. This is unbelievable."

"We didn't drug him, did we? You aren't making any sense."

"I wish I wasn't," Carl said, still in that eerie distant voice. "This is a much bigger mess than we knew. I know exactly who Hong got involved with. I wish I didn't know, but I do. The bastard is my worst nightmare."

He stopped there. Questions crowded into Justin's mind. He asked the only one that mattered: "Can we take him down?"

"I doubt it," Carl said. Some of the life came back into his face and voice. He took one step back towards the prep area and swayed unsteadily. "But Eddie's been waiting five years for an excuse to try."

Parker tossed a wad of fabric at Justin and caught Carl before he fell. Justin took the hood in both hands, fought the urge to stuff it in Hong's mouth and choke him to death with it. He jammed the cloth over Hong's head instead. Then he stared at the black, blank lump. His arm drew back as if the limb belonged to someone else.

His left leg cramped just as he swung his fist. His knuckles crashed into the back of the chair behind Hong's shoulder, and wood shattered in a hail of splinters. Justin fell to one knee. Concrete crumbled under the impact point.

His anger cooled under a wash of horror. If that punch had landed, he would have smashed Hong's skull. He knelt there thinking about that until Parker grabbed him by the collar and dragged him away.

Out in the prep area, Carl was sitting with his head down and his forehead braced against his wrists. Alison looked up from stroking a hand down his back to frown at Justin. Parker started calling orders to the Mayhem crew, and a bustle of activity ensued.

Everything felt disconnected, as if Justin were watching reality from a distance. Then Alison came up and kissed him on the cheek.

"Welcome to the scary club," she whispered.

"STOP SULKING," Carl said.

Justin turned away from a bank of windows that showcased the city skyline. They had ended up in a very nice hotel suite after a stop to pick up Tyler and his bodyguard, and another stop to drop them off elsewhere, and Justin had been standing in this spot on and off since arriving. The windows offered a magnificent view of the cool gray sunrise over Lake Michigan.

Parker had joined him for a while before dawn, pushing him through their morning exercises without bothering to turn on lights. The t'ai chi forms seemed to be a constant in Parker's life. Sleeping and eating might occur at unpredictable intervals, but at five in the morning, with the exception of the day after he'd played tag with an automobile, he ran his routine.

The workout had done more than warm up Justin's muscles and make the worst aches recede. It had forced him to stop *thinking*. He understood now why someone with a job like Parker's would make time for the routine.

Carl was taking up most of a couch in the seating area. He seemed lucid enough, and he'd showered and changed clothes, which was more than Justin had done yet. His eyes were still dilated, though, and Justin didn't trust the look on his face. He also didn't trust himself to speak. He took a seat across from Carl and waited.

"Go to bed," Carl said. "Everyone else is tucked in, even Eddie. I can't sleep now. I'll keep an eye on Hong until the team can reinsert him. You'll want in on that, I expect. He's rebounded from the episode last night, and he's yours to squeeze, at least for a day or two. Whatever you want, he'll give you."

Justin knew he should feel bad about that, but instead he was savoring the idea of making Hong sign tons of legal documents in front of impartial witnesses. Reestablishing creative control of the stolen tech would be simple now, if he could find a way to dissuade the new mystery player from their interest in it.

First he had to get Carl to tell him the man's name. Icy frustration locked his muscles tight. Then the feel of the chair shattering under his hand washed through him, and he flushed in shame. "How's Parker's hand? I asked. He ignored me."

"Bruised," Carl said with a small smile. "Not Eddie's brightest move. He's lucky he didn't shatter bone on you. Did you feel it?"

"Barely. Blunt force has to be pretty traumatic to penetrate. Never did test against bullets. I'm more worried about accidentally killing someone than getting hurt."

"I know that. You're practically screaming it with every breath." Carl sighed. "You'll find a way to cope with it. Work with Eddie. He'll help you work it out."

"I need to work with you." Justin leaned forward. "I need you to tell me who I'm fighting now. Who is he? What is he to you?"

Carl met Justin's eyes and held them, something he did only rarely. The pain in that dark blue gaze was overwhelming. Justin's back went tense, and he fought to hold up his chin. Carl dropped the stare first and sighed.

"Dominic Walton was untouchable when he engineered the Rydder Institute abductions, and he's more powerful now than he was five years ago. I honestly don't know what to do. He's as big a name in the military support business as you are in general industry. We can't *fight* him, Justin. He owns an army."

Justin's heart beat hard against his ribs. "He doesn't own me. I have something he wants. We'll start there."

THUMPING NOISES and murmured conversation awoke Alison midmorning. She peeked out her door to see what was going on.

Justin had David Hong cornered by the windows. They were both dressed in business suits. Hong was reading whatever Justin was showing him on a datapad, and he nodded every few seconds as if his head were on a string. One hand kept rubbing at the other wrist as if it hurt.

Carl stood at the door to the suite, dressed in black, which was always a bad choice given how pale he was. One of the security team's big black duffle bags sat at his feet. His hair was falling in his face, and the tired smudges under his eyes looked like bruises.

Yoshi and Kaylie were waiting alertly on either side of him. Both were dressed in crisp gray slacks and fitted blue blazers today. Yoshi was practicing his inscrutable stone-face, and Kaylie kept sliding glances sidelong at Carl.

Justin steered Hong across the room by an arm and handed him off to them. They walked him out the door. Carl bent to consult with Justin in a whisper, and then Justin was gone too.

Carl made his way to the couch, regarded it with a scowl, and went to the table instead. Alison beat him there and pulled out a chair for him. It took him almost a minute to negotiate full contact with the seat.

Alison asked, "How on earth did you shower and dress yourself?"

He slanted a look up at her. "Kaylie and Yoshi helped, after they warned me that they still expect a bonus once I'm feeling better."

One comment with a mischievous look and just the right inflection, and Alison had a much more vivid understanding of various casual intimacies she had glimpsed over the past weeks. "Thank you for that," she said. "You and Yoshi and a three-way in the shower. There's an image for me to cherish on lonely evenings. "

Humor helped her balance a twinge of envy with the surprise of being trusted with private knowledge. Carl offered up very little of himself, and there had been true affection in his voice just now.

He said, "Be sure to leave out the part of the picture where I was sobbing and writhing around from the pain. Unless you like that sort of thing. I don't."

That was not the retort Alison had expected. Harmless flirtation to bitter self-deprecation in two seconds flat; it was an impressive mood swing. "You can have coffee, can't you?" she asked. At the affirmative nod, she retreated to the kitchenette.

He slouched forward to face the floor. "Oh, by the way, Terry wants to offer you a job. Are you interested in administrative work for an exclusive security firm? I know from personal experience that they do good work."

The final statement carried enough innuendo to sink the conversation. Alison let the silence hit bottom before she cleared her throat. "Personal, huh?"

Carl put his elbows on his knees and rested his forehead against his wrists. "I hate muscle relaxants. I was—Terry is—serious. Maybe I should leave this conversation to Eddie."

"Converse with your brother? You can't mean that. Get your head together. I promise I won't take offense at anything you say."

She busied herself with the coffee supplies to give him a little time. "Okay, what are you trying to say? It must be important, if you're putting yourself through this. Is it about whatever's going on with—what does Justin call him?"

"Hong? 'Greasy lying murderous motherfucker' is the phrase that stuck in my mind." Carl paused. "I imagine 'weasel' is the one you're looking for. They're filing legal documents. Do you know who Dominic Walton is?"

"No." The name rang a bell, but it was a distant one. The coffeemaker burbled. Alison reminded herself that even an incoherent Carl was more comprehensible than Parker. "I'll look it up. Why?"

"He's Hong's partner, or more accurately, his puppet master. Justin's still at risk, but it's a different game. The new rules are simple: we want to get word out that he's still a going concern without going public. Rumors, personal contacts—anything that might tempt Walton to go for containment. Then we contain Walton instead."

"In other words, you're setting a trap with Justin as bait."

Carl gave her a sad smile. "Essentially, yes. We start by going from low profile to invisible. That means cutting the Mayhem crew loose. It's hard to move around unseen with an entourage, and physical defenses are no help against an opponent like Walton."

Alison might've believed that story if she hadn't spent two weeks in the security team's back pocket, but she had spent that time learning. The truth was that Carl, Parker, or both of them wanted their friends out of the line of fire more than they wanted backup.

"We're down to five?" she said. "Not much of a party."

"Four. I have unfinished business, plus this—" Carl shrugged slightly, "—needs checking out. I'm useless as it is. For the next few days, you three will be lying low here with Eddie to keep an eye on things."

Alison got a grip on her tongue before she said something

regrettable. She filled a mug and brought it to Carl. He blew across the hot liquid and took a cautious sip.

"I am not at my best today," he said. "You're angry."

He sounded hesitant. Alison made a cup of tea before sitting down and trying to put her emotions into words. "First, I'm annoyed, not angry," she said. "Second, you're not useless, you're injured. Third, I'm not arguing about losing the security, but don't bullshit me about the reasons. Fourth, can neopsychs get trauma counseling? You seriously need some, and I think you know it."

Carl's breathing went ragged, and he set down his cup in a gesture that looked casual until coffee sloshed out. "It isn't that simple for me."

Alison made big round eyes at him. "And it is for the rest of us poor mortals? Nice excuse."

He snorted. "You don't pull punches, do you?"

"Not when I'm fighting out of my weight class. Please, Carl. Promise you'll talk to someone. If you get yourself or anyone else killed because you're not thinking straight, you *will* see me angry."

"All right, I promise. Since you asked so nicely."

"I'm not nice. I also think you're stupid for booting Terry's team, but that's your decision. I decide for me. I'm staying with Justin. I need to see this through to the end."

Carl's eyes crinkled slightly, but the smile got lost before it reached his mouth. "You stay," he said. "That's what you said last night when you backed Eddie down, isn't it? Thank you for your help, by the way. You understand that this will get dangerous, don't you?"

"Danger is everywhere. I nearly died standing ignorant on a sidewalk. I'm alive, and I'm seeing this through to the end, and don't bother telling me I'm being irrational, because I already know." She paused. "I can't stop you from tying me up and leaving me behind, but I'll warn you, I'll be very, very angry if you do."

The threat won her a small but genuine smile from Carl.

"I'm going to ask you another favor," he said after a pause. "Eddie can do anything it takes to keep other people safe, but he isn't good *with* people."

"I can wrangle Justin and Tyler for him while you're gone."

"Them and Eddie too, if he needs it." Carl took a deep breath and released it in a long, relieved sigh. "Good. Tyler's a pain in the ass when he feels left out. Help me put together a brief for him? I can't even dictate clearly right now."

"I'll handle it," Alison assured him. "Taking care of things is what I do best."

TYLER DROPPED the heavy carryall and the lighter plastic bag onto the coffee table at the same time. They hit with a clatter and a squish, respectively, and Alison looked up.

She was seated on the couch in a tank top and shorts because the room was Justin-comfort tropical. She filled out the top quite nicely. A bowl of popcorn, a bottle of root beer, and her datapad hinted that she'd been there a while.

Justin was at the table in the dining area with his back to the room. He wore a rumpled business suit, a look he carried off better than Tyler would've expected. The city skyline glowed through dark windows beyond him. Tyler peeled off his jacket and sank into the couch, stretching out his legs to rest them on the coffee table.

One heel nudged a pill vial. "Who's sick now?"

"Nobody. They're sleeping pills." Alison peeked into the bags. "Mission accomplished, I see. He'll be ecstatic."

"If he ever notices they exist," Tyler said. He grabbed a handful of the popcorn. His last meal had been grabbed on the run in the morning, while he was wandering around the sprawling University of Chicago campus.

Alison brought him a bottle of beer and a restaurant box full of sandwiches before he finished the popcorn.

"How's he doing?" Tyler asked while he ate. "What's he doing?"

"Writing letters. Calling people. Baiting Dominic Walton by being alive. I actually met him, you know, at the funeral. He looked so ordinary."

That was one of the unfortunate differences between fiction and reality, and one of the reasons Tyler was preferring fiction more and more these days. In novels and movies the bad guys looked *bad.*

Big, graying, and heavy around the middle, Walton looked a lot like a Caucasian version of David Hong. Both men had that air of calm authority that came from years of success in their chosen fields.

Tyler had never heard of their new enemy, but he knew how to research a topic. After Alison's message had landed in his account at midday, he'd spent his few spare minutes looking over the information.

Walton was no politician, but he had spent decades in appointed roles within state and federal administrations. In the last few years he'd taken up the hobby of buying minor firms in various fields and growing them into influential international ones.

A lot of his holdings were in industries supporting armed conflict. He'd been accused of arms and drug smuggling by competitors, but the charges never stuck. When he held news conferences or accepted awards, people looked comfortable around him. He made them laugh.

Tyler said, "I'd never believe he was a big bad chunk of evil by looking at him either. Still, the world will be a nastier place if he starts selling pocket-sized explosives to the highest bidder. It's bad enough that he has control of whatever voodoo Carl uses."

"It isn't voodoo," Alison said, "and it's been proven you can't steal the people who can do it. Carl thinks Walton is dabbling in brainwashing with drugs from Restoration-era military experiments. Access and training are restricted, but it's possible. The Civilian Security Bureau works with Rydder to keep the information out of circulation."

"When did you become such an expert on history?"

Alison sniffed. "I majored in it. Carl also forwarded me a stalker's gallery of material on Walton, and I had all day to waste going over it. Is it weird to say I hope he's the right bad guy? This seems to be an obsession for Carl."

"If it isn't Walton, then we're back to zero." That was a thought Tyler would rather not consider. "Where is Carl, anyway? He usually hovers over Justin like a mama bird."

"By now he's in Minneapolis. Unfinished business, he said. I didn't pry."

That was understandable. "Who are the pills for?"

"Him." Alison shot a glare in Justin's direction. "I'm under orders to get him to sleep tonight if I have to knock him down and shove the pills down his throat. I thought it was a joke, but I swear I can't hold his attention for five seconds. I've tried everything except slapping him."

"Not a bad idea." Tyler grabbed the bag. "He gets obsessive like that. I'll show you how to set him straight, and you can take over from there."

CHAPTER FIFTEEN

TYLER LOBBED THE PLASTIC BAG at the back of Justin's head. It bounced off and landed on the floor with a squishy thud. Alison made a protesting sound, but Justin's only reaction was to pick up the bag and look inside. "Hey, is this it? Nice."

Alison went into the tiny kitchenette. Tyler closed his eyes and yawned. "Them, not it. I ran off three sets before we ran low on components. You have no idea how much I wanted to key in fluorescent green and yellow dyes like that crash helmet you had up north."

"Thank you for resisting temptation."

Tyler grinned to himself. "The only body specs I had were from Mayo. You were even scrawnier then, so I scaled up. Sling 'em on, let's see how well I estimated."

Fabric whispered. Tyler chose to keep his eyes shut, and he kept his mouth shut too. If Justin wanted to strip naked in front of the windows, then that was his choice.

Several moments passed, during which popcorn began popping in the kitchenette. Then Justin said, "They fit fine. How much of a hassle was it?"

Tyler sat up. The windows were now an opaque white wall.

The feature made him glad he'd resisted the urge to say anything about exhibitionism. The blank background nicely framed Justin's new outfit. Black fabric clung almost skin-tight from throat to ankle, lightening to gray where the textile stretched over contours. Justin put on the dress pants and belted them in place. The shirt and shoes were left in a pile on the floor.

"What's wrong?" Justin looked down.

"Nothing." It was easy to forget that Justin wasn't soft under the saggy clothes he preferred. Dressed like that, the muscles were impossible to miss. "But you could've bought base layer at any decent outfitter."

"Not *this* material. It's inductive, with a customizable heat-dissipation threshold. I could power it for cooling instead of heat retention or generate an electrical field. For all I know, there'll be a situation where not having *that* would kill me. If I layer two suits to mask my heat signature, it might get close to real invisibility. That would be interesting."

He fell silent and gave his bare toes a speculative look.

Tyler weighed the potential reaction to calling it a ninja suit. "To answer your other question, it was no hassle. The techs helped me set up the CAM unit, and we ran them as soon as the courier dropped off the liquid components. I'm not going to ask why a textile firm in Chicago owes you a favor, but they tripped over themselves being helpful."

"Dawnstar funded them," Justin said absently.

The people Tyler had met had been responding to a personal connection, not a financial one, but it wasn't worth arguing. Justin was impervious to some concepts.

Alison came out of the kitchen with a bowl and a mug and a bemused look on her face. Tyler made room on the couch, but she took a seat at the table where she had a better angle on Justin's rear view and put a finger to her lips.

Tyler grinned at her.

Justin came into the seating area to look through the bag full of cells and new accessories. "They're all recharged?" he asked. "You worked out the flow issue?"

"We did. Built a charger that works off standard outlets too. We also made two of the little flat cells you mocked up. If I'd known you wanted them to power the supersuits I would've asked Perez to keep working on spares."

Tyler waited out Justin's indignant glaring reaction to "supersuits" before adding, "Building the transformers, now *that* was a hassle. It never occurred to me to ask how you powered the cells in the first place."

"I used dedicated generators in the design phase." Justin made a little pyramid of cubes and then stowed them away. "That was back in Lincoln. I always knew I'd have to find a way to charge them off an existing grid eventually."

Justin's hands were shaking. Time to distract him. Tyler asked, "Did you get any power flickers up here? We caused a blackout on campus, but we were too busy containing the damage to worry about if many other grids went down."

Justin made a face. "Shit. Were my calculations that far off? Did Perez throw a tantrum? I trust him implicitly, but he was always yelling at me about sloppiness."

Tyler had meant to offer a diversion, not crush Justin's confidence. "Your numbers were fine. There was a glitch in the university system. Perez didn't yell at all. He cried when he looked over the recording and the note you sent, though."

Justin settled onto the couch with a puzzled look. Tyler's patience snapped. "Tears of joy, Justin. He's glad that you're still alive. How can you not grasp that people care about you?"

Justin ducked his head and ran both hands through his hair. "I try not to think about it. It makes me squirm."

And just like that, Tyler wanted to kick himself. The only person in the world who truly would've mourned his death had died first. That was a little sad, when he thought about it. He picked up the bottle of pills and set it down again with an emphatic click. Justin frowned at it.

"Look, you need sleep," Tyler said. "Take as many of these—"

Alison said, "No more than two. Carl's orders."

Justin whirled to look back at the table. A blush crept up his neck, confirming that he had forgotten that Alison was in the room. "How long have you been there?" he asked.

"Long enough." Her bright smile was the one that took her face from ordinary to beautiful. "I had a very nice view from the kitchen for a while."

"Sorry about that."

"Oh, I'm not, but when you start forgetting people, it's time to call it a day. You need to eat dinner and then take your pills. I've been saying that for hours. Will you please listen now?"

Tyler would've cheerfully walked off a cliff if she'd asked him to do it in that tone. Justin showered, ate dinner, and took sleeping pills without a single protest, which was equally impressive in its own way.

After literally tucking the man into bed, Alison returned to the living room and got herself a fresh drink.

She brought a bottle of beer for Tyler too, and they toasted their joint success. Tyler hid his smile and his envy in a long pull from the bottle.

CARL DIDN'T REACH his destination in the quiet Minneapolis suburb until nearly nightfall. He'd been halfway to the airport that morning before he turned around, daunted by the idea of having to make excuses to Alison. Working up the nerve to *keep* his promise had taken him hours longer.

The sky overhead was cloudy and dark when he left the bus stop. Trees arched over the shadowed streets on both sides, and autumn colors were visible in the washed-out glow of streetlights at the end of each block.

Windows glowed behind closed curtains in most of the dignified old bungalows. Dry grass crunched underfoot as Carl walked across a precise square of lawn. Children were laughing in a neighboring backyard, where tiny white lights bobbed and flickered on the branches of a tree.

It was happy and normal and alien all at once.

Carl knocked on the front door. It swung open in a rush, and a mellow tenor voice said, "Guys, you have to stop begging for candy. Halloween isn't—" The man in the doorway raised his eyes a meter from where they'd been focused. "—for weeks yet. Hello, there. You're not the pesky neighbor child."

"No," Carl said. "Hi, Pete."

"Hiya." Deep-set pale brown eyes twinkled at Carl from a swarthy face framed by curly black hair and a close-trimmed beard. "God, you look awful."

Laugh lines framed Pete's eyes and mouth, but Carl couldn't trust the cheery countenance. Fifteen years in public relations and pediatric counseling had taught Pete Hamil exquisite self-control. Five more years spent as Rydder Institute's coordinator with the Civilian Security Bureau had polished the mask to a mirror finish.

Carl gave up trying to guess what feelings it was hiding. "Can I come in?"

"Stupid question. Of course you can. When I said, 'Anything you need, ever,' I did mean it." Pete stepped aside and looked past Carl. "Where's Eddie?"

"Working."

"And you're here without him dragging you in? Wonders may never cease. Inside, before you let out all the warm air."

Pete took the duffle out of Carl's hand and pulled him into the house by the arm. Both shoulders shrieked protest. Medical scans had confirmed that nothing was permanently damaged, but lots of things had been strained and wrenched. The door shut, and he leaned against it.

Pete said, "So you feel as awful as you look. Lovely. You are allowed to refill analgesic scrips before you run out, and I have mastered the art of discreet shipping. No need to endure my company for the sake of a restock."

"I promised I'd come. To talk." If Alison hadn't metaphorically twisted his arm, he would've called instead.

"A day of miracles indeed. Hand over the kit; I'll fill it." Pete went tense when he saw all the empty slots and pockets. "I'm bumping up the rating from awful to dire. You haven't needed most of this in ages. Never all at once."

"Long story," Carl said. "Can I stay here tonight?"

Pete's eyebrows went up. "Stupid question number two. Refer to previous answer. Please sit down before you fall over. You're far too heavy to drag across the room."

Just like that, Carl was blind, trapped in the dark, and he felt a hand on his calf while a petulant voice said as clear as a bell, "He'd fit in the box better if we chop him off at the knees. He'll be dead in a day anyway. Why wait?"

Carl dragged in a deep, gulping breath. The air smelled like warm spices, not mold and filth, and that was enough, barely, to override the memory rerun. He staggered across the room to the couch and collapsed there.

Pete said, "That's awful to the umpteenth power. Jesus, Carl. You're a mess."

"Stress reruns. I had a bad episode. Eddie had to drop me hard. I'm still getting aftershocks."

Pete's manner shifted to a brusqueness that was easier to handle than the pity and sarcasm. "I can't refill your whole kit from mine, but I'll lift the rest from work tomorrow. What do you need? Are you on anything? Have you slept?"

Carl worked his way back through the sequence. "A few hours

last night. There's nothing in my system but backwash. Fentanyl would take the edge off."

"You're all edges if you want Fentanyl. Hold on."

A few efficient minutes saw Carl relieved of coat and shoes and provided with a mug of something hot. He sipped at it and watched Pete rummage in drawers. The mug held apple cider. The small living room was a happy clutter of toys, stuffed animals and sporting equipment. There was a hand-quilted throw on the couch. It all made him ache.

He'd had a home, once upon a time.

Pete brought over a side chair to face him, sat down and held up a foil-wrapped patch, dangling it in two fingers. Carl ripped it open and counted every heartbeat after its application until the pain began to recede. Five hundred and seventeen.

"Start talking," Pete told him with perfect timing. "Whole story."

He got through the past few improbable months in less than two hours, using documentation and recordings whenever possible. Pete picked up three lightweight plastic balls early into the presentation and juggled them throughout, even while watching the interrogation imagery. Afterwards he tossed the balls at Carl one by one.

Carl deflected the first, and the second bounced off his chest and rolled under the couch. He caught the third one. For an instant, he saw shattered bloody pieces. His fingers throbbed. He opened them and let the ball drop.

"Do you believe me?" he asked. "Am I right about the tampering job on Hong? About Walton?"

Pete looked up from the recording that he was viewing for the third time. His obvious surprise began to unravel the knot of self-doubt that Carl had been pulling tighter for days now.

"The tampering is subtle, but it's clear to me." Pete slapped Carl on the leg. "Don't doubt yourself."

"I have every reason to be cautious about trusting my own

judgment in this. I was hyped, and I still missed it until he went into that aversive fit."

"Well, I'll second your verdict. Illegal tampering. What was the goal? Any idea?"

"Guaranteed results in upcoming public negotiations, I think. That, and protection from exposure or blackmail. Nothing complicated."

"Child's play, then," Pete said. "But inducing session amnesia takes a different tool kit, and I haven't seen a crude guilt-punishment loop like that since my classes about the bad old army loyalty programs. It's an unusual triple play."

He paused. "I'd even go with *unique*, and your abductors triggered conditioned allergies in two neopsychs with the same approach. That points to a common source. The kidnappers all died during the rescue op, though, and the Feds never traced their paymaster. How can you be so sure it's Dominic Walton?"

The memory hit like a punch, and Carl reeled back, dizzy and cold and burning, and not blindfolded this time because they wanted him to see the damage, and he saw it and he saw *them* and it hurt, it hurt, it hurt—

"Hey!" Pete's raised voice would've cut through steel. It cut through the ghosts. Carl blinked away sweat and tears with a shudder, and Pete sat back, staring. "You never named names in the debrief. Never. Jesus, why not? It would've been a huge break for the investigators. I would swear Walton's name was on the Security Bureau short list for some reason. Politics, I think."

"I didn't know him by name. I saw him in a news story a year later. Down in Panama, with Eddie. I lost whole days to reruns." Carl wiped his face on his sleeve. "It wouldn't have been proof, even then."

"True." Pete continued as if nothing had happened, throwing out brisk objectivity like a lifeline. "He must save the good stuff for very special occasions. The Security Bureau liaisons monitor like crazy for that kind of thing. Christ, I hope the reactionaries never find out this is popping up again. It's exactly what Rydder Institute was founded to prevent."

"Prevention was never the goal. Integration was. Our security, the protocols, our conditioning, the ethics codes: they were supposed to be transition tools. To control the cultural spread, not seal it up."

"You're preaching to the choir, but you know that's not how it's playing out," Pete said. "Not since we closed Chicago and Baltimore. I agree that it's like trying to bottle up a volcano, but ever since you and the others—Admin gets more scared and stagnant every year. They encourage living inside the walls now to cut security costs. Barely a hundred of us still live off campus."

Carl let the old bitterness settle. He hurt enough already. "Well, I've done my best to stir things up. I dropped off Hong's blood sample at Rydder yesterday along with an edited recording of the interrogation."

"Yesterday? You've been in town for two days already?" Pete scowled. "Wait. You were on Institute grounds? They'd disappear you in a hot minute if they recognized you, and you're not exactly inconspicuous. What were you thinking?"

"Somebody had to get proof to Admin, Pete. They need to know their bottle's cracking, so they can make repairs."

Finding who had sold drugs or their formulas was only a stopgap solution, but damage control was the name of the game. Taking out Dominic Walton wouldn't put the secrets back in the bottle either, but it would send a message to the people under him and to people like him.

Carl added, "Besides, it wasn't much of a risk. It's not as if anyone expects me to be me. My back-door deal with the Feds included a records purge on my biometrics, and big blond men aren't exactly rare around here."

Pete walked away, picked up a hockey stick, and poked at a soccer ball. "And how did you spend the extra day?"

"Shaking off the Institute Security who tailed me. A restock and a chat weren't worth risking your career. I had to get a physical anyway. The university clinic does good work. I waited until the tailing team lost interest."

Pete laughed without a trace of humor and swung the hockey stick. The soccer ball went flying into a pair of toy penguins on a side table.

"You're a bad liar when you're dopey," he said. "You stalled because you still can't stand the sight of me. You stalled when you should've come here first."

It was true, but truth could hurt, and Pete kept right on jabbing at the open wound. "I would've run that sample in myself. I would've gotten you a doctor, discreetly, and you could've been resting this whole time. You know I would help. No, wait. You should know, but you can't shake the bitter bullshit. Even after all this time, you're still stewing in distrust and betrayal. You should be past this, Carl."

A shudder ran through Carl's body, and all his muscles snapped tight at once. Not just a rerun of nightmare memory. Worse. A million times worse.

Trapped. Beaten. Degraded and humiliated. Broken and bleeding. Disintegrating. He squeezed his eyes shut, but it didn't help. The world inside his head began to crumble, one mended, lumpy patchwork piece at a time.

"Oh, Christ. No, no, no, no, no. Don't you dare." Pete dropped the hockey stick with a clatter. Hands pressed against Carl's face on both sides.

Pete leaned in, forehead to forehead. "Get a grip, I'm begging you. I don't have your conditioning triggers on the tip of my tongue these days, so if you let yourself fall apart, you'll stay that way this time, and Eddie will hunt me down and kill me. Don't do that to me. Please don't."

The warm pressure held him anchored, and the babbling sound of Pete's voice plucked at all the right strings: discipline, duty, defense of others. The universe stopped shaking. Carl inhaled past the icy tightness in his chest.

"Caught it." It was little more than a croak.

Pete's relief had a sharp, resentful edge. "Tell me you didn't know you were teetering on the verge of *that*. Tell me you were too deep in fugue rebound to see the biochemical shitstorm brewing. Tell me that you didn't come here to kill yourself in my living room on purpose, out of spite."

Carl swallowed hard. "Nearly didn't come at all."

"Thank God you did. Those aren't aftershocks. You're spiraling. This isn't going to fix itself. You'll kick a keystone trigger in an elevator, or on the subway, anywhere you're confined and stressed—Jesus." Pete sank into a chair across the room and put his head in his hands.

A clock with a cartoon cat on the face ticked quietly on the wall behind him. "You need rest more than anything else," he said at last. "You know where the spare bedroom is. Go sleep yourself out. I'll take care of everything."

His voice was too controlled, too calm.

"Pete—"

"No. Not another word. I'll take care of everything, I promise. Go on, now. Go to sleep and let me take care of you properly."

Carl paused on the stairs when Pete added softly, "This time, I swear I will do right by you."

He couldn't have known the last few words were audible. The sadness they'd carried had been far too raw. Carl gave back two words that he should've said years earlier but never had spoken: "Thank you."

CARL'S PHONE WAS PINGING. He heard it, but the noise was a distant addition to a very nice dream involving silk and sunlight and lots of bare-skinned bodies, and he was much too preoccupied to answer.

Someone answered it for him. "Pete Hamil. No, he's still asleep." The voice fell to a murmur, and murmurs fit the dream. Carl let it go.

"I hate to wake you early, but it's important." Pete was loud and intrusive, and he didn't belong in the dream. Carl ignored him.

Someone grabbed his big toe and twisted it. "Up. Now."

The dream evaporated when Carl sat up. The sunshine stayed. It spilled through a window across a bed that nearly filled the small room it inhabited.

Pete stayed too. He was standing in the doorway at the end of the bed, and he said, "Don't move too fast, you're going to be queas—"

Carl shoved him aside and stumbled towards the bathroom before the nausea got the better of him. Once he got himself settled, he washed up. His eyes wouldn't focus, and his head felt too heavy for his neck.

"Fentanyl doesn't do this," he said groggily when he returned to the bedroom. "What time is it?"

"Nearly one o'clock. It's also Wednesday." Pete was sitting on the end of the bed now. He waved the phone. "The natives are restless. I warned them that I was benching you, but my updates are no longer having the proper reassuring effect."

"Wednesday." More brain cells came online. Carl collected vague impressions: dim light, quiet conversation. "Four days. You sedated me."

"Oh, we had a great big festival of pharmaceutical fun. Thus, hangover."

Apart from the ebbing nausea, he felt much better. He felt good, and not only physically. That meant that someone had been meddling in his psyche.

Pete answered the unspoken question. "I dug up your profile, and I called in Mitani for help with the major stuff. *Please* be more careful, Carl. The only reason you survived the initial crash was that your core integrity slotted right into the broken conditioning framework. Integrity can't shield you from everything, and you're held together with tape and gauze. We used a lot of extra tape this time, but if you don't respect the weak spots, they will kill you."

"We talked. You and me."

"You bet your ass we did. That's how therapy works, even when therapist and client are both boneheaded control freaks." Pete waved the phone again. It was emitting small angry squeaks. "Could you please tell Mama Bear that I haven't beaten you up and locked you in the basement?"

Not even a flicker of anxiety rose in response to the phrasing. Pete raised his eyebrows.

"I already said thank you." Carl went hunting for his shirt and pants. He was not facing Alison half-naked, not even on the phone. "Put her on speaker."

Alison's voice burst into the room as Pete tossed the handset onto the rumpled quilt. "—said sit *down*. No, I won't use the screen. If you're going to make me talk for you, then you can wait until I'm finished. Sit. Down. *Now*."

If Carl hadn't already been sitting down, he would've dropped like a rock. Pete grinned and mouthed, "Nice."

Carl zipped up his pants. "Alison, is Eddie getting out of hand?"

"Oh, thank God." Her voice rolled down from command to warmth. "Can you please tell Captain Crazy here that you're fine and make him—hey, no grabbing. Don't *test* me. I will stab you in the eyeball with a stylus. Back off."

Silence fell. Pete choked and covered his mouth. Carl could picture the staring match. He knew who would win. "It's okay, Alison. Give him to me or go to speaker. I'll talk him down."

"He doesn't need talking down. He needs to use manners." That part wasn't directed at Carl. The next question was. "When are you coming back? We're not in the same—*ow*." A pause. "How would I know not to say that? You didn't tell me."

Pete had fallen back on the bed and was silently laughing so hard his face was turning purple. A rough, weary voice emerged from the phone. "Carl."

"Yeah, Eddie. Pete says he kept you briefed, and you've always trusted him, so what's the problem?"

The wait was painfully long. "Trouble," Parker said at last. "Bad, Hamil said. Bad jitters again today. Itchy now. Worse every minute."

The bottom dropped out of Carl's stomach. "It isn't me. You hear? If you're jittering, it's there."

There was a clatter. Then Justin said, "Can you explain why Parker just dropped this and hit the exit like a bat out of hell?" His voice faded. "Tyler, go close the door. Allie, get away from the windows."

He'd already grasped the essentials. Carl said, "Eddie's clearing an escape route. Grab what you can. My bet is that you have about ninety seconds."

"What are we escaping from?" Justin asked with commendable calm.

"No idea, but the first time Eddie had a major itch, an air strike hit his position five minutes after he shifted his unit. Move, Justin. I'll find you later."

Carl cleared the call and set up a new account.

Pete sat up. "And to think I almost ignored the call."

"They'll be fine." He had to believe that. "We didn't expect this kind of trouble this fast, but we knew it was coming. I need to hit the road. Alison won't be able to manage him when he's jittering. No one can."

"Alison is the tiny thing who made baggy black cotton look like a cat suit? I'm surprised she can bring Eddie to heel at all."

Carl threw dirty clothes into the duffle. "As far as I can tell, there's no one in the universe that Alison can't manage. Myself included. Lucky thing, as it turns out."

"Oh, she's the one who guilt-tripped you here, not Eddie? Good for her. Give her my thanks."

Downstairs in the kitchen, Carl made a beeline to the coffeemaker. A single setting at the table testified to an interrupted meal. Pete handed over the refilled medicine case, energy bars, and a data clip. "I reached out to my friends at the CSB and collected Walton's profile for you. The political thing I remembered—he's on sedition watch lists. All those private military holdings make the Bureau nervous. He does nothing to draw official interest, though, and at the moment he's overseas."

He sat down and pushed away the cold rice and vegetables. "They wish they had more, but he's careful."

"Every little bit helps." Carl packed everything except two energy bars into pockets. Then he sucked down coffee and choked down the energy bars. "He's going down, Pete, even if I can't get enough evidence for legal action out of him. I will never get a better chance. Do you have a problem with that?"

"Not a bit. Dr Wyatt is cooperating, isn't he? Which is the real one: the madman in the recording or the calm guy on the phone?"

"Both, I think. Rydder has his chart. Look him up."

"Now I'm intrigued." Pete gave Carl's state of readiness a quick up-and-down. "You'll do. I'll get you to the airport."

It wasn't a question, so Carl didn't answer. He nodded.

"Give me a call once you're tucked away," Pete said as they shook hands outside Departures. "If you get a chance."

He didn't sound hopeful. Carl pulled him into a hug. "I will call," he said. "This time I will."

CHAPTER SIXTEEN

THE ESCAPE ROUTE PARKER CHOSE got everyone out of the hotel to the street by way of stairwells and an underground pedestrian walkway. He didn't run, exactly, but he walked *very* fast. Tyler had to jog to keep the same pace. Alison could barely keep up, and Justin was even slower than she was.

They were not allowed to stop and catch their breath until they were six blocks away from the hotel, standing on a train platform. The question of why they were taking public transit rather than the perfectly adequate vehicle in the hotel garage was met with a glare.

The ride to the airport was both nightmarish and unexpectedly funny. The train was crowded, the rail noise was deafening, and Parker watched everyone getting on the train with a feverish intensity that invited confrontation.

Tyler distracted their fellow passengers with smiles and charm. He was the only person Alison had ever met who could charm at a shout. Justin helped too, carrying on a one-sided conversation with Parker that made the man look less conspicuously insane.

Once they left the train behind and took a shuttle to one of the airport parking lots, Parker's tension subsided below redline.

Once they were standing alone at the stop, he said, "I don't have a plan beyond *get away*. Got a feeling our location was compromised, but I wasn't expecting overkill like that. Someone has to be tracking us. No idea how they're doing it."

"What overkill?" Tyler said. "You have a *feeling*? I'm standing in the cold with barely the clothes on my back, and you don't even have a plan or a reason for running?"

"Go back for your toothbrush if you want," Parker said. "Take the three goons pretending to pick a sedan with you. As soon as we're off a camera grid, they'll hit us. We shook off another team downtown, and I downed two to clear the stairs. Call it a squad—means at least a short platoon on the op. Sending that much muscle after three civvies and me? That is massive overkill."

Tyler went pale, but Alison wasn't sure whether it was in reaction to Parker's anger or the news that there had been an ambush on the stairs. Parker glanced at the three large men in football jerseys who were inspecting the trunk of a car in the neighboring aisle. Justin broke the silence. "I cannot get used to hearing you talk like a normal person."

Parker looked up at a departing plane. "Nine years in the armed forces, Justin. Perfectly capable. Ideas? We have what we're carrying. Minimal firepower, no money without clean IDs, no IDs until Carl can get us new ones."

"Which he can't do until we get clear of this," Justin said. "We're screwed. Is that what you're saying?"

His face had the same look Alison had seen on it right before he'd attacked Hong, the expression that looked preoccupied but was really a sign of temper slowly and quietly reaching its explosive limit. She took his hand. Justin flinched away. She said, "We're not dead yet."

He gave her a wan smile and squeezed her fingers. She asked Parker, "Do you have a destination in mind? How fast do we need to get there? I have an idea, but it might keep us in town."

Parker said, "I'm at 'drop the goons, steal a car, and drive until we run out of charge.' I'm open to anything."

"I need to call someone."

"Need to drop them, no matter what," Parker said, watching the men at the car. He handed Alison a handset. "Only two clean calls left. You get one."

She stepped away and made a voice-only call from memory. "May I speak to Adam Berenson, please?" she said to the man who answered. "This is Alison Gregorio. Do you remember me? You set up a properties tour for me."

There was a long silence, and she held her breath.

Berenson said, "If this is a joke, I'm not laughing. I'm unlikely to forget the name of a woman responsible for seven separate sessions of police questioning. Who is this? What do you want?"

Alison's hands went cold, and she had to control a sudden fit of shakes. This was no time to break down. She took a vacation, her office blew up, she disappeared. Of course she would be a suspect. "It's me. I was in Lincoln when C&A blew up. I had nothing to do with it, but I know who did, and why Lincoln went boom too. Here, I can prove it's me."

She activated the camera. Berenson's face scowled against a background of wood paneling and framed artwork. His gray hair was mussed, and his chin bristled with stubble. "I can generate phone imagery too," he said, flat and cold. "If this is real, then call the authorities. Turn yourself in."

"No, wait. Please. I can't go to the police. It's complicated."

Berenson glowered. This silence was more delicate than the first, and it ended in a sigh. "Complicated is my least favorite word, young woman. I can't help you. Call the police."

"Police? Alison, you know we can't afford—hey. Adam, is that you?"

Alison nearly jumped out of her skin as Justin peered over her shoulder. He said, "Alison, how do you know Adam?"

Berenson looked stunned. Alison could sympathize.

She'd known that Design Unlimited did a lot of work for Wyatt Enterprises and the Dawnstar Foundation, but she'd never assumed that there was a personal connection. "You two know each other."

Justin covered her hand with his own, steadying the phone. His fingers were warm. Alison released the conversation to him. "Good to see you, Adam," he said. "Napping on a work day, you lazy bastard?"

"Good. God." The image blurred. Berenson came into focus again, sitting in a high-backed recliner. "I'm home with a cold, not that it's relevant. It's you. You're alive. Where have you been?"

"Hiding from people who want me dead," Justin said. "No police, all right? We're in a major bind here. Can you help us?"

Berenson's gaze shifted to Alison. "This is your complicated?"

And Parker called, "Justin!"

Justin said, "I'm sorry, Adam, this is a bad time."

He released Alison's hand and hurried after Parker.

"Mr. Berenson?" Alison turned her back on them and tried the smile again. "We're stuck at the airport. We need—I don't know, exactly. Help."

"I'll be there in ten minutes. Are you in immediate danger?"

Tyler took her by the shoulders and faced her towards the parking lot. "You don't want to miss this," he whispered.

JUSTIN PUT his hands in his pockets and strolled towards the group inspecting their car. His finger trembled on a power cell switch, and the timer Parker had given to him sat quietly in the other pocket.

Parker wanted a distraction. He could be distracting. The men looked ordinary enough: three friends, rumpled and tired after a long trip, arguing over whether they'd found the best vehicle in the available selection. Then all of them straightened to attention.

Justin's blood chilled.

"Our lucky day," one of the men said. He lifted a shotgun from the car trunk and handed a shock baton to one of the others. "You get him. We'll take the rest."

The last one pulled a pistol from under his jersey. Justin's pulse was racing now, but he kept walking towards them. No one else was going to be killed on his account. "Was it something I said?"

The timer beeped. Justin hit the power cell switch and stepped between two cars. All three men kept staring at the empty space in the aisle where he'd been.

"What the—" was as far as the talkative one got.

Parker came around the far side of their car and delivered a sharp punch to the back of his head. The man dropped like a stone. The other two bolted in opposite directions. The spontaneous retreat caught Justin by surprise, and the one with the pistol ran right into him.

The collision took them both to the ground in a tangle of limbs and weaponry. The pistol's muzzle looked huge as it veered towards Justin's face. He blocked it with his forearm and swung his other fist at the man's head.

Flesh sank beneath his knuckles. Bone cracked.

The man went limp. His pistol clattered to the ground. Blood seeped from the ruin of his face.

Justin's stomach heaved. He hit a car when he lurched back, and then Parker hit him, pushing him aside so that he could reach the body on the ground.

Parker hefted the man up and efficiently broke his neck with one forceful twist. The corpse hit the ground again with a meaty thump, and Parker frowned down at it. Then he gave his vicinity a narrow-eyed stare.

"*Distraction,*" he said. "Destruction's my job."

Justin switched off the power and tried to pretend that the resulting wave of nausea and pain was rooted in physics and not emotion. Fist to flesh, bone collapsing under his knuckles. His stomach lurched again.

Losing his lunch didn't rid him of the cold, shaky horror. Parker helped him to his feet and propped him against a car while he stowed the bodies inside. "Them or us," he said. "No time for weepy guilt."

Justin spat to one side and wiped his mouth. "What's guilt got to do with it? I'm afraid I'll do that to someone I *don't* hate, that's all. You know a million ways to hit people. Help me figure it out before I kill someone I like, will you?

The concern in Parker's eyes shifted to puzzled interest. "Boxing lessons?"

"Please."

"Later. Once we get out of this trap."

Another plane roared overhead. In the relative quiet afterwards, Justin heard Alison speaking loudly to someone else. "We can wait," she said. "Things are under control for now."

Justin hoped she was right.

TWENTY-FOUR HOURS LATER, Justin was halfway across the country from Chicago and felt too tired to be hopeful about anything.

He scanned the busy restaurant for Tyler and Alison. The decor reached for folksy western but settled in the vicinity of tawdry, and the air smelled like grease and coffee. The dining room was packed full of guests.

Everywhere he turned, he saw evidence that Albuquerque was reaping the benefits of tensions elsewhere in the Great Southwest. The situation to the north and west was deteriorating, according to the chatty check-in clerk at the adjoining hotel. Vacationers in search of desert scenery and handicrafts were sticking to spots less likely to explode into open conflict.

Open conflict was something Justin was all in favor of avoiding. He spotted Tyler and Alison deep in a hushed conversation in a booth at the rear of the room. Navigating a course across the crowded floor to them took some time. Tables had been jammed into every available spot, leaving no clear aisles.

Justin moved through the tripping hazards without stumbling once, which was a miracle, considering how little sleep he'd gotten recently. Other than short service stops, they'd been on the road since leaving Adam Berenson's home in the Chicago suburbs.

Justin owed the man a huge debt. Berenson had brought them all home and fed them dinner, which had been so pleasant and normal that it had felt surreal. Conversation had revolved around everyday events in Berenson's life, including complaints about various project sites sitting idle and unoccupied. By the end of the meal, Berenson's car keys, credit chits he'd mentioned filling as gifts for grandchildren, and a datapad containing files on the properties they'd discussed were all sitting on the table.

Then he'd gone to the kitchen to make coffee. The man knew all about plausible deniability.

Parker had scooped up the offerings, and they'd left without good-byes. Their destination was a building in northern New Mexico currently mired in zoning negotiations, and Albuquerque was the last town of any size on their route. Justin had put his foot down and called for a halt half an hour ago now.

For once the decision had been easy. Exhausted drivers had no business on dirt roads in the mountains at night. Getting this far had taken forever. Interstate travel restrictions in place due to the ongoing squabbles meant that the faster routes were closed to them. Local roads were low profile but slower as well. Twenty-plus hours on the road was enough.

When he reached the booth, Tyler and Alison sat back with an air of interrupted intimacy that made Justin's stomach knot. At times like this his conscience started to sound a lot like his first wife. People were not property. They didn't belong to him. They were not things that he could control.

He couldn't control where Alison chose to turn for comfort. It wasn't surprising that she turned to Tyler—disappointing perhaps, but hardly surprising. Tyler was a comforting person in his own thoughtless, tactless way.

"Having a nice chat?" Justin asked.

"I doubt you'd enjoy it." Tyler studied the menu. Justin slid in beside him. That side of the booth was safer emotional territory, even if Tyler did smell like a goat.

Alison said with appalling bluntness, "We were talking about sex, actually."

A woman at a neighboring table turned to look at them in horrified amazement. Justin handed a room key to Tyler and slid another to Alison. "Thanks. I just lost my appetite."

"Euphemisms again, Justin," Alison said with a touch of exasperation. "It's a game. What is wrong with you? Are you allergic to fun? And where's Captain Kickass?"

"Captain Cranky," Tyler said, and he snickered.

The pair of them had started playing games in the middle of the previous night to keep Parker from falling asleep at the wheel, and they'd made up new ones with every change in drivers. The Nicknames game was worse than Euphemisms, and even Nicknames was preferable to the baffling word association exchange they'd kept up for two hours straight.

They couldn't have picked a better way to make Justin feel like shit. He couldn't help with the driving, and half the time he couldn't even follow the nerve-shredding chatter long enough to get the jokes. All he wanted was a quiet, peaceful meal and a few hours of sleep.

"Captain Taciturn," Alison said in response to Tyler's last comment.

"Sure, show off your vocabulary, English major."

"History major, math geek."

Justin said with rising desperation, "When did I become the only grown-up around here?"

"Five a.m., I think." Alison gave him a mournful look. "I am sorry, Justin. We get carried away. Where is Captain Insomnia, anyway?"

"Do you mean Parker? He's checking the rooms. He's spooked because someone tracked us down twice despite all his precautions."

Tyler said gravely, "If evildoers somehow followed us over the farm roads of Kansas and across the unremitting hell of north Texas, I will slay them by removing my shoes. The stench is almost as deadly as the one created by raising both arms. Would you like a demonstration?"

"*No.*" Justin rubbed at a stabbing pain over his right eye. "I've forgotten what I was say—oh. We need to eat, get upstairs, and get the doors locked so Parker can wind down. Can we please do that without turning it into a joke or a game? Please?"

Alison nodded, wide-eyed. Tyler muttered under his breath. Justin pretended to read the menu and pretended not to hear Tyler. If he heard the insult then he would have to pummel Tyler into the floor, and that would be dangerous.

Fist to flesh. Bone shattering. He felt the impact all over again. The menu drifted out of focus. He gave up. "I'm going up," he said. "Maybe Parker will sleep if I promise to sit watch."

He could feel Tyler and Alison staring at his back all the way to the exit. He refused to limp until he was out of sight.

TYLER TOOK another hike around the outside of their newest bolt hole just as night was falling. It was his fourth walk of the afternoon. He went out through the lowest level onto the patio, and he felt better the instant he left the building.

He hopped off the edge of the patio to the canyon floor almost two meters below. A breeze flowed strongly through the narrow stone channel, and a broad ribbon of water flowed down the center of the rocky riverbed more than ten meters away. Between the whispering air and the burble of water, the canyon was never silent.

Tyler *liked* silence.

He stopped by the water's edge and turned back to examine the house. A fold in the interior east canyon face cradled the tall structure made entirely of earthen material. It was stained to match the surrounding rocks in striated bands of yellow, red, and gray, and the building would've been indistinguishable from stone except for the narrow windows. The thin golden lines glowed within the shade of the surrounding rock.

The interior of the unfinished building was huge and airy, but even two thousand square meters of enclosed space wasn't enough. Justin and Parker had spent the afternoon throwing punches and kicks at each other, bouncing off walls, floors and the staircase. There wasn't enough space in the world to make that endurable.

Tyler climbed up three stories to the top of the canyon on rock steps that had been cut so that the progression looked like natural erosion. The uneven treads were well-placed, but it was still a steep and strenuous climb.

At the top of the cliff, the house rose into a two-story tower of faux stone. Horizontal layering echoed the canyon rock below, and sheer mass minimized the presence of modern accessories. Low walls extended off one side to shelter a large garage, and parapets on the flat roof hid antennas, solar collectors, and wind turbines. Fuel and water tanks were buried in the surrounding grounds.

Construction fencing contained a hefty chunk of real estate, sweeping along the sloping eastern side of the butte in a broad arc from rim to rim of the canyon. Security lights had been rigged on the posts, but Parker had disabled them on arrival when he set up surveillance with equipment purchased in Albuquerque.

They'd bought a lot of things in Albuquerque using IDs that Carl forwarded: camping gear, tons of food, and other miscellaneous indulgences. Tyler had a new datapad for grinding numbers through the formulas he was developing. Justin had picked up one too, along with boxes of tools, but he'd been more excited by the shin guards and other protective headgear that Parker had bought for him.

Gravel crunched behind Tyler. He tensed.

"Relax. It's only me." The breeze whipped Alison's hair across her face and blew her new sweatshirt hood up against her neck. She looked cold and unhappy. "Can you please keep an eye on Sturm and Drang and the cameras for a while? I did it all afternoon."

Tyler winced inside. He should've offered earlier. "Sorry, the weirdness factor was too high for me. Justin kickboxing is like a parrot doing algebra."

"He's also been one big, silent ball of *angry* for two days now, and I'm afraid to leave them alone in case somebody gets hurt, and Carl is late, and I'm worried, and I need air. You won't help even a little?"

"No, I didn't mean that I wouldn't—"

Alison dissolved into tears. Tyler patted her arm and tried explaining that he'd been apologizing, but she kept crying until he gave up and opened his arms.

Alison barely came up to his chin, and she felt nice pressed close against his chest with both little hands clutched in the back of his jacket. Very nice. Soft in some places, firm in others, and delightfully female all over.

Alison jerked her stomach away from his lower body. "Mother of God, Tyler. Seriously?"

"What? Male, healthy, celibate for way too long. Take it as a compliment."

"Take your compliment and stuff it—" She pushed away and wiped her eyes. "Forget it. Do what you want. I'm done."

She squeezed through the chain looping the security gate shut and headed down the drive at a stomping fast pace, wiping at her eyes as she went. Tyler followed to make sure that she wasn't really running away, because he would kill himself before breaking that news to Justin.

Alison sat down on a rock marking the first switchback in the road. The ribbon of graded dirt ran along the shoulder of the eastern bluff, descending the slope in tight curves and then meandering into scrub towards a paved road in the valley and the highway beyond. Dusk had swallowed the horizon now. Stars were visible halfway up the sky.

Headlights and a cloud of dust were visible far out along the road, well over two kilometers away. The light disappeared as the car went through a copse of trees and then reappeared closer. Tyler hoped with all his heart that it was Carl, because if it wasn't, then they were in big trouble.

Light from the interior of the house spilled out along the walkway in a wash of glare. Parker came outside, pulling on a shirt while he walked, and he stripped off a pair of knuckle protectors and dropped them on the ground so he could pull his phone out of his shorts pocket.

"Got you on visual," he said a moment later, and he headed down the road, where he unlocked and opened the security gate. A moment later Alison joined him there. If they spoke, the sound didn't carry, but Tyler decided that a retreat was in order.

The indoor temperature was nearly as chilly as outside, so he went up the stairs to grab his jacket from the loft that he'd claimed for personal space. He wouldn't be allowed to sleep there, he'd been told, but he could sleep anywhere. What he wanted was space to work and think.

He shrugged on the extra layer and leaned over the chest-high interior wall to look all the way down. The scattered security lights made for lousy ambiance. The view was still impressive. Below him the entry level and two more floors radiated off an open central stairway that descended in a spiral to the lowest level on the canyon floor. The upper floors were cantilevered off the central column, with more than two meters of space between protective chest-high walls and the rough inner face of the cliff. Air constantly whispered up and down the ring.

The inefficient use of space made a pattern like flower petals or a nautilus curve. Framing showed where doors, interior walls and partial ceilings would eventually be placed, but right now Tyler could see most of every level. Each floor had its own bathroom, also currently visible from above. At least the fixtures were plumbed. The water heaters and septic system worked fine. It was far more civilized than camping, and far prettier than the flop house in Chicago.

Down on the bottom level, a kitchen was separated from the larger living area by a wood-topped island. The seating space would be nice and roomy, once random piles of flagstone, tile, and planking turned into a fireplace. Now it was a cluttered space with a large alcove in one wall and a spectacular view of the canyon floor through French doors.

The primary building material was gritty, and a powdery residue covered every surface. Dust hung in the air. Bits of protective gear marked Parker's path from the lowest floor to the top, one piece of padding every few steps.

Justin was sitting at the bottom of the stairs with both knees bent and his head resting on them. Dust was caked in a long stripe down the spine of the bodysuit. His sweatpants were torn at the knees, and the shin guards were as dusty as his back.

"Carl's here," Tyler called out.

The sound had a muted quality. Justin looked up. His arms and headgear were dusty too. "I heard. I'll come up as soon as I catch my breath," he said.

It wasn't reasonable to walk up three floors on a bad leg after getting kicked around like a soccer ball for hours, but Justin wasn't known for his sense of reasonable. He would do stupid things right up until someone else stopped him.

Tyler's conscience woke up from the vacation it had been

enjoying since the road trip began. He hadn't meant to revert to adolescent irresponsibility the instant his ass hit a car seat, but that was exactly what he'd done. No wonder Alison was in tears tonight.

He owed her an apology, and more importantly, Justin owed him one. Or maybe they owed one to each other. Tyler knew better than to let Justin get away with going all secretive and obsessive, but Justin deserved better than heebie-jeebies and avoidance too.

"Don't walk up," Tyler said. "They can come to us."

CHAPTER SEVENTEEN

TYLER COLLECTED PARKER'S DISCARDS ALONG the way down the stairs and dropped the equipment in a pile behind the curve of the stairs. Justin had taken off the headgear, but he had dust smeared on his face too, which was still flushed from exertion. He also hadn't bothered shaving in who knew how long.

"You look like a bad joke," Tyler said as he helped the man to his feet. "Black and white and red all over."

"Fantastic." Justin scrubbed at his face. "Are you ever going to run out of bad jokes?"

"Never." Tyler dove right in. "Justin, what's wrong?"

The door into the foyer from the garage opened, and the noise startled both of them. Justin's left leg buckled when he turned. Tyler grabbed his arm and steadied him.

Some things never changed.

Tyler didn't recognize the man who walked into the house carrying an armload of boxes and bags. For one horrible moment he thought Parker had been ambushed. Then Parker and Alison came inside carrying more bags, and the blond bearded giant peered down the stairs with his head tilted to the side.

"Holy crap," Tyler said. "What's with the lumberjack costume?"

Carl was wearing jeans and a black-on-red plaid quilted jacket. He said, "It's warm, and it fits."

"I think it looks good," Alison said. She stretched up to give Carl's hair a tug and then went bouncing down to the level where she'd dumped her gear earlier. "Sorry, Tyler. No peep show for you after all," she said as she moved out of view. "Viking Santa brought me all the tarps and tools on my list."

"Rats," Tyler said with a sense of relief. Alison wouldn't be teasing him unless he'd been forgiven for being male. "Carl always ruins my fun."

"I do my best." Carl brought a load of supplies downstairs. He stopped to give Justin a long look.

Justin returned the evaluation with a raised chin and an air of belligerence. Parker took the bags and boxes from Carl and started spreading items all over the floor.

The majority of the supplies—food, clothes, climbing ropes, and a space heater, among other things—were mundane, but some of the hardware piqued Tyler's curiosity. He'd used similar components when building power cells for Justin. Many of the parts cost a fortune. He wondered what Justin planned to do with this batch.

So far Justin had been incapable of explaining how he knew minute changes to the cell design would produce dramatically different results. He also swore that he wasn't guessing. He *saw* it, but he didn't have words. The conversations kept ending with frayed tempers and the invocation of either "moron" or "freak," depending on who lost his temper first.

Carl said to Parker, "Refresh my memory, please. I did use the phrase 'improve coordination and muscle tone' when I suggested that he work out with you, did I not?"

"Yes." Parker didn't look up.

"So, then. I did not say, 'inflict full-contact jujitsu on a convalescent.' Good. I'd hate to think I'd lost my mind in my old age."

Parker sat back on his heels and glared.

"Really?" Carl turned to Justin. "*You* instigated this insanity?"

"It seemed like a good idea at the time." Justin pulled off the forearm guards and sat down to work on the straps of the shin protectors. It was a measure of his exhaustion that he didn't protest when Tyler took over. Afterwards Justin gathered up the padding and got to his feet, again accepting help without argument.

Carl was still using the stare that made talking infinitely less painful than saying nothing. Tyler edged out of the target zone and picked up Justin's headgear. Justin said, "I'm perfectly safe, except against head strikes, which Parker is avoiding."

"Why bother wearing guards then?"

"Cushioning. Hit or missed block, either way there's contact. I don't know what I'm doing, and my trainer's breakable, even if I'm not."

Tyler hadn't thought twice about the possibility of Parker being in danger. The man was lethal, and it wasn't as if Justin were super-strong. He was only stiff-at-speed.

Then again, stiff-at-speed could pulverize brick. Tyler had seen that in the lab in Lincoln. His hands went sweaty as he recalled the fight in the parking lot. "Hey, back in Chicago, didn't you punch some guy—"

"Not now!" Carl pinched his nose between his fingers. "This is your idea of coping, Justin?"

"Yeah." Justin staggered and sat down. "And yeah, Tyler. I hit the guy who aimed a gun at me. He's dead."

He looked calm, but his hands were clenched hard on the protective gear.

"Wow," Tyler said. "That's heavy self-defense."

He couldn't understand Justin's carefully blank expression or his white-knuckled grip. It didn't look like guilt so much as fear, and Tyler couldn't imagine why Justin would be afraid. Unless he was waiting for condemnation.

Carl said, "You have the most incredibly expressive face, Tyler. Yes, he values your opinion. That's why I reamed you over the toxic teasing. Think before you open your mouth for once, will you? Please?"

Tyler handed the headgear to Justin, changed his mind, and took all the equipment away. As he tugged shin guards out of Justin's clutches, he said, "Does this mean I can't call you 'killer' now, just like I'm not supposed to say 'freak'?"

Justin made several choked attempts to speak before he said, "You've never called me killer in your life."

Carl gave Tyler a thoughtful frown, then nudged Parker, herding him into the kitchen area to unpack boxes there.

Tyler sorted out the straps on the guards. "Yeah, but now I'm regretting all the missed opportunities. If I start now, then you might cry, and I can't stand crying. This is the reason for the sudden interest in manly sports? You got one physics lesson and decided to take a full course?"

Justin's chuckle sounded pained. "More or less."

"You can't cram that into one day, for pity's sake. You need to take a shower. You need to shave. You need to eat. You need to talk—"

He looked up and stopped in time to avoid mentioning Alison's name. She was eavesdropping from halfway up the stairs. Justin followed Tyler's eyes and went tense again.

"Hey," he said.

"Hey? *Hey*?" Alison took a deep breath, which was always impressive. "For two days I've been wondering what I'd done wrong, all because you couldn't be bothered to explain why you were upset? Can't you think of anything better to say than *hey*?"

"Sorry?"

Alison sighed and stomped out of view. Justin stared after her with an expression so raw and confused that it made Tyler feel sorry for him.

He gave the emotional dust a few seconds to settle before saying, "You're a mess, Justin. I'm upgrading myself from comic relief to loyal ally for the evening."

"Should I know what that means?" Justin asked wearily. "Upgrade whatever you want, as long as you help me get my sorry ass upstairs to a shower and into a bed."

"Good plan." Tyler held out his hand, and Justin took it.

ALISON SET her cup and her computer on the kitchen island, and then she stretched to place a mug of coffee at Carl's elbow. "All right, I'm ready for my busywork."

Carl glanced down. "It isn't busywork. I've told you that nine days in a row. Do you have a long-term memory problem?"

"Hah, very funny. Boost me up there."

The work island was a good workspace for Carl, since standing was easier on his back. Alison's chest barely cleared the top. Carl lifted her up so she could sit cross-legged there. The lowering sun reached the top edge of one of the French doors, and light flooded into the room, illuminating Alison's still-doubtful expression.

Carl said, "What you do is important. Someone has to keep Justin on task when he makes his morning calls, and when you take over the surveillance workload in the afternoons, I can focus on other projects."

"It's still busywork," Alison said. "But thanks for pretending it matters."

She shunted the surveillance to her unit so she could run systems checks and keep an eye on the perimeter. The space heater in the far corner ticked into a warming cycle, and the measured sound of Tyler's boots on the floor upstairs was a steady counterpoint to the scuffles and thumps of Justin and Parker sparring outside.

It was another pleasant afternoon in limbo. Until the fallout from Walton's blitz play in Chicago settled, they were stuck in a holding pattern.

Everyone had their own ways of filling time. Justin spent a few hours every day renewing his acquaintance with academic and professional associates, getting confidential legal affairs in order, and spreading disinformation. He split the remainder of his waking hours between his construction projects and physical therapy disguised as fight training.

If his condition kept improving as fast as it had so far, he would be able to fend for himself if the operation went sour. And if his gadgets worked as advertised, they might even succeed in bringing down Dominic Walton without bloodshed.

Tyler filled the loft walls with diagrams and numbers and calculations, and he was starting on the floor. He said the space helped him think. He spent hours nagging and distracting Justin with questions, and at least once a day he and Parker went on a cross-country run.

Parker used the treks to familiarize himself with their territory. He also put everyone through emergency drills, worked with Justin on the plans for defenses, and he kept the night watch.

Alison had run out of diversions after three days. What she had done in that time still amazed Carl. She'd used plastic, staples, rope, and creativity to convert all the uncomfortable exposed spaces into a collection of tented areas that evoked the feel of an exotic bazaar.

Once she was done with that, Carl had been more than happy to give her a new focus for her energies. His job was to make certain that they weren't taken by surprise again, and there was plenty of work to go around.

"I have the cameras," she said. "There's a new sidebar."

"I gave you the cache from the watchdog programs too.

There's one for any mention of our names or associated accounts, a tracker on Walton's security-related assets, and a program that maps results from the other two. Review any red highlighted items and blue map tags, and flag repeated items for me. I want to concentrate on some Civilian Security Bureau records that one of my friends forwarded from the Chicago local division."

Alison watched information roll down her screen while Carl confirmed that the collateral damage from the Chicago departure had been sanitized. That was the silver lining to the cloudy problem of going up against organized criminals. They cleaned up after themselves.

The data flow could be fascinating, and Alison didn't look up until Justin came downstairs again after a post-workout shower. He made a beeline for the rat's nest of a work area he'd established in front of the unfinished fireplace, and Alison watched with a little smile on her face, because Justin had only tossed on jeans over the skintight black bodysuit.

Justin, on the other hand, was as oblivious as usual.

Carl said softly, "In case you're wondering—"

"I don't wonder. I know I'm pathetic," Alison said morosely. "If I sent out signals any hotter, the smoke alarms would go off."

Carl slipped an arm around her shoulders and pulled her closer so that he could whisper in her ear. "Tyler—our very own fiercely nonviolent Tyler—has told me he's ready to knock Justin out, strip you both naked, and lock you in the garage until you bang like bunnies. His words."

Alison's shoulders shook. Carl could feel her giggling against his chest, and he could feel when the laughter turned to tears. She put both arms around his chest, wrapped both legs around his ribs and clung to him. He rested his chin on Alison's head, and let himself enjoy the moment. It wasn't every day he got to be an oversized teddy bear.

"For what it's worth, you aren't pathetic," he said quietly.

"He's unbelievably gun-shy, but he isn't blind. Trust me, he notices you."

Alison leaned back. Her face was blotchy, and her hair was mussed from contact with his shirt. "Do I look blind?" she asked. "You all notice me. Trouser adjustments occur in my wake whenever I wear tight shirts. If I weren't the only woman in ten square kilometers, it might be flattering."

Carl burst out laughing.

Justin naturally chose that moment to realize he wasn't alone in the room. He took in the situation with a blink, and a stricken look came over his face. He ducked down fast, and Alison let her head drop against Carl's chest with a groan of despair.

"There's always the garage option," Carl reminded her.

Alison put her hair back into its ponytail holder and wiped her face against her sleeve. "I'm considering it."

She slid off the counter and took her cup to the stove. The break for tea led to a long quiet period punctuated by the working noises Justin made in his section of the room.

Alison eventually broke the silence. "This whole plan of waiting for Dominic Walton to pounce on us out here—are you sure it's a good idea? He could bring in an army and bomb us off the map, given the number of mercenaries he employs."

Carl said, "We're more like spiders in a web than sitting ducks. Predators, not prey. Justin's putting out word that he's back in control of the technology Walton wants, along with the news that he's established an inheritance chain for it. That channels Walton's strategy. He needs Justin alive and cooperative. There won't be an army. Covert personnel retrieval is a tactical op, six to twenty, depending on the scenario. When we're ready, we leak our location and control the confrontation."

"Yes, but if—"

"There's no *if*. Walton's ego won't let him delegate this, and taking him out of the picture will leave Justin—and you, and Tyler—free to start rebuilding your lives. It should work, but you're right. There are risks. Frankly, I'd be happier if everyone else went to ground somewhere else and waited for news."

"Frankly, I would go crazy with worry. We're doing escape and evasion drills, aren't we? We won't get caught up in the endgame. Relax." Alison shook her head. "And that wasn't what I was going to say. I'm wondering why you need Justin as a lure at all. Why didn't your brother climb into a bell tower and blow Walton's brains out years ago?"

Because the odds of Parker getting away with it had never been good enough. Because Carl wanted to *destroy* Walton if possible, and that meant separating him from his protection. Merely killing him would be a consolation prize.

Aloud, Carl said, "Walton is surrounded by professional bodyguards around the clock, and he has military and law enforcement connections that are far better than Eddie's or mine. One of our advantages here is that even reaching the site forces him out of his normal security bubble."

"Bodyguards." Alison pulled up her computer. "Crap."

She ran a search and then sat back to stare at the result. Carl raised a questioning eyebrow, but Alison only shook her head and raked an errant hair behind her ear. "Justin, I need you over here," she said.

The statement raised no response.

"Justin."

On the third repetition, he looked up. "What?"

"I don't want to shout across the room," Alison said. "Come here, please."

Justin came over, although his body language screamed that he would rather be anywhere else in the universe. His face was a mask by the time he got to the work island, and he kept the barrier between himself and Carl. He conspicuously focused on Alison alone. "I'm here. Talk."

Alison flexed her hands into fists to keep from reaching for him.

She said, "You need to call Helen. Now."

ALISON GAVE Justin an hour alone before surrendering to temptation and going to check on him. Justin hadn't asked to be left alone. He hadn't said anything since Alison told him that his ex-wife's security team might not have her best interests at heart. That because of Justin's existence, they might even be a threat to her.

Every day for the last two weeks he'd pushed Helen's name to the bottom of his call list and said he wasn't ready. Privacy was the only kindness Alison could offer him now.

She'd given him Helen's contact information, gotten him seated at the plank-and-fieldstone desk where they both spent most mornings, and left him there.

A red tarp hung between the office and the stairwell. Alison ducked under it. Justin was slumped in a folding camp chair with his legs hooked over the second one, where Alison sat in the mornings. He held a phone handset against his forehead as if he planned to absorb it by osmosis.

Alison wanted nothing more than to walk over to him and give him a hug or a kiss or most of all—God help her—a full-body tackle, followed by banging like bunnies. She didn't move.

Justin flinched whenever she got too close to him. She watched the clock on the workstation screen behind him. Three minutes passed before he noticed her and tucked one arm over his face. "I got through, but I'm not done," he said. "Do you want your room?"

"Not necessarily." She'd hung two tarps, blue and green, as curtains between the workstation and two makeshift bedrooms. The extra privacy was nice, and Tyler practically lived in his loft. "What does 'not done' mean? Did you talk to Helen or not?"

"She's calling back." Justin added his other arm to the facial armor. "After she makes contact with the shadow team I dropped on her last month."

"You put extra security on her? That was considerate." Except for the part about not *telling* anyone, but that was classic Justin as well. "Not the same firm, I hope."

"No, I checked. They're clean. One of the Mayhem crew suggested them. I was worried, after Tiffany. I don't know how long it'll take Helen to shake her regular team. She'll call."

"No problem. I'll hang downstairs with Carl."

"You do that." Justin peeked out from under his arms. His face was blank, his voice dry, but the glint in his eyes was cold. "Run off to Carl and leave me to wait for Helen to finish eviscerating me. Thanks so much."

"What did you expect?" Alison's unresolved feelings imploded into anger. "She thinks you're dead, turns out you're not, and the first thing she hears from your lips is that you've put her life in danger? Of course she's furious. You can't handle that? Fine. I'll talk to her. Get out."

Justin sat there as stunned as if she'd slapped him. Alison yanked the second chair from under his feet. "Go on, leave. Sorry that I thought the mother of your child deserved to hear from *you* that you're alive. Sorry that I thought you might want privacy to talk to your own wife." Alison grabbed the handset out of his hand. "And leave Carl out of it, you idiot. *God.*"

She brushed past Justin and retreated behind her curtains. Her bed was the only place to sit. She sat and squeezed her eyes tight shut to keep the tears inside. Her sinuses hated her already.

The tarp rustled. She didn't acknowledge it. The sag of the mattress under the weight of a second body was harder to disregard. Justin's breath against her cheek as he sighed heavily right beside her—that was impossible to ignore.

"Get out," she said. "If you need a nap, go use your own bed. Or Tyler's."

"He's not mine," Justin said. "Ryan. There were tests."

Alison bit her tongue. Screaming, "Are you blind?" wouldn't help anyone.

"And Helen is my ex," Justin said. "I can miss the way I used to love her and worry about her and hate her guts at the same time. I'm begging you, don't abandon me out of courtesy. Probability of civilized behavior is directly proportional to the number of witnesses. Please stay."

He waited another ten seconds before he went back to the office side of the curtain. Alison stared at the lattice of plastic strips she'd made into a ceiling, and she considered hiding forever. Then she returned to the office and kicked her feet up on the desk as if this were any of the last ten mornings they'd spent there.

Each day Justin had endured repetition after repetition of the same questions and shock, without once letting on that he'd heard it all before. He dispersed the emotional overload with jokes, and when he forgot names or lost himself midsentence, he relied on Alison to intervene with a steady faith that awed her.

Courage, generosity, and kindness were only the beginning. He also had a laugh that made things go tight in Alison's belly, and he looked fantastic in tight clothes. The physical avoidance might be frustrating, but it was still a nice way to spend a few hours every day.

"You have such a beautiful smile," Justin whispered.

Startled, Alison turned and caught a glimpse of desire so intense that it literally took her breath away. It was gone in a blink, and Justin smiled. "I guess I am an idiot," he said. "Can I add jealous to that? Jealous idiot?"

"If it's true, sure." Alison said. "Justin, I'm touchy-feely. Yes, I hugged Carl. I hug everybody. If you want a hug, all you have to do is stop dodging."

"I don't want a hug."

The simple statement was a knife right in the gut. Alison held her breath against the pain. "Okay, good to know."

"I don't want a hug. I want—" Justin glanced at the buzzing handset. "Shit."

The workstation screen flickered through the protocol for an incoming call, and then Helen's face was there. "Justin, I've found your people, and we're on the—oh, I can't say where. Are you satisfied? Are you happy now? Once again I've uprooted my life for your convenience."

She was dressed in a vintage coat and scarf, speaking into something held at eye level like a makeup mirror. Ocean was visible behind her, along with glimpses of a vehicle interior.

Justin sat frozen, staring straight ahead. Helen's voice took on an edge. "Are you listening to me, Justin?"

Alison reached over and squeezed his leg. The contact jolted him back to life. He said, "Lower the phone, Helen. Don't show me where you are. You have Ryan with you? You're both all right?"

"Yes, Justin, we're both perfectly fine." Helen spoke with martyred patience. "This paranoia is absurd, you know that? If I hadn't already been looking for an excuse—"

She broke off to glance away. "No, Ryan. He most definitely isn't an angel. Yes, all right. Sit in my lap."

Ryan popped up on the screen in front of his mother. Alison compared his small, serious face, tousled hair, and dark eyes to the disheveled, scowling, mature version sitting next to her, and she wanted to pull out her own hair.

Helen looked down at the boy, and her mouth flattened to a line of disapproval when she raised her head again. That one unguarded glance confirmed everything for Alison. The woman's eyes were hot with frustrated spite.

Helen had once said that Ryan was *hers*, with an emphasis that explained the deception. She'd deliberately shut Justin out of his son's life, except that Justin had neatly sidestepped her strategy and showered Ryan with affection merely because the boy was *Helen's* son. That must have been maddening.

Ryan wore a striped uniform shirt and had grass in his hair, and he was fretful and squirming. "How come you're not dead, so I can talk to you now?" he demanded. "You were dead for my birthday and didn't call. How come you didn't call *before*?"

Justin, who had kept his composure through every other variation of those questions, completely lost it this time. Unfiltered pain and regret went charging across his face before he got his expression under control and pasted a smile over the chaos.

"It's too complicated for phones, kiddo." His voice shook. "Put it on your New Year's list. All right?"

Ryan nodded with a solemn acceptance that indicated his familiarity with the odd stalling tactic. "What if you're dead again on New Year's? How long do I have to wait then?"

Justin winced, but thankfully Ryan moved on without waiting for an answer. "And how come I have to miss soccer? How come Mariana couldn't come with us?"

"That's my fault. Who's watching you now? Can you go sit with them so Helen and I can talk?"

Ryan craned his head around. "She plays basketball."

Helen handed him off and settled a frown on Justin. "This had better not be one of your oddball jokes. I had to call Rob and my agent and the studio and the Primary Ed programmer, and you're lucky I'm not working this fall. You're lucky I wasn't on location. You're lucky—"

"Will you shut *up*? I'm lucky you're not being used as a hostage against me, all right?"

The raw outburst stopped Helen's rant dead in its tracks, but she adjusted her scarf and her collar and rallied for another assault. "You need a haircut," she said. "When was the last time you shaved? And what kind of shirt is that? Don't you ever care what kind of impression you make? When will you learn that you can't—"

Alison swung her feet to the floor and leaned forward to mute the sound. Justin had been shrinking lower in his seat with each word as if Helen still had a right to criticize anything he did. Alison said, "I like the way you look."

He ducked his head with a small, private smile.

Alison flicked the sound back, but Helen was glaring now. "Who are you talking to, Justin? I know that expression. Put her on so I can see her."

"Shit," Justin said under his breath. Louder: "Helen, you know Alison, don't you?" He adjusted the camera, and in the review screen Alison saw that her hair was ratted and her red fleece jacket had dust on one shoulder.

"Hi, Helen. Bet you're surprised to see me."

"Oh, my God." Helen whipped off the glasses and peered at her own screen until her face loomed large. "Oh. My. God. Alison, the Civilian Security Bureau is looking for you, the Seattle branch and Central too, and—and you've been with *him* the whole time?"

"Not that you have a right to ask, but yes. Helen, the people we're trying to protect you from nearly killed me less than an hour after we hugged good-bye. For your own sake and Ryan's, stop fighting. Please, stop. Please be safe."

Helen nodded quickly, and put a hand over her heart. "Oh, Alison. I never be—" she said before she was drowned out by a high squeal of "ALLIE!"

The screeching dialed back to excited babble that distracted Helen for a moment. She said with indulgent bafflement, "Ryan wants to know why you left his bunny in a box. Does that make the least bit of sense to you?"

The stuffed animal Ryan had given Alison in Lincoln had been left behind in a Chicago high-rise hotel. She'd only had time to grab one armload of clothes and a bag.

Comprehension kicked Alison in the guts. Ryan had given her the toy *so she wouldn't be alone*. "Helen, ask him how he knows where it is."

Ryan said, "Mariana made my bunnies special so they can

visit, but I can't visit without her. I want to visit. I want Mariana. *I want to go home.*"

A full-fledged tantrum ensued in the background, and at last Helen looked worried. Then she closed her eyes, and in seconds was calm and poised again.

"She is a very good actress," Justin commented softly.

Alison made a mental note to let Parker know that his defenses hadn't failed. The security breaches had been her fault: innocent, inadvertent exposures caused by a combination of opportunity and bad luck.

Ryan's going-away present had been inside a bag from the night they left the bunker in Lincoln to the day before they were targeted in Chicago. A camera and a wireless burst transceiver were all a tracker would need to pinpoint a target. Except when it was transmitting, such a device would be undetectable. Alison had learned the theory from Terry's Mayhem and Havoc crew. She'd never imagined living the reality.

Walton's agent might have been seeding any number of offices and bedrooms and other locations with whimsical gifts from a celebrity's child. Alison wondered how much intrigue had been generated by poor Ryan's generosity.

She hoped no one ever told him.

Snippets of conversation came and went before Helen said in a tone of loathing, "I'm told we need to stop and *strip*. God, this is a nightmare. I swear, Justin, if I could go back in time and never meet you, I would do it."

She disconnected.

CHAPTER EIGHTEEN

"WOW," ALISON SAID. "I USED to like her. Now I want to slap her across her selfish face."

Justin's laugh was bitter. "I know the feeling."

Silence fell, punctuated by small noises: Tyler in his den upstairs, running water from the kitchen.

"Are you sure you don't want a hug?" Alison asked. She was aiming for a dry tone to lighten the mood but missed, landing with a splash in an ocean of wistfulness.

"No. I mean yes, I'm sure."

Alison leaned back in the chair and watched the plastic overhead move gently in a draft. "Too bad, because I could use one right now."

Justin's chair scraped back as he stood up. His movements were jerky and slow, and when he grabbed for Alison's wrists he missed on the first try. Then he had a warm grip on both of her arms and tugged her onto her feet and off-balance.

She landed heavily against his chest, and they both staggered because Justin stepped back on his bad leg. He hitched his weight against the desk to steady himself, and he pressed both hands against the sides of Alison's face.

His fingers were trembling. The look on his face was hungry and rapt and as far from rejection as looks could get, and when Alison put her hands against his chest, she could feel his heart beating fast.

The kiss was all tongues and suction and nipping teeth, and—on Alison's part anyway—a certain amount of desperate clinging. After a few exquisite moments, Justin pulled back, only to bury his face in the bend between Alison's neck and shoulder. He exhaled. Heat shot through Alison's body.

"You hug everybody," Justin whispered. "I don't want a hug. I want this."

His hands slid up beneath her shirt to cup her breasts, thumbs flicking across the nipples, and he kissed her again. "And I want this," he said against her lips. She let the world melt away in the glory of taste and warmth and texture. Then Justin's hands slid downward as he said in a low, shaky voice, "And I want this."

Alison's sanity made a belated reappearance. She caught at Justin's fingers before he finished unbuckling her belt and things got out of control. "Wait. Justin, wait."

"Shit." He jerked away from her and stood with his hands spread wide. His breathing caught harsh in his throat, and his eyes had a wary look that Alison very much wanted to kiss away.

"Seriously?" she asked. "You're seriously worried about rejection?"

She kept a hand against Justin's chest as she kicked her chair out of tripping range. Then she grabbed Justin's shirt and turned them both so she could hop onto the desk. Then she wrapped her legs around him and pulled him up close. Everything felt so good and so right that she was tempted to let all the complications wait.

Waiting would be a mistake. "Now we talk," she said.

Justin did nothing but look at her with his arms outstretched as if he'd forgotten them. Alison reached out and put his hands on her waist, then brushed stray curls of hair back behind his ears.

"Remember talking?" she asked. "That other nice thing we can do with tongues and lips? Your timing is rotten. I'll settle for a pity fuck because I am that desperate, but I won't be just another way for you to piss off Helen."

She was close enough to see every tired, stressed line around Justin's mouth, and it was clear that he was having difficulty thinking. She waited for him to work through her words.

Justin leaned forward to rest his forehead against hers. "You terrify me."

"Not what I was aiming for, honestly," Alison told him.

He was still shaking, or else Alison was. She couldn't tell. In about ten seconds her self-control was going to vaporize, and she was going to be kissing him again whether he was acting out of pity, revenge, or sheer boredom.

Justin moved back a little and squinted. "I promise you, this is purely about you and me."

"Good." She shifted closer and tightened her legs. "We can stop talking now."

"No, let me finish explaining before I lose my mind." Justin laughed and put his face against Alison's throat again, breathed out a ripple of heat that sank into her skin.

"I want you so much it terrifies me," he said. "But I don't want a pity-fuck, and I can't think of a single reason you would want—"

Alison put her hand over his mouth to stop the stupidity from leaking out. The sensation of lips on her fingers was so distracting that she missed the next few words. When she regained her senses, she heard, "—let you decide."

Her chest went tight. "Then we're good. My mind's made up. I want you despite that unflattering remark about me scaring you."

"I'll stop being scared if you'll promise me one thing."

Anything. Everything. Alison barely censored the words in time. Justin was already scared. "What?"

"Can you please never *ever* mention Helen within an hour of me having my hands on your tits? Please?"

Alison had been holding her breath, and it came out in an

undignified bark of laughter. Happiness spiraled up, and she said, "I can do that."

ALISON CAME AWAKE in utter darkness to a flash of light, the sound of thunder, and a blaring squeal from the proximity alarms. Before she was fully conscious, a body slammed her onto the mattress and knocked the breath out of her. She didn't scream. She'd shrieked the first two times they'd done a worst-case drill, and once she'd accidentally given Parker a black eye.

There was little chance of anyone reaching the building without some warning, much less coming through the canyon-side wall at this level, but it was called *worst-case* for a reason. Parker had body armor. If a breach blasted chunks of concrete and metal rebar across the house, better that it hit him first.

If they were caught by surprise after all their planning, they would have to assume the worst.

Ever since Justin had mentioned their location to about a dozen people over the past few days, they'd all spent more and more of their time in drills. Alison hoped she wouldn't have to hike in the rain again. This was the second thunderstorm in a day, and the second drill.

The tarp overhead glowed briefly again, and thunder rumbled. Parker reached over her to check on Justin too.

That was the closest Parker ever came to acknowledging that Justin slept in her bed now. Sleeping was all that happened at night, with Tyler on the far side of the tarp and Parker sitting wakeful on the stairs a few meters away, but it was a tactile comfort Alison was unwilling to deny herself.

She wondered why Carl was taking so long to call out tonight's scenario. Parker's equipment harness ground painfully into her thigh. She pushed at it with one hand to relieve the pressure. When Parker hissed, she hurriedly moved her hand. The disputed area contained *personal* equipment, not buckles or harness.

Her embarrassment vaporized when she realized she could also feel Parker breathing fast and shallow. He was usually as quiet as a stone. When another flash lit the building and the floor shook, Alison's pulse jumped. That wasn't thunder. This was not a drill.

Parker abruptly rolled off and grabbed Alison's wrist, laid hand signals against her sweating palm. Wait, was the first, followed by taps for thirty seconds and go.

Go, go, go.

Then he was gone in the dark, and his footsteps pounded up the stairs. Alison grabbed the coat, the radio earpiece, and other gear that never left her side these days, and she reached for Justin's hand. He placed a kiss on her knuckles and gave her a shove towards the window. And then he was gone in the dark too.

He wasn't coming with her. In all the drills they'd practiced, he'd gone with her. The brutal collision of those two facts defied comprehension. Nearly the full thirty seconds had passed before Alison's brain coughed up an explanation.: Justin had been running drills with her, but he'd been planning something else *without* her.

Alison slipped into her shoes, hopped onto the partition wall, and went out the window that was barely large enough for Justin even after the glass and frame had been removed and replaced with plastic. It didn't matter whether the opening was big enough. Justin wasn't there.

Outside, the window inset created a narrow ledge beneath an overhang. She would edge along that until she could use the rigged ropes to climb to the canyon rim and meet Tyler. He didn't fit through the windows at all, so he had to leave through the garage and come along the wash behind the house. Unless that had been a lie too. Maybe he wasn't coming either.

Alison shoved aside her doubts and followed the drill.

TYLER KNEW he shouldn't be up in the loft in the middle of the night. Deathtrap, Parker had called it, when he'd ordered Tyler to stop sneaking up there. The windows were sealed shut, so escape was constrained to the single stairway.

Tyler understood the restriction, but sometimes he needed to be in his own space, to stare at the walls in the dim night-lighting, to let the hard visuals scratch at the itch of an idea in his head. He went and sat in the center of the room and let the shapes of the math dance in his mind.

He knew he was in trouble when the alarm went off and the night-lights went out and a blast lit up the room in stark white for an instant before full darkness fell. He knew he was in trouble, knew he should run, but his heart was beating too fast, his chest hurt so much he couldn't take a breath, and his legs felt disconnected from his helpless body. He sat in a ball on the floor and sweated, unable to move a muscle.

When he heard someone running up the stairs, he knew he was doomed. Looking over a rifle barrel at an faceless shadow, he knew he was staring at death.

Parker slapped him to his feet, kicked him down the stairs, slammed his pack into his arm, and shoved him out the garage door into the dark. All in total silence. A shudder racked Tyler's body. He took one stumbling step and another, and then he ran.

ALISON FOUND her way along the route by feel and ignored the terror gibbering in the back of her mind. The dry wind blew cold through denim and fleece, and her fingers went numb. The river below rushed and roared, still flowing strong with runoff from the day's storms, but once her eyes adjusted, the canyon rim loomed against a brilliant field of stars above her. All the thunder tonight had been man-made, not natural.

The hundred meters of trail felt like infinity.

When she got to the top of the bluff, the first thing she saw was a light like a bonfire in the near distance. Then an arm clamped around her body, and a hand clamped over her nose and mouth to stifle her scream of panic. What happened next was a drilled response. Elbow straight back into the attacker's diaphragm, stomp on the instep, twist, push back and kick up, creating distance for escape and causing distraction or injury.

It had worked in self-defense class. This time it resulted in Alison lying with her forehead pressed into rocky soil and her body squashed beneath a heavy weight. She tasted metal and sand. Whoever still had a hand across her mouth was out of breath and seriously needed to shower. He also felt improbably familiar.

"S'me." Parker sucked in a breath. "Ow. Fuck."

Alison shoved at him, and Parker rolled away onto his feet, crouched low. Then he checked his gear and retrieved the rifle he'd dropped before grabbing her.

He adjusted the angle of his helmet, and his teeth flashed. "Nice moves for an amateur," he whispered.

"*Nice moves*?" Alison parroted it in a singsong. "That was another drill after all?"

Anger and relief swirled through her. She felt sick to her stomach and prayed that her sweatpants were damp with sweat and not urine, but she was pretty sure she was praying in vain. She rolled onto her back and jammed her cold hands under her arms. "Jesus, I think I wet myself I was so scared. If you ever fall asleep again, I'm pouring a bucket of ice water over your head, or down your pants might be a better—mmph!"

Parker planted a hand over her mouth again, hard enough to cut her lips against her teeth. "No drill," he said quietly. "Launched seekers to trip the close proximity alarm. Blew the shit out of the road and canyon. Then broke outer perimeter and squatted. Trying to spook us out. Got it?"

Out there in the dark, someone was watching right now. If Parker hadn't caught her, then she might've run straight into people who could do far worse than scare the piss out of her. Escaping past an incoming assault was a calculated risk. This was a feint; that made it a trap.

Alison nodded understanding, which got her mouth returned to her. When she sat up Parker put a hand against her back. Heat radiated off him, and Alison settled as close as he would allow. She ran her tongue over her teeth and spat grit.

Parker tapped Alison's ear. Carl's voice spoke right next to her: "—still sitting tight on all routes. They might have a drone up top."

She jumped and looked all around.

"Copy no-go," Parker whispered.

It echoed. Alison touched the earpiece she'd forgotten putting in. She had donned it out of habit, but she'd never switched it on. "I'm so sorry. I could've saved you the rescue if I'd kept my head."

"Did better than Tyler."

A new wave of fear washed over her. "Is he safe?"

"He's fine. Froze like a rabbit."

Alison braced herself. "And Justin?"

Parker waited a long time before answering. "He's setting up a perimeter trap. Didn't expect a siege op. Would've been better if he could've laid it closer."

Alison shoved away most of her confusion and asked the important question. "What is he setting a trap *with*?"

"He built big chunks of boom powered to last a week or so. Lots of them."

"Bombs? That's what he was working on all this time?"

"Mines, not bombs."

"I don't care. Why aren't you setting them up? Why didn't you do it before? I thought you only needed him as bait. Why does it have to be him? Why isn't he leaving?"

Even in the dark Alison could see the answer in the way Parker looked away: Justin wanted to stay.

Parker said, "Couldn't set up early. The damned things have a time limit. Why him? Fucking invisible. Plus it left me free."

Free to shadow her and Tyler. Free to keep them safe. The logic of it made Alison want to scream. "Now what happens?"

Parker sighed and stood up. "The bad guys reset. We regroup. You and Tyler bail as soon as there's an opening. That's the plan."

On the way back, they picked up Tyler, who was shivering and white-eyed, and not even trying to hide the fact that he'd been crying. He'd barely gotten fifty meters away from the building before word came down to stop. Alison let him hold her hand and pretended she was taking solace from his presence rather than comforting him.

The light and warmth inside the house felt unreal. Alison paused in the foyer and rode out another wave of shakes. Tyler hesitated halfway up to the loft.

"Can I take a shower?" he asked Parker, and his voice was so high and nervous that he sounded like a child.

"Don't know." Parker headed downstairs. "Can you? You need one, that's for damned sure. You stink."

TYLER DIDN'T WANT to leave the shower stall.

He'd been sitting under the hot spray long enough to prune up his fingers and toes, but the splashing hot water was calming. He might never leave.

Parker lifted the tarp in the bathroom doorway. The man was still suited up and equipped for combat. The sight of him turned Tyler's blood to ice all over again, but having Parker barge in while he was crying and naked was nothing compared to what he'd already been through.

He raised his voice to be heard over the water. "Give it your best shot. Bitch-slap me for being a possum. Ream me for panicking. Lecture me about cowardice. I'll warn you, I've heard it all. My own brother gave up on me. I only stayed because Justin needed somebody to help him, and I *promised*. I thought I could be brave, but I was *wrong*."

Parker said nothing, and Tyler turned off the shower. He couldn't snivel with an audience, and the silence was nerve-racking. He toweled off. "Say something, will you?"

Parker came inside instead. The bathroom was huge, but his armored, bulky presence made the space too small for two. Tyler backed into the counter. Parker stepped up close. His green-brown eyes were as hard and opaque as polished stone, and he had a smear of dirt on his cheek.

A muscle under his jaw jumped, and he jerked up his chin. Tyler cringed before he could stop himself.

"No fucking guts," Parker said.

Tyler didn't bother denying it.

Instead of sneering, Parker lifted one dirty hand to tap a finger against Tyler's forehead. "Great big brain." The finger tapped lower. "Great big heart. Two out of three. Better than most."

The slap against Tyler's shoulder knocked him off-balance. Parker said, "You'll do." Then he turned and left.

For some reason, Tyler no longer felt like crying.

When he picked through the pile of clothes in the loft, he learned that all of his pants had migrated to the pile by his mattress downstairs. Reusing the dirty clothes he'd worn earlier was out of the question. Those he intended to burn as soon as he could. He slipped into running shorts and went down two levels in search of something warmer.

Alison was sitting at the workstation barefoot and wet-haired, wearing a sweatshirt and jeans, with a sleeping bag wrapped around her shoulders like a quilt. It was Tyler's sleeping bag.

He ducked past her, dressed fast and came back out to claim the other chair. He wouldn't be sleeping. He might as well join this party, invite or no. It was closer to being his room than hers anyway.

"I guess we're not cut out for a life of thrills and adventure," she said.

"Not if adventure means people trying to kill me, no."

He sighed. Alison reached out, offering a hand. "I hate this. Can I say that? I hate it."

He squeezed her fingers. "Me, too."

After another silence Alison said, "I was okay with Carl's little revenge scenario until now. It's his life to risk, and I understand that none of us are safe unless this guy is stopped. Now I'm afraid they're all going to get killed. Tell me honestly if you think they have a chance."

"My brother was the soldier, not me." Tyler thought back on knowledge picked up by association rather than intent. "This is a good, defensible position, and on top of that, they're weapons-free and the other side isn't. As long as it's tag versus tackle, they should have a win against any covert approach."

He belatedly realized that something was missing. "Hey, speaking of covert, where's Justin?"

Alison wiped away tears. "Nobody knows. He wanted to play commando games, Carl and Parker let him do it, and now he's missed his check-in."

CHAPTER NINETEEN

JUSTIN DIDN'T GET BACK TO the house until after sunrise. The canyon was still in darkness, but the sky overhead was bright behind a rippled veil of cloud. The river was flowing fast and muddy, and water spread in a deepening lake against the explosive-generated rock fall.

It would flood the house before afternoon if nothing changed, which made him glad that the French doors and sidelights were heavy-duty acrylic and not glass. The water pressure wouldn't break them. Neither would bullets.

Those doors were also now boarded shut. Demanding that the defenses be dismantled simply to save him a climb up to the barred and dead-bolted front door seemed selfish and lazy. The long walk back up the stairs would be easy enough if he rested a little first.

His breath fogged in front of his face, and the power cell in its pocket at the back of his collar rubbed against his spine. It was still channeling power into fabric, through fabric into skin. He sat down with his back to the wall to rest for a while.

He was warm now and still nearly pain-free. And invisible, of course. That would have to change soon. Six hours of charged time meant he would pay heavily for the indulgence. Worse, he'd hiked over ten kilometers and for most of it he'd been burdened with equipment. When the displaced aches and pains came back, they were going to hit like a hammer.

The door opened, scraping against the concrete sill. Surprise erased every thought in Justin's head. Carl leaned against the frame and scowled at the area. Size alone made him imposing on any given day. Today he was dressed in the same kind of ballistic protection that Parker regularly wore on night watch. On Parker, armor looked casual. On Carl, the additional bulk was intimidation personified.

"I know you're out there dithering," he said. "Either that, or invisible rabbits have decided to nest on the patio, which I think unlikely. Get visible and get indoors. I can't wait to hear why you left us hanging for almost four hours."

Justin had been listening to Carl's worried voice in updates and queries for hours now. He could forgive some rebound anger. "I'm not dithering," he said. "I'm resting. Do my feet really look like rabbits on the sensors?"

"Visible. Inside. Report. In that order. Now."

Carl's sense of humor was evidently buried under the extra layers of clothing. Justin narrowly prevented himself from responding to the hostility. Both of them losing their tempers would help no one, and only Carl had a good excuse for the anger.

Justin reached back to the nape of his neck and popped the switch. A few heartbeats later he was looking at his muddy fatigues and the toes of his muddy boots. The chill air enveloped him like a blanket of ice, the cramp in his leg went from uncomfortable to agonizing, and fatigue crashed over him between one breath and the next. Worst of all, backlash pain radiated from his bones, far worse than he'd anticipated. The desire to scream took a lot of containing.

Carl lost patience before it was over and hauled him up by one arm to drag him indoors. He was gentle about it, though, and

Justin dug in his heels just inside the door so he could stand and wait for the dizziness to diminish. Chills waved over him. He clenched his teeth to keep them from chattering.

Tyler was frying eggs and onions in the kitchen. Alison sat on the work island with Carl's computer in front of her, and Parker was napping on the floor with his back against the work island.

"What took so damned long?" Carl said while he barred the door. "You were supposed to check in."

"Even if it got me killed?" Anger ate at Justin's self-control. "I'm double-suited so I don't pop IR or UV sensors, but I don't know how far my voice carries. Silent was safer. Oh, and have you noticed the limp? I'm *slow.* I only should've had to cover half that distance, remember? Less than half."

That reminded him that he needed to mention something. He had it on the tip of his tongue—and it was gone again, buried under Carl's voice saying, "Fine, blame it on the leg and not the I-always-know-better attitude."

"Don't let the bitchy tone fool you," Tyler put in. "He was worried. Me, I'm glad you were careful. You're not usually sensible that way."

Wood thumped against the wall as Carl finished reassembling the barricade. Parker raised his head, looked around with a yawn. He gave Justin a nod that showed *he* hadn't worried.

"Map time" he said.

Carl said. "No, Eddie. He's shaking like a leaf. Justin, go upstairs and get a hot shower before you flame out on us."

One of the perimeter alarms went off. Alison silenced it with a glance at the screen and said, "Over and back again. It would be scary if it weren't so funny."

Parker had said that triggering alarms at unpredictable intervals was a standard strategy for wearing down defenders' nerves. In this case the aggressors s were missing a key bit of intelligence: the system they were tripping was half a kilometer inside the real surveillance shell Justin had designed.

Once Parker had explained the problems involved, putting together a solution had been fairly simple. It was just another power application. Justin still wasn't entirely sure *what* it tracked, but he could calibrate the unit to show only living animals forty kilos and up, and it worked equally well day or night.

"It won't be funny once the cells on those sensors run down," he said. "The charge won't last long; that's why we weren't relying on them the whole time."

He'd set it up mainly so that Carl could help Parker get Tyler and Alison safely past any opposition. He looked to Parker. "The bad guys pulled back hours ago, right? I heard Carl's reports even if I didn't answer. Why is everybody still here?"

Alison had been making a point of *not* looking at him all this time. Now she smiled—if bared teeth could be called a smile. "I do what I want," she said. "And I wanted to stay and give you a piece of my mind. I hate surprises."

It sounded a lot like she hated him.

"I didn't want to argue with you," Justin said. "I wanted you safe."

"Turnabout is fair play. I'll leave now that I know you're safe."

Carl got a grip on Justin's arm and manhandled him to the stairs. "Do I have to carry you up there?"

He made it sound like a threat. Justin pulled free and glanced over his shoulder as he limped up the steps.

Alison rolled her eyes. "Don't worry. I won't go without saying good-bye."

A LONG HOT shower erased most of the backlash pain. The headache stayed, and the vertigo stuck around as well. Dressing should've been simple, but everything Justin picked up belonged to Alison, and whenever he leaned over, the inside of his head tried to fall out. He sat down and held his skull in place with both hands. At least he had the base layer on. He wouldn't freeze.

"Hey, lunatic. How are you holding up?" Tyler slipped into the room and set a plate full of food and a water bottle beside the bed.

Justin looked up without moving anything but his eyeballs. Even that much motion made his head swim. "Fine."

"Liar." Tyler went digging through the clothes. "Eggs. Eat."

"You're hanging around Parker too much."

"You have no idea. Fuel up, or I'll do my cranky Alison impression next."

The eggs were wrapped in tortillas, and the scent of them made Justin's stomach growl. He finished the first wrap in four bites. After he ate the second one and downed a bottle of water, the headache began to ease.

"Did you even chew those?" Tyler tossed jeans and a gray pullover onto the bed. "Here you go. That's the best I can do. You're on your own for socks."

Justin said, "Did I ask you to root through my things in the first place? Did I ask for help?"

Guileless blue eyes met Justin's with a hint of challenge. "No, you didn't ask. I don't expect miracles."

The verbal slap hurt all the more for being richly deserved. Justin absorbed the impact and got himself dressed, socks and boots included. "Sorry," he said afterwards, because Tyler was still waiting. "And thank you. For everything."

"Listen to that. You do know the words. Stop before I get all weepy and we have a moment or something."

Justin threw the empty water bottle at him, and they went downstairs together. Carl was nowhere to be seen. Tyler pointed up when he saw Justin looking around. "Workstation level," he said. "He went up right after you did. Sleeping, I hope."

"I doubt it," Alison said. "Here, I have the maps up."

She refused to leave her perch, but she moved the screen to one side so Justin could make notations on it. Parker came to watch from Justin's other side, and Alison leaned in so she could observe as well.

It put her breasts at a distracting elevation, and Justin was close enough to smell soap and warm skin while he took in the view. He tagged the emplaced devices as quickly as possible. Close proximity only made him want to be a lot closer and a lot less clothed, and this was neither the time nor the place.

"I'm still furious," Alison said, leaning even closer so that she was breathing the words in his ear. "But mostly I want to screw your brains out. That's how relieved I am."

Justin's body abruptly stopped paying any attention to concepts like time and place and propriety. He swore under his breath.

Parker shouldered him towards Alison. "Go. Make up. Make out. Both."

He sounded amused, and he swung himself onto the top of the island, boots, equipment, and all. He reached for the surveillance computer and made shooing motions with the other hand. Alison blinked at him, and a blush colored her cheeks. Then she hopped down, which put her within Justin's reach, and then he had both arms around her.

"You have got to be kidding me," Carl's voice carried across the whole house from the stairway landing. "That merry band of pranksters out there might get serious at any time, and you two want to waste time sucking face?"

His face was creased from lying too long in one position without moving, and his eyes were bloodshot. He walked heavily down the stairs and stopped at the end of the kitchen island. Parker put a hand on his arm.

When Parker was the one showing self-restraint, something was deeply wrong with the proper order of the universe.

Alison slipped away from Justin, moved right into Carl's personal space, and poked him in the chest with a finger. "Back off."

Carl looked down with a startled expression. "What?"

Justin smiled. This would be good. Alison versus Carl might look like a kitten facing down a bear, but a smart man would put his money on the kitten to win.

"Back. Off." Alison punctuated the words with jabs. "You can put up with a little face-sucking, or I'll give you a real reason to bitch and jump his bones right there on the counter. Right now. Call my bluff. I dare you."

Justin's imagination imploded, and his lungs stopped working. Parker cleared his throat and looked away. Carl backed off a step, then another, and his shoulders sagged.

"He's back, you've talked, you go. That was the deal," he said. "Every extra minute is an unnecessary risk. We should've kicked you and Tyler out before dawn. We should've made you go *days* ago."

"I second the leaving idea," Tyler said. He was edging around the perimeter of the room to reach the stairs. "Allie, I'll grab our bags, okay?"

"Okay," Alison said. She closed her eyes. "Five minutes, God. That was all I asked. Why was that too much?"

Time.

The elusive thought wandering the back reaches of Justin's mind slid to the front again. "Walton isn't out there. He's flying into Kirtland this morning," he said as fast as he could, before it disappeared. "With more people. Fifty-something, and they weren't sure when, exactly. Sorry, it kept slipping away."

Parker hunched over the map with a muttered curse. Justin hoped he found answers there. Fifty was a ridiculous number. Even he knew that. That many people would only get in each other's way, but Walton was bringing them. There had to be a reason.

"That's a hell of a thing to drop on us now," Carl said. "You didn't think that was worth calling in? You couldn't *remember* it?"

Carl's force of personality could be daunting even when he

didn't mean it to be. When he wielded it like this, the weight of it was crushing. All the pressure condensed Justin's emotions into a single driving need to push *back*.

Alison returned to his side. "That's your scary face, Justin," she whispered. "Don't you start too."

Justin struggled to hold his voice and temper down. "I overheard it, and no, I didn't want to risk someone hearing *me*. And then you got in my face and drove it out of my head."

"Yes, blame me for your faulty wiring. How did you get close enough to eavesdrop?" Carl put one hand to his forehead. "You walked straight up and down the road, didn't you? Right through their lines." He dropped his hand and picked up the glare where he'd left off. "How could you take a risk like that?"

"What did you expect me to do?" Justin didn't mean to shout, but he did. "My balance and my endurance suck. I didn't want to fight through brush and sand all the way. The zigzag sweep was hard enough."

"It was foolish and reckless and flat-out stupid. If they'd captured you, all this would've been for nothing. You are not replaceable, and if you're too weak and slow to handle a little extra hiking, then what the hell were you doing all the way down in the canyon at the end?"

The edges of Justin's vision started to go red. "None of your business, you arrogant prick. Take your self-righteous bullshit and shove it up your ass."

Carl was moving before Justin finished speaking, and Justin pushed forward too, more than ready to meet him on his terms. Parker dropped to the floor between them, and Justin found himself confronting Alison.

She latched onto his lips as if she wanted to inhale him and got both hands on his shoulders, pushing him back. Justin's leg collapsed under the extra weight. He paid a lot more attention to the kiss than the impact.

Alison rose onto her elbows. "Sorry," she said. "I had to do something to distract you."

She didn't sound sorry.

Carl was still fighting mad. Parker had one arm against his throat and was using body weight and leverage to keep him from moving forward. His boots squeaked as he was pushed back, and he shifted into a tight clinch, pinning Carl's arms tight.

"No," he said. "Absolutely not."

Carl blinked at him, and then inexplicably began to laugh. It sounded strained, but anything other than blind rage was an improvement.

Justin started laughing too, when he realized that Parker wasn't warning Carl to stop; he was telling Carl not to expect a kiss as a distraction.

"Hey," Tyler called from upstairs. "What's all the commotion? And whose phone is ringing down there?"

The phone belonged to Carl. He answered it, listened, kept listening while he paced from the stairs to the kitchen and back. Alison wondered what she was missing, while Justin let his head drop back and continued to chuckle.

All the antagonism had vaporized as if it never existed. Death match to snickerfest in five seconds flat. Parker gestured for her and Justin to stand up, and then he vaulted onto the work island again as if the whole exchange had been perfectly normal.

"You are insane," Alison told Justin. "All of you."

She took a quick personal inventory as she got up. Right knee bruised where it had hit the floor. Heart hammering in her chest, skin sweaty and damp. Every muscle tense. Some of the stress escaped as a pained sigh.

"Are you hurt?" Justin went tense. "Shit, did I *hit* you?"

"No, no, I'm okay."

He touched Alison's face lightly and then wrapped both arms tight around her. "Don't *ever* do that again," he mumbled against her neck.

His whole body had gone rock-hard for an instant when he'd hit the floor beneath her. It was the weirdest sensation Alison had ever felt, and dodging past his fists to grab him suddenly seemed a lot less clever.

"Damn Carl," Justin said in her ear.

Alison detached herself before her resolve weakened. "If testosterone poisoning was fatal, you'd both be dead."

Justin followed her to the stairs. "Then damn me too," he said. "I can't stop thinking about that countertop now."

Alison turned back and found Justin much too close, wearing a smile that tried to make light of the emotions in his eyes. She let him kiss her because they really didn't have time for that conversation. This time no one interrupted them before they had to come up for air.

"Leaving," she said. "Right."

"Hold," Parker said. He jerked his chin at Carl, who was leaning on the kitchen counter with one hand pressed against his forehead.

Tyler came thumping down to the first landing with a knapsack over one shoulder and another bag in his hand. "I got your kit, Alison. We're out of here."

She pointed to Parker, since he was the one making cryptic objections. He said, "Sit tight."

Tyler took the order literally, sinking to the stairs and slinging his backpack onto his lap. Alison took her bag and joined him. Justin settled in as well, and Alison couldn't summon up the discipline to push him away, especially when it became clear that he was starting to doze off.

Parker raised his voice to say, "Intel. Share."

Carl pocketed the phone with a darting glance up the stairs. The amount of pain in that short look stunned Alison. He was always so aloof, indulgent at best, cranky at worst. Pity welled up. No wonder he'd lit into Justin, unwarranted as it had been. If any of them were hurt it was going to kill him.

"I have just been reminded that I am a boneheaded imbecile with control issues," Carl said to his feet. "No surprise to any of you, I'm sure."

Parker perked up. "Pete?"

"Yes." Carl dropped into one of the camp chairs by the fireplace after turning it away from the room as a whole. It creaked under his weight, and he slumped down until only the pale top of his head was visible.

"This is what happens when I keep promises," he said. "People can call at inconvenient times to drop confidential information on my head. We're about to be in a war zone, as if we didn't have enough problems."

"Fed contacts." Parker returned to his typing.

"Pete says the Bureau says the CAF's mobilizing to shut down Colorado's hydroelectric blackmail scheme. Borders close midnight tomorrow, and the big hammer falls if they don't cave by Monday."

"Out, ASAP." Parker pointed two fingers at Alison and Tyler, wiggled them. "Creekside. Talk it."

Tyler said, "Down the wash low and slow, onto one of my three running trails, depending on where you report trouble, swing back down into the riverbed. Go as fast as we can from there to the highway. Hitch if we can get a safe ride; otherwise a long hike into Eagle's Nest. Use the IDs and funds to catch a bus. Try for contact in a week."

"Go," Parker said, and that was that. Alison shifted Justin's drowsy weight off her arm and followed Tyler up the stairs. Justin tagged along behind. As Alison left the garage, Justin caught her hand and pulled her close one more time.

"I love you, you know," he whispered.

And then he shut the door in her face.

"Bastard," Alison said, with feeling. Tyler looked shocked by her reaction. She didn't have the heart to explain it. Tyler was a romantic. He wouldn't understand that Justin had only said the words because he was afraid they might never see each other again.

It took an hour to reach the point where canyon cliff mellowed to steep hillside, and Alison was exhausted by the end of it. When Tyler stopped to rest, she was ready to lie down for a week. Sneaking used whole sets of muscles she hadn't known she had.

They were under observation for most of the distance. Carl's cool advisories had kept them at the maximal distance between watchers, and Tyler had enough knowledge of the terrain to make the most of their cover, but progress was slow. Better slow than shot or captured, but it was going to be a long trip, even traveling in the river bottom, where they could walk rather than creep.

There were still four kilometers or more to go cross-country before they reached the highway on this route, and with all the military activity, hitching might not be an option. They were looking at a long, long walk.

Things could be worse, Alison knew. It wasn't dark or freezing cold, and she hadn't pissed herself. She sat down close to Tyler and considered scooting on her rear end all the way down the steep slope. No matter what method she chose, she was resting first.

Tyler handed over a water bottle with a worried smile.

Their enemies had made a mistake trying to soften them up or smoke them out. The dry run had given Tyler a chance to find his feet. Out here in the open air and daylight, he was in his element.

Alison's feet ached. Her heels felt chafed raw inside the boots. "Not fair," she said. "You're in shape."

"Not my fault that you sat on your fine ass all those times I went out running."

"Now I know why Captain Killjoy laughed when I asked for a bulletproof vest." Alison stretched. "I would've dumped the extra weight."

Carl's voice crackled in her earpiece. "Cut the chatter, please. Last sentry is fifty meters ahead, a little over a hundred to the right, up top. Stay in the valley on his side, and shut the hell up. Good luck."

His words faded in and out, after that, and they lost contact for good once the trail took them downhill. They would still be visible on the house system for a little while, but they would get no more warnings. With luck, they would be in the clear soon.

"Luck" was an ominous word.

A rhythmic thudding came and went in the distance as they made their way to the river bottom and began hiking along its course. The hillsides were shallower here and farther from the flowing water, leaving room for trees to grow in the rocky soil.

The footing was uneven, and Alison concentrated on avoiding roots or loose stones. Only when the thumping noise grew louder did she finally recognize the sound. "Tyler, that's a helicopter."

THE HOUSE WAS MUCH TOO quiet. No pacing footsteps in the loft. No scraping of chairs or voices from the workstation level. No whistling kettle, no rummaging in the refrigerator. There was no sign of Justin thumping or bumping upstairs either. Carl heard only the tick and hum of the space heater and tapping from Parker working on the kitchen island above and behind him.

Carl watched two dots cross the terrain map on the device in his lap and willed them off the screen. The sentry was ahead to their west, and the sun was just past zenith. If the man looked the right direction and they were in the open, they would be easy targets.

The screen fuzzed briefly. The anti-jamming and ranging measures Justin had cobbled together were failing hours earlier than he had predicted. Carl sought distraction before his adrenaline level spiked any higher. "Eddie, what's your take on Walton dropping a crowd into this?"

"Cover," Parker said. "CAF outsources support. Hundreds of contracts out, last week or so. Maybe he'll spring an additional squad. No more."

"Is that speculation?" Parker still had his own contacts in and out of the Combined Armed Forces. The amount of typing he'd been doing indicated conversation in progress.

"No. Yes. Postings account for fifty and more. Designated buffer zone out there. Marshaling areas, medical units, supply drops." Parker hesitated. "Best bet is to cut and run. Shit-stupid luck, Fed moving in this big. Should've been a perfect setup."

Should-have-been didn't count. It was time to admit defeat. Carl sighed. "We can't risk any more surprises. Justin won't pull the plug. We'll have to do it for him. Do you go upstairs after him, or do I?"

Justin answered from the left: "I'm right here."

Shock coursed through Carl. The back of his head slammed against the side of the counter hard enough to make him see stars, and he flailed for balance.

Parker laughed at him.

Justin watched the whole show without a hint of emotion. His eyes held steady on the tracker unit until he was sure Carl had it under control. Then he looked up.

His cold resentment smashed down Carl's rising temper.

"Yes, I know you can take care of yourself," Carl said. "That isn't the point. I yell at Eddie too."

"Truth," Parker said cheerfully.

Carl ignored him. "When did you tiptoe down here?"

"An hour ago." Justin leaned back with his weight on his hands. "I've been sitting there—fully visible—all that time. You need sleep even more than I do. I'll still follow your lead on this. I could talk myself back and forth all day."

Parker abruptly sat up straight, head tipped to the side. He slid to the floor an instant later and gestured for silence. A distant muttering became audible. He jogged up the steps to the first landing, stopped there to listen again.

"Topside," he said. "Now."

He returned for his helmet and equipment, and then he charged upstairs again. Justin followed at the best speed he could manage, which wasn't fast. Carl glanced at the surveillance screen one last time before he closed the unit, and a chill ran through him. Tyler and Alison were at the focal point of a new arc of glowing contacts.

He grabbed the rest of his gear and followed Parker outside through the garage. Justin joined them in the open area behind the building a minute later. Metal clanked as his pack hit the ground. A small helicopter passed low and fast along the canyon, rotors tilted for maximum forward acceleration. Another was maneuvering out over the broader valley, and a third larger one disappeared below the slope of the hill along the road, roughly where Walton's team had set up their op center.

There was no point in sharing the news about what Alison and Tyler were facing. There was nothing anyone could do about it now. There was nothing anyone could do to help any of them now.

Despair was harder to control than panic, and Carl barely tried. Numb acceptance would be a better defense than fear against what was coming.

"Interesting," Justin said as the larger helicopter rose into view again and headed south. "Why are we out in the open where they can see us?"

"Because I'd rather die with sun on my face," Parker said.

Justin's mouth dropped open.

"We're screwed," Carl said in translation. "Those are CAF units, not private birds. Walton is either calling in major debts or accruing them. That's a million dollars a day flying around out there, minimum, and no reason for it to be here now."

Parker had his binoculars out and tracking the pair of smaller helicopters as they crisscrossed the area. "Showboating," he said.

His gaze and voice were both bleak when he turned to Carl. "Satellite imagery explains last night. I never in my worst night-mares thought he'd have a full CAF logistics train to draw on. I'm sorry, Carl. I'm so fucking sorry."

"You didn't know. None of us did until too late."

The numbness was creeping into his voice. Parker heard it. He looked away fast. Justin said, "Someone needs to explain, please. Walton still has to come in for us, right?"

Parker said, "He doesn't have to come in *covert*. No chance for us to counterambush or use that rat trap you set. He doesn't have to expose himself. He can let his people hammer us flat in broad daylight with gas and sonic assault and stun grenades. And once you're a captured domestic combatant, he can drag your ass out of here and do whatever the fuck he wants."

"Oh." Justin squinted off into the distance. "Shit."

CHAPTER TWENTY

A SHADOW FLASHED ALONG THE ground in front of Alison, and the thuds of sound were joined by engine roar and a howling burst of wind. She hit the ground and put both arms over her head. Tyler landed beside her.

Gravel and twigs bounced off her arms and back, and then the cacophony receded. The helicopter lifted over the hilltop and disappeared. Rotor noise echoed down the valley. Tyler stood up and spun in place, trying to track the helicopter's course, but it had vanished.

As soon as Alison got to her feet, Tyler grabbed her wrist and took off running.

Alison tripped and stumbled and sent them both into the dirt. Tyler came up onto his elbows, twisting and turning to look all around. Alison grabbed his arm to keep him down. "Don't panic on me, Tyler."

He put a hand over hers. "I'm not. I'm looking for a hide. We need to get under cover before he comes back with guns blazing. And yes, I saw guns. Look, there."

He pointed ahead, over a hundred meters through the trees and scrub to the side of the valley. The eroded hillside had collapsed into a shallow cliff and a pile of jumbled rock slabs. "We need to get there before he gets back."

The rotors were getting louder again. Alison said, "I can't do it."

"Yes, you can," Tyler said, intense and certain. He took her upper arm and hefted her up again. "Lean into me. We have to do it."

This time Alison trusted Tyler to balance and carry some of her weight, found a last burst of energy to push off with her toes and push again and again, and they *ran*. Her heels were on fire and she could hardly breathe and she had a stitch in her side. It felt a little like flying, until her toe hooked under an exposed root, and something popped inside her ankle. It bent under her weight on the next stride, and pain flared up her leg like fire. She lurched into Tyler's side and bit her tongue to keep from crying out.

Tyler swung her up and then around to his back, all without stopping, and for the last fifty meters she was clutching at his neck and his pack, clinging like a limpet with her chin bouncing against his shoulder. They rounded a boulder and came under a huge slab of stone that had fallen at a tilt to face the cliff.

Tyler stopped so that Alison could slide down. For an instant, after her foot touched the ground, her vision snowed over from the pain. She couldn't help sobbing.

The helicopter flashed past, heading towards the spot where it had passed them earlier. It barely cleared the top of the slope afterwards, and someone shouted indignantly in the distance.

After the noise receded again Tyler collapsed to his knees and then onto his side, gasping for breath. Alison crawled past him, deeper into the grotto. The ceiling dropped lower, and she crawled right into the narrowest space at the back and made herself as small as she could.

Her hands began to shake, her ankle throbbed and pulsed, and the world went away for some indefinable time.

Only a thin sliver of sunlight hinted at the existence of the outside world. Tyler was invisible. Bulges and ridges of stone hung down from the overhang, and the sand underneath Alison's legs was cool, dry, and clean.

Time passed. Alison stopped shaking.

Tyler was lying somewhere making a muted gurgling sound. Alison tentatively identified the vocalization as laughter, and she hissed Tyler's name.

He had to remove his pack and scrunch up his shoulders to fit into the space next to her.

"I don't know what's going on," he whispered. "Let's sit here and wait. What happened out there?"

"I twisted my ankle. Thanks for the ride. How did you know this spot was here?"

"Habit." Tyler shifted position so that he could pull Alison's leg into his lap. "On runs I'm always looking for campsites, hides, blinds, things like that. What-if spots. Parker and I did some boulder-hopping here. Wow, that looks bad. Sorry, I know I'm supposed to say you're fine, but it's turned totally sideways."

He pulled a roll of stretch bandage out of his pack and began wrapping it around Alison's ankle, right over the boot and sock. She knocked her head on the low roof and bit her lip. Spots floated in front of her eyes.

"What-ifs?" she asked to keep herself from sobbing.

"What if a tornado came out of nowhere? What if a polar bear was chasing me? What if I needed to hunt a deer with my bare hands? What if a giant lizard appeared? What would I do? Where would I go?"

"Like, what if helicopters attacked me out of thin air?"

"No, I admit this scenario never occurred to me."

Rotor noise came and went again, and then voices drifted through the air. Feet scuffed against stone. Whoever was out there wasn't even trying to be quiet.

Tyler rolled up against Alison, cramming himself as far from the light as he could get. Alison felt him trembling too.

She pressed her face against Tyler's chest and prayed.

JUSTIN'S PATIENCE and nerves began to fray by the end of the first hour. After three, he was ready to snap. He leaned over the parapet of the roof to look out. They'd retreated there for the commanding overlook, after all. The panoramic view was impressive, but he didn't see what he wanted. Walton was not out there.

The building was effectively surrounded. Ten people patrolled along the eastern slope in a loose cordon, and the river was lapping at the lower doors of the house. Foam swirled in the deeper water beyond the patio.

Walton might not make a final move until tomorrow or the next day, after hostilities officially began. He might even try to have his prey brought to him elsewhere, the way Parker had predicted, although the waiting game argued against that.

Justin couldn't let him call the shots, not and have any chance at beating him. This had to end *here,* and it had to end *soon,* and he had the means to force that confrontation to happen.

If surrender was the only way to take the fight to the enemy, then that was what he would do.

He had done as much preparation as he could. He knew what terms he had to set. Now his biggest problem was that his allies had inexplicably turned defeatist on him.

Carl sat against the wall nearby with his eyes closed, literally shutting out the world. He wasn't asleep. His breathing was fast, his body tense. Parker was no better, although his spin on despair was more subtle: his summation of their predicament had seamlessly gone from "us" to "you" at the mention of first contact.

He clearly planned to make the initial clash a bloody and final one. Every five minutes like clockwork he checked over rifle, pistol, and knife; hands and eyes moving in a twitchy repetitive ritual. As company went, he and Carl together were more than a little depressing.

"Leave," Parker said. He gave the same advice every five minutes like clockwork. The first time, he'd said it in direct response to Justin's current plan.

Justin could escape even now. He could walk away with no one the wiser. He could do it, as long as he was willing to spend the rest of his life knowing he'd fled. Knowing he'd left the other two behind to die.

He was tired of losing. Tired of running. Tired of it all.

"I am not leaving," he said. He knelt in front of Carl. "I'm taking him down, one way or another, and I want you to stick around for the ride. Both of you."

Carl opened his eyes. "I will not be taken prisoner again. Not by him. I can't."

The flat voice was as bad as the bleak blue stare. Justin went straight to the selfish point. "I'm taking him down with or without you. I will let him take me. I can get to him. I'm sure of it. No matter what happens, you won't stay a prisoner. If it all goes wrong, then we all die, but so does he, I promise. I have better odds of surviving with you than without you, that's all. Please. Help me."

Minutes passed. Pain etched lines in Carl's face, and he finally said, "*Dammit.*"

Justin went to look over the valley again.

Sunlight glinted off small planes flying into and out of the airstrip outside the closest town over ten kilometers distant. Helicopters worked up and down the main valley towards the state border now. Justin thought about Alison and Tyler and their chances of escape, and then he locked the feelings in a box.

A mutter of engine noise came up the hill.

Parker joined him at the wall, pressed him down below the parapet. "Game time," he said. "Make it count."

THE FIVE MILITARY transports that stopped along the last switchback all had darker patches on their dusty hoods and doors: identification decals had been recently removed. That identified them as private contractors. The men who piled out of the vehicles wore uniforms without unit badges, rank insignia, or names. That identified the operation as not only private but illicit as well.

Consultation occurred behind the center vehicle. Equipment was unloaded. "What is all that?" Justin asked as he eased below the parapet edge.

"Standard tactical assault loadout," Parker said. "Breaching cannon. Grenade launchers. Riot gas."

A loudspeaker delivered an order garbled by echoes. "Come out or we come in" was the gist of it.

"Don't shoot," Justin shouted. "I'm up here."

He lifted himself onto the wall to sit. The world wavered as he swung his feet over the far edge. Nervous energy was not enough to counter the effects of sleep deprivation; he kept a firm grip on the wall.

Activity on the ground ceased.

"Let's not play games," Justin said. "I know Dominic Walton is calling the shots. Make this easy and get him here so I can surrender in person. You know there's only three of us. We don't have many options. We do have guns and other weapons. Don't push it. Nobody has to die today."

They stalled and protested and made noises that proved they were not taking him seriously. Justin kept one hand down for balance and turned. Parker handed up the pistol. Then he picked up the control unit for their perimeter defenses and checked the list of codes with an air of resigned desperation.

Justin gestured with the pistol. Carl stood up, head and body above the low parapet just out of arm's reach. He folded his arms over his chest and raised a pale eyebrow. Justin swallowed dread and steadied his aim on Carl's face.

He was pointing a gun at a man who could kill himself without touching the weapon. All Carl had to do was open his mouth and tell Justin to pull the trigger. Justin could see the temptation in Carl's eyes, and fear made his fingers tremble on the sweaty pistol grip. Carl shook his head, an almost imperceptible negation. He wouldn't lay that weight on Justin's conscience.

"What was the name on the obituary?" Justin asked. "Sorry, but was it the same? Names don't stick. This won't work if he isn't sure it's you."

Carl raised both eyebrows. "Every time I forget how sideways your brain works—Carl Jenson. I went back to it a couple of fake histories ago. Stupid, maybe, but I missed it."

Justin called out, "Take a picture, people. Carl Jenson is the label for it, and he dies too, if Walton doesn't get his ass in here fast. He'll want to hear that name. I'm not feeling very stable and I am sick of being a pawn. Walton takes us both, or no one does. This thing has nine bullets. I only need two."

The threat sounded brutally sincere. Justin was a little worried by how real it felt.

Ten minutes later a car arrived behind the line of trucks and disgorged five passengers. They came right up to the house. Walton looked at ease in his combat utilities in the same way Parker did. The body armor was tailored, and he knew how to move easily despite the extra weight. His hair was gray, his skin was ruddy, and his round, smiling face could serve as a textbook illustration for "male Caucasian: middle-aged, smart, sociable, and trustworthy."

He was sweating, the holster on his belt hung crooked, and his entourage looked pissed off. He'd moved fast to get here and changed plans to do it. It was all about finding the right leverage.

Carl growled, and Justin's blood ran cold at the sound.

"Satisfied?" Walton had a boardroom smile: all teeth, no sincerity. "You asked for me by name. Here I am. Come off that wall, Dr. Wyatt, and bring your friend with you."

"I'll be down in a minute, Dominic. Can I call you Dominic? Or do you prefer asshole?"

At the mention of Walton's name, Parker keyed in the commands to arm every device that Justin had placed that morning. The two suit units that Justin had squirreled away more recently came to life as well.

Walton was not getting out of this alive. That much of the gamble was won and done, and Justin was going to cherish the man's outraged reaction to being insulted for as long as he lived. However long that turned out to be.

"Before I join you, I should warn you about something," Justin said. "There is now an active mined perimeter approximately twenty meters behind your cordon, following the same arc. It's about a hundred meters wide, and the mines are motion-activated with a detection range equally wide."

He watched Parker's fingers count down. Walton was struggling to keep his face neutral, and the soldiers behind him were in deep and earnest discussion.

"You're bluffing," Walton said. "There's no way you—"

The demonstration unit blew sky-high. It was a lot more impressive than Justin had expected. Tyler was going to have a field day figuring out why the things worked. All Justin knew was that they did what he wanted.

Best to avoid thinking about Tyler, he decided. "I didn't *get* them. I made them, using the specs you're after. They won't detonate sympathetically, there's significant overlap, I doubt that you can pinpoint them, and clearing lanes by brute force won't work unless you're willing to sacrifice personnel along with equipment. They won't trigger unless living bodies cross the sensor lines. Test that if you want. The murders are on your head."

The statements hit Walton like physical blows. His face drained of blood, which was dramatic given how flushed he'd been. "You couldn't—you—how did you make them so fast? Out of what?"

The eagerness behind those demands made Justin shiver. He said, "I'll tell you all about it, but it's complicated. For now, your people can stay put or die. Unless you can call more helicopters without awkward questions, of course. If you can call them at all. Your radios are down, by the way. Comms interference is a useful side effect."

Walton's face turned red again.

"There's one more device on the top floor here," Justin told him. "Set for proximity and signal-loss detonation. I'm generating the signal. If my heart stops beating for any reason, it goes boom. In the interests of self-preservation, I'll ask that you don't take me more than fifteen meters from the building. That's the signal range, and as you just saw, that's still well inside the *blast* range."

He shrugged. "I'm not stupid. I want to live. I'm just sick of being pushed around. Sit down with me and negotiate like a civilized human being, and I'll give you whatever you want."

He handed the pistol back to Parker and took the control box. Parker held onto it until Justin met his eyes. "Been an honor," he said. He left the pistol and the rifle behind when he headed to the roof hatch.

Justin took the controller into the loft, keyed in one last sequence, and then backed carefully away. The other two were waiting at the front door.

"This is a stupid plan," Justin admitted.

Carl said, "You have no idea."

CHAPTER TWENTY-ONE

THE PLAN WENT OFF THE rails the instant the door opened. After a flurry of shouting and pushing, Justin was shoved to his knees. Gravel ripped his pants when he hit the ground. His arms were yanked back and secured with something, his head started throbbing, and his vision blurred.

Someone put him in a chokehold from behind, and a crowd of boots and legs milled around him. Parker and Carl were wrestled to the ground on either side, restrained with plastic ties, and pinned with their faces in the dirt.

Walton came up the walkway to stand in front of Justin.

"You're none too impressive in person," he said.

He was silhouetted against the sun. Justin knew the positioning was a ploy meant to intimidate. He knew, but it still worked, and he held his breath to keep from hyperventilating.

Walton must be furious that he'd been outmaneuvered and trapped, but it didn't show. He studied Justin's face with sharp interest. Justin studied him in return. He was close enough, but there were too many other people with weapons too close to Carl and Parker. The outcome would be too bloody to risk.

Justin said, "This is the kind of bullshit that makes me uncooperative. I said I'll give you the tech free and clear."

"This may come as a shock to you, Dr. Wyatt, but I don't care." Walton's smile was still devoid of humor. "I will take your tech, but what I want most from you is your long-term cooperation, and I didn't hear you offering that. I did come prepared to get it."

His voice went hard as the anger seeped through. "And now I'm going to make you *beg* me to use you. I do not take orders from a lousy piece of salvage. You don't trap yourself with me and escape the consequences."

The animosity in his expression was tightly controlled. Anger was a weapon, and he was using it to look for a weak point.

Justin's mouth went bone-dry. Walton said thoughtfully, "Your disdain for the military is well known, and I recall that Jenson is almost devoutly pacifist. Where did your demolitions expertise come from? Don't say you looked it all up. You had help."

He looked from Justin to the men holding Parker. "Not hard to guess. You need to know how far I'll take this, Dr. Wyatt. He'll make a good demonstration. Sergeant, please."

The man sitting on Parker's back stood up, lifted a foot.

Brought it down.

The crack of breaking bone yielded to a crunch as the soldier leaned into Parker's back. Carl threw off all four men holding him. He rolled into one man's legs, and took out another with a kick to the kneecap, and then they buried him in bodies.

Justin's stomach fought into his throat. He fought back and won with discipline forged through weeks of practice. Walton watched with a chilling detachment. Justin had no idea what his own face showed. He felt numb.

Even if Parker might prefer death at this point, Justin could not stand by and watch the slaughter. He couldn't sit there and do nothing, so he said, "That's Carl's brother you just broke, you know. Good job destroying great leverage."

The taunt might keep Parker alive a little longer. Walton

wouldn't let the broken dregs go to waste, not when Justin had just rubbed his nose in the original mistake.

Walton stepped forward, fist raised, but at the last second he transformed the swing into a broad gesture to someone behind Justin. "Set up inside. There has to be a disarming procedure. One of them will give it up. Strip, shave, and sequester them all, run patch-tests on Wyatt, and go ahead with clonazepam and B47 for Jenson. Tape his mouth shut till the drugs kick in."

Justin felt grateful when they hooded him. What he'd seen already was more than he could bear.

Alison's elbow dug into Tyler's kidney. "I need to pee," she whispered.

He moved over, bruising a shoulder on stone. "Do your worst. I'm uphill."

Disapproving silence met the suggestion. He met it with more silence. Silence was safe. Finally, Alison said in a tiny, shocked voice, "You're serious."

"Hell, yes. Piss where you sit. I'll be doing the same. We're not moving from this spot until I'm absolutely sure there's no one out there waiting."

Concealment was their only defense, and the hunt had come too close more than once. Twice Tyler even saw boots, but none of the searchers ever dropped flat to look all the way back underneath the ledge.

The helicopter made three passes before moving northward away from them. When the ground search flushed out a pair of mule deer near the river, the pilot took the blame for mistaking wildlife for human beings. Under other circumstances Tyler would've felt sorry for him.

No one on the ground seemed to take their job too seriously. They talked. Incessantly. Snippets of wind-carried conversation indicated that they had been expecting garrison duty, not a day of slogging through sage and piñon in search of fugitives who might or might not exist.

That search was abandoned after an hour or so, following an explosion in the direction of the house. The next hunt was more serious, judging by the lack of chatter from its participants. Tyler nearly walked into that one. He'd been on the verge of crawling out to see if it was safe when a sudden cessation of birdsong tipped him off.

That group had gone down the riverbed along Alison and Tyler's intended route. A return sweep by the noisy crew a while later had covered the valley from side to side.

The sun was going down now. It was already pitch-dark in their grotto, and it was getting cold. Emerging from beneath solid rock would bring them up like spotlights on any thermal scanners pointed their direction. Tyler couldn't convince himself that no one would be looking. Something had gone horribly wrong, and he wasn't going to stick his neck into the mess until he had to do so. That wasn't fear; it was good sense.

If this were a good movie, he would be heroic and steal a weapon from someone, kill everyone else by stealth, hotwire a convenient car, and triumphantly drive Alison to safety. In this reality he was going nowhere, and Alison was going nowhere without him. Those were cold facts. They had water, an emergency blanket, and shelter. Tomorrow would come soon enough.

He ignored the soft rustling and other noises until Alison whimpered. That sound sliced into Tyler's heart. "I'm sorry, Allie."

"Don't be." Her voice was stifled. "You're not uphill."

He moved in a hurry. A short time later, Alison said, "You laugh at the weirdest things."

"For the second time in a year I'm freezing my ass off in the middle of nowhere with a cripple whose goal in life is to cover me in bodily fluids. What are the odds?"

"Pretty long, right?" Alison said. "A lot like our odds of getting safe to the highway."

Neither of them felt much like talking for a long time after that.

THE FIRST HOUR of captivity took the prize as the worst in Justin's life. The second hour knocked it off the podium. Around hour ten he stopped keeping score. Walton and four disinterested handlers were the only people he saw, he was certain the handlers didn't care, and the whole competition was Walton's idea.

It started when the allergy tests sent Justin into itching, choking fits. He shouldn't have laughed, but at the time he was wheezing too hard to do anything more useful, and the irony struck him as hilarious.

He could've told Walton at the start that the drugs used to warp Hong wouldn't work on him. He'd known since spring, ever since walking away from Rydder Institute with nothing but the knowledge that he would never get better. The intake team had sent him off with a long list of medications to avoid if he sought therapy elsewhere.

He could've told Walton a lot of things, but when he started laughing, Walton lost his temper and ordered the handlers to "beat him until he pukes his guts out."

They abandoned that effort after breaking knuckles and truncheons on him, and the stun gun was retired after a second use confirmed the initial results. They lost interest after establishing that the effects couldn't be circumvented, and they gave back the bodysuit when he went hypothermic and then spiked a fever.

After that, the challenges got serious, but Walton always hung back at a distance to observe. Justin cultivated patience. An opportunity to get closer would open up eventually. Until then, it was all about endurance.

No food, and no rest longer than ten minutes. Walking up and down the stairs until he tripped and knocked out two teeth. Walking in circles after that. Standing or sitting restrained until muscles cramped solid. Being held underwater until he inhaled it and choked and vomited. He hated that the most, which they must have noticed, because they kept at it until he could no longer swallow properly.

Walton never *ever* got within arm's reach again.

They hooded him whenever they changed locations and at random times in between, and they spooked him and tripped him and startled him so often that even a change in air pressure left him hyperventilating. At unpredictable intervals they pulled him from the physical grind to stand in the warm, empty garage while they asked questions. They never liked his answers, and displeasure inevitably led to a new round of endurance testing.

The workstation level had been emptied to a bare-swept expanse of concrete floor, and the lighting was repositioned to make an impenetrably bright cone of illumination along the back wall. Between other activities Justin was left there in the glare and the draft from the tarp-covered broken window.

Sound was a constant. When no one was personally harassing him, he was provided with recorded distractions. He couldn't hold onto coherent thoughts, much less conceal complicated secrets, so he was grateful that he didn't have to try. Cooperation didn't interfere with his goal. The remote unit for the mines was sitting beside a bomb with a proximity trigger that they could not disarm. That was truth. Justin stuck to the truth and bided his time.

When he could think straight, he wondered why Walton would bother making him a puppet now that his corporate and financial significance was gone, but clear thinking happened less and less often as the hours passed. He'd thought he was intimately familiar with pain and exhaustion after the last few months. By hour sixty it was all of his reality.

He endured.

At hour sixty-six his handlers rolled out a new addition to the routine. When they finished, he started crying and couldn't stop.

A PIECE of gravel slipped loose under Alison's hand and slid into a mound of its fellows with a cheerful noise.

She froze in place, heart suddenly pounding. Her arm muscles quivered, holding most of her body weight at an awkward angle as she moved her knee up and planted it in a position to push herself forward.

The soldier standing a hundred meters away began to turn towards them.

Tyler put his face into the dirt and held still. Alison followed suit. They waited so long that she would've sworn the shadows had lengthened by the time Tyler brushed his foot against her hand in a signal to move again.

The sentry was back to contemplating the trail.

They crept onward towards the river. Alison's hands were abraded and coated in sand, as were her elbows. Her clothes and hair were also sandy, although some of that was deliberate camouflage.

They had no food or water and couldn't hide forever. Alison's ankle wasn't getting better. They *had* to move, and so they were moving. Slowly. Every time Tyler put his head down and disappeared against the scrub they were crawling through, Alison reassured herself that this might just work.

Another foot or hand placed, another interminable wait based on Tyler's count of heartbeats, another infinitesimal advance. Alison had no idea how Tyler kept himself occupied, but she spent a lot of time thinking about ways to help Justin once she reached civilization again.

It was always when, in her mind. Never if.

She came up with a lot of ideas: too many of them. There were too many unknowns to plan effectively, too many factors out of her control. Alison worked up through decision trees and down trails of speculation and developed alternative strategies based on assumptions.

Polishing rough edges off her various plots kept her from worrying about Justin, Carl, and Parker. It also kept her too busy to think about herself. Alison looked over her shoulder at scrubby piñon pine, sagebrush, and cactus, then ahead to willow bushes and cottonwood at the river's edge. The scenery wasn't changing.

At least she was moving. She could creep along on elbows and knees just like Tyler. Walking would be another matter entirely. Her ankle crunched when she tried to flex it, which felt disgusting, and the pain was a solid entity. No more throbbing. The hurt couldn't get larger. She was afraid to look at it.

She followed Tyler to a tumble of brush and boulders near the water's edge. He started moving again before she even sat up. Tyler's lips quirked at her look of dismay, and he lifted their water bottles. Pointed at her, at the ground, himself, and the river. He made walking motions with his fingers. Alison made a more universal gesture with hers. Tyler grinned and crawled away.

He thought they could get a kilometer today if they were lucky. Unless they were lottery-winning lucky there would be no hiding from any long-range surveillance tonight. There were still three more kilometers to go after the first one, just to get to the road. Alison wished she could jump to her feet and run screaming the whole way.

Tyler returned moving, and they crept onward together.

CHAPTER TWENTY-TWO

TYLER HEARD TRUCK TIRES CRUNCH on rock, and soon afterwards shouts and whoops echoed up and down the valley. Running footsteps and displaced gravel warned him that the party was heading his way a few minutes later. He tried to become one with the earth.

The two departing soldiers were only fifty meters away when they passed by, but then they were safely past, scrambling up the slope and gone.

Shadows were all the way across the valley now. The sky darkened to sapphire, and insects began making noise. The never-ending breeze whispered through brush and rattled cottonwood leaves. An airplane passed far overhead.

Tyler stood up and walked back to Alison. She was lying on her back smiling at the sky. "I think we're safe," she said. "Want to know why?"

"Not really." There was no telling how long the respite would last. Theories could wait. Tyler carried her piggyback, first to a stand of trees for a pit stop and then to the river. Alison made little grumbling noises in his ear the whole way. By the time they both had empty bladders and full water bottles, Alison was bursting at the seams with impatience.

"All right, tell me," Tyler said while he checked her foot.

"They close the borders at midnight, right?" she said. "I'll bet that the army ordered them away. If they stay away, then we can hike right out. I'll bet they don't. Come back, I mean. Hey, that tickles. *Ow!* And that *hurts.*"

Tyler had cut off her boot to restore circulation long ago. Her toes were the size and color of cocktail sausages. They were still warm, and that was the best Tyler could say about them. He touched the black, swollen ankle, felt the heat, and tried to keep his fears off his face. Alison watched him with big dark eyes and a scrunched-up nose and pretended she wasn't in agony. Her skin was gray under a nasty sunburn, and her forehead was as hot as her ankle.

They would not find decent shelter tonight, and it was getting cold. They hadn't eaten in two days. Alison couldn't walk. A desperate sense of failure rose up and choked Tyler. He was still horrible at taking care of people.

"Ready to do some dancing?" he asked.

Alison smiled. "I'd rather talk. We can't just leave them all trapped back there, but the only organization big enough to take on the CAF is the CSB. Tell me if this sounds crazy, because I think I know how to get them into the game."

Her ideas were crazy, and she sounded feverish, but the plan might actually work. Tyler told her so, and then he proceeded to help her build a coherent narrative out of her scattered thoughts.

He hoped it was all unnecessary. He really hoped that they'd spent two days hiding from people who weren't hunting for them. He hoped that in a few days' time Justin and the others would rejoin them, and everyone would make fun of him, and everything would be fine.

Hope aside, he was intellectually certain that Alison's more morbid guesses about Justin's situation were closer to the truth.

They'd never expected to face full-on pursuit in broad daylight, much less helicopter surveillance and a protracted ground search. Something had gone horribly wrong.

Orion rose. The soldiers didn't come back.

Alison fussed when Tyler picked her up and started walking. He threatened to sing her lullabies to make her be quiet.

"Let's keep working on our plan instead," she said.

It was their plan now, not hers. That was the one positive development in an unspeakably awful night. Before long, Alison was too weak to hold herself in place. Tyler rigged a sling under her butt, tied her arms to his belt in front, and kept walking. He was so tired by the time he reached the highway that he walked right across the shoulder onto the road and stood there looking at the smooth surface in complete confusion.

Walking right off the other side and over a small rise made perfect sense at the time. He set Alison down next to a boulder and shook her awake so they could watch the sun rise together.

A CAF TRANSPORT picked them up just after dawn.

Alison didn't question Tyler's decision to flag it down. She was too tired and too woozy to waste energy on little things like whether hitching a ride with the military was safe. Tyler had gotten her this far. She would trust him to take her the rest of the way.

He not only picked a safe ride, but also wheedled information out of the female driver and her truckload of passengers—including the one important fact that might make all of Alison's speculative plans necessary.

There had been no official military operation in their area. Unauthorized excursions had occurred. A certain amount of official fallout had rained down on an air unit that this group disliked. Details were gleefully shared.

Alison thought about the important things while they drove into town. She could be throwing away everything Carl and Justin were trying to accomplish. She was guessing blindly that they had failed. There was evidence, but evidence wasn't proof. Ignorance was not bliss. It was hell.

The soldiers dropped them off near an emergency clinic with a friendly warning that evacuation of the area would likely go from voluntary to compulsory in a day or two. Tyler bought new phones and clean clothes while the clinic decided that Alison needed more treatment than they could provide, and Alison made her calls on the way to a hospital.

She couldn't get past the local police station's main reception menu or the one for the closest Central unit, which was in Albuquerque. Making contact with a live representative of law enforcement took a call to Pete Hamil, who called someone he knew, who called someone else, who called Alison back. From there she was passed along to enough people and repeated her story so many times that Tyler had to make notes for her.

She'd imagined that turning herself in would be easy.

She was sitting on a gurney in Santa Fe waiting for surgery on her ankle before a CSB agent finally came for her, and the doctors wouldn't let him in, citing dehydration and shock, and throwing around the weight of medical judgment. When Alison woke up with a cast on her foot, the agent started asking questions again, but she couldn't understand him. The doctors chased him away for another twelve hours, with annoyed comments about general anesthetic and exposure and abuse of power.

"This is your official statement," the agent told her when they finally sat down to the task of bedside interrogation. "Start at the beginning."

"The beginning for me," she said, "was when I was recruited to become part of Dominic Walton's conspiracy to usurp the authority of the United States government."

Things got a little complicated after that.

THE VOICE that woke him said to walk, so Carl walked, stubbing bare toes on stairs as he climbed them. When the voice said sit, he sat blind. A tremor of emotion tugged at the indifference that held him captive like a leash and collar.

He could still feel fear. Mostly it lurked in the depths, a reminder to behave, to obey, to wait. Hate was swimming around down there too.

It wasn't Justin's fault that Carl had been too weak to ask for a bullet, but hate didn't have to be fair. Caution kept the hate buried, and the memory of pain held it in check, but hate was a patient thing. Its time would come.

The voice said to dress, and the hood came off. He was alone before his eyes adjusted to the glare illuminating a semicircle of floor. Cold air whispered across his skin. He put on the uniform waiting on the floor, stretching past the ache of bruised kidneys and separated ribs.

Those were the only injuries he'd taken, and those few had been inflicted during the initial struggle. Walton knew his weaknesses already. This time there had been no artificial barriers to protect him, nothing but his will to stand between resistance and compliance.

Willpower wasn't enough, not when he knew the consequences of rebellion so well. A few small reminders had broken him to obedience in no time at all.

It wasn't a proper harness. His leash had to be held tight to keep the hate from breaking free. He couldn't be used for much more than bullying, and he wouldn't last long under the strain.

That was one small, sick comfort. Another was that Parker had been such an early casualty. In his mind he saw a boot come down, heard the crack of breaking bone. He rode out a brief flare of grief.

His brother was nearby and past feeling pain, he knew that,

but that was no solace. He could only hope neither of them lasted much longer.

Two of the guards hauled a body into the light by the legs and shoulders. It was bound hand and foot and dressed in dirty, skintight black, and it lay where it was dropped when they yanked off the hood and departed.

Carl cleared his throat, and Justin jerked at the noise. There was a fearful, defeated quality to every line of his body language, and vindictive approval surged through Carl's mind. Misery did love company.

"Suck your toes," he said for the intense satisfaction of watching Justin try. And a few seconds later, ashamed of the impulse, he relented. "Stop."

Justin turned onto his side and groaned. Every bit of exposed skin was caked with dust, and a thin bruised line ran over one filthy cheekbone. A jagged scar showed against the stubble behind his ear, the first external evidence Carl had seen of the head injury from the plane crash.

"He left your hair." Justin's voice was a slurred, shattered whisper. Bloodshot eyes evaluated Carl's condition. "You're dressed. You're clean."

They'd kept him on the flooded lower level, bound, gagged, and lying blind with the cold water rising over his ears. They'd said the hair was too pretty to cut. They'd said and done a lot of things.

When the brain stewed in its own juices long enough, it was easy to mold even without pharmaceutical aid. Physical abuse triggered predictable reactions, carved deep channels that could take a lifetime to erase. Those channels were easy to reopen and flood a second time.

Hatred swelled. Carl's lips lifted in a snarl. "You think I'm grateful for it? You think Eddie was grateful? All he wanted was a fast, clean death. You dragged us into this, you arrogant bastard. You deserve whatever that sadist can dream up and worse."

Justin's eyes filled with tears. "I never—" he stopped to swallow. "They broke his arms like sticks and he never made a sound, and I was right there and I couldn't—*God*. Oh, God." He rolled over to hide his face.

Walton had shattered Parker's arms, not his spine. Carl slowly processed that revelation. A complex swell of emotion surfaced, yawned wide and swallowed the hate. Clarity washed through his mind in its wake and carried away everything else.

He'd been tossed together with Justin so that they could hurt each other, and that was exactly what they'd done: Justin out of ignorance, Carl for spite's sake.

He sat down and lifted a hand, waited out Justin's reflexive flinch, and wiped away tears and snot with his sleeve. This was beyond apologies. Cold advice was all he could offer.

"You need to kill me. I can't run neo protocols without the drugs, but I can read you and I can force snap responses. I will do it, Justin. I can't ..." He was weak. "Take me out while you can. One good solid kick to the base of the skull. I won't feel a thing."

"We're dead already. Why rush the finale?"

"I'm serious."

"So'm I. We're on hour eighty-three, give or take. Only twenty-two left. You don't get to go early if I don't. Wait." Justin sighed, sounding relieved. "I dropped a ten. Twelve hours max. Hundred hours total, plus or minus a few."

"You're so tired that you can't even add, but you think you know how long this has been going on? You're insane. Twelve hours until what?"

"Until the cells upstairs detonate regardless. The configuration isn't stable. Even if I don't make it, I still get the bastard. He dies, we die, everybody dies. One way or another, it's done."

The last words were emotionally flat. Carl looked at Justin without the filter of animosity and saw the price that had already been paid. Pinpoint pupils and glassy sclera, gaze unsteady. Skin dry and tight over the bones of hands and face. Tiny bruises at the hairline and jaw, muscles racked by shudders every few seconds.

Before too much longer he would do anything he was asked if it brought an end to the abuse. He had persuaded Carl with hope, but he had planned against failure. Not arrogant after all, only desperate and inspired.

"You never mentioned a deadline," Carl said.

"I didn't?" Justin's eyebrows drew together, and his eyes wavered. Then he moaned softly and thumped his head against the floor over and over. "No, of course I never said anything to you or Parker. Stupid skull full of goo. *Shit.*"

They had to be under surveillance even now—especially now—which meant Walton knew Justin's backup plan now too. If he wanted, he could leave Justin to die, take Carl as a consolation prize, and blow the perimeter by sacrificing whatever or whoever was necessary.

Carl pushed aside the terror of that future and moved to restrain Justin before he hurt himself. Justin struggled until Carl dragged the man all the way into his lap. Then he wriggled around until he was spooned close for maximum contact, buried his face against Carl's arm, and wept like an infant until he passed out.

He started to shudder soon after that, and his skin grew fever-hot. The handicap had to be a known factor, or Justin wouldn't have clothes at all. Walton wasn't going to let him die if it could be prevented, and he would never let him rest when he could push him harder instead.

Carl held on tight and waited. He sensed motion, out in the shadows, and then Walton brought him to heel with six heart-breaking words: "I can still hurt your brother."

"NEEDS TO BE WARMER, doesn't it?"

The voice was cheerful and loud, and it jolted Justin awake. One elbow slammed tile. Broken ceramic fell pattering down. His hands and feet were loose, and he was sitting cold and naked under a fall of water that was not quite hot enough to ease the chill in his body.

A work light set over a mirror blazed into the shower stall, and a figure moved across the glare. Justin stared at it until it came into focus. Parker met his eyes with a level, sardonic gaze. "They were afraid to scald you. Fucking morons. Go ahead and turn it up."

A shudder that had nothing to do with cold ran down Justin's back. He adjusted the water controls, and the hot water pounded into his skin.

Parker stood by the counter and watched. Like Carl and all of Walton's troops, he now wore a camouflage uniform. The blouse was open to accommodate straps holding one bandaged arm to his bare chest. The other arm hung in a cast at his side. The bandages were black with dry blood, and the fingers peeking out of the cast were dark red and swollen.

His head had been shaved like Justin's, although it wasn't much of a change from his usual cropped cut, and his left eye sported a greening bruise. The bandages smelled putrid. He tried out a cynical smile on the smug face. Stillness looked unnatural on him. It made him look like a statue of himself. A fake. A replacement.

Justin felt a new chill as Walton's long-term plan suddenly resolved into focus. Walton didn't want him as much as he wanted access to people Justin knew. To do unto Justin's friends and acquaintances what he'd done to Parker, what he'd already done to David Hong and who-knew-how-many others. Which brought Justin right back to: why? The situation was like a nesting doll that got uglier with each revealed layer.

He said, "Your left arm is rotting. Maybe both."

"Likely." Parker sounded unconcerned by the prospect. "It doesn't hurt. Can't feel my own prick, the drugs I'm on."

"What drugs? What did they do to you?"

"Don't ask me questions." Parker's smile grew sharp. He tapped his cheek, drawing Justin's attention to an earpiece. "They don't like it. How do you know when your toys will blow? How do you keep your internal clock up?"

Every word coming out of his mouth made Justin want to scream at the wrongness of it. "How doesn't matter, does it? I'm right. Ten hours now, or less. Has Carl seen you?"

"Not yet." Discomfort flickered over Parker's face. "Disarm the bomb and the mines and be done, Justin. They'll hurt you if you keep asking me questions."

"They'll hurt me anyway." Justin took a deep breath. "You're awful at good-cop, Parker. Why are you even trying? Why can't I ask you anything?"

Parker stepped back, and two more men came in. They efficiently hooded and hogtied Justin, and then they made him pay for disobeying the directive about questions. He'd all but invited the punishment.

They punished him, and they asked about disarming the power cells again, and they hurt him when they didn't like the truthful answers. He roused under the shower spray with Parker by the counter as if the interlude had never happened, except for the bruises marching up and down his arms and chest. Except for the blood seeping up. Except for the pain.

Flinching was no longer a reaction Justin could control. Nor was cowering. He did both when Parker knelt beside him, and even when nothing more happened for heartbeat after slamming heartbeat, the tears started.

He could not face that again. Couldn't do it. Couldn't.

"I'm fine," Parker said. He was barely audible over the shower. "It's all right. I know you don't understand, and I'm sorry for that. Sorry for this."

"*Stop.*" Justin whispered. He would've yelled it, but his voice was shredded from screaming. "You are dying on your feet. How can you not see that?"

Stark horror chased after Justin's realization that he'd unintentionally asked a question, but Parker only said, "Oh, I see it. I'm fine with it, that's all. They made me agreeable and docile like a big, neutered pit bull and moved right on to Carl and then to you. You two, you're prizes. I'm an expendable resource."

Justin blinked water out of his eyes. His jaw clenched tight against speaking. One question might be overlooked. A second would never pass unnoticed, and terror held him silent.

The corner of Parker's mouth rose. "I gave them the idea for that, you know. I spend a lot of time thinking about vulnerabilities, and they asked me how to hurt you."

He studied the thin rivulets of blood swirling down the drain, and his eyebrows quirked up. "That's how this works. You get that, right? I'm useful and functional, but it's a rush job, and it's all artificial."

His eyes were hard now, at odds with the weird smile. Justin wondered what message he was missing because his head was full of slushy pain. And then one of his handlers came in and asked, "Is he stable enough for another session?"

Parker rose to his feet, wobbling as if unsure of his balance. "As good as he'll ever get. Dress him up so we can all go have a chat with Carl."

The idea of that made Justin shrink inside, but it was what would come afterwards that he truly dreaded.

Soon. One way or another, it would be over soon.

CHAPTER TWENTY-THREE

JUSTIN'S HANDLERS DRESSED HIM, SECURED his hands behind his back, and brought him stumbling out of the bathroom into a room unexpectedly lit by sunshine. A cold fresh breeze blew inward from the uncovered row of shattered windows. The tops of the tarps still darkening the lower floors were secured to the lower sills.

All the open space felt unspeakably perilous. The world had been a place of glare and shadows for too long. Justin's brain locked up. When his body went limp, his handlers dropped him to his knees and held him there.

Walton stood in the doorway to the stairs, an impossible five meters distant. Carl was kneeling at his side. His eyes were shut, and he was being held upright by a tight-fisted grip in his hair. Someone had stripped off his shirt, and his hands were bound behind him. Old scars knotted his skin from shoulder to waist, an elaborate tracery of dots and lines that dove below the beltline. He swayed in place as Walton spoke to two soldiers in the stairwell.

The pair were strangers to Justin, and both carried slung rifles. They accepted their orders—keep everyone clear until further word—and once they left, Walton tugged at Carl's hair while he frowned into the distance. Finally he said, "You are an unbelievably aggravating little motherfucker, Dr. Wyatt. Tell me how to disarm whatever the hell that thing is upstairs."

"You can't," Justin said.

One of his handlers shifted a thumb onto a bruised point and leaned. Pain flamed up, and muscles cramped in response. Justin lay on his side quivering until it ebbed away. Walton said, "I'm running out of kinder gentler options. How do I disarm that booby-trap?"

"You can't," Justin whispered as he was lifted upright. "That's why I put the remote for the minefield up there. There are motion detectors, there's a dead-man trigger, there's inherent instability. That's all. It was a dirty improvisation. I never thought you would reject a perfectly reasonable deal."

Walton frowned and pointed to Parker, still waiting at the door to the bathroom. "You. Over here. Face-to-face."

Parker sent an unreadable glance at Justin in passing. He sank to his knees facing Carl as smoothly as if it were a choreographed routine. He was smiling again. "Hey, bro. You really need a harness and a ball gag to complete that look."

Carl's eyes popped open, and Walton yanked at his hair. "Prove you're worth keeping alive, blondie. Analyze my work. Tell me what I used on him."

"Neoscope and Provimate." Carl's voice shook at the ends of the words. "CSB calls the combo 'catnip,' court-approved for hostile interviews, lasts up to twenty-four hours per dose with diminished duration after repeated use. Pros: extreme pliancy and loss of inhibition, full access to knowledge base. Cons: euphoria, widespread somatic analgesia, high risk of permanent brai—"

Walton yanked his hair, stopping the recitation. "That's right. He's numb. Not suffering. Now Wyatt. Assess him."

"Severe wake-state instability, minimal self-awareness, diminished mental faculties, physically compromised, fully responsive to threat of duress. Withholding and deception defenses are eroding."

"Not fast enough. I need to know what he's hiding under that deception." Walton pulled Carl's head back. "Find me a shortcut, for your brother's sake."

He released Carl with a shove.

Carl came to his feet and circled Justin. He looked long and hard, with his head tipped to the side, and his eyes were full of loathing. Tangled hair fell across his face. He shook it back, returned to his place and dropped to his knees again to match stares with Parker.

"Bruises," he said. "How? He can take a hammer to himself without leaving marks."

Parker glanced up, and Walton said, "Go on, tell him."

"Needles," Parker said. "Inserted in or near nerves—slowly, to avoid triggering the hard-shell effect. Hit him, and they break off in place. Very effective, and they haven't touched anything major like nail beds or genitals yet. I'm thinking that's what they usually use the kit for."

Carl's chin sank to his chest. "There's your shortcut. He'll shatter in no time. You're at his stressor limits."

"Yes, but I need him visually intact and free from permanent damage." Walton contemplated Carl with a frown. "I wish it didn't have to be you, but he doesn't respond the same way to your brother, and too much is invested in this to give up now."

He gestured to one of Justin's handlers. The man went away and returned with reinforcements. The final tally for their side was six, and it took all of them to hold Carl down so they could administer a shot without ripping out a vein.

He sat up, after their retreat, and between gasping breaths he said, "This is a mistake. We've both betrayed him now. This isn't a stressor. It's reinforcing resistance."

Walton snorted. "You'd say anything right now. He cares. It

shows. Knowing he's responsible for—well. It will hurt him. Granted, it won't hurt him nearly as much as it'll hurt you."

Carl turned to Parker, "Kill me."

Justin's heart felt like a lump of stone in his chest.

"You know they thought of that," Parker said. "Direct order. 'Do not do anything your brother says to do.' "

His free hand moved towards the spot on his belt where a knife sheath usually sat, and understanding started to come together in Justin's head. All thought fled when Walton strode towards him.

Walton stopped well short and laughed. "The look on your face —you should've kept your mouth shut and let me slit your guard dog's throat at the start. He gave up your murder plot fast once we figured out what to ask. Here's what happens now. They will suffer for your lies until we run low on time here. I will clear a lane by calling in an air strike and blowing a crater in that hill if necessary. We will stand well out of range and watch you die here, and after that, they'll continue to suffer even if you won't."

He pitched his voice louder. "What does the Civilian Security Bureau call that dose we gave you, Dr. Jenson? You have to be feeling it already. You must remember it."

"Ballbreaker," Carl said in a dead tone. He was bent forward with knees splayed, head to the floor. Every breath was a gasp. "Avanifil, PT-141, and a neurotransmitter cocktail that induces cutaneous allodynia. Popular in the BDSM community on release, fell out of favor fast. Also known as Pray-for-Death."

Walton gave Justin a smile that was worse than Parker's for insincerity. "In simple terms, it'll get him up, keep him up, and leave him in screaming pain when anything touches him." He cleared his throat. "We'll add water to the stimulus menu since we have it. It should be an interesting exercise."

The lump in Justin's chest rose into his throat.

"I doubt the repair job on his sanity will hold. Cardiac arrest and internal damage are also dangers." Walton shrugged. "If he doesn't last, I will jack up the brother. You can sit and watch until they are catatonic or bleeding out, or you can tell me how to disarm your trap. Do that, and we all walk out of here alive and mostly intact. Your choice. I have nothing to lose."

He backed away and gestured to the handlers. "Downstairs."

THE CSB AGENT next to Alison cleared his throat. "Your story had more holes in it than a block of Swiss cheese," he said. "You know I know that, right?"

He was tall, with cinnamon-brown skin, dark chocolate eyes, and a crooked nose that kept his face from being too pretty. He had a kind smile and an easy manner, and he was relentless.

Alison shifted her weight off her crutches to gesture at the scene in front of them. "And yet here we are, and there *they* are."

The CSB units had mobilized before dawn, but the sun had been well up before they arrived here. She and Tyler stood beside the agent's rental car, which was parked at the rear of a protective herd of more substantial vehicles. Local and district-level police trucks and patrol units were taking up a healthy chunk of roadside near the bottom of the hill leading to the canyon house.

The house roof and a piece of mangled security fence were visible from Alison's position. She could also see the six unmarked trucks and forty-odd uniformed people near the top of the slope. Between the two groups sat a wide swath of desert that no one wanted to test.

The first arrivals had been frantically waved back by the soldiers inside the perimeter, and after a shouted exchange of no-one-wants-to-shoot-anyone assurances, things had settled into the current frenzy of nothing happening.

The immediate area was swarming with armed personnel doing incomprehensible things, and off to either side in the scrub, pairs of men in gray coveralls with "CSB" across the back were using backpack paint sprayers to mark a safe line using maps that Alison had marked for them.

Communicating with the trapped soldiers was proving difficult. Phones weren't working. Neither were radios. Shouting wasn't terribly effective.

Alison's fear was like a hole in her gut. Her narrative had contained all the right keywords to get official eyes pointed in the right direction, but all she'd done was break a stalemate. That crew had been up there for well over three days.

Justin was there too, with Carl and Parker—and Walton. She knew that in her bones, but she didn't know what had happened. This might all be a useless effort. The people she wanted to save might not welcome this interference. They might've had everything well in hand all along.

Then again, they might be dead already. Worse, they might be dead *because* of her if they'd been captured alive and Walton's response to exposure turned out to be "bury the evidence and talk fast."

She pushed aside the fear and said, "I said you had an unsanctioned paramilitary operation behind your lines. I said the situation was contained but unstable. I even gave you all the tactical data I could remember. I've delivered."

"Touché. There are definitely shenanigans going on." The agent snorted. "Double-checks on your statement set off alarms all over the place. This response team would be here even if we weren't."

Tyler slid his arm around Alison's waist and took some of her weight off her injured leg. "Why *are* we here?" he asked. "I mean, we want to be, but I thought we'd have to fight to get clearance."

The agent had a wicked smile. "Think of it as protective custody. We don't let people who drop leads like this on us fade into the woodwork. I believe you've fallen into something so bad that you committed perjury to see it straightened out. I respect that enough to let you see it cleaned up. Now respect me and tell me what it really is."

Alison took a breath, then let it out. She had no idea where to start. Tyler said, "Look, Agent—what's your name again?"

"Patterson. Dan, if you finally want to be friendly."

"Agent Patterson, the truth sounds crazier than Allie's fairy tale."

"Crazier than a scorned lover going straight and betraying a multigenerational conspiracy that's been starting domestic conflicts with corporate support since Restoration? Nothing can top that."

Alison exchanged a look with Tyler, and he started talking. She filled in gaps. When they were done, Agent Patterson looked uphill. Muscles knotted and relaxed under the warm brown skin of his jaw as if he were holding in a smile.

"Well," he said heavily, "I can't be right every time."

CARL MADE it to the lower level under his own power before he couldn't take any more. Air hurt his skin. The rasp of cloth was beyond excruciating. The hands against his back, pushing him forward, left seared imprints on his flesh.

The bottom floor was still a shadowy cave, and the icy floodwater was well over his ankles now. The water was blackly opaque, its rippling surface broken here and there by lumpy islands of debris pitched down from higher floors. A tool kit and an attaché case sat on the kitchen counter in a zone illuminated by flashlight.

In minutes his nerves would move from clamoring overload to shrieking madness. He let himself fall forward. The chill water that should've been soothing felt worse than the air. Too much pressure. Too much sensation.

Too much.

With an inaudible snap he was a passenger in his own body: a numb, peaceful passenger in a body lying facedown in dirty water in the dark. Water rushed down his throat when he gasped in relief.

They rolled him over and hauled him to his feet again. There were three of them, two nearly as big as he was, one closer to Parker's rangy height.

Parker himself was standing on the last dry stair watching the commotion with a single guard at his side. He looked as placid as a cow, but he was fighting the giddy compulsion to be helpful with all his might. Carl had seen that in the guarded flashes of hatred. He'd heard it in the hints Parker kept tossing in vain at Justin.

Justin was too far gone to understand clues, so tired that he was blinking out for seconds at a time, wholly unaware of the gaps in consciousness. Even when he was nominally awake, his forebrain was drowning in toxins that would warp logic and make irrational choices seem inevitable.

Carl retched up water, but he felt no real connection to his body even when he started to quake with an urgency bordering on delirium, even when every touch ripped loose sobs and screams, even when agony flared impossibly high. He was numb *inside,* detached from it all where it mattered.

Gratitude and fear were what he felt most. Gratitude, because defenses he hadn't known existed were holding firm against the fires of hell and preventing total obliteration. Fear, because he needed Justin to be hardheaded and calculating and stick to his own plan for a few more hours so that this could *end*.

And he knew Justin wouldn't last.

JUSTIN'S two remaining handlers kept him alert by the simple expedient of hurting him whenever he closed his eyes. They also secured his hands in front so that they could hold him upright. Walton sat above them on the stairs, well out of reach. He offered dispassionate commentary while he folded the discarded uniforms his subordinates had stripped off before getting to work.

Parker was ordered to sit down because he was blocking the view, but he said nothing—*did* nothing—about what was happening right in front of him. He watched with a bland, disinterested stare from the lowest dry step. The guard sitting above him looked more disgusted than he did. That was almost the most obscene aspect of the situation.

The worst part was that Justin could have stopped it before it started. He didn't. He waited.

He waited until long after Carl was bleeding, choking, crying. He held out until long after he hated himself for it. Finally he heard himself saying, "Stop it. I'll tell you what you were missing. I'll tell you what you want. I'll do whatever you want. Just please make them stop."

"You first." Walton sounded indifferent, but when Justin stood up and turned away from the horror show, his handlers allowed it. He felt the steps wobble, knew that he was the one wobbling, and moved up a step to brace his hand on the wall.

One step closer. One step away from his handlers, who were paying more appalled attention to their comrades than to him. He said, "I need a screwdriver or a pen or a knife."

"What? I can't hear you."

Justin repeated it as loudly as his abused vocal cords would allow, adding, "You can't stop the timer, but I can. You've seen what a shock does to me. With access to the electrical system I can spoof the sensors, walk in, and deactivate it. That's what I was hiding. That's all I have to do, I swear."

"Hey, big dog, is he telling the truth?" Walton asked.

Parker said, "More or less. He doesn't need tools. None of the outlets are covered yet. Look at the ones on the stairs here. He can pull out any live wires he wants."

The murderous look on Walton's face came and went in a

blink. "Still trying to work the angles even now. You'll pay for that later."

He let out a piercing whistle that froze all motion for a moment. The moment didn't last. His three men went back to what they were doing after only the barest hesitation. The sobs and other noises didn't pause at all.

Walton snapped his fingers and sent Parker's guard to intervene, but the others shoved him out of the way. After a moment, Justin's handlers waded into the fray to help.

Fear and doubt shrieked at Justin to wait, but he could not waste the opportunity he'd worked so hard to create. He was elbows-deep in the wall outlet two stairs up before he could second-guess himself into paralysis. A half-second after that he wasn't tired, he wasn't hurting, and he wasn't visible. He went up one more step and another without hesitation or limping or pain, and Walton was unconscious on the stairs before he knew what had hit him.

Unconscious or dead: Justin couldn't tell which. He didn't care.

"Hey, Parker." His voice wasn't even a whisper. He swallowed hard, tasted blood. "Parker, look at me."

Parker didn't turn. Justin sank to the stairs as his strength began to seep away fast. Desperate panic rose. He couldn't do the rest alone. "Parker!"

Nothing. *"Eddie!"*

Parker swung around, and his eyes flicked up and back, seeing nothing. The smile vanished.

Justin said, "Go rescue your brother."

THE AIR BURNED against Carl's skin. He opened his eyes, squinted them shut again. Light burned too. His legs were cold and wet and burning all at once, and his jaw ached. Every last cell of his body burned and pulsed with pain. He willed the numbness to return, but it had worn off.

When he moaned, the vibration seared his throat.

"Can you hear me?" Justin whispered. "Please wake up. We don't know what else is safe to give you. Is it helping at all? Can you please say something?"

Water rose against Carl's legs. Blazing pain shot up his spine and charred the inside of his skull. "Are you trying to kill me?" he snarled.

"No, I'm trying—" Justin's voice cracked. He coughed and shifted his weight.

Water splashed again with agonizing force, and Carl came to his feet cursing. The only reason he didn't fall down again was that he had the kitchen island at his back. Adhesive pinched at throat, elbows, belly, and thighs. The anesthetic patches slowly dulled his nerves to a manageable level of input.

The room was no longer dark. The tarps were down. The muddy water outside the French doors was well over a meter high. Water poured into the room through pressure-weakened joints between the two panels. The pattering fall of liquid sounded like a fountain.

Justin and Parker were in front of him, and beyond them, six bodies were draped over six different stacks of debris like bizarre works of art. Two of them were secured with zip ties. The other four were past needing restraints. A seventh man lay bound, gagged, and blindfolded in the fireplace alcove with little more than his face above the water.

Ripples traveled in all directions as Walton struggled to free himself. Carl caught his breath. It hurt.

Justin whispered, "He's real, Carl. He's all yours. We saved him for you." He lurched sideways, the water surged again.

Agony lanced through Carl's body again, wiping away all ability to comprehend Justin's words. "Get the hell away from me," he said through gritted teeth.

"I'm going." Justin sloshed towards the stairs. "See? I'm already gone."

Carl turned to Parker and finally managed to inhale. "You took him out? I don't know how—I don't care—thank you."

"That's a joke, right?" Parker gestured with the arm that was in a battered cast. The nails on that hand were black. The other arm was freshly bandaged and freshly stained with blood. "Thank Justin. It was all him. Fucking maniac said, 'Rescue your brother,' and while he was patching me up it was 'Stop creeping me out and talk like yourself.' My favorite: 'Do what you think you should, not what anyone else tells you, until that shit wears off.' Which it hasn't."

"Obviously." The easy verbal response and the relaxed expression proved he was still under the influence of the interrogation drugs. Carl's mind blanked trying to wrap meaning around the situation while he stared at his brother's arms.

The bandages were clean, his injuries stabilized, and he was feeling no pain. Justin had already done everything for him that could be done under the circumstances, just as he'd done for Carl.

A crinkling sound brought his attention back to reality. Justin stood on the stairs halfway up to the next level. He wore an outsized camouflage shirt over the bodysuit now, and he was stuffing empty foil wrappers into a pocket.

The man had done the impossible, and Carl had kicked him in the teeth over the petty details. That had to be the single cruelest thing he had ever done in his life. Pain or no, it was inexcusable. Shame welled up. "Justin, I am an ungrateful asshole. I'm so sorry."

"Don't be," Justin replied in that ragged whispery voice. "Clothes here should fit you. Walton's medical kit is on the counter. When you feel up to yelling at me little more, I'll be in the loft with the ticking time bomb."

He awkwardly pulled on a pair of pants, rolled up the cuffs, and started up the steps. Parker called after him, "Front door first —make sure it's locked."

Justin slipped and nearly fell when he tried to wave.

Carl stared after him, baffled. "Yell at him *more*? Why?"

"Let it go," Parker said once the man was out of sight. "Don't expect sense from a sleep-deprived torture survivor. Get your own brain in working order."

Being alive took some time to accept. He was alive with Parker silently fidgeting at his side when he had fully expected them both to be long dead by now, and that was too much to believe. He got dressed and sat on the stairs, and Parker brought the pills and the injector he requested, and little by little the physical clamor died down.

Rational thoughts crept out of hiding. "You want to go stomp on Walton's arms?" he asked Parker. "You're looking at total rebuilds on both yours if the left one's salvageable at all. And Justin deserves a better apology. I can wait."

Parker snorted. "You want Justin to feel better? Go and squeeze Walton dry. I'll watch over Justin until you're done."

"Thank you." Carl went to the counter to grab the rest of Walton's supplies. He had ghosts to exorcise.

CHAPTER TWENTY-FOUR

CLIMBING THE STAIRS TOOK EVERYTHING Justin had left. He leaned against the wall inside the loft doorway and waited for his vision to clear. When it did, Tyler's mathematical notations caught his wandering attention.

The control unit for the mines and the little explosive gadget he'd slapped together were sitting on a scrawl about power conservation and wave forms. He crawled into the room and pulled two wires.

The sound of footsteps behind him tightened all his muscles into knots, and he caught himself on one hand to keep from pitching onto his side.

Parker stood in the doorway with an odd look on his face. His gaze went to the disabled device and back up.

"Bluff." The look was smug glee. "Knew it. You needed the power boost for the strength to take him out."

"I'm so damned weak." Justin felt hollow inside. "Early on I could've hit him cold, but he wouldn't get close because you spilled that plan, and I got so tired, so shaky. So *stupid*. I thought of the cells here. I didn't even see the stairwell outlets. When I realized that you'd caught on, I was terrified that you'd warn him."

"Only if he asked a direct question," Parker said. "Was it all bluff?"

"No, there are proximity and signal-loss triggers keyed to my biometrics. They would've gone dead in a few days when the maintenance charge bled down, just like the mines. I slipped a lie about a detonation deadline to him through Carl. That was a lucky break. I thought I'd have to play delirious to get them to listen."

Parker was staring. Waiting for the rest.

"I had to push him to switch tactics. He had me. One more session of—" he couldn't even bear to talk about it. "—and I would've done anything they asked, I would've lost my nerve and shut this down, and we all would've died at the perimeter line."

The weight of Parker's gaze was too heavy to bear. Justin went to the window to escape it. "I never thought he would do what he did. I thought he would use Carl to push me directly, with neo tricks. That would've been perfect. It would've been easy."

"Easy," Parker said. "Except that Walton only trusted the tried and true. You couldn't know that."

"I thought he'd go after me." Justin rested his head against the window pane. He didn't have the energy to cry. "But he went after Carl, and he had to believe that I didn't want to give in, or he never would've let down his guard. I had to *wait*."

People had moved into the area outside the minefield, but he couldn't bring any of it into focus. Literally too tired to see straight: Tyler would see a joke in that.

That thought cracked open the box holding all the precious things Justin had laid aside because they were too painful to contemplate. He stopped the fear before it clawed its way out and closed the lid on it again. Alison and Tyler had gotten away. He had to believe that.

Parker crowded him away from the exposed position and peered out the window from the side. "No blame on you," he said. "Guilty one's downstairs getting what's coming to him. Don't take

Carl's bitching seriously. He's a shit when he's in pain, and he can't help—holy fuck."

"Trouble?" Justin's knees went weak. He sat down, huddling into a ball. "Already? We should have hours yet before anyone tries to get in. Walton left orders."

"No." Parker laughed, then looked down at Justin and sobered fast. "Not trouble, Justin. Cavalry's here. That isn't Walton's crew, out past the perimeter. Those are Civilian Security logos."

That was a good thing. Justin put his aching head on his knees and wondered why he couldn't seem to care. Parker scuffed past him and shouted downstairs. "Carl! Put that on ice, and come see this."

Justin heard more shuffling and felt a sense of heat and presence. Parker nudged him with a toe. "You can't see, can you?" he said. "Alison is down there in the middle of the CSB rank and file."

The second round of happy news was just as hard to process as the first had been. Justin knew he should be thrilled, but the only emotion he could raise was a sense of wretched misery.

Time stopped, and then he was on his feet gasping, fighting something soft and yielding. Carl caught him by the shoulders. "Easy, now. It's only a sleeping bag. You need to stay warm. Settle down."

Justin stopped struggling and dropped to the floor again. He hit Parker's feet on landing. Everything hurt, and nothing made sense.

Parker dragged the sleeping bag over him one-handed, then awkwardly wrapped himself in a second one. He shoved a knapsack and a canteen against the wall with his foot, and then settled on the window sill.

"From the second floor," he said when he saw Justin staring at the gear. "Their prep area. Where I slept and you didn't, lately."

The world slowly put itself back in order, and Justin choked on emotions so mixed that he couldn't put names to any of them. The floor refused to swallow him whole.

Carl knelt down. "Me and my big mouth."

He took Justin's chin in hand and forced eye contact. "Don't you dare implode now. Not over me. Not over this. If I have to tell Alison I broke her boyfriend, she will skin me alive, and I would deserve it. Don't blame yourself."

He looked concerned, when he had every right to feel hate. His voice was firm and warm, not bitter, not full of justified wrath. Justin whispered, "I'm so sorry. I never imagined he would do something like that. He wanted *me* suffering."

"And you did. Probably more than me, frankly. I owe Pete a huge thank-you for his extra tape and glue."

"What?"

"Never mind. Think on this: you *played* him." Carl's smile was feral. "I can do a lot with that. I can't wait to see his face when he hears it."

"Carl—"

"Stop."

Justin stopped. Carl released his jaw and stood up. "I need time to work on Walton. You need to sleep before you go psychotic on us. Eddie needs to let that catnip wear off before he gets anywhere near the Feds. Give me a few hours, and then we'll go and face the world together. That's all I ask. Until then, stay there and rest. Will you do that?"

Justin nodded.

CARL WENT UPSTAIRS, and the past stayed in the dark and the wet and the cold. It felt good. As soon as he cleared the loft doorway, Parker said in a low voice, "Still can't kill the fucker?"

"I'd rather see him suffer," Carl said, equally quiet. "What's the status on that catnip dose? You must have a good idea, often as you've been on it."

"Pain's bleeding through. Hour or two more, at most." Parker pushed himself to his feet. The sleeping bag slid to the floor near Justin, who grasped at the quilted cloth and pulled it around himself without waking.

Carl knelt to take a closer look.

Justin's sunken eye sockets were almost as dark as the scruffy beard covering his hollowed cheeks, and three days fasting had melted flesh off his bones. The pinpoint bruises were larger and darker now, and the tan of his skin was shading towards gray. He'd used weakness as a tool, counted on vulnerability being seen and used against him. He had known he was going to hit bottom and used the downward momentum to get where he needed to go.

Carl wondered what the man had been like before his brain was half-jellied in a plane crash. "How is he?"

"Better." Parker waggled his head. "Bad. Missing teeth, can't chew. Bolts awake at every loud noise, crashes again fast. Got energy gel and water into him."

Carl gently touched one of the dark spots on Justin's wrist. A hard knot shifted, glinting in the light. He eased up the man's sleeve. Metal slivers pattered to the floor. Bloody dots marched up Justin's forearm. Carl's skin crawled. "You are one twisted individual, Eddie. Lucky his body's rejecting the needles like this. Imagine digging them out one by one."

"Their needles. They asked."

The tight words buzzed with guilt and came out a little too loud. Justin woke in the same rocketing panic as earlier: on his feet and flailing before his eyes opened. This time he recovered without the wholesale disorientation. He lay flat on the floor with an aggravated expression while he got his breathing under control. It took a while.

"How long can I expect that to keep happening?" he asked. "Because it's getting really old, really fast."

Criticism would break that calm shell like a hammer on ice. Even humor might shatter him. Analysis was Justin's way of coping, even when it sounded whiny. Even when he could barely speak.

Carl gave him cold facts. "Assume every time you sleep for the first few months, unpredictably forever afterward. The faster you get into therapy, the better. Be smart. I wasn't."

"Wonderful." Justin's sigh turned into a squeak, and then he started stripping off the uniform and the base layer with frantic haste. A few undignified minutes later a substantial pile of needle tips had been collected, and he was naked and shivering.

"This sucks," was his succinct commentary on finding himself unable to dress again without help. He glanced at Parker and winced. "Sorry. It isn't self-pity. It's only that I promised myself we'd all walk out of here on our own or not at all, and I don't think I can walk."

"You got us this far," Carl reminded him. "Let us carry you the rest of the way."

Justin looked up, and dark emotions rose in his eyes. "Carry me downstairs first," he said. "I want to talk to him before we go. I want to give him a *choice*."

TYLER WAS TAKEN off to one of the vans for questioning by a new pair of agents, and Agent Patterson spent the whole morning asking Alison questions at a table in one of several tents set up in the center of the staging area.

The side flaps were up, and the canopy overhead snapped in a constant breeze. Alison huddled in her seat and kept a tight rein on her temper while she went over everything again and again. Shortly after she'd resorted to playing "what-would-Parker-say," Patterson called a break for lunch.

Shouts from the top of the hill interrupted a silent meal of awful sandwiches and oversweet hot chocolate. Alison looked up towards the house she couldn't see, and her mouth went so dry that she couldn't swallow.

Patterson's face was an officious blank, but his eyes were warm with sympathy. He handed over Alison's crutches and escorted her to the van where Tyler had disappeared earlier.

The rear doors opened on a bewildering forest of consoles, screens, and control panels both virtual and physical. Tyler was kicked back in a station chair with a datapad in his lap and two agents bracketing him. All eyes were on a display showing a fuzzy high-angle shot of the house from the roof. The front door wasn't visible, but a gathering crowd was. Then a second view split the screen, this one from the north with a sightline on the garage and the front door.

"That just started," one of the agents said. "Phones are back up too."

The front door of the house opened. Two men stumbled out, and one fell to the ground. Their hands were bound behind them and their feet were shackled. Alison's heart lurched, but the panic receded when she saw they were strangers.

"Human shields," Patterson murmured, probably for Alison's benefit. "For whoever started the broadcast, maybe. What next?"

Parker emerged next. He prodded the first two men forward with kicks, and then Carl came out. He was carrying something close against his chest. Alison stopped breathing when she recognized the limp form, and she gasped when Justin finally moved. Tyler came to kneel beside her at the back of the van.

"They're okay," he said as if convincing himself as much as her. "They're alive."

"Yes, but where's Waldo?" Patterson shook his head when the techs darted irritated looks at him. "What? You were all thinking it. Somebody had to say it out loud. I meant Walton, of course. He has to be there."

Discussion ensued on the hilltop, and Parker started ordering people around. The CSB side of the no-man's-land buzzed with activity as well. Carl set down Justin so he could play with what looked like a remote control, then scooped him up again despite visible protests. They headed for the road.

Alison turned away from the screen and moved as fast as her crutches would allow. Tyler and Patterson cleared the way. At the edge of the safety zone Alison put both feet right on the paint line and waited.

Carl and Parker were trailing a crowd as they walked slowly down the hill. Patterson said, "And that, boys and girls, is how the Pied Piper got all the rats out of the city." His smile faded when the parade reached the point where all the faces were clear. He pulled out a phone handset.

"Hi, Deecie," he said. "I need Neil here soonest. Bureau flight, CAF, charter, priority commercial, whatever it takes. I'll run it through channels, but get him out the—what?"

He sent a snapshot of Carl. "That's why, plus a story that nearly beats yours for knots. Neil can untangle this total goatfuck. I can only contain it. I'll make sure he gets comp leave. Thanks. Kiss the babies for me."

The phone went back onto its clip. Patterson said, "So much for all that earnest full disclosure. You never once mentioned that one of your buddies was a CSB security asset. That would've been useful to know before now."

Alison was too busy holding her breath again to ask him what he meant. Carl stepped across the paint line, and Justin was right there in front of her. He was scruffy and nearly bald, and he looked so sick and fragile that Alison had to wrap herself around him to reassure herself that he was real. His arms shook as he hugged her back.

"Hey, gimpy," he whispered in her ear. "Good to see you."

It was perfect until all of them were swarmed by CSB personnel who wanted to talk and push and shove and help.

Patterson pulled people aside and created a bubble of private space within all the activity.

"Your file says 'all possible discretion,' " he said to Carl. "You've made that tricky, but I have clearance to debrief, and proper authority's en route to repair all the holes in your camouflage. Tell me what you need."

Carl looked as confused as Alison felt. His eyebrows drew together, and he took several deep breaths before attempting speech. "Let's start with someplace warm to rest, ASAP. Priorities are medical attention and chain-of-custody assurance for legally radioactive evidence."

Justin whispered at him. Carl added, "Also, keep your people on the road and away from the house."

Inside ten minutes they'd been cleared by some grumpy medical personnel, and Agent Patterson herded them into a work tent. The side flaps came down, and a space heater was cranked up high. Justin dropped into the seat closest to the heat and punched numbers onto the keypad of his gadget. When he sat back and closed his eyes, he went from looking exhausted to looking dead.

Alison sat beside him and slid her fingers over the pulse in his wrist for reassurance. Tyler took the chair on her other side, and Parker settled at her feet with a groan. He leaned against her leg. She patted him on the head.

Carl remained standing. His visible bruise collection included bite impressions and dark finger marks on the sides and back of his neck. Alison stopped staring when he slid a frown her way.

"Discreet and medical aren't easy to put together," Patterson said with a worried look at all of them from the doorway. "Not locally. Since the EMTs say no time-critical issues and doled out happy juice and antibiotics, I'd prefer to let proper clout get you to decent facilities. Three or four hours. There's water, coffee, and bad sandwiches coming."

"I'm out of patience," Tyler announced. "What's a security

asset, what does it have to do with us, and what the hell is going on?"

Carl looked to Patterson before saying, "I'm a security asset. The CSB built me a new identity, back when Rydder Institute would've buried me. I occasionally do work for them that Rydder won't approve, and the CSB occasionally provides me with investigative data. Beyond that, I'm as confused as you are. I have no official status."

"Yes, but you are memorable," Patterson said. "And I'm a Central asset too. The kind who approves requests from other Central assets in the field." He added to Tyler and Alison, "If we need him, we get in contact through cutouts. Keeps him off-book and gives us deniability. If his biometrics pop up on our radar—if he gets in trouble playing hero, for example—we keep the locals pacified and slide him back into hiding."

"That only happened once," Carl said, sounding peeved. "And when did our barter arrangement get upgraded to a full aid-and-assist?"

"Officially? It hasn't. But if you tell me you weren't up there milking a traitor dry, I'll call you a liar. You've earned whatever support we can give, and I intend to see that you get it. My boss says I should use initiative. I'm initiating."

"Fine. Initiate this." Carl shrugged a shoulder to slide the knapsack to hand, offered it up. "Careful of the sharps. I collected all the medical waste along with the unused drugs. Some of it has Rydder stock labels. There's a huge, gaping security breach you'll want to plug. There's also a long written confession from Dominic Walton in there."

"Written? No visual record? What did you do to him?"

"I left him in the house to wait for arrest. Parading him in front of his men would've been crass, not to mention dangerous. There's video too, but the cracked jaw made his words a little garbled. Blame Justin for that."

Justin's arm flexed under Alison's hand. He whispered, "Tell me when you're ready to retrieve him. Right now the place is rigged to blow if he moves off the lower level. I don't want your people getting hurt."

He didn't even bother opening his eyes. Alison tightened her grip on him.

Parker craned his head around. "Rigged?"

Justin's lips curved into a thin smile.

"That's why you were down on the patio that morning," Carl said with an air of revelation. "You booby-trapped the house that early? You never said a word about it."

Justin shifted his hand to twine his fingers with Alison's. "I was feeling paranoid, and you were already yelling at me. They were my real backup plan, in case things went wrong, which things did. Even if Walton got me to disarm the showpiece in the loft, he still died. We died too, though. All the rest of it was my fault, because I was selfish and I didn't want to have to die to win."

Carl sat back. "One way or another, you said. Damn, Justin. That's why you wanted to talk to him, isn't it? It wasn't gloating. You needed his biometrics to reprogram the trigger specs."

"One way or another, he lost. I promised you that. I promised myself. Now he can face arrest and trial or not. He gave me a choice. I gave him one."

"Can I get a summary of his statement while we're waiting for my omnipotent partner?" Patterson asked. "I'd like to know how many lies I'll be putting in the official report. Walton's been building a private army, right?"

"By subverting low-level CAF commands, yes. You already suspected that, but did you know that he was doing it by guaranteeing personal loyalty? Your psychs will recognize the formulary. He had hooks into decision makers for over a dozen major businesses too. He didn't pull the lines often, but he admitted to causing two market crashes and some other chaos. There's probably more if you dig . I have pretty extensive records of his activities over the last five years. I'll get the Bureau copies. You'll need major support from Rydder Institute for the cleanup, but you're on your own with that."

Patterson's eyebrows shot up. Carl watched and waited until the agent said, "Personal vendetta?"

"At first. Now it's more. Today, I learned that Walton was never working solo. He's one of a loosely affiliated group of people who have no real agenda beyond creating one crisis after another for mutual profit."

Alison jerked upright. Carl paused to observe her and Tyler while Patterson laughed under his breath. Carl said, "Did you make up a conspiracy theory to get the authorities out here? I wondered. This was a welcome sight, I admit. I wasn't looking forward to wheedling our way past Walton's pack of angry underlings."

Tyler said, "Yeah? Well, we were worrying that we'd get you killed by trying to help."

"You're lucky you didn't. If Justin hadn't maneuvered Walton into a lockdown, that's what would've happened."

"If I'm not allowed to feel guilty, no one is," Justin whispered. "Finish the story. I'm enjoying it."

Carl rubbed both hands over his face. "I don't have much more. There are two names in the report. The group is heavily compartmentalized, and they're the only ones Walton knew. He spent most his time ranting and cursing them for getting him into this."

Patterson made a move-along gesture.

"His original focus was the paramilitary buildup but he's an opportunist. That's what got him into trouble. When David Hong came fishing for a partner, it was like handing whiskey to an alcoholic. Walton's confederates had been encouraging him to target Wyatt Enterprises for reasons of their own. They knew about his CAF schemes. They played his weakness; if he took out the head of the company and shook it up again less than a year later, he would scoop up technology that would be invaluable to his military plans."

"But Wyatt wasn't dead after all," Patterson said with a look at Justin. "So Walton wasn't going to get his shiny toys *or* ruin the company he was supposed to sink. Not without Wyatt. Oh, man. You lured him out here?"

"Motherfucker called me salvage," Justin said.

Carl said, "We only knew about the tech facet at first, but yes, we laid a trap."

After a peek into the knapsack, Patterson said, "Nice work."

A bright flash like reflected sunlight lit the tent wall, and a cracking rumble of noise followed. Debris pattered down with a sound like rain.

"You did tell him that the diagrams in the loft held the keys to building the mines and everything else," Carl remarked into the silence afterwards.

"I left his handset and a knife on the stairs, too." Justin yawned. "Careless of me."

He opened his eyes, and the look he sent Agent Patterson was cold. He lifted his gadget in both hands. "You don't get this. Nobody gets it. Not Walton, not the Fed. I will blow the whole perimeter as soon as I won't blow us all up doing it. Don't mess with it. You'll kill people. It's mine, I'm not sharing, and all I want is for me and mine to be left in peace. Clear?"

Patterson's nod was firm and serious, but his mouth slowly worked itself into a smile. "Clear as glass, Dr. Wyatt. You've done more than enough already. Sit back and relax."

Alison scooted over despite a pained protest from Parker and put her head on Justin's shoulder. "Me and mine?" she said softly, and Justin tensed.

"Only if you want to be."

She stretched to kiss him on the ear. "Mine."

AFTERMATH

CLEAR SKIES AND SUNSHINE were winter rarities in Seattle, but the weather for Alison's real estate closing cooperated by providing picture-postcard views from her new loft studio. All the mountains were out, and Rainier was majestic against the rosy evening sky.

Justin sat on the floor inside the door and watched Alison, not the view. She sat on a box and stared out the window until the pink clouds dimmed to blues and black. The whole time she wore a smile that hinted at secrets and sadness, and Justin couldn't take his eyes off her.

She had to know he was here. The elevator was efficient, not silent, and hers was the only unit on the floor. She hadn't even turned to look when he'd arrived an hour earlier. Justin had no idea what to say, so he sat and waited.

She'd let him in. That was a start.

"Mine," she'd said, but that had been three months and a lot of changes ago. They'd taken a long crooked path to this day and place and abandoned a lot of things along the way. Certain topics were ignored. People moved on.

Tyler was at the University of Chicago exploring a world Justin could no longer visit except in short, bright glimpses that were as frustrating as they were transcendent. They spoke nearly every day, but it wasn't the same, and Justin missed him fiercely. Selfish maybe, but he couldn't help it, just as he couldn't help tuning out painful details when Tyler went on and on about ideas. He tried to be happy for Tyler's sake and mostly succeeded.

Parker was here in Seattle, but between surgeries and therapy and anti-infection isolation, he might as well be on the moon. Carl's time was split between supporting his brother and helping the CSB wrap up the aftermath of Walton's confession. He was friendly and welcoming, whenever Justin worked up the courage to visit the rehab center, but the demons they were both still wrestling showed up at awkward moments.

His own psychologist said that his insanities were healthy enough to go on with, in her pithy phrasing, and she gave Justin patient looks when he admitted that he still felt guilty. Alison had recommended her.

"Mine," she'd said, but Justin hadn't been easy to live with, the last little while. Not that he'd ever been easy.

In the kitchen area to his left, inset lights over the counter and stove turned themselves on. Alison turned, and her smile brightened. "Hiya. How was your day?"

"You should know, you scheduled it. Endless back-from-the-dead bullshit. Dawnstar wants me back on their board. I'm stalling."

His voice rasped. He would have that souvenir forever. As scars went, he'd gotten off easy. His teeth had even grown back, which was a puzzle to his doctor and a relief to him. "You've been busy here," he said.

"I have, haven't I?" Alison went up on her tiptoes and spread her arms wide, smiling in a way that brought Justin's aching heart into his throat. She wore a soft dress with a peasant top, and the skirt spun out in gauzy layers as she twirled in a circle. "I love it already."

She stepped out at the end of the spin, caught off-balance by the brace on her ankle, but she laughed as she came hobbling across the wood floor to bring up the rest of the lighting.

"Do you like the place?" she asked.

Justin thought that he should probably be feeling hurt by her refusal to let him have any part in building her nest. She'd bought the place with her share in the C&A survivors' fund, one of the many topics they both avoided discussing.

"I'm glad you love it," he said, and Alison dragged him on a tour.

She'd been in possession of the loft less than twelve hours, but despite an echoing lack of furniture it was already indelibly her space. Woven bamboo room dividers split the huge open floor into quadrants, leaving an extra-broad corridor along the window wall. The largest room was already filled with a colorful explosion of cloth, yarn, wood, paint cans, and tools. Boxes were stacked against the interior brick wall.

In a second section, a bed covered in pillows and throws had been tucked into a nook created by the master bathroom build-out. It was a single bed. Alison dragged Justin onward when he hesitated there.

The next space was empty, and beyond that, they moved into shadows. None of the overhead fixtures targeted the last and smallest room. The skyline glittered in the window like framed art.

A couch and two heavily upholstered chairs faced the window wall, and a standing lamp cast a warm glow. The brick walls at the back and side of the nook were covered in photos, text pages, sketches, and fabric swatches. All the flotsam and jetsam drew the eye from point to point of the installation.

Crumbling bits of concrete, a jagged shard of glass, and a phone earpiece sat on one shelf. Pictures of people Justin didn't know spiraled and spread around panoramic shots of the Seattle skyline before and after C&A's destruction. There was also an image of Parker in a hospital bed. He had a sour glare on his lean face and a bruise-blackened middle finger raised, even though he'd had to press the whole hand against the opposite upper arm to make the gesture.

Headlines about Walton's death wove over and under snippets of biographical material and pictures of the crater where the house had collapsed.

There were many more pictures: Tyler asleep on a sofa, shots of women from the Mayhem & Havoc team in various poses and locations. Images of Helen, Ryan, and people Justin didn't recognize. Lots and lots of those.

Only one picture of him: scruffy-jawed and nearly bald, leaning hard against Carl and clutching a control box in both hands. Justin didn't remember Carl being worried at the time, but he looked that way in the picture: worried, bruised, and haggardly pale.

Alison had captured the detonation of the mines in a series of stills that gave the destruction a brutal kind of beauty. "Steep hill with ruins" became "scoured-flat island butte" in ten frames. The man that Dan Patterson had called "Agent Clout" was in the background. He looked like a rumpled accountant, pale-skinned and pale-eyed, with dark hair that curled even more than Justin's did.

He'd shown up shortly before the pictures were taken, and he'd smiled when Justin told him to fuck off and stay out of the way. Alison had taken over negotiations at that point. Justin still didn't know the man's name, but his clout had proved to be as good as advertised. The incident in New Mexico had officially never happened, and they'd all been inserted back into civilization with cover stories that were backed by irrefutable documentation.

Justin touched one little arc of images, arranged to be viewed best from one of chairs. Alison had placed chunks of rock, a twisted piece of metal, a copy of the New Mexico property deed, and a wheedling note under Design Unlimited letterhead above the stills. Adam Berenson wanted to hire him for demolition work.

Alison sat down with a troubled expression. "My place, my

life, my people," she said. "I thought you'd like it. You look miserable. You've looked miserable for days now. What is your problem?"

"You are." He mulled over his answer in the resulting silence and restated it. "I'm your problem. You have a life, you have work that makes you happy, you have—" he gestured. "*This.* I don't know what I have."

He still didn't know what he was going to do with himself in the long term. He'd never been an executive by choice. Meeting with people who had known him before the crash was already eating away at his soul. Being a figurehead would destroy him. The mental blanks still came and went, as did his struggles between impulse and indecision. He wasn't getting any better. He had to face the reality that deterioration was as likely as improvement.

He still had more than enough money to live on, if he lived simply and made some prudent plans. The decisions of where to go and what to do weren't critical except for this one point. "I don't fit here. I said I love you, and I do, like breathing, but—"

But she never had said it back. "Mine," she'd said, and it wasn't the same.

Alison's laugh startled him into a flinch. Most loud noises still did.

She cupped a hand against his cheek. "Sorry. Justin, do you really think you are small enough to ever fit into someone else's life? Seriously?"

"I don't even know if I fit in my own life. I want to fit in yours."

Alison grabbed him by the collar, sat him down in the chair, and straddled him. "Good, because I left you a whole room. Didn't you see?"

She leaned forward to kiss him with an intensity that left him dizzy. "You'll need a separate bed because you still wake up kicking and yelling. We can have sex anywhere, and I intend to —*Justin*—"

He stopped moving his hands. Her smile turned sad. "You can fit here with me for now, but it's good that you brought it up. Love isn't all there is to it. You know that already, mister twice-bitten. We might as well talk this out sooner rather than later."

"You do love me?"

She thumped her head against his chest. "You are *hopeless*. Yes, I love you. You are in my heart for always. But love won't hold you back, and that will be a problem eventually."

"Where do you think I'm going?" He steadied his voice. "No plans here."

Alison retreated to the other chair. "None yet," she said. "But when you do make them, you won't consider anything except what will make the plan work. You'll work until you forget anything else exists, you'll step into the scary and dangerous without thinking about anyone else around you—you'll do heartbreaking things, and at some point I *will* push you away to protect myself. I could delude myself and lie to you, but I won't. I love you too much to do that."

Her analysis hit like the solution to a puzzle, pieces locking into place in a sudden shining moment of clarity. And it hurt, because she was right about him, which meant her prediction was probably right as well. "I could change."

Alison said wryly, "And give up what makes you so special? No. I don't want to end up hating you for it, that's all. I'm not saying now or tomorrow or next week. Maybe it'll never happen, and I'm borrowing trouble. I don't *want* to leave, not ever. You would starve if I did."

"I had lunch."

"Only because I messaged you from the property closing. For me, being needed is like red meat to a tiger, and God, do you need me. We should get the everyday things formalized, so that everything else between us—"

"Sex?" Justin said, hoping to see the smile again.

"Among other things." Alison gave him the grin he needed so desperately to see. "So that we have tight lines to tie us together even when I can't hold you too close without bleeding. I couldn't bear to lose you forever just because I'm not big enough to hold all of you."

She'd needed to build this place without him so that she could make room in it for him; space where he could stay or go without ripping out her heart by the roots. Sensible, practical Alison had done that for him and for herself. Justin's heart lifted.

"Will this work?" Alison said, hesitant now. "Is that enough for you? This is why the room's still empty, because it's that or nothing, and oh, God, don't look at me like that, because just saying it is like gutting myself with a spoon. Please say that this is enough for you?"

"More than enough. Allie, I don't have any future right now. Not one I can plan. Can you promise me one thing?"

"Anything. Everything."

"Promise you'll always be honest and blunt and *you*. Don't hold back because you think I can't stand the truth."

"When have I ever—" she said, but her phone burbled at her before she could finish. "Saved by the doorbell."

She pointed Justin back into his seat and went to meet the new visitor, and Justin thought his brain was playing tricks when he heard Tyler say, "Happy house day, Allie. I brought beer and the dynamic duo. They took the stairs."

Footsteps thumped closer, and then Tyler was there, sun-kissed and fit and outdoorsy in flannel and jeans. He set down a plastic pet carrier in front of the couch so he could go look at the walls. "Nice work," he called. "Most people collapse in a heap and order pizza on move-in day."

"I'm ordering Chinese." Alison's voice drifted over the divider wall. "Don't shout. Were you raised in a barn?"

"More or less," Tyler said. "Why?"

Justin tried to make senseless things fit together. When the plastic box made a mewling noise, he recoiled hard enough to make the chair creak.

"Still twitchy, huh?" Tyler removed a squirming double-handful of fur from the carrier. "This is Allie's first install-ment on her crazy-cat-lady credentials."

The fur belonged to a gray spotted kitten. Tyler said, "Courtesy of Agent Neil McAllister. His uncle breeds fancy critters. Remember Neil? The guy you called 'fucking asshole' for a week? Dan Patterson calls him Agent Clout."

Justin swallowed the lump in his throat.

"Oh, Christ." Alison came around the corner. "Tyler, what did you do to him?"

"Nothing! I was showing him your new kitten. No teasing, not even a single joke. Justin, what's wrong?"

Justin wrenched his mind into gear. "Nothing. You're here. Damn, I've missed you. How long are you in town?"

Alison gave Tyler a look that could've melted steel. He wilted. "I swear I told him a hundred times. He only ever pays attention to the math."

"Yes, but you never told *me* that he wasn't listening." Alison scooped the kitten away from Justin and walked off. "Hopeless. Both of you. No wonder you get along so well."

Once she was gone Tyler said, "I've *told* you this.. I helped Neil and Dan locate and bury most of the literature on the power cells, and now I'm back to play supersecret science with you. Perez helped me put together a shopping list."

Carl's voice arrived before he did. "I can see why he's confused, if that's your idea of an explanation."

As soon as he was in the room, he started handing things to Tyler. "What part of my warning about phone conversations didn't sink in? Eye contact. Repetition. Require response. I've told you this, to use your words."

He was bristling with aggravation, and for the first time since leaving New Mexico, Justin started to believe the man didn't secretly hate him. "You're back for good?" he asked Tyler, because he wanted to be sure.

Tyler said, "Yes, Justin, for good. Or evil. Who knows? And don't tell me you won't help. We need you."

"Need me for what? I can't explain what I do, and I don't understand what you do. Haven't we proved that?"

"No, we've proved that you suck at phone conferencing. Your voice is barely there and sounds like sandpaper, and I can't hit you with soft objects. Do you think I care if you can't explain? Just sit in a corner and build shit, all right? Is that too much to ask?"

"Was there a real question in there?" Carl pushed cat toys and equipment to one side and took over the couch. He leaned towards Justin and said in a stage whisper, "The correct answers are 'no, all right, and no.' "

A laugh crawled up from somewhere deep in Justin's chest. He was still chuckling when Parker came trailing in. He had Alison tucked under one arm, and the smirk on his face said that he was enjoying the support more than he needed it. The sweaty pallor and the slow progress betrayed how much he did need it.

Alison deposited him on the couch next to Carl and deposited the kitten on his lap. "How long?" she asked.

Parker looked to Carl, who said, "We can spare three or four hours. He's in for work on the right wrist tomorrow. They'll check him for pre-op at midnight."

"Plenty of time for a decent housewarming party." Alison put her hands on her hips and beamed at all of them. "Party: a social gathering of invited guests, typically involving eating, drinking, and entertainment. I'll pick up the food. You guys start working on the rest of it, okay?"

Silence fell after her departure. Parker sank back to let the kitten romp over his immobilized arms. Carl got it to pounce onto his lap instead.

Tyler sighed. "This isn't entertaining, and in my experience it's usually best to do what Alison says."

Parker smiled as the kitten rejected Carl and came back to him. Carl looked at Justin and waited expectantly.

Justin stood up. "I'll go get the beer."

The End

ABOUT THE AUTHOR

K. M. Herkes writes and publishes books that dance in the open spaces between science fiction and fantasy, specializing in stories about damaged souls, complicated lives, and triumphs of the spirit.

Professional development started with a Bachelor of Science degree in Biology and now includes experience in classroom teaching, animal training, aquaculture, horticulture, bookselling, and retail operations. Personal development is ongoing. Cats are involved.

When she isn't writing, she works at the Mount Prospect Public Library. She also digs holes in her backyard for fun, enjoys experimental baking, and wrangles butterflies.

Visit dawnrigger.com and check out extras like free short stories, story-inspired artwork, links to the author's media, and blog rants on life, the universe, and writing.

Lastly, subscribe to receive rare Dawnrigger Publishing email alerts and get an exclusive free short story just for signing up.

CPSIA information can be obtained
at www.ICGtesting.com
Printed in the USA
FSHW021232010321
79025FS